THE SENATOR SERIES

EL SENADOR

ALAN D. SCHMITZ

BLACK HAWK PUBLISHING

Black Hawk Publishing
Blackhawk340.com

Ordering Information:
Quantity sales. Special discounts are available on quantity purchases by corporations, associations, and others. For details, contact the "Special Sales Department" at the web address above.

El Senador/Alan D Schmitz – 1st. ed.
ISBN 978-0-9973573-1-8

Acknowledgments

I want to thank my readers, for it is you who keep me writing during the most tedious of times. *El Senador* is the second of the Senator series, and it's here because you were so supportive of Senator Steven Westcott in *DNA Never Lies*. I hope you're as excited to see Steven in this new environment as I am, along with exciting new characters and familiar faces from our last adventure.

As this book comes to print, I am already working on the third in the series, having retired to become a full-time novelist. There are more stories waiting to be told, each packed with high-stakes political conflict and life-or-death struggle, and I'm glad you're along for the ride.

Last, but not least, I want to thank my editor, Robert Wood from Standout Books. His guidance and contributions keep my own creative juices from turning stale. He understands Steven Westcott and my entire cast of characters, ever prodding me to keep them true to themselves and helping me hone the twisting plots that test them to their limits.

Chapter 1

Senator Steven Westcott didn't have to be told twice to keep his head down as another bullet whistled over his head. The bullets were ripping apart the thick foliage of the forest around him. Suddenly, he missed his army gear, especially his helmet and flak jacket; his Mexican escorts were better protected.

They were select members of the Fuerzas Especiales, better known as FES, and they were armed with new M4s, which demonstrated just how special they were. They were the Mexican navy's answer to US SEAL teams and had proven themselves incorruptibly loyal to the government .

The strong scent of pine needles was being overtaken by the smell of gunpowder.

"Filipe, give me a weapon so that I can at least shoot back!" Steven shouted over the gunfire.

"Sorry, amigo," replied the team leader, who crouched in the protection of a large, fallen tree. "You are an American citizen. My orders are to protect you at all costs but not let you interfere in our business, which, in this case, includes killing Mexican citizens."

Another flurry of bullets cut into the jungle around them as Steven watched Filipe load up a grenade to launch with his M4.

Steven pressed his head against a small rock and took advantage of a break in the gunfire to remark, "When I was told you could arrange an introduction to Antonio Ortega, nobody told me that introduction would come after I was dead."

"Certainly, you did not expect I could arrange such a date with El Pequeño Diablo for you without engaging in a bit of chit-chat first? But I must admit, it seems they are not in the mood for visitors today."

Filipe made a few hand gestures to his team. Steven understood exactly what he was instructing, because they came right out of the playbook of his own Special Forces training. The three other FES soldiers passed on the signals until all knew exactly what was going to happen next.

"El Pequeño Diablo?"

"In English, it means 'the Little Devil'."

"I know what it means, but why?"

"His father, El Diablo, not so nice a man. When his father was killed, Antonio took over, much stayed the same. So, he became 'El Pequeño Diablo'. Pretty soon, we will be able to make your first introduction. These are only poor farmers, but they can get your message through to El Pequeño Diablo. Of course, they can't do that if we kill them first."

Filipe looked at his watch. He started to count down with his fingers to let Steven know exactly when all hell was going to break loose.

When he had only one finger up, he aimed his M4 toward a nearby hillside and launched his grenade. At exactly the same time, three other grenades pounded the same hill. The explosions were deafening.

The gunfire stopped, but Filipe waited another minute before shouting out in Spanish, "We are government forces; we do not want to hurt you or ruin your crops. We are here just to talk. Lay down your weapons and stand together in the poppy field. I promise we will not harm you." He turned to Steven. "Pray they are smart enough to comply."

"If we do not give this crop to the cartel, we will be killed," a farmer shouted back.

"I understand, we only want to talk. You can keep your lives and your crop if you do as I say. We are the FES; if you shoot at us, you will all die."

"Don't shoot, we will obey."

The earbud in Filipe's ear confirmed their compliance.

"Snipes says they are moving into the open. They do not particularly like working for the cartels, but it is the only way they can support themselves. I have no wish to harm them. Stay here until I signal that it is safe for you to come out."

Involved in a firefight without a gun in his hand, Steven felt naked. He watched cautiously as two of the FES members came out from the protection of the forest with their M4s pointed at the farmers. The farmers huddled in their field of poppies with their hands up in the air, clearly afraid for their lives. Filipe joined the other two soldiers and ordered the farmers further into the clearing of the field where the FES sniper still hidden in the forest could clearly see them.

Steven listened as Filipe ordered in Spanish, "Down on the ground, hands behind your heads."

Steven had reservations about the wisdom of the president of the United States in sending him out on this particular mission, but he certainly didn't have doubts about how dangerous the mission was. The men that he would be forced to deal with were all exceedingly dangerous.

The forest was now eerily quiet. The birds, usually numerous and noisy, had all fled. Filipe was talking to the farmers, but Steven couldn't hear what was being said.

How, he wondered, could a United States senator become so embroiled in another country's problem? He was no longer a young man seeking adventure in the Special Forces, yet here he was, far away from home, being shot at once again.

Steven thought of his family, especially his young daughter. He had responsibilities now; his daughter needed her father alive and well. He was here because the president wanted him to be. Actually, *two* presidents wanted him here: Señora Alejandra Espinoza Torres, the current president of Mexico, and Julius Walker, the president of the United States. As far as he knew, they were the only other two people on the planet who knew what his mission was. Now, Steven wondered if he had made the right choice.

The radio Filipe had left behind started to squawk.

"Senator, it is safe now."

Slowly, Steven climbed over the tree and towards the edge of the clearing. The jungle camouflage Steven was wearing kept him invisible until the moment he stepped out into the clearing. He carried the non-distinct uniform well; he was solidly built and, at just over six foot, looked like a giant compared to the farmers. He had been rigorously training for this mission for months.

Filipe ordered one of the farmers to stand. The old man stood up slowly, looking like he expected to be shot at any moment. With a nervous stomach, he waited and kept his eyes down and non-threatening.

Eventually, the farmer peered up at Steven. Steven caught the surprise in his eyes when he realized that the VIP who wanted to talk to him was a gringo. Steven's white skin had been covered in camouflage paint just like the soldiers, but even so, there was no doubt he was a white man, though his face looked younger than his forty-five years of age. Out here in the jungle, with camouflage on his face and his broad shoulders squared, he looked dangerous. In Washington, dressed in the custom suits he wore, his clean-shaven face and round jaw looked more amicable.

The farmer looked at his two sons and son-in-law lying face down in the field. Suspicion was written all over his face when he looked back at Steven.

"This is Hector," Filipe said.

"What is your full name?" Steven asked in fluent Spanish.

"Hector Soto De Balsas," the farmer murmured without looking directly at Steven, his body arched from years of fieldwork.

"Señor," Steven said respectfully, "I need you to carry a message for me."

The farmer looked up with confusion in his eyes.

"Sí."

"My name is Senator Steven Westcott." Steven handed the bewildered old farmer a card with his name on it and his picture. "This is me, yes?"

"Sí."

"I am from the United States. I am a US Senator. I am an important man in my country. I need you to tell the cartel that I need to talk with its leader. I need you to tell them that the man who is on the card has to talk with Antonio Cruz Ortega, or there will be much problems."

"No, no! Señor, I cannot do that. You cannot do that. Señor, I do not know Ortega, he will not listen to me. They will kill me just for speaking his name. I tell you that you do not want to meet with El Pequeño Diablo. He will kill you."

"Tell the man who buys your crops that he needs to get a message to El Pequeño Diablo and that I want to talk to him. Make them understand or, the next time we visit, we will destroy your crops and others to get his attention."

The old farmer shook his head, even as he agreed, "I will try!"

His sons looked up at him, worried for their father's safety.

"Not 'try'! You must do it, or your crops will be destroyed," Steven promised. "Get that message to him. I don't care how you do it. A way for him to contact me is on that card."

The farmer looked at the card and understood he was talking to an important United States politician, but it was too late. A look of fear washed over the old man's face as he glanced towards the sky.

"You must go, you must go now," he demanded.

Filipe was trying to make sense of the sudden bravado of the farmer. He scanned the jungle for a trap, and that was when he saw it. There was a small radio propped up against a tree at the edge of the forest where the farmers had come from.

"Oh shit!" Filipe cursed, loud enough for all around to hear. "They called in our attack. Reinforcements are on the way. Run, we gotta get out of here!"

Chapter 2

They were on top of a mountainside. On either side, a thick forest of pines surrounded the two acres of poppies in which they stood. A hushed sound started to break through the pines.

"Run, run!" Filipe ordered, pointing. "Into the forest and down the mountain."

Just as they started running, a helicopter emerged from behind the treetops. The highly trained soldiers knew that they couldn't outrun the bullets that were sure to be coming, but perhaps they could hide from them.

As Steven ran one way, the old farmer and his sons ran in the opposite direction. The family had just barely gotten out of harm's way when the bullets started to pound the ground. At this point, it was every man for himself, and the soldiers spread out to make it harder for the shooter to get more than one of them. Luck would have to be their armor until they reached cover.

The helicopter was making an attack run. Bullets shredded the poppies behind Filipe. He could hear them getting closer, and he knew he wasn't going to make the cover of the forest. Filipe stopped, hurled himself sideways as hard as he could and curled into a ball, trying to roll even further.

The bullets pounded the field where he had been, just missing him but covering him in dirt and poppies. The pilot couldn't move quickly enough to follow the sideways leap. The helicopter lifted its nose just a bit and turned to the left. That put the stream of bullets moving toward Steven.

Out of the corner of his eye, Steven saw Filipe go down and assumed he had been hit. Steven knew he would be the next casualty as twin lines of fire hurtled towards him. Adrenaline pumping, he could hear the muted sound of earth churning under repeated fire. In seconds, the bullets would be upon him, but the forest was at least ten seconds away.

That was when he heard a high-powered shot from behind the trees. Steven knew the protocol; Snipes, their sniper, was positioned to cover them, and he had taken his shot. The helicopter wasn't military; it was a private make outfitted with automatic guns. That meant the windscreen wasn't bulletproof.

The shot pierced the large protective windscreen but missed the pilot and copilot. However, it did manage to distract the pilot, and his finger came off the guns' trigger for a moment.

The extra seconds counted, and Steven raced into the trees and jumped over the log that again became his shelter. From the edges, he watched the helicopter turn from him as he caught his breath.

The pilot had seen where the shot had come from and twisted the guns towards it. With a steady hand on the trigger, the bullets raked the ground. The 'copter fishtailed in the air, obliterating a hundred square feet of forest.

Steven had miraculously survived, but Filipe and Snipes were down. Steven looked overhead to where the canopy was the thickest and ran towards it. There was a rendezvous point down the mountain, and he needed to get there as soon as possible, without getting killed in the process.

Steven slowed his pace once he was fifty yards into the forest. He climbed partly down the mountainside, carefully picking the most protected route back. He hoped the helicopter couldn't hit what it couldn't see.

Behind a cluster of boulders, Steven watched the helicopter getting closer, scanning the mountainside. He couldn't let curiosity get the better of him. One glance towards the helicopter at the wrong time and he would be spotted. Steven's operational logic was simple: if he couldn't see the helicopter, it couldn't see him. Following it with his ears, and ears alone, would be his safest play.

Steven tensed his body ready for a fight when he heard a rustle in the trees.

A moment later, Filipe slid down next to him nearly prone and said, "Nicely done, amigo. As you can see, introductions are coming along just fine. We already have a welcome committee."

Steven shook his head in disbelief, saying, "You're alive! I thought you were dead. You are one crazy son of a bitch, you know that?"

Filipe smiled back, replying, "Maybe just a little, but not half as crazy as you. Anyone who asks to meet with El Pequeño Diablo, one of the most dangerous men in Mexico, is truly the crazy one."

Filipe rolled onto his back to keep his profile down and, hidden by foliage, looked off towards the helicopter.

"I wish my friend El Cazador was here. He is a special friend with special talents. I know I am safe around him; he is like a brother."

"I have a friend like that; you're a fortunate man," Steven said, as he tried to slow his heart and the pace of his breathing. After a few calming breaths Steven asked, "Where is El Cazador?"

"He is on another mission, but God willing, you will meet him soon."

The helicopter hovered in place, pointed in their direction.

"I will make you a deal," Filipe offered. "If I give you my weapon and you shoot down that helicopter, will you promise not to tell anybody?"

"I won't tell a soul, I promise. But, if you give me your weapon, what will you shoot?"

Filipe handed his M4 to Steven.

"If you bring down the helicopter before it shoots at me, I shouldn't need it, right?"

"What are you talking about?"

"We need a rabbit to draw this hunter out."

"Filipe!" Steven cried, grabbing the soldier by his arm to stop him. "The helicopter took out Snipes."

"Maybe, maybe not. First, we take out the helicopter. After that threat is gone, we go back to find Snipes."

Filipe slid down the mountainside to a clearing. The opening was wide and off to the side. Filipe had to time his run just right. He wanted the pilot to see him but not too soon.

Steven realized what Filipe was up to and that it was up to him to keep Filipe alive. Steven risked a look around the boulder. The copilot spotted him instantly; there weren't that many places on the mountainside to hide, and the timing of his quick look couldn't have been worse.

The helicopter turned towards him.

"Oh shit!" Steven breathed, knowing what was coming next.

He ducked for cover just as the big guns mounted on the fuselage turned the rocks around him into shrapnel. Steven curled up in a ball to protect himself. The gun was of little use to him, but at least he'd distracted the helicopter and given Filipe a chance to move into position.

The pounding seemed like it would never end, but the rocks had protected him so far. Suddenly, the firing stopped, and the sound of the helicopter changed as it moved off.

Steven risked a look and saw Filipe below him trying to attract the gunfire. The helicopter hung in the air in front of Filipe, drawing its sights on him.

Filipe ran from his cover and across the open ground. The helicopter twisted towards him. Disaster struck: Filipe fell to his side and grabbed his ankle in pain.

The pilot took his time; his quarry was helpless and about to be plastered against the mountain. But, just before he could get lined up for his shot, Filipe rose to his feet and ran in the opposite direction of the helicopter's turn.

Filipe's plan was that the pilot would have to stop his pivot and change direction to follow him, hopefully making him an easier target for the American. The downside of his plan was that he would have to run through a surplus of bullets first. The question was, was this his lucky day?

The pilot was taken by surprise and realized he had been baited. The man was far from injured, but the fool was still running into his sights. The pilot pulled the trigger; he would need a few seconds to aim the gun, and the best way was to follow the trail the bullets were making.

Filipe decided today wasn't his lucky day after all and suddenly turned away from certain death, only to be faced with a long, open run for life. The bullets were chasing him once again and gaining.

Steven stood on the rock and braced himself. The M4 was a solid weapon, and the .223 caliber round was powerful, but the short barrel sacrificed accuracy over distance.

The copilot spotted Steven taking aim at them. The pilot, however, was busy tracking Filipe, bullets already nipping at his heels.

Steven steadied himself, took a breath and let it out as he aimed and squeezed.

The helicopter was pivoting as it tracked Filipe with a full fusillade of bullets.

Steven pressed the trigger for a three-shot burst. The first two weakened the acrylic windscreen, and the third exploded the copilot's head.

Steven pressed the trigger for another burst, but the helicopter gyrated wildly, and the shots missed. Steven saw the sparks as the bullets ricocheted off the fuselage. No doubt the pilot had lost control because of the carnage inside the cockpit.

He watched Filipe take cover as the helicopter twirled in the air, falling from the sky. A body dropped to the ground from the helicopter, and the pilot somehow regained control. Now, Steven was the primary threat, and the helicopter swung back towards where he'd fired from. Steven dropped behind the rocks and was protected for the moment as the sound of the helicopter stayed steady.

It was a standoff; as long as Steven didn't move, it couldn't attack, but leaving the security of the rocks was his only way to reach the rendezvous point in time for the extraction.

The helicopter moved off; it still hung in the air, but it had taken a higher position for reconnaissance. Soon, Steven knew why; from the multitude of voices coming from below, he realized that his downward escape was blocked.

"You missed."

"Damn you, Filipe! Will you stop scaring the shit out of me? And I didn't miss."

"I disagree: the helicopter is still a threat."

"Tell me something I don't know."

"The others are alive, even Snipes, but he is injured."

"We have company coming up the hill."

"Tell me something I don't know," Filipe replied, grinning.

Chapter 3

W e go to plan B: now, we go up instead of down," Filipe said, nodding towards the top of the mountain.

"I hate plan B."

"Ahh... Americans; they want everything to be easy."

Further up the mountain, the five men regrouped. Steven helped to treat Snipe's wounds by stuffing expanding sponges into the leg wound to stop the bleeding. After wrapping it tight and administering morphine, he broke down one of the M4s and made a splint out of it. While he worked, the others formulated a plan of escape and assessed their resources.

"From now on, we stick together. If we get cornered, we form a perimeter, but whatever we do, we must not become exposed to the helicopter."

"Sorry I let you down, Sergeant," Snipes said, feeling better now that the morphine was kicking in.

"You did no such thing. You'll be making out with the nurses at the base by sundown."

Snipes looked at the sun, struggling to stand as he bravely suggested, "We had better get a move on."

Two soldiers moved to either side of Snipes and helped him as the group kept climbing under the cover of the forest canopy.

Steven and Filipe were climbing together when Filipe confessed, "We will never get off this mountain alive as long as that helicopter is tracking us. As we climb higher, the tree cover will dwindle. If we aren't out of here before sundown, it will be a long and dangerous night."

Steven nodded in agreement, looking at Filipe as he reached out for a branch to pull himself up the mountainside. The higher up the mountain they went, the steeper it became. Snipes was struggling not to be a burden over the difficult terrain.

As they climbed, Steven suggested, "I've had practice with a sniper rifle. If I can use Snipes' gun, I can take out the helicopter and keep it occupied while you get him down the other side of the mountain."

"The other side of the mountain is steep and exposed. If you fail, we will be open targets."

"Your team risked their lives to get me here; let me help. It will take all of you to prep for the descent and get Snipes out of here."

Filipe paused and reflected. He took off his camo-pattern helmet with one hand and brushed the other through black hair wet with sweat.

"OK, amigo, his gun is yours. When was the last time you practiced with a sniper rifle?"

"You don't really want to know, do you?"

"Holy Mary, please help us," Filipe said, looking toward the sky in earnest.

"So, here's what I'm going to do and what I need you to do, because we still have the army of men coming up the mountain towards us."

Steven took up his position near the top of the mountain. He was protected from a frontal attack, though his sides were exposed. Filipe helped him camouflage himself and the rifle. Just like before, Filipe needed to create a diversion and draw the helicopter up the mountain and hopefully into the sights of the powerful sniper rifle.

Steven tried to calm himself and watched the treetops below him slowly turn in the wind. Using that as a gauge, he assessed how the wind could affect his shot. The sporadic gunfire was getting closer and closer. Steven realized that one shot would be all the advancing soldiers would allow.

Steven steadied his breathing and looked at his watch. They didn't have much time to clear the mountain before dark. If Filipe wasn't successful at baiting the helicopter, and if Steven wasn't successful at shooting it out of the sky, their plan wouldn't work. As far as Steven knew, there wasn't a plan C.

He listened for the sound of the helicopter coming closer. Apparently, the pilot had gained some respect for the firepower of the men he was hunting. He obviously didn't want the same thing to happen to him as his copilot.

Unfortunately, the sporadic shots of their pursuers were getting closer. The other side of the mountain, and the escape route, wasn't that far from his location, but he would still need time to get there, hopefully without being seen. The closer the drug lord's army came, the more likely it was that after he took his shot, the noise from the gun would help them find him.

Steven waited patiently; his cover and camouflage had been carefully done, and he knew he was nearly invisible. The FES soldiers couldn't make their escape until he brought down the helicopter. The plan was that, as soon as they heard the unique sound of the sniper rifle, they would begin their descent. They had to make the assumption that it was a successful shot. Steven made up his mind: he would wait until he could take the shot and make it count, whether it led to his capture or not.

Finally, the helicopter was moving closer. Steven could only imagine that Filipe was exposing himself just enough to be seen but also disappearing long enough to force the pilot to come in closer so he could report the position to the ground forces.

The tactic seemed to be working, though the helicopter still wasn't in his line of sight. Steven looked at his watch. At the rate the militia below him were advancing up the mountain, they would be upon him soon. This was going to be close; very, very close, if it worked at all.

Steven triple-checked the gun: the safety was off, and he'd adjusted the sight as best he could. He wouldn't have time to recalibrate the distance to target. He would just have to make a manual adjustment; in effect, take his best guess at the time.

The helicopter was getting closer; it sounded like it was coming from just behind the lower tree line to his right. He could hear the voices of the militia; they were being guided to a destination. Steven prayed that Filipe knew what he was doing.

Steven crouched down, trying to make himself invisible. Through the treetops and between the branches, he could see the helicopter. At least, he could see parts of it in small glimpses but nothing he could risk taking a shot at.

Glancing further down the mountain, he got his first look at the men hunting him. They had an uphill climb to find him, but being able to see and hear them unnerved Steven. The shot to bring down the helicopter would have to be taken soon for him to escape.

Slowly, the *thump-thump* of the helicopter was getting closer. It was in range now, but it still wasn't in the clear.

"There, over there..." one of the men said, pointing across the mountain.

The man was pointing at Filipe, who was much further down the mountain than Steven had expected. Without moving from position, Steven could see Filipe running across an opening to his left.

"Crazy son of a bitch," Steven whispered. He knew that Filipe was once again risking his life to pull the helicopter towards him and into the opening.

And it was working.

Steven steadied his breathing.

The helicopter banked towards Filipe. It shot out of its hidden perch much faster than Steven could have imagined, and he wondered if the pilot knew they were creating another trap.

The target was moving fast. This was no longer a fixed position shot; now, it was a case of hitting a small, moving target. He had to take it out before it was upon Filipe and back in hiding behind the next ridge. This had to work.

Steven stood from the safety of his hidden perch and tightly tucked the rifle into his shoulder. He moved the barrel of the gun across the sky, tracking the target. The gun sight wasn't adjusted for this kind of shot; he would have to aim where he thought the helicopter would be, not at where it was.

Steven gauged the speed of its arc through the sky.

He squeezed the trigger. The rifle recoiled into his shoulder.

But the helicopter was gone, disappearing behind the ridge.

A bullet ricocheted off the rock behind him. He'd been spotted.

Taking the gun with him, he ran up the mountain with bullets pounding the ground all around him. Somehow, he had to find the helicopter again and take another shot.

Voices were screaming orders and locations. Filipe was even further down the mountain than he. Both of them would be captured and killed, though not necessarily in that order.

Steven reached the top plateau; the equipment to descend was on the far side, the steep side. From here, he knew he should be able to spot the helicopter again.

That was when Steven heard the sound that brought a smile to his face. He was running across the plateau and couldn't take the time to look, but he was sure of the sound: the helicopter had exploded. Nothing else could possibly make that kind of explosion, let alone the screech of steel against rock.

Steven twisted his head and saw his pursuers. He couldn't fight them with the single-shot rifle. Besides, in the time it took him to shoot one, four more would get behind him. He had to run and hope his luck would continue to hold.

Filipe emerged from the cliffside and ran towards Steven, his gun aimed right at him.

"Drop, *now!*" Filipe screamed.

Steven dropped to the ground and a burst of rapid fire screamed over his head. Two attackers directly behind Steven fell to the ground dead.

Steven rushed to his feet, and he and Filipe ran for the cliff. The equipment for both of them was ready.

"Toss the gun over the mountainside; they must not get it."

Steven took the gun by the end of its still-warm barrel and swung it around his body and out over the sheer cliff. He didn't have time to hear it splintering into a thousand pieces as it hit the rocks hundreds of feet below them.

Filipe was already wearing his body harness as he ran up holding out Steven's. Steven grabbed it from him and swung it over his head and, when it rested on his shoulders, he tightened it across his waist.

Filipe ran to his rigging and clipped his support harness to it.

"Go, go! You have to jump now," Filipe urged. "I will cover you. Just grab on tight and jump."

Steven looked back and saw the enemy gunmen getting into position behind some rocks.

"It's now or never, amigo."

"Damn it, Filipe; I told you I hated plan B."

Steven picked up the frame of his hang glider and secured his harness. He ran towards the cliff, jumping into the void in front of him.

More shots came just as his feet left the ground.

Filipe fired off one more blast towards the attackers and jumped off the cliff just as Steven dropped off the edge.

Steven worked the control bar he was suspended over. The wide wings caught the air, and he was flying. In front of him, the other team members were well out of harm's way, heading to the lush valley below.

Steven felt himself fall a bit from his perch. When he looked up to see why, he realized that a bullet must have hit his support harness. His entire body weight was suspended on a fraying nylon strap.

More bullets shot past him but missed. After a quick glance around, he saw Filipe off to his right with a wide grin on his face. The kites they were riding were accelerating them towards the valley far below. Filipe was obviously unaware of Steven's new predicament.

Steven glanced up again just in time to see the strap break.

His body dropped towards the craggy rocks hundreds of feet below, and he held onto the control bar with all his strength.

Steven was hanging from the bar by only his hands. The kite caught a gust of wind, and he lost his grip from the jolt of the wing. There was nothing below him but the valley floor thousands of feet below. Steven was glad for all the pull-ups he had done as he hung on by one hand, but he still didn't have control.

"You must pull yourself up, amigo," Filipe shouted.

His sweaty hand was slipping on the bar, and the broken strap was dangling down. He wrapped it around the hand that had slipped off the bar then did the same with the other. The immediate risk to his life was averted, though he was still swinging from the kite with no hope of controlling it.

Things turned worse for him when he heard bullets whizzing by him and the sounds of rapid fire. His kite was turning towards the small militia, who were lined up on the cliffside and shooting wildly.

Steven needed to somehow get control of his glider, which meant he had to get his body back up on the control bar. If he didn't change his situation, his arms would lose whatever strength they still had. Pulling his body up would become an impossible task if he didn't do it soon.

Steven was intently studying his dire situation when he heard, "Get ready, my friend."

Suspended thousands of feet in the air, Steven was shocked to hear such a close voice. He turned toward Filipe, who was floating towards him.

"When I fly under you, kick off my glider and get your feet onto the control bar. It's the only way."

Steven stretched his neck and watched Filipe maneuver his glider closer. His hands were turning purple from being tightly wrapped in the straps of the harness. He gasped for air, his breathing erratic.

Steven shouted to Filipe, "No, don't try it, it won't work, I'll just throw your glider out of control too."

Steven could tell that his pleading wasn't being heeded as Filipe tugged on the controls and nudged his own glider behind and under Steven's.

"Try not to break my glider, if you please."

Steven was too tired and out of breath to come back with a pithy reply. He prayed the dangerous stunt would work.

Filipe timed his actions as best he could. He forced his weight back, and the nose of his glider shot up sharply.

Steven used all his strength to pull his knees to his chest and got ready to release his hands from the straps.

Filipe banged his glider into Steven. Steven pressed his coiled legs against the crossbar of Filipe's glider and, with a mighty effort, jumped straight up.

Steven was now suspended in clear air; if he missed his target, he would fall again, and this time he wouldn't be able to save himself.

Steven reached for the upper wing support and caught it with his left hand. For a moment, he dangled by one arm as the glider fell out of balance and out of control. With a mighty tug, he lifted himself up enough that he could also grip the support bar with his right hand, but the glider had never been meant to be controlled in that way.

Filipe's glider stalled from the tactic and fell off to the side. Steven didn't notice, because his own glider was pitching violently up, his center of gravity now too far rearward.

With considerable effort, Steven steadied his feet on the control bar and moved his body weight just a bit. The fragile aircraft was highly unstable, but he was able to turn it away from the cliffside. Even subtle movements changed balance and weight enough that maintaining a steady glide was near impossible.

Filipe had, through considerable effort, regained control and brought his glider out of the stall. It had wind under it again, though he had lost height in the process. Filipe let his heart settle down after he realized that he wasn't going to slam into the mountainside at any moment. He looked up and saw that his new friend was also still flying, though erratically. It looked like his daring maneuver had worked.

The mountainside was fading away. Though uncomfortable and highly unstable, Steven was slowly getting used to flying the glider in this unique style. The team was safe; their extraction point was in the valley below, along a clearing by the river. The sun was setting, and Steven took what time he could to enjoy the view.

Chapter 4

Steven laid a modest bouquet of flowers on the ground. It was strange to see his name etched into the gravestone in front of him. He had taken the liberty of giving his daughter Destinee his last name upon her death. The stone read 'Destinee Sanford (Westcott)'.

Steven had only known her for a short while before her death. Her mother had kept her a secret from him. Steven said a short prayer and made a promise he whispered to the grave.

"I will not forget you, I promise, and I will share a secret with you that I can't share with anyone else on the planet: I'm going to get those cartel bastards. You, and too many like you, suffered at their hands. If I can, I'm going to shut them down."

He looked over towards the waiting taxi and then bent down, repositioning the flowers for no particular reason. He felt like he should do more, say more, but that time had long past. Destinee was gone and he felt like he had failed her in life. It was too late now to make amends.

Steven turned and slowly walked to the cab. Another daughter and another grave waited for him in Peabody. A visit home to Massachusetts was in his future, and another sad visit to the resting place of another daughter he felt he had failed.

****

Steven was sitting in his taxicab, enjoying the sunshine and the view of the Washington Monument in the distance. It was only days since he had flown back from Mexico. Shannon, his scheduler, had given him a note that a Colonel Tripp wanted to see him. Along with the note were instructions to go to the Eisenhower Executive Office Building. It was located next to the West Wing on the White House premises.

He didn't know a Colonel Tripp, and a military meeting at the Eisenhower Building didn't make much sense. The Pentagon would have been more logical, but somebody in the military had his back in Mexico, so Steven didn't ask questions.

Feeling relaxed, he watched the colorful blossom of the cherry trees pass by the window of his taxi. It was a week since their harrowing escape from El Pequeño Diablo. Now, he was safely back in Washington, dealing with the usual day-to-day details of Senate life. It wasn't lost on him how seamlessly he had fallen back into his daily routine.

Steven had to admit that the last week of dealing with constituent's problems, committee meetings and re-election fundraising had soon become monotonous, although not being shot at or jumping off cliffs to cheat death had its appeal too.

In the distance, the White House stood proud. What had the president gotten him into? The better question was: was he glad for the risks he was being asked to take? The last year had been exceptionally difficult for him, and that was putting things mildly. Now, for the first time since his divorce, he felt alive again.

Steven had always wondered if quitting Special Forces had been the right thing to do. Yes, of course he had been successful in business, and now he was a United States senator; not a small accomplishment. But something had been missing from his life since he left the service.

His mind knew his body couldn't take the punishment, nor could his family take the uncertainty of whether he would return safely from each dangerous mission. But in his heart, he knew something was missing; something he had thought he would never feel again.

Now, suddenly, thanks to the president, that special feeling had returned, and it felt good. Steven admitted to himself that the danger and excitement in Mexico made him feel young again; it made him feel more alive than he had in years.

The cherry trees that lined the boulevard had just blossomed. The end of March through the beginning of April seemed to be a favorite time for the blossoms to peak. This year, they were peaking late and were spectacular. The day itself seemed glorious, because spring had finally broken the long, dreary winter in Washington. Lazily, Steven watched the colorful trees blur past the window of the cab. Was he glad for the risks he was being asked to take? He realized he had answered his own question.

He cracked open his window to let in the fresh spring air that was infused with the sweetness of the cherry blossoms. Nobody in their right mind would even debate which lifestyle was preferable. The life of a senator, surrounded with safety, prestige and luxury, or crawling through the mud, often tired, hungry and thirsty while fighting to live another day. Steven realized that he was looking forward to his next trip to Mexico despite the obvious danger.

As the Eisenhower Building came into view, he tightened his tie and checked that the lapels of his suit coat were flat and straight. The Eisenhower Building wasn't a military building, at least not anymore. Today, it was the official office of the vice president of the United States. Steven wondered if the vice president had found out what the president had asked him to do. If so, Steven wondered what he would say to the vice president if asked about his recent visit to Mexico. He was under orders from the president himself to tell no one of their plan. Working in secrecy was a necessary special operations protocol. He accepted the importance of it and knew that this secrecy, at least for now, included the vice president.

"I never dropped anybody off here before. This is where the vice president lives, isn't it?"

"No, my friend, he takes up offices here for his staff, but he lives at the Naval Observatory."

"Oh..." said the cab driver, accepting the answer, though he wasn't sure he should believe it.

Steven had spotted the cabbie watching him through the rearview mirror more than he was watching the road. Now, the question came.

"Do I know you from somewhere?"

"I'm Senator Westcott; it's possible you saw my picture in the paper at one time or another."

"I knew it! You're the guy the whole country was looking for. You're Senator Westcott. No shit, I knew I recognized you! Wait 'til my wife hears I was talking to you today. Personally, I thought you were kidnapped by Iran or something. Are you going to see the vice president?"

"Not that I'm aware of."

"Well, here you are."

Steven looked up at the driver's ID and taxi license rubber-banded to the sun visor.

"Thanks, Joe. This should take care of the fare."

"More than enough."

"Keep the change."

"Hey, you're an OK guy. And thanks for capturing that murderer guy. What a wacko."

"Thanks again, Joe," Steven said as he stepped out of the cab.

The cab took off down 17th Street. The door Steven was told to go to was around a corner that was blocked off to street traffic. Not only was Steven Westcott a United States senator, he was also a Washington, DC history buff. Steven looked at the etched cornerstone and remembered some of the details of its construction and use.

The Eisenhower Executive Office was massive. It had been built in the late eighteen-hundreds on the land that had originally been the White House stables and had over ten acres of office space over its five floors. In many ways, it had been the first Pentagon, first used to house the various war departments at its inception. It had taken a hundred years or so before the huge edifice had grown too small for the original tenants and they had moved.

Steven stepped through one gate and down a small walkway. Still outside, he was checked through security. The walk opened up to a wide staircase, ascending to the second level. Inside, Steven looked around. Even though he wasn't new to Washington, it was the first time he had stepped foot in this building.

He glanced at the line of doors, all fronted with the exact same opaque glass in the upper quadrant. With something like two acres of office space per floor, finding the right room would be daunting.

"Hello, Senator Westcott. We've been expecting you."

Steven turned hurriedly, and his eyes widened in surprise.

"I'm sorry," he said. "You startled me."

The young man, impeccably groomed and wearing a dark suit with a white shirt and red tie, explained, "I was asked to escort you to your meeting."

"I was just about to take my best guess at which direction to head. Your guidance would be appreciated."

"This way, Senator, it's not far."

As he tried to memorize how many halls they went down and how many turns they took, just in case he had to find his own way out, Steven was glad that there was a guide to take him to the appropriate room.

The guide left Steven standing in a marble hallway just outside a non-descript office door. It looked like one of the hundreds of other doorways, with a simple number printed above it, and Steven turned the handle.

"Senator Westcott, I hope the day is treating you well."

A good-looking, dark-haired woman stood from behind a reception desk. She was wearing a blue blazer that mostly covered a white blouse with the top two buttons opened. As she turned away, Steven's trained eye notice a bulge in the small of her back; a weapon covered by the smart blazer.

"This way, please."

She led him around a corner and to another door. The frosted glass panel of the door didn't have a name or marking on it.

As they waited, his escort spoke quietly into a hidden microphone. Steven had to look closely to see the clear earbud. The microphone, he thought, was probably hidden under her lapel.

The door opened from the inside, where two more Secret Service agents greeted him. These two were males, big males, one white and one black. Out of habit, Steven sized them up and wondered if he could take them in a fight if he had to. He decided he didn't want to have to find out.

"Steven, it's so good to see you again."

Steven turned towards yet another inside office to look towards the voice.

"Mr. President?" Steven spoke softly, not certain the voice was as it seemed.

"Sorry to surprise you in this way. Come on in, let's talk."

The president of the United States held the door open. Steven entered the side office and looked around. It wasn't elaborate in the least. In fact, it was somewhat spartan.

He turned to face the president as the door closed. That left the two of them alone. The president turned on a small radio that was sitting on the desk, and country western music filled the small room. "Just in case our voices carry in this old building," he explained. "I heard your first mission was successful."

"We got out alive, if that's what you mean. One of the FES soldiers was injured, but he's expected to make a full recovery."

"You did make contact, though?" the president asked, sitting against the simple, wooden desk.

"We got a message through to Antonio Ortega. He is, understandably, a cautious man. I haven't directly talked with him yet. However, he bought into my mountaintop visit and has agreed to meet with me."

The president motioned to one of two chairs opposite the desk.

"Please sit, Senator. Make yourself comfortable."

Steven was uncomfortable, and it showed. Being alone with the president in such an obviously clandestine location made him appreciate the seriousness of his visit. He sat down as suggested, thinking of it more like an order than a request.

The president changed subjects, and Steven sensed it was his way of relaxing them both.

"You know President Herbert Hoover took up his office here for a while? Oh, not in this very room, of course. There was a Christmas Eve fire in 1929 that severely damaged the Oval Office, so he moved into this building until the Oval Office was repaired.

"Many didn't want this thing built. Can't say I blame them; it looks like it belongs in France. In fact, it's even grander than the Élysée Palace, the home of the French president. There's lots of history here, though. The Japanese emissaries met here with Secretary of State Cordell Hull after the bombing of Pearl Harbor."

Steven nervously rubbed both of his hands against his pants leg, saying, "If I recall correctly, Mark Twain actually called this the ugliest building in America."

The president laughed.

"That he did, in fact at one point, it was close to being demolished. And now, well... now, it's been officially registered as a National

Historic Landmark. Never predict the future; you're bound to be wrong.

"So, Senator, as you can guess, the reason we are meeting here is that it is much more private. Many people scour the White House registry for who has visited, but here, most are hardly noticed. Not many people know that this building is connected through an underground tunnel to the White House. That means I was never here.

"I'd offer you a drink, but..." The president waved his arm dramatically to emphasize the emptiness around them. "How about a cigar, though?"

"No thank you, sir."

"You're sure? These babies are of the highest quality; a gift from the president of Nicaragua."

The president reached into his breast pocket and proffered an open cigar case. Steven looked down; the cigars were clearly some of the best in the world, each embraced by a golden band. But a good cigar like that was meant to be enjoyed over time. He was sure he wouldn't be with the president that long.

"I'm sure, sir. Not today, but perhaps we could golf someday when I would have the time to enjoy it."

"A cigar and golf, sounds like a capital idea. I would like that. You've refused a cigar from me before, if memory serves."

"Yes, my last visit to the Oval Office, sir."

"I remember now. Same reason?"

"It was, sir. I do enjoy a fine cigar from time to time, as you do, but to light up such a fine cigar for just a few pleasurable puffs seems a waste."

"I agree. Golf it is, but I insist on supplying the cigars."

The president smiled, trying to put his visitor at ease. He slid down into the simple, wooden chair next to Steven.

"What can you tell me, Senator?"

"These guys play for keeps. Mr. President, I don't mind reminding you of how dangerous this assignment is. There were four young men with me, and we could all have been killed."

The president bit his lip just a little and agreed, "I know. Trust me, Steven, I get it. If you have a better plan, let me know."

"I can assure you that I don't have a better plan, sir. I... I just want to make sure that you and President Torres realize that you are putting some fine young men in harm's way."

"You're not getting cold feet, are you?"

"No, sir! I lost two daughters to drugs; I am more than happy to take out those sons of bitches. I have a score to settle, and you've given me an opportunity for a little payback that I'm not going to waste."

President Julius Walker rubbed a bit of stubble that was already forming on his chin. It was obvious to Steven that the president had shaved early that morning, meaning he was well into a very long day. He looked up at Steven, making sure the senator was looking into his eyes as he spoke softly.

"It's a tragedy about your daughters. As a parent myself, I can't imagine what you've gone through, and I couldn't agree with you more that these cartel bastards all deserve to die. But Steven, this isn't some sort of license to kill. Protect yourself and your team, of course, but we need them alive to cooperate with us. That is, at least most of them."

"I understand the mission, sir, and its importance. However, I won't think twice about taking one or more out if necessary."

"I remind you again, only if necessary, but it *will* be your call; no second-guessing. And I do understand your anger, hell, *my* anger. You and I both know how many people have died in Mexico over the last five years alone due to the cartels and drug trade.

"Some estimates are as high as sixty thousand, and who knows how many more are forced into the sex trade? That's not even counting the people whose lives were ruined by the drugs or died from over-doses and contaminated product.

"Steven, President Torres and I have given this much thought. This is literally about the national security of our two countries. Our national security costs money, lots of it, and if our economy doesn't get better, and fast, we won't have any money for national security.

"God help us if interest rates rise even further. The math is pretty simple: five percent interest times twenty trillion of debt is one trillion dollars a year in interest alone. Can you imagine that, Senator? Twenty-five percent of our annual budget would go towards just the interest on our debt. We need some exceptional economic growth, and we need it fast. The only way I can see that happening is if Mexico becomes the trading partner President Torres and I know it can be."

Steven finished the thought for the president, letting him know that he understood the significance of his job.

"And that won't happen unless Mexico becomes safe for investment. And *that* means the cartels have to go. Sir, I've been to Mexico on numerous occasions and have seen the violence and poverty firsthand. The hard-working people of Mexico deserve a safe place to live and work. They need safe schools, factories, and colleges. I understand and agree that once that happens, Mexico's economy is going to take off like a rocket and take us with it."

The president stood and paced the room, choosing his words carefully.

"I know this is a lot to put on you and a bunch of twenty-year-olds still wet behind the ears, but it has to be done. I don't have anybody else that could possibly do this, and neither does President Torres.

"Plain and simple, the cartels have to be shut down. Unfortunately, taking the bosses out one at a time only encourages somebody else to take their place. If the last twenty years have told us anything, it's that every time we remove one boss, two more emerge. We need to get them all at once or we will accomplish nothing.

"If you told me that this plan was foolhardy and had absolutely no chance of working, I would have to respect that. I couldn't and don't expect you to risk your life or the lives of others on a fool's quest."

Steven stood up to face the president.

"I don't for one second think that this is going to be easy Mr. President. However, I don't think it is a fool's quest either. One thing I do know for certain."

"Oh? And what's that, Senator?"

"The longer the cartels operate, the stronger they get and the more people die needlessly. This is our one best chance, so I say let's take it."

"Thank you, Senator; the country owes you a debt it will not be able to repay, regardless of whether this is successful or not."

"I understand. What say we shut the sons of bitches down?" Steven directed his eyes away from the president for a moment and realized there was nothing in the room but blank walls. He turned his eyes back towards the president, saying, "Mr. President, there is one more thing I need to ask of you."

"Anything, anything to make this work. That is, anything I can pull off clandestinely."

"It's not for the mission, sir."

"Oh, what is it?"

"My family, my daughter. If something should happen to me, do I have your word that you will do what you can to help my daughter through life? To ensure she's safe and gets the finest education possible? You see, sir, I need to know that she will be OK."

Without hesitation, the president put his hand on Steven's shoulder and said, "You have my word. Whatever school she wants, and I'll make sure she chooses wisely."

"Thank you, sir. And there is an FBI agent that I would like to know is being watched over, for her own safety."

"You mean that feisty former detective, Chelle Saltarie? Your current girlfriend?"

Steven felt anger flow through him as he realized he had been followed and investigated so thoroughly, though he shouldn't have been surprised.

"Yes, sir," he said with a look of suspicion.

"Sorry, Steven; I had to know everything about you. I'm placing all of my bets on you. Anyhow, what makes you think she would even want help?"

"I'm sure she wouldn't, but she wouldn't have to know."

"Steven, if you're referring to her new job at the FBI, she got the job on her own. Your recommendation was noted but unnecessary. As a friend, I can tell you this; she would probably drop you like a hot potato if she thought you were meddling in her career."

"Yes, sir, I'm sure you're right. Our secret?"

"Our secret. If I am in any position to help, and only if she needs it, I will. I promise."

"One other thing. My brother, sir; I need to know he will be all right."

The president withdrew his arm and the confident smile on his face retreated.

"Steven, Ernie broke parole. You know that, don't you?"

"Yes, sir. I'm not looking for a pardon for him. Just that he gets a fair shake and isn't thrown to the wolves in prison."

"You want me to get him sent to a country club?"

"No, sir, just someplace he won't get killed; someplace he'll at least have a chance at rehabilitation. Maybe some sort of pilot program could be established to help him break the cycle? He's a good person, Mr. President, I just want him to have a chance at life."

The president looked away in thought; he didn't make promises lightly.

"Your country owes you a debt already, I owe you a debt, but you know he's on the run. The FBI thinks he's in Mexico. Hell, Steven, he might be working for one of the groups we're trying to shut down! He doesn't have much going for him down there; he'll have had to take whatever work he could get. That means illegal and dangerous work."

"Like you said, sir, he doesn't have much going for him."

"He could have just not broken parole. He could have played by the rules like other law-abiding citizens."

"One difference, sir. Ernie is my brother."

"Steven, you know I can't promise anything when it comes to an escaped felon. But, if something should happen to you, and if Ernie turns up in the US alive, maybe, *maybe* I can help him in some way."

"That's all I wanted to hear and all the guarantees I need to continue this mission to the end."

"So, Senator, what do you think, now that you're into it?"

"Operation Persuasion is underway. I think it has a chance."

President Walker handed a leather-crafted briefcase to Steven, saying, "We collected profiles of the leaders of the various cartels, mostly put together by the Mexican authorities, though we contributed what we could. For your sake, I hope they're accurate. At any rate, it's the best we have. Only you can open this case once the lock is set." The president slid open a hidden cover. "It uses touch ID technology. It will take three fingerprints, your choice what fingers and what order. Colonel Tripp will help you set it up.

"Steven, I must admit that your first foray into Mexico was much more dangerous than I had expected, so I took the liberty of arranging some backup for you. We cannot become directly involved in military operations in Mexico, but I think I've found a way for the US government to assist you in a more clandestine way.

"Colonel Tripp and his team are waiting for you downstairs. He's experienced in classified operations and is in charge of your special support. He's a good man, and I trust him. He has some interesting ideas for your safety, and you may want to listen to them, but Steve, remember, He does not know your mission, nor may you share it with him. He only knows to assist you in any way he can."

President Walker held out his hand and smiled widely, saying, "Steven, you have good instincts; follow them. And, Senator?"

"Yes, Mr. President?"

"Don't get yourself killed; I'm counting on you." The president looked up, staring into Steven's eyes. "They play rough, so watch yourself."

"Yes, sir, I will, but I can play pretty rough too," Steven said as they shook hands.

"Now, wait here until I disappear. Agent Troy will be along shortly to escort you to see Colonel Tripp."

Chapter 5

"Cabbie, pull over by that woman standing alone."

The sun was setting, and the air was developing a night chill. Chelle's long, white dress coat was unbuttoned, and she waited with her hands in her coat pockets.

"You mean the one in the white coat?"

"Yes, she's expecting me."

"Wow, she's a looker, ain't she?"

Senator Steven Westcott didn't feel compelled to answer the cabbie, but he did so anyway.

"Yeah, she is a real looker. Mind your manners, now; she can get mean if you get on the wrong side of her, she's a cop."

"Oh... thanks for the heads up."

Steven grinned and sat back in his seat.

The Washington, DC cab pulled over to the curb, and Steven exited and helped his date into the car. Chelle was easily a foot shorter than Steven, and his arm seemed to surround her as he guided her gently by the shoulder. Steven picked up a slight scent of her perfume as he bent to help her into the back seat. He liked the way she had let her curly, auburn hair grow out from the shorter look she'd had as a police detective.

"Chelle, you look stunning."

Chelle's shoulder-length hair was curled to the point of being a bit frizzy, but, with the way it framed her face and bounced on her shoulders as she got into the cab, it looked attractive on her.

Steven hurried around the cab and slid into the back seat, next to Chelle. Chelle's coat was open, and under it, Steven could see a silky, red blouse and the lapels of a matching leather blazer.

"'Stunning'? Senator, are you trying to get my vote?" Chelle asked as Steven settled in next to her.

"I thought I already had your vote."

Chelle laughed and agreed, "Yes, you certainly do, and you look well."

"Your smile does that to me. It seems to take all my cares away."

"I'll bet you say that to all the FBI agents you meet."

With a laugh, Steven disagreed, "Not all the agents, trust me, just one."

Chelle's background as a cop, and now as an FBI agent, had taught her not to take her good looks too seriously. She was much more comfortable on the shooting range than getting her nails done. However, for tonight, she had treated herself to a bit more face time in front of the mirror. She still knew how to be a woman, and she wasn't afraid to act like one. That didn't mean the gun in her purse wasn't as convenient as possible. She knew the world could be a dangerous place, and she didn't want to be caught flat-footed.

Chelle glanced up at the rearview mirror and saw the cabbie smile. That was how some cabbies were; some couldn't care less what was said in their cabs, but to others, as soon as you entered their realm, you were fair game for whatever voyeuristic tendencies they might have.

The cabbie seemed to be checking her out regularly in the rearview mirror. He pretended he was looking at cars behind them, but Chelle could see his eyes lock on her from time to time. She sort of didn't mind; it was a cabbie's best compliment.

"Where are we heading?"

"That would be a surprise," Steven said, gazing directly into Chelle's sparkling blue eyes with a mischievous grin.

"Say, I know you two. You're that senator guy, and you're the cop that was on TV all the time!" exclaimed the cabbie.

Chelle and Steven just looked at each other and laughed. They were getting used to being called 'that senator guy' and 'that cop'.

After a ten-minute drive and a bit more whispered small talk, the cab pulled over. The small, old, two-story building looked exceedingly out of place surrounded by a large parking lot and the shadow of the US Capitol Police Headquarters, hundreds of times its size.

"You're kidding," Chelle laughed. "The Monocle Restaurant? Right in the shadow of my old office."

They stepped out of the cab, and Steven handed the driver the fare plus tip. Steven slipped his arm over Chelle's shoulder and ushered her to the door.

Immediately, the maître d' greeted them, saying, "Senator Westcott, how nice to see you again."

"Alec, how are you this evening?"

"Most splendid, sir. I have your table ready. Please, follow me."

The maître d' took them up narrow stairs. Chelle examined the brick wall on one side of the stairway and the photos on it. The wall had, at one time, been the exterior of one of the buildings that had now been merged.

The upstairs was a bit cozier than the open concept below them. The Monocle Restaurant was as much Washington establishment as you could get, and it reminded its visitors of that with a motto written on the wall in bold type: 'An empty stomach is not a good political advisor.'

"I understand this is a haunt for you senators and congressmen," said Chelle. "Is that true?"

"It is, this and a few others. If we need somewhere to hash things out in a neutral area, we can usually arrange a private area. Sometimes, a little privacy is essential to keep things moving."

Steven and Chelle sat at the table, Alec assisting Chelle with her chair. The table was set for two guests sitting directly across from each other. Steven ignored the setting and took the seat directly to Chelle's left to keep their conversation more intimate.

"So, how did your trade mission to Mexico go? I didn't see anything in the paper."

"It went as well as I could have hoped. As unbelievable as it will seem, we're trying to avoid publicity for now. Negotiations can be a delicate thing; I've found it's best to keep the press out of it."

"A politician who doesn't want press. You certainly are full of surprises."

"And how's your new job?"

"In a word, exciting. I think I made the right decision. It was time for me to move on. Your little escapade last year changed things for me at the department."

Steven gently took Chelle's hand in his.

"I'm sorry, I didn't mean to create so much havoc in your life."

Chelle squeezed back, saying, "It's not a bad thing; it's a good thing. I'm still in law enforcement, and I'm learning things I didn't even know existed. I have a lot of practical experience that will work in my favor. I think I'm going to become a good agent, if I do say so myself."

"I know you're going to be a damn good agent. After all, you were one hell of a detective."

Steven was starting to feel relaxed; the mission had been on his mind constantly, and it was nice to have a distraction for a night. He looked at Chelle and smiled. Chelle Saltarie was a very pretty distraction.

"Care for a glass of wine with dinner?" he suggested.

"I'm not on duty for a change, and you're not driving. How about the whole bottle?"

"I like the way you think."

Steven ordered the wine, and soon Steven had Chelle filling him in on some of the more exciting training exercises in Quantico.

Chelle was enjoying her almond-crusted salmon and Steven his thick, red, bone-in ribeye.

As Chelle prepared another bite with her fork, she asked, "You mentioned on the phone that you were talking with your daughter. How is she doing? Do you think the counseling sessions are helping?"

Steven sipped his wine and took a moment to think about how to answer.

"You're so kind to ask," he said, smiling to let Chelle know she hadn't broached a taboo subject. "Tracy's grades are improving, that's a good sign. She's such a strong young woman; I'm so proud of how she's handling all of this. I can't even imagine being a teenager and being exposed to everything she was.

"I never told you: she invited me to one of her counseling sessions. I was so impressed. She's certainly taught me a few things about life. In short, despite what she has had to get through, I think everything will be OK."

"And Lucille?" Chelle asked; she had never been one to stay away from a needed conversation because it would be uncomfortable.

"I thought men were supposed to avoid talking about their exes?" Chelle said with a laugh, "My fault, I asked."

"Lucille was at one of the counseling sessions with Tracy and me. It went well; I mean civil and all. My anger at her divorcing me is gone. The divorce was for the best. I understand she's still fighting depression, but she's taking pro-active measures, and I truly wish her the best."

"I guess you can't fault her too much. You could make the argument that she has a right to be depressed. I mean, anybody who went through everything she has..."

Chelle stopped mid-sentence, realizing what she was implying. Steven had been through that and more.

Steven reached his arm over her shoulder, smiling as he hugged her closer.

Looking deep into her eyes, he said, "Thank you for caring. We both lost a lot, but the worst thing was, we lost faith in each other. Lucille was, *is*, a wonderful woman. She is a terrific mother and, if I had to have an ex, well, I'm glad it's her. We were fortunate in that we had a wonderful and loving marriage for twenty years. Chelle, I need you to know that my feelings for her changed when I realized she had lost faith in me."

"I'm sorry, Steven, I didn't mean to press you. Maybe it's the cop in me. I ask too many questions for my own good. It's none of my business."

Steven gave Chelle's hand another gentle squeeze, saying, "I hope it's your business." He took another thoughtful pause and another sip of his wine, adding, "I was mad as hell at her for a while, but not anymore. I think of it as our marriage having been exposed to both a physical and mental trauma that forever changed it. We are not the same people, nobody would be. Rebecca's death changed us; we lost a daughter, and we were already struggling with that. Then, well, you know the story. It wasn't Lucille's fault, and it wasn't mine, but it happened just the same."

The maître d' came by, and Steven and Chelle put a polite stop to their conversation as he emptied the wine bottle, sharing it between them. When he was gone, Steven shrugged, exhaled, and shared a thought.

"Maybe if I hadn't done what I did, what I had to do, we would still be struggling through our marriage, trying to make it into something it could never be again, but it's better this way, both for us and for Tracy. I let my attorneys handle the divorce, and I tried to stay emotionally unattached. I'm not holding any grudges. Life is too short."

"Steven, you know I understand, probably better than anyone else on the planet. I guess what I'm asking is how you're doing. You've been through so much and mostly all of it bad."

"Not all bad; I'm sitting with a gorgeous woman, holding her in my arms, gazing into her beautiful eyes and having a conversation that I couldn't and wouldn't want to have with anyone but her." Steven's face changed from serious reflection to friendly optimism. "And as long as we're putting all our cards on the table, and in the interest of full disclosure, I have something I need to say.

"As far as you and I are concerned, I'm not hoping for anything from you other than your friendship. At this point in my life, I think you understand me better than anyone. It's hard to explain. I mean, my life is complicated, and I don't expect anyone to become entangled in it. You have a new career, and who knows where that will take you? I hope it's obvious that I love your company, but I'm sure you know I'm not ready for another committed relationship."

Chelle took a long sip from her glass, covering her face as she digested Steven's bluntness.

"Wow, we certainly are putting all of our cards on the table, aren't we? How on earth did you ever get elected as a senator with that kind of honesty?"

"You wouldn't want it any other way, would you, Chelle?"

"No, I wouldn't, so let me put my cards on the table." Chelle set her glass down and turned towards Steven, leaning in. She looked at him with an impish smile and whispered, "I find you very attractive, my career doesn't intimidate you like it does some men and you're right; I think I do understand you. After all, I had you thoroughly profiled by the best experts in the field, and I do know what you've been through over the last year. I also know that I don't know *everything* about you. You have a secretive side and, like most politicians, you're good at changing the subject when I start getting close. But that's OK, I don't mind a little mystery.

"Steven, we're two adults. I'm not looking for any complications in my life right now either, I don't even know where I'll be living in the near future, but that doesn't mean I don't have feelings right now or that I want to ignore them."

Steven and Chelle's lips were only inches apart, and it seemed only natural for them to meet. Steven stopped; if Chelle wanted the kiss, the invitation would be obvious. He didn't have to wait long. Her warm, tender lips met his. The kiss seemed so natural, like it had always been there, even though it was their first. Steven couldn't help but wonder: was he being selfish? Soon, he would again be in harm's way. Was he taking unfair advantage? Was it right of him to develop this relationship, regardless of what they called it?

Chelle slowly broke off the kiss, and Steven wondered if she had felt the same deep stirrings. Chelle gently licked her lips, making sure Steven caught the gesture. She picked up her wine and changed the subject to the reason, or at least the pretext, for their meeting.

"I told you I have a bit of information to share with you on the people who you believe killed Destinee," she said.

Steven's demeanor changed substantially. The businessman in him came out as he set down his wine and listened intently.

Chelle continued talking in a subdued voice, saying, "I used some of the FBI's assets to track down more information on the Woods Trust."

"Chelle, I appreciate what you're doing, but I don't want you to get in any trouble with the bureau over this," Steven whispered.

"I'm calling it a training exercise. I don't think it's wrong for me to use the FBI computer system to find out who might be trying to blackmail a senator, whether he's a friend of mine or not."

"I thought you didn't buy into my theory?"

"Let's just say I wasn't as enthusiastic about it as you, but I'm slowly changing my opinion. I went on your assumption that Sam Kreiser's death wasn't an accident and he was murdered because he knew too much. So, who would want Sam dead?"

"His accidental death was certainly convenient for you, and the timing is strangely coincidental, but I don't think his death was for your benefit; I think it was for theirs."

"So, you're not suggesting I killed Sam?"

"No, of course not. The expertise to fake that kind of accident was beyond you. No offense. You could have hired somebody, but that would expose you to potential blackmail, and you're too smart for that."

"Ah... no offense taken, I guess."

Steven stabbed his fork into the last of his ribeye and asked for a Drambuie on the rocks as an after-dinner drink.

Chelle continued, "Sam's death was ruled an accident for good reason; an investigation was thoroughly conducted and foul play was ruled out. But—"

"But, you're not buying it."

The waiter came back with Steven's drink, and Chelle declined one for herself.

"If Sam was telling the truth about the Woods Trust, they would certainly have the resources to create the illusion of an accident. If they were also behind the attempted blackmailing of a US senator, they certainly had motive to dispose of Sam. The last thing they would have wanted was a public trial. Just the mention of their name could have been problematic for them, and Sam could have known much more than he let on."

"That's an awful lot of 'if's, Detective. And you forget that nobody tried to blackmail me."

"'Agent', Mr. Senator. I'm not a detective any longer."

Steven smiled, saying, "Sorry, Agent Saltarie; old habits. I'm just happy I'm not one of your suspects for a change."

"You're not even on the radar on this one, though I think it revolves around you for some reason. There is definitely a legal entity called the Woods Trust, specifically one founded in 1955. I ran across an old file that was loosely linked to the trust. It mentioned Philip Alan Woods, a seasoned diplomat and leader of humanitarian efforts during World War Two, who became an international consultant for the US government. In fact, he was instrumental in the creation of the United Nations. He died in 1962 at the age of 87."

Steven had to give Chelle credit; she had discovered what the president of the United States had already told him. But that meeting was confidential, so he couldn't let Chelle know he could confirm her information.

"Chelle, you're suggesting that, somehow, and who knows for

what reason, a man who died years ago is responsible for Destinee's murder? Not just that; he was actually gunning for me, but he didn't want me dead, just locked away for the rest of my life?"

"In a word, yes. There are a few other strange things. When I tried digging deeper, I kept getting locked out of files. 'Higher authorization needed'."

"I would imagine that you have only the most basic authorization at this point."

"A little more than that, but still not much. But when I can learn more at home on my personal computer than I can access on a government database, I get real suspicious."

Again, Steven wished he could share the information he had. The president had also said that the trust was a major player on the international stage, though staying out of the public spotlight was its specialty. Steven had been disturbed to learn that presidents were still regularly invited to the conference it sponsored.

Chelle continued, "Woods was extremely wealthy when he died; a trust started in 1955 could be an exceptional amount of money now. The trust is still active, *that* I found out, and being denied access tells me that the files definitely exist. I think the government is, or was, interested."

"Agent Saltarie, you certainly do have an active mind."

"Well, my intuition was right about *you*, despite the evidence."

"Believe me, I don't question your intuition."

"Well, my intuition is telling me that Sam's death wasn't an accident. He said he stole from the Woods Trust because he thought they wouldn't miss the two million dollars."

"Apparently, he was wrong."

"He sure was, but it must be a huge trust for him to have thought he could get away with it. I'm guessing they didn't prosecute Sam because they didn't want the publicity. He owed them big time, so they used him to get to you. Why else would Sam do it? He had no grudge against you; he didn't even know you. His entire relationship with Lucille was calculated to help him compromise you. Furthermore, I can't find one instance of the trust's charitable giving or any other disbursements, so why does it exist? What's its purpose?"

Steven sipped his Drambuie and spent some quiet time reflecting on Chelle's logic. Chelle sat silently and finished the last of her wine. Eventually, Steven signed off on the bill and asked the maître d' to call them a cab.

"I admit there are a lot of 'if's and 'maybe's in all of this," said Chelle, "but if somebody wanted to destroy you for some reason, we – I mean *you* – should know."

"I have to admit, I still can't fathom why anybody would want me in jail for murder. What would that gain anybody?"

Chelle made sure she had Steven's eye; she wasn't ready to abandon her thoughts.

"Maybe they didn't want you in jail."

"Well, framing me for murder would have been a strange way of keeping me out. What are you getting at?"

"The other reason for framing somebody for murder, especially a senator."

"Another reason?"

"To be able to blackmail them with the promise of coming up with the evidence to prove their innocence. What if their intent was to switch the blame to Sam? That is, if you cooperated with them."

"So, they didn't want me in jail, they just wanted to use the threat of jail to make me cooperate?"

"Not just jail, lifetime for murder, if not the death penalty. Pretty strong persuasion."

Deep in thought, Steven helped Chelle with her chair. Chelle thought it chivalrous, unused to such tender treatment, especially from her cop friends.

"If you can't buy somebody, blackmail them," Steven said as he opened the door of the restaurant for Chelle.

Chelle rephrased it for Steven, saying, "Somebody – say, the Woods Trust – wants something from a certain incorruptible senator. Only solution: blackmail them into cooperating, make them an offer they can't refuse."

Outside, the evening air was warm but refreshing. Chelle's curly, brunette hair wafted gently in the fresh night breeze.

Steven thought about Chelle's theory. He had suspected that Sam's death had been arranged by higher powers to free him for his current mission. Now, he was concerned that Chelle was right. It was entirely possible that Sam's death was covering up a much more sinister plot in which he and his family were just pawns. That made Steven worried for Chelle, and he didn't want her digging into her theory any deeper.

"I... I know this was all my idea, and don't misunderstand me; I would love to find Destinee's killer, but I've got a lot on my plate right now. As strange as it may seem, I'm not interested in chasing ghosts, even if they might be real, at least not right now. Maybe what's in the past should stay there."

Chelle reminded him, "They underestimated you. That might not happen next time."

Steven smiled, replying, "This time, Agent Saltarie, I do believe you're the one with the outlandish theory. I would appreciate it if you didn't waste any more of your time, or the FBI's, on a wild goose chase."

"Maybe... maybe you're right. It is just a theory. Still, it intrigues me."

Chelle looked down the road for the approaching cab, and Steven stole an extended gaze at her face. He could see the crease of her smile. Chelle was wearing a near-constant smile tonight; he didn't need to ask if she was enjoying the evening.

The side of her face looked baby smooth, and the breeze played with the front of her light-red blouse, sometimes pressing it against the outline of her breasts.

Steven gazed up the street just as Chelle smiled and twisted her arm around him, snuggling up to his side. It was time to put the detective in her to rest.

The taxi pulled alongside the curb, but before Steven could open the door, she said, "I don't have to work tomorrow. And... well... if you would like some company tonight? What I'm trying to say is, you don't have to take me back to my apartment if you don't want to."

Steven looked down into her eyes to judge her sincerity.

"I would like that. It's been so long since I felt this close to anyone. I don't want to go back to my apartment alone again. To sleep with the scent of your hair and to have the softness of your skin against me would be the most wonderful thing I could imagine."

Steven took Chelle's face gently in his hands and tilted her face upwards as he kissed her deeply. He didn't have to wonder; there was no doubt Chelle was as emotionally evolved as he, regardless of what they had both said earlier about not becoming committed.

Chapter 6

Filipe, you're a sight for sore eyes," Steven said, giving him a light salute and, before Filipe could react, a giant bear hug.

"Amigo, not here, the men will talk."

Steven dropped the slightly smaller man with a playful push.

"Let them talk. How's Snipes?"

"He gives his regards. But, sadly, he cannot be here. It will be another month or two before he is ready to join us again."

Steven was warmly shaking the hands of the other team members as he said, "So, now what, no sniper?"

"That would be unacceptable, let me introduce El Cazador."

"'The Hunter'," Steven said, repeating the name in English with a wide smile to let the man know he approved. "I've heard a lot about you. Anybody who Filipe thinks so highly of is more than good enough for me."

El Cazador nodded, saying, "Filipe has told me much about you also. You are a very brave Americano."

"I can afford to be brave with you and the team protecting me."

Filipe wrapped his arm around El Cazador and said, "I share everything but my wife with El Cazador. He is my second in command."

Steven could tell that El Cazador was both flattered and embarrassed, but the man smiled and added, "We think like each other, and that makes us dangerous to our enemies. Our superiors have told us that our president is counting on us to protect you while you are in our country. I promise you that we will."

"That promise, coming from you, means a lot to me," replied Steven. "Come on; I need to address the rest of the team."

Steven motioned for Filipe and El Cazador to follow him, and they proceeded to a spot at the corner of the airport tarmac where the rest of the team had congregated. They were at the Pedro Jose Mendez International Airport. The airport was situated east of the city of Ciudad Victoria, which was the capital of the gulf state of Tamaulipas. Ciudad Victoria, a city of over a quarter million, was nestled between two mountain regions. To its east was the Gulf of Mexico, and its northern border abutted the southernmost parts of Texas. Unfortunately for the population of Tamaulipas, it was perfect for smuggling drugs into the US, which made it a dangerous place to live.

The group of five huddled, and Steven started talking over the sound of a helicopter engine starting up.

"Everything is on a need-to-know basis here. I am prohibited from divulging the exact nature of our mission. I will tell you, and it is my duty to tell you, that this mission is extremely dangerous. It is critically important to the United States, but, and let me make this very clear, it is also critical to Mexico. If we are successful, your families, your homes, your work will all become safer.

"We are going into the belly of the beast. You are to deliver me to Antonio Cruz Ortega. You know him as El Pequeño Diablo, the head of the Gulf Cartel. I will meet him alone. You will wait for me at an extraction point that only Filipe and I know.

"If I do not show by the assigned time, you are not, I repeat *not*, to come for me. I will probably already be dead. Is that understood?"

The men around Steven looked up at him with blank stares, not willing to agree to his terms.

"Look, men, I get it. No man left behind. But I can't be responsible for your deaths." Steven looked directly at Filipe. "I mean it, Filipe; if I'm not there, get out. If they torture me, I might break. Hell, everybody breaks under the right persuasion. If I give them the extraction point, I want you to be gone by the time they get there."

Filipe stared into the eye of the United States senator in his care and reluctantly agreed.

"Sí, we will leave at the designated time."

"OK guys, let's get going. El Pequeño Diablo isn't going to wait all day."

Dressed in military fatigues, the group of men ran with their guns and full gear towards the waiting Black Hawk. The exception was Steven; he wasn't dressed as a soldier. Instead, he wore tan jungle fatigues along with heavy jungle boots.

The lone helicopter took off, heading west towards the coastal mountains and the drop area.

Filipe was sitting next to Steven inside the noisy fuselage. He spoke loudly so Steven could hear him.

"Amigo, you know that El Pequeño Diablo is not going to be waiting for you with open arms. He may be meeting with you just for the opportunity to kill a nosy American as a warning to others, or he may want to hold a US senator hostage for special dispensation. I hope what you have come to tell him is important enough for that kind of risk."

Steven stared out of the open door opposite him, watching as they flew over the university city of Ciudad Victoria and knowing the landscape would now swiftly become mountainous. Steven watched the city fall away as the helicopter climbed over the treetops and proceeded north.

Filipe was right. The cartel bosses were ruthless, many coming up in the ranks of the cartel partly based on how many people they had killed. El Pequeño Diablo was no different. He had been taught the finer points of the trade by his father, who had been killed during one of the many skirmishes between rival cartels. The question wasn't if what he had to say was important or not. The question was whether El Pequeño Diablo would believe him.

It was only twenty minutes later when the pilot announced they were almost to the coordinates they had been given by the cartel leader.

Steven studied the rugged terrain below him. He knew that understanding it could mean the difference between life and death. Undoubtedly, the cartel leader had picked a spot where he could make sure the helicopter was alone. Steven was sure that El Pequeño Diablo would also have picked a spot where he could find plenty of cover for hiding and an escape route to boot.

The pilot called over the intercom, "Get ready, we're at the coordinates."

Filipe ordered his men, "Guns ready; it could be an ambush to steal the helicopter." He looked at Steven. "Good luck, my friend. See you in three hours."

The helicopter landed in the clearing, which was situated in a small valley. El Pequeño Diablo's men would have little difficulty in observing the helicopter and its occupants from any of a number of vantage points. If they wanted to ambush them, they had picked the perfect spot.

Steven shook hands with Filipe and stepped out. He felt he was foolishly giving himself up to the enemy as he walked away from the Black Hawk unarmed.

When it took off again without him, his last sight was of Filipe saluting him with a casual flick of his wrist. Steven stood in the middle of the clearing and put his hands behind his head, waiting for instructions to come from the hillsides.

The sound of the helicopter was gone when he heard instructions come from the trees behind him.

"Throw your passport towards the big tree in front of you."

"I don't have my passport."

"We need your identification."

"My wallet has my driver's license, it has my photo on it."

"Throw your wallet towards the tree."

Steven slowly took his wallet out of his pocket. He made a point of showing it in his hand before he tossed it the ten feet towards the tree.

Someone dressed in camouflage khakis, the kind a soldier might wear, picked up his wallet.

"Make one move and it will be your last," somebody else warned him from the edges of the clearing.

Steven stood motionless, waiting for the next command. It didn't take too long for the soldier to shout out.

"Take off your clothes, all of them: watches, rings, everything. Comply immediately, or you will be shot."

Apparently, they believed he was who he said he was.

Steven made a show of demonstrating his compliance. He took off his watch and tucked it into his pants pocket. He unbuttoned his shirt and took it off. Then, he undid his boots and took them off as well as his socks. Finally, Steven undid his pants, took them off and laid them on top of the growing pile.

"Everything!" came a shout from the trees.

Steven sighed; he'd been hoping they hadn't actually meant everything. He slipped his thumb under the elastic of his jockey briefs and pulled them down and off, tossing this last item onto the pile.

"Step away and move to your right. That's far enough. Now, face down on the ground. If you look up, you are dead."

Steven did one of the hardest things he had ever done in his life: he stayed still as he heard the rush of men coming towards him. It didn't take long before he felt rough knees pressing into his back. His hands were twisted behind him and secured roughly with a thick cable tie.

Before he was hauled back to his feet, a thick, cloth bag was drawn over his head. Steven was now naked, secured and blinded. He was at the mercy of his captors.

Chapter 7

His feet were tied just before he was pushed into some sort of vehicle. Lying on his side, Steven felt the vehicle move. He knew, from the boots that kicked him from time to time, that he was being closely watched.

Trying to memorize speed and turns, or even sounds and smells, was impossible on the bumpy ride. The vehicle was obviously off road. No words were spoken, including by him. He could only assume he was being left alive for a reason. He had no reason to doubt that he was, in fact, being taken to a face-to-face meeting with El Pequeño Diablo, the Little Devil.

The blindfold was a good sign; it was being used so he couldn't identify anybody or assess a location. Stripping him down was meant to prevent any tracking devices on his clothes from giving away their position. All reasonable precautions if they intended him to survive the day.

Finally, the vehicle came to a stop. Where? He had no idea. They could have been driving around in a circle for all that time. At last, the hood was unceremoniously taken off. The ties around his wrists and ankles were cut free.

"Here, put this on."

Steven was handed a one-piece coverall. It was reasonably clean, and he was surprised to see that it was about his size. He could count at least six rifles pointing at him.

After he had the coverall on, he asked in fluent Spanish, "Does anybody have a cigarette?"

Nobody answered and nobody flinched; these men were fairly disciplined. It was just as well, since Steven hadn't smoked in years. Right now, though, he had to admit it might have been calming.

He looked around the compound and saw tents and a few lean-to structures. This was a camp of some sort, not permanent by any means, but it had been in place for longer than a week, by the looks of things.

The encampment was under the protection of some trees, but at this elevation, the canopy wasn't thick. He slowly took a few steps and worked his way into a bit of sunshine, making a point of smiling when the sun touched his face.

There were guards surrounding a tent. Steven hoped the occupant was none other than El Pequeño Diablo. He guessed it was about ten minutes later when a man actually emerged from the tent.

"Señor Senator, sorry about the bumpy ride, and of course the necessity of taking your cloths. When you are a wanted man such as myself, it can't be helped. I'm also sorry your clothes and your watch cannot be returned to you; they are floating down a river, moving further away from us each moment. However, I do have your identification."

The man from the tent pulled out Steven's ID and held it up, examining the photo on it against the man in front of him.

"Señor Ortega, I presume."

Steven didn't have to guess; he'd known Ortega as soon as he saw his face.

"Senator Westcott, what a truly unexpected visit from such an esteemed man."

"It isn't because I'm an admirer. We need to talk privately. Very privately."

"Maybe I don't want to talk. Maybe you need to be dead."

"Do you think I came here to martyr myself?" Steven looked at all the guns pointed at him. "I have an important message. Several, actually, but we need to talk in private. This is for your ears only."

"Maybe I should just kill you here and now. Maybe I don't want any messages. Maybe I should send a message by sending you back home in small pieces. Why should I listen to a man from north of the border?"

"Your life depends on it, so why wouldn't you?"

"Before I contacted you, as per your instructions, I of course researched you. I must say, I am impressed. You obviously took great risk to get the message to me, and you have taken an even greater risk to meet with me in person. That is the only reason you aren't dead already."

Steven slowly bent over, stretching his back and sides.

"Look," he said, "it's been a long day. I've been stripped naked, kicked, bounced along the mountain on the floor of that pick-up and now my back is sore." Steven stretched some more, swinging his arms a bit. "We need to talk right now."

"You do not give orders here." El Pequeño Diablo clearly wouldn't accept being bossed around. "I could extort a grand bounty from your country, were I to tell them I am holding one of their senators."

"That would be a huge mistake. Obviously, they know I am here, and precautions have been taken for my safety."

"We watched things closely. Nobody followed us. You are very much alone, I am afraid."

"You know, I was wondering if you can see the next ridge from here?"

"And why would you care? It seems you have more pressing problems."

"It's not for me, it's for you. I have something to show you. I hope there is nothing of value there."

El Pequeño Diablo's face instantly changed. He had one of his men get on a radio and call. Steven overheard the communication as his men confirmed that everything was OK.

"What game are you playing?"

"Like I asked, can you see it from here? There's something you might want to see."

Antonio barked some more orders, and Steven was soon back on the ground, his face in the mud and four men sitting on his arms and legs.

****

Antonio rushed to his jeep and shot off down a mountain road. There was an open bend in the mountain path. From there, the opposite ridge was visible. One of his major processing plants was there.

He was in constant communication with his men there, and the team left to guard it were put on full alert. It was a heavily armed compound on an easily defensible ridge, and they reported nothing out of the ordinary. Despite all this, Antonio raced to the opening and slammed the jeep to a halt.

He grabbed his binoculars and could see nothing but peacefulness. He scanned the only approachable roadway, but it was empty.

"Are you sure?" he asked over the radio.

He looked at the factory where he mass-produced methamphetamine or, as it was called on the street, crystal meth. The raw materials came mostly from China and were unloaded at sea from ships into smaller boats that docked at secret ports along the gulf coast.

A man with a deep voice shouted back over the radio, "Nobody has set off the alarms. All is quiet. The men are on full alert, but we have seen nothing."

Antonio was scanning the wider area with his bare eyes when he caught a glimpse of something. By the time he realized what it was, the ridge was destroyed. From miles away, it looked surreal – an immense, silent explosion.

He felt the silence until the roar of thunder caught up with him. He could have sworn he even felt the heat from the blast. It was gone. His largest meth factory and most modern production facility was gone.

The American had done it. The American would pay. Some of the smoke cleared, and Antonio scanned the ridge in disbelief one more time, only there was no ridge. He twisted the jeep back onto the roadway and raced back towards his American captive.

Antonio pulled into camp and exited his jeep in anger. The men were just staring at their boss; they had heard the roar of the explosion and knew something had happened but not exactly what.

"Stand him up. Stand him up now!" El Pequeño Diablo demanded.

Steven was lifted into place by two guards. Antonio punched Steven hard in the stomach. Steven slumped over, the guards struggling to hold the big man up so their boss could take another swing.

"That was a million-dollar facility you just destroyed; you have put my production back a year! I have commitments, people who will be angry with me when I can't deliver."

"I told you we needed to talk," Steven managed to gasp out once he caught his breath.

El Pequeño Diablo turned to walk away, rubbing his head. Suddenly, he twisted with his hips and punched Steven hard in the stomach once again.

"You are a dead man! A dead man, you hear me? I am going to kill you so slowly that the maggots will have time to eat you from the inside out."

"If you listen to me, I will tell you how to make your money back. If you don't, you will die." Steven looked towards the sky. "They know where you are, now. You can't escape. If they suspect I'm dead, another missile will come and another after that until they're certain you've joined me."

Antonio was so angry he wasn't listening. He grabbed Steven by the hair. Even if it broke his hand, Antonio was going to smash the man's face in with it.

"Look," spat Steven, "I know Miguel killed your parents. I can help you get him *and* his business."

Antonio held back. They were the first words he had heard.

"El Ángel!" Steven shouted the name. "I can help you gain control of El Ángel's cartel. Do you want that, or would you rather die from a missile aimed right at your head?"

"Tie him up, tight, and take him to my tent," ordered Antonio. "Michael, take the truck to the processing plant and see if anything or anybody is left."

"'Left'? What do you mean?"

"Just go!"

Chapter 8

Steven was dragged roughly into Antonio's tent with his hands and feet tied. The four men who were guarding him tied him to a chair. Only after they were sure he was secured did they leave him alone with their boss.

Antonio was pacing in front of Steven, playing with a pistol. He flicked the safety on and off as he checked the clip to make sure it was full. Eventually, he snapped it securely into place.

"You are two sentences away from being a dead man. How do I kill Miguel Ángel Vega?"

"You don't. *We* do. That is, if you cooperate with us and he doesn't. Otherwise, it will be the other way around. But, if I had to guess from Miguel's profile, I'd say he won't cooperate, and that would mean you could be the one to take over his operation."

Antonio stared at the photo ID in his hand. For an el politico, the man had balls of steel. Antonio was fascinated; what could be so important for this man from north of the border to risk his life to tell him?

"I believe you are who you say you are," he said. "You are an important man in the United States government. Is that true?"

"You could say that. I am one of one hundred US senators, and I've met with the president a few times."

"Why is the United States interested in helping me?"

"Because we want something in return."

"What could I possibly do for you to get such a favor?"

"We think that you can help us in a way nobody else can, at least not in this part of Mexico. The missile attack was to demonstrate that we're serious. I have a small window to report back that I'm OK. If I don't, you will be killed. Escaping will be impossible."

"Do you think this is the first time I have been threatened?"

"By the United States military, yes, yes I do. This isn't a threat, it's a promise. I can arrange another demonstration if you would like."

"You do not threaten me!" El Pequeño Diablo shouted, pounding on the tabletop. He racked the slide of his gun, flicked the safety off and held the pistol against Steven's head. "No, a bullet to the head would be much too quick."

El Pequeño Diablo tossed aside his gun and took a long knife from inside his desk.

"I do not like to be threatened," he said as he held the knife against Steven's throat. Steven didn't flinch.

"If I don't walk out of this camp alive," he said, "neither will you."

"Tell me, what is this favor?"

"Oh, it's no favor to us, but it is the only way you will live. I'll tell you exactly what you need to do. In fact, I – *we*, my government and yours – will help you do it."

"Tell me, and I will decide if I will comply."

"No, Antonio. I am here to tell you that you are a dead man if you do not agree to our plan."

"You bastard, you gringo bastard! How dare you threaten me? This is my land; I control everything from here to the coast. I can kill you with one slice across your neck."

Antonio sliced the knife through the air in front of Steven.

"I never claimed you couldn't kill me. I'm just promising that, if you do, you might as well slit your own throat as well. They have you on surveillance cameras, facial recognition. For all I know, they're listening to this conversation right now. If they suspect I'm dead, my government has the permission of your government to destroy this mountain and everything on it.

"From the moment you came out to meet me, you were tagged, and now you will be followed. My government has technology you haven't even dreamed about." It was a bit of a bluff, but then again, Steven was sure the government did have technology even he hadn't dreamed of.

The plan had simply been to blow up the closest processing plant without blowing up the senator as well. Steven's eccentric movement when he'd stretched had been a signal to the surveillance team that he was ready. The trick was locating him after the winding truck ride through the forest, but apparently the plan had worked.

Antonio thought back to the horrific explosion and the complete destruction of his production facility and the mountaintop itself, along with all the men and women working there.

"I do not take kindly to threats, Senator." Antonio snarled. "No government can track me through these mountains."

"We can and will; you have been exposed to a dose of radiation that our satellites can see. You can't wash it off or hide it."

"How? That is impossible." Antonio angrily tossed the knife across the room. It stuck into a tent pole, shivering with the impact. "Perhaps I will use you for a bit of sport, some target practice with my knife."

"Listen to me, Antonio. The second you touched my ID, you were exposed. The radiation is harmless unless you decide not to cooperate. Then, of course, it will be deadly. Live or die, your choice."

Antonio stared at the ID sitting on his desk. Steven could see him contemplating whether what he said could possibly be true.

"You are a foolish man if you expect me to believe you. I think that I will kill you and take my chances you are bluffing."

"If you kill me, it will be worth the sacrifice of my life to know that you will be dead. You and others before you killed my daughter with the drugs you sell. I would gladly die in exchange for your death." Steven cocked his head to the side and cracked his neck. He smiled and calmly offered, "Perhaps another demonstration would help convince you?"

"Perhaps, but first a question. If you would gladly see me dead, why would you want to help me?"

"Because my president and yours asked me to."

"And you say I can keep my money?"

"Yes, and your soldiers."

"And my soldiers?"

Antonio couldn't imagine such a scenario.

"And you will no longer be considered a criminal."

"How is this possible?"

"Because you will be working for us."

"And if I stop working for you, then what?"

"We will kill you. You can't hide from us anymore. We will know where you are at all times."

Antonio glanced again at the ID on the table.

"Why should I believe such a preposterous threat?"

El Pequeño Diablo studied his prisoner. He felt he could sense a lie when told; right now, there was a strange feeling in the pit of his stomach. If the man was telling the truth, he could indeed already be in their trap.

"Antonio, there is no decision here. I'm not lying. Either you cooperate with us and enjoy your wealth and freedom or you die. It's that simple."

Antonio sat down on the chair behind his desk, but he spied the ID in front of him so he stood and moved away from it. The explosion he had seen earlier replayed in his mind.

"No, Señor Senator, I think you are lying. You knew where my processing lab was, and your military blew it up, but that is the end of your tricks."

"What if I made the truck that brought me here disappear? It's headed to the same ridge. We could all watch; you know, like a movie. We could make popcorn, have a beer. It'll be fun. What do you say?"

"I think you are bluffing."

"Let's find out. After all, it's your life we're talking about."

"No, Señor Senator, it is *your* life," Antonio replied with anger in his voice. "OK, we will do it your way." He picked up his gun. "I will have a beer; you can drink your own blood."

Antonio shouted some orders when he stepped outside, and two guards came in and untied Steven from the chair.

One of the guards roughly pulled Steven's arm behind him to tie it, and that was when Steven twisted his body around and slammed the guard in the chest. In the same moment, he picked up the chair with one hand and brought it down hard on the other guard's neck and back. The first guard caught his balance and rushed the American.

Steven flew up against the tent pole. The second guard now had a part of the broken chair in his hand, intending to use it as a club over Steven's head. Antonio rushed back into the tent and shot his pistol in the air.

"One more move and I will shoot you right now." Antonio walked up until his gun was no more than a couple of inches away from Steven's head. "Tie him."

With his arms retied behind his back, the two guards marched him out to Antonio's jeep, hoping for the chance of some payback.

Steven stopped for a moment and squinted at the sun as if he hadn't seen it for months. The guards pushed him ahead.

"Hey," Steven protested, "I'm just trying to stretch out my back a little. You guys were pretty rough on me back there."

As he talked, Steven bent at the waist and twisted his back a bit.

"Señor Ortega, are you sure you want to lose more men? The truck headed for the ruins of the processing plant doesn't have a chance."

"Stop your stalling, get in my jeep and we will see who is bluffing!"

Steven sat up front next to El Pequeño Diablo as his two guards jumped in back. El Pequeño Diablo reached into the back of the jeep and pulled out a beer from a cooler.

"Salut, my friend!"

Soon, the jeep with the four men was parked on the same ridge from which Antonio had watched his factory disappear.

Antonio called over his radio, "How close are you to the mountain?"

"We are starting the climb up the road to the factory now. Antonio, from what we see, there was great destruction, it appears that the factory is gone."

"Go see for yourself and report back."

"You know you are condemning those men to die," said Steven.

Antonio threw his beer bottle over the ridge and opened another.

"Beer tastes good on such a hot and humid day, don't you think, amigo?"

"There's still time, you can stop this."

Steven knew the men in the truck weren't exactly innocents, but he didn't like being an executioner.

"You said I could have El Ángel's territory."

"Like I said, for your ears only," Steven said, nodding to the two men in the back.

Antonio motioned for them to step away, but he added, "If the prisoner tries to escape, shoot him."

They waited for the guards to get out of earshot and Steven sighed.

"As I was asking," said El Pequeño Diablo, "what about El Ángel's territory?"

"Somebody has to run it if El Ángel doesn't cooperate. If that becomes the case, and we're forced to kill him, we'll want you to use your army and his to keep peace and make sure no other cartels take over."

"You want me to grow even bigger? Why... why should I believe you?" Antonio was slowly accepting that things might be out of his control.

"Antonio, your men are going to die. Untie me before it's too late."

"Why should I believe you?" Antonio demanded again, louder and angrier.

"Why else would I have come here? My president and yours wanted me to personally deliver this message. I risked my life just to talk to you, just to convince you to work with us. If we wanted you dead, you'd be dead."

"As soon as I let you leave, maybe I will be dead. Maybe this is just another trap by the FES."

As they talked, the truck came into view on the winding road up the mountain.

"You will just have to trust me," replied Steven. "Join us and you will live. If you don't let me go, I can guarantee you will be dead, just as your men will soon be. I see no choice for you."

Antonio followed the truck below with his eyes and contemplated the situation. Soon, the truck would be halfway up the mountain. It was at least a mile away, Steven judged.

"What is it you want me to do?"

"We just need you to change your business plan a bit. We'll help you. Not only will you make more money, but you'll be able to spend it freely and live freely."

"That is far enough with the truck, walk the rest of the way," Antonio said into his radio.

There was some mild protest from the man on the other side, but Antonio convinced him to do as he was told.

"That was a wise decision, amigo." Steven smiled. "I have no wish to kill more people."

"You didn't mind killing the men and women at my factory."

"Would you and I be talking if I hadn't? Would I still be alive?"

"Well, amigo, you won't be for long." He finished his beer and glanced at his gold Rolex. "Your time is up."

"I'm not bluffing, give it another five minutes."

"Why, why? Five minutes? Ten? I do not like your threats or your president's threats. Out of my jeep, I do not want blood all over it." Antonio cracked the gun butt over Steven's head. "Now!" he shouted. Steven turned his back towards the door so he could open it with his tied hands. He found the lever and twisted it. The door opened and he stepped out backwards, keeping his eyes on Antonio.

"To the cliff. By night's end, there will be no remains for anybody to find. The coyotes have to eat too."

The two guards only meters away watched, smiling and laughing at the soon to be dead gringo.

"Please, if you don't mind, move closer to the cliff," El Pequeño Diablo requested. "There is no sense in making my men get their hands dirty dragging you there. Now, first, I'm going to shoot your legs full of holes. When you are withering in pain, I will push you down the mountain so you can slowly and painfully die. Maybe, if you are lucky enough, you will stay alive long enough to make friends with the coyotes before they rip you apart."

A mile away, the truck vanished in a cloud of fire. The guards froze as a loud explosion followed.

Antonio stared down at the giant hole in the road where the truck used to be. He forgot to breathe for a minute or more before he whispered just loud enough to be heard by his men, "Put your guns away. Untie him. This is my new partner."

Antonio sat in his jeep, waiting in silence. He was relieved when Steven joined him. It was only then that he was sure he wasn't going to be blown sky high.

"How do I know that you won't kill me after I have served your purposes?" he asked.

"We won't have to or want to. If we're successful, you will become an important man in Mexico's history and its future."

As Antonio started driving the jeep back to camp, Steven saw him considering the truth of his last statement.

They climbed the bumpy road slowly, and he asked, "I would become important to Mexico's future?"

"Very. That is, if we make this work. I never promised it would be easy."

"Make *what* work? You have told me nothing."

"When the time comes, I will, but that time is not now."

Back at camp, Antonio's men were shocked to see the gringo untied and leading the way. Now, it was Steven's turn to pace the small tent. He picked up his ID and slipped it back into his wallet. He slid the wallet back into his pocket as he strode over to the knife sticking in the support pole and pulled it out.

Antonio was clearly shocked to see him handle the poisoned ID so casually. The fact that his former prisoner now held his knife was lost on him.

"Now, I have a few questions," said Steven. "Your drugs flow north towards Nuevo Leon. That is correct, isn't it?"

Antonio wasn't used to giving out such information, though it was fairly common knowledge. He hesitated, not afraid to let his guest know he was thinking over how to respond to the question.

Steven reached out and grabbed Antonio's hand, twisting it behind his back and bringing the knife up against his throat.

"We are partners, do you understand? You tell me everything; your life and mine depend on it. I will not play games with you."

"Sí, sí! Yes, of course, they go north."

"To Laredo?"

"Sí."

Steven kept the knife but eased off Antonio and stepped back a few paces.

"Do you use the group called 'El Dragóns', led by a man named Francisco Delgada Reyes?"

"Sí, they move my narcotics to the northern states, and I use them if I need to send a message to anyone trying to move into my territory."

"Can you control Francisco? If not, he will have to be eliminated."

"He is a dangerous man; cutting off heads to make a point is his personal specialty, but he is effective, and I cannot control the movement of my drugs without him. For the right amount of money, he usually does what I say."

"For now, tell him nothing of our meeting. You can continue to use him, but if you suspect he will not do as you say, let me know, and I will either have a talk with him or we will take him out of the equation all together. Right now, I don't want anything to change, especially your control of an area. If you have to use the El Dragóns to do that, so be it.

"My information has the Black Knights, the 'Cabelleros Negros', as your competitors from Puerto Vallarta through central Mexico north to El Paso. Is that correct?" Steven used exaggerated motions as he talked with his hands, waving the knife in front of Antonio's face to make a point.

"Yes, the Caballeros Negros control that area."

With each question, Antonio was becoming a believer that the crazy American was dangerous and to be taken seriously.

"Our information has it that they are led by a man called Juan Guerrera Carlos."

"Your information is, again, correct."

"Can you set up a meeting for me?"

Antonio's face turned white, and he stammered, "El Padrino? No, no." How could his world have been turned so upside down in one afternoon? "The Godfather, he will kill you."

"So, you *can* set up a meeting."

Antonio started to think that wouldn't be a bad thing. Maybe he could arrange a meeting for the American. If he was lucky, El Padrino would kill the American and his life could go on as normal.

"It is possible. I could tell him that I want to make a deal with him. Extend a territory to him in exchange for something."

"You have illegal oil taps going on right now in Hidalgo. He controls Jalisco, you could propose giving those taps to him."

"Why would I do that?" Antonio didn't like the way his new partner was thinking. "And how do you know about those?"

Steven ignored the questions.

"El Padrino also has oil transport trucks and steals oil himself. If you tell him that you want to give him those taps in exchange for something, he would meet with us."

"You're loco! I'm not meeting with him, and I'm not giving him my oil. That's turning into good revenue."

"It's not your oil, you steal it from the oil companies."

"After I steal it, it is my oil, my money. You said I could keep my money."

"Look, if the plan works, we won't give him your oil, but that's if the plan works. We need Juan Carlos and the Black Knights to cooperate, or it won't."

"What plan? I know of no plan."

"The plan where you keep your life and your army and your money. What do you think would convince Juan to join us? If we were to blow up his main hacienda in the mountains?"

Antonio's face turned even whiter as he dropped into his chair and protested, "No, no, you must not do that, he would send his entire army after us!"

"Señor Ortega, are you OK?" came a call from outside the tent.

"Sí, sí... Go away, I am fine," El Pequeño Diablo said tiredly to the side of the tent. Looking back at Steven, he explained, "You are loco; you do not want El Padrino angry with you. Juan is a family man, his family lives at the ranch in Tepic. You kill his family and nothing else will matter; he will kill you, even if he dies himself."

"OK, bad idea. Wait, I think I have it. A simple but effective way to prove to him we mean business. Yes, it's obvious: we'll blow up one or two of his oil trucks."

Antonio rubbed his head like he had just developed a migraine.

"Maybe you won't kill me, but I think El Padrino will."

Steven took the knife in his hand and tossed it across the tent. With a *thud*, it stuck into the corner of a slender tent pole.

Steven reached out to shake Antonio's hand; if not a sign of friendship, a sign of cooperation.

"You can contact me the same way you did to bring me here. I strongly suggest you stay in contact. If you are declared rogue, you will be killed. I will have further instructions on how to proceed."

Antonio took the American's hand suspiciously and returned the handshake.

"My men will take you wherever you need to go."

"One other thing, Antonio."

Antonio looked up as if one more bomb was to be dropped on his lap.

"You can't tell anyone, not a soul, that I was here, and you must instruct your men to hold their tongues also. Our plan must remain a secret until we are ready; it's in your best interest.

"That also means that, until I say otherwise, all of your enemies are still your enemies. I can't protect you in any way. If you are caught by government forces or another cartel, you'll be just as dead."

Steven knew that keeping secrets was something Antonio understood. He had many of them. More importantly, being asked to keep this visit secret made the promise of not killing him more real. As Steven had thought when El Pequeño Diablo's men blindfolded him, one doesn't need to ask a dead man to keep secrets.

****

"Amigo!" Filipe was happy to see his American friend. "We have been watching you for the last hour. The forward scout said you were safe and alone, nobody has followed you."

Steven was happy to be back in the safety of the FES. They skipped the formality of a handshake and went to a solid hug.

"You have more lives than a cat, amigo, but where are your clothes?"

"They had me strip down to nothing. They tossed my clothes and my watch into a plastic bag and floated it down the river, suspecting an embedded tracking device."

"And they were right, of course," Filipe said, grinning. "It appears that your watch was too great a prize for one of the soldiers. Somebody kept it, and we followed it with the built-in GPS tracker. I believe we know exactly where you were taken."

"It was El Pequeño Diablo's camp. Doesn't matter; I'm sure they're long gone from it by now."

Steven didn't share the missile strikes with them, or that a nearly invisible drone had been following him and listening to his conversation with extremely sensitive equipment. Nor did he share that, from now on, El Pequeño Diablo would be working for him.

"Time to head back to camp," he said. "And Filipe, I have another mission for you. I assume you've heard of El Padrino?"

"Certainly, my friend, in America you would call him 'the Godfather', like in the movie."

"I need you to locate the tapping points he uses to steal oil and time their truck movements."

"I like the sound of that. I think El Padrino and his Black Knights are going to lose some of their tankers if you're thinking what I think you are."

"Sorry, Filipe, that's on a need-to-know basis. Of course, you're free to speculate all you want."

Chapter 9

Steven climbed back into the Black Hawk for the ride back to Pedro Jose Mendez International Airport and closed his eyes for some well-deserved rest. The familiar thumping of the chopper blades slicing through the air comforted him.

The men around him were all relaxed; they were safely on their way back home. Steven closed his eyes and retreated towards the most comforting thoughts he could. Those thoughts were of his daughter, Tracy, and his last visit with her only weeks before.

****

As usual, his first stop had been to see his daughter Rebecca's resting place. She had been seventeen when she died of a drug overdose. Steven imagined he could feel the sun on his face as he gently placed the bouquet of flowers down and said a prayer, apologizing for the thousandth time for not saving her.

The living needed his love more than the dead, however, and he had suggested to Tracy that they go horseback riding. Spring break had given them the chance to get away together, and Tracy was growing up so rapidly that Steven had jumped at the chance. Sometimes, it was hard on him, as his younger daughter had started to remind him so much of her sister. She was now only two years younger than Rebecca had been when she died.

"Are you enjoying your spring break?" he had asked as he coaxed his horse down the lane with a few gentle kicks of the stirrups.

"No, Dad, why would I like a break from high school? No

homework, I don't have to get up early, I can do anything I want. I guess I can't imagine why anybody would like that."

"High school has made you into a little wisecracker, hasn't it?" Steven had chided playfully.

"Yes, I'm enjoying spring break and thanks for taking me horseback riding. I hardly get to see you anymore. Ever since you and mom divorced, life has been a little weird."

"I know what you mean, it's been strange for me too."

"Are you still pissed at Mom for not believing you were innocent?"

"I am not pissed at your mother."

"You were."

"OK, I'll admit that I was, but I'm not anymore, and I wasn't when we finalized the divorce. Your mother is a fine woman, and I will always love her, it's just that things changed."

"Dad, I'm not a little girl. I know what happened; I could see it start right after Rebecca died. I thought it would go away in time and things would get better."

"So did I, honey, so did I."

"I don't blame you."

"Well, good, but don't blame your mother either. A lot happened in our lives, both of ours, and yours too. We became different people, and we just weren't meant for each other anymore."

The path had narrowed after that, Tracy clicking her cheek to get her horse to pick up its pace a little while Steven followed a horse-distance away. The canopy of trees had shaded them as they took a path through Willowdale State Forest, the light that escaped through the leaves flickering off his daughter's shoulders.

After a half-mile, the path had widened again, and Steven had caught up with his daughter.

"Do you miss her, Dad?"

"You mean Mom, I assume."

"Yeah, do you miss her?"

"Of course, her and you, our house. I miss carrying you on my shoulders to watch the Fourth of July parade and seeing you at Christmas all excited because Santa came. I miss all of that, but I can't bring those days back; they're gone forever. Now, it's for us to fondly remember the past and look towards the future."

Tracy had considered her father's advice and enjoyed the sun on her face.

"Do you have a girlfriend?"

"Tracy! That's none of your business."

"You do!"

Steven had looked away down the path and galloped his horse away from the conversation.

"That proves it!" When she finally caught up, she had asked, "Is it that detective?"

"What makes you think it's her?"

"I could tell she liked you."

"You only met her once."

"I know, but I'm right, aren't I?"

"She is not my girlfriend."

Tracy had looked at her dad with a disbelieving stare.

"Look, we've seen each other a few times. She has a different job now and might even be moving away from Washington."

"Do you want her to move?" Tracy asked, but Steven had ridden on, deep in thought. "Well?"

"I guess it doesn't matter, I'm way too busy for a relationship. I wish her the best wherever she goes."

"You're not getting any younger, Dad, and she's cute."

"I'm not exactly over the hill, you know."

"Not yet, but..."

"Thanks a lot. What about you, any boys?"

"Naw, I'm too busy too. I'm studying hard, and a boyfriend would just want me to hang out with him."

"It can't be easy for a girl as pretty as you to fight off all the boys."

"You have to say that, you're my dad. But Jeremy McConnel did ask me to prom."

"Well?"

"Well what?"

"Well, what did you say?"

"I said no."

"No? You don't want to go to prom, or you just don't want to go with him?"

"He's pretty nice, but I don't want him to think I'm his girl or anything. I'm just a freshman, I didn't want to get a dress, I don't know, other things."

They had ridden on a bit in silence before Tracy volunteered, "I'm having lots of fun, my grades are pretty good. I don't know, I guess I just didn't feel like going to the prom."

"Trust me, honey, you'll know when you do. I think you made a very wise decision, and I'm proud of you. Anyway, sun's going down soon, time to get back."

"I miss you, Dad. I'm glad you came back to visit."

"This is still my district. I have meetings, and I want to meet with the people I'm representing. I'll be back often, and I promise I'll see you whenever possible."

"How long will you be home?"

"Another week, then I'm afraid I'll have to leave again."

"Are you going on another trade mission to Mexico?"

"I am, honey, so I might not be able to call you. It gets crazy busy when I'm down there."

"I understand. I'm sure it's important."

Steven had looked toward the setting sun. His daughter had no idea how right she was. It had been that day, after they'd hugged good-bye, that Steven pledged to himself that he wouldn't fail Tracy where he had failed Rebecca and Destinee. If he had a chance to put a dent in the cartels and their trade of illegal narcotics and human trafficking, he would.

****

"Amigo, Señor Senator, we are here."

Steven felt a gentle shaking of his shoulder. He opened his eyes and nodded that he understood as he felt the wheels of the chopper gently touching down. *Damn reality,* he thought. He wanted to retreat back into his memories of home and his daughter.

Steven looked at the smiling face of his friend, who was sitting next to him.

"Filipe, how would you like to share a beer with me in my quarters? I have a question to ask you."

Filipe had some errands to see to before that, so Steven went back to his small quarters alone. They were lavish by some measures; he had his own bathroom and office, and thankfully the air conditioner was working, or at least the small ribbons tied to the vents were blowing limply in its breeze.

There was a knock at the door.

"Come in."

"Señor Senator, you wanted to see me?"

"Please, please come in, can I offer you a Corona?"

"Sí."

Steven grabbed two beers out of his refrigerator. Thankfully, it was working much better than the air conditioner.

"It's a beautiful night, care to go for a walk?"

"A walk would be nice."

Steven offered up the glass neck of his Corona. Filipe tapped his own against it in a small, mutual salute.

Outside, in the darkness, they saw a commercial flight coming in with landing lights blazing a hole in the night sky.

"You have a beautiful country, Filipe."

"Thank you, Señor Senator, I agree it is most beautiful."

"Please, call me Steven, amigo."

"Esteban."

"What's that?"

"'Esteban', it is Spanish for 'Steven'."

"Ah, yes, I remember now from my high-school Spanish. I was Esteban all year. That was in Mrs. Hoogan's class. Failed the first time through. Didn't like it much."

"But your Spanish is excellent."

"You can thank the army for that. I got serious, the army got serious and I learned Spanish."

"Esteban, you said you have a question for me?"

"What do you know about Miguel Ángel Vega?"

"El Ángel?"

"Yes, though from what I've heard, he's no angel."

"He is particularly ruthless, possibly insane. It is said that he boils people alive, slowly if possible. He controls the west coast with entry points to the US in Tijuana and Mexicali. There's a war going on now between the Black Knights and the West Coast Cartel that is ruining the vacation area of Puerto Vallarta. The tourists are afraid to go there and with good reason."

"Your information sounds pretty solid."

Filipe tipped his beer to his mouth and finished it.

"The military, mostly the navy, has been caught in the middle of that war. I have friends that have seen things nobody should ever see."

Steven stopped walking; the light from a security post lit his face from the side.

"Filipe, after we let the Black Knights know there's a new sheriff in town, I need to see El Ángel."

"A new sheriff?"

"Sí, a new sheriff, a new chief of police."

"Ah, and you are this sheriff?"

"In a manner of speaking, yes."

Filipe shook his head.

"Señor Senator, with all respect, your luck cannot hold out forever. This is a dangerous game you are playing."

"This is no game," Steven said solemnly. "I know the risks, but I also know the rewards for your country and mine. I need you to trust me and to use your connections to get me set up with El Ángel." He sipped his beer. "Ready for another, amigo?"

Filipe considered Steven's request in silence as they walked back to the barracks for more drinks. Steven and Filipe took two wooden desk chairs and set them just outside the door, enjoying each other's company, a few more beers and the cool night air of the Mexican night.

"I might know someone who could help us find El Ángel," Filipe said solemnly, "but I am doing you no favor, my friend."

Steven emptied his beer and twisted the empty bottle around in his hand.

"I understand; it's not your responsibility if something happens to me."

"Señor Senator, when will you tell me what you are trying to accomplish with these dangerous meetings? I could be of much more help."

"I can't; it's up to our bosses. But I can tell you it's worth the risk."

Filipe stood up; it was time for him to go.

"El Ángel does not just kill his enemies, he first makes an example of them. If El Ángel does not like your message, and that is assuming he even listens, you will be brutally tortured. He has had years to perfect his craft; you will die very slowly. You will pray for your own death."

Filipe started to walk away into the darkness but stopped and turned around.

"Please, think long and hard, amigo. If, in the morning, you still want that meeting, let me know. I wait for your decision."

Filipe turned and walked towards his barracks.

"Filipe," Steven called out. "I *have* thought it over. Set it up."

Filipe stared at Steven, whose face was lit by the light from the window. He saluted, acknowledging the request, then turned and walked heavily into the darkness.

Chapter 10

Chelle's head popped up into the sunshine as she climbed the stairs leading from the Archives Metro station. It was a beautiful spring day in Washington, not too hot and not too humid.

Chelle turned north towards 9th and Pennsylvania. The fountains of the US Naval Memorial Plaza were attracting scores of birds, chirping as they flitted in and out of the trees around the fountain area.

The huge FBI center she worked at was only a block away. Chelle was early; her new boss didn't expect her in for another half-hour, but Chelle liked to take her time and enjoy the morning rather than rushing to her work.

She stopped for coffee; it wasn't Starbucks, but it was hot and steamy. This time of morning was a personal time, and her thoughts went to something that couldn't have been more personal. Chelle rested on a bench near a fountain. It was one of two, and together they stood guard over a giant map of the world etched in the granite between them. The map showed the lands and the oceans the navy protected, and her thoughts moved towards Senator Steven Westcott.

She reminisced about the last night they had been together. Between both of their hectic schedules, they had finally had time for dinner. Chelle smiled and felt warm inside as she remembered the long, cozy and exhausting night together.

****

In the morning, when they awoke and lay in each other's arms, Steven had been so deep in thought he hadn't realized he was twirling his finger through a few loose strands of her dark, curly hair.

That was when she had rolled over and slid herself halfway on top of Steven, her bare breasts against his chest.

"A penny for your thoughts."

"I'm sorry, I was a few thousand miles away."

"Mexico?"

"I wish I didn't have to leave again," Steven had said, gently stroking his fingertips across Chelle's back.

"I don't suppose I could talk you out of it?"

"You can try," Steven had said, smiling.

"Would I have any luck?" she'd asked, kissing his chest.

Steven had sighed, replying, "No. Negotiations are at a delicate spot right now."

"How long will you be gone?"

"A week or two, I suppose."

"Must be some negotiations."

"It will be far-reaching when it's done, but don't expect to see any results for years."

"In other words, you won't be able to take credit for all your hard work and sacrifice."

"That's OK, I'm not doing it for that. Maybe someday, years from now, people will remember how it started. Oh well... doesn't matter, not important. So, will you be in Washington when I get back?"

"I'm still not sure. The job opening I've been waiting for came through today. I've been offered a training opportunity in LA. It wouldn't be permanent, but it does start in two weeks."

"Besides the timing stinking, what aren't you sure about?"

Steven had rubbed the soft flesh of her buttocks with his big, strong hands as she said, "I don't know if I want more training. I want to get out in the field and actually do something."

"What's so funny?" she had asked.

"Nothing, it's just so you. I think you would be happy if I went on the run again and you had somebody to chase down."

"If you go on the run, I will chase you down, and it won't take me months to catch you."

Steven had looked up at the ceiling and said seriously, "Chelle, don't turn down the position because of me. My life is anything but stable, and I don't expect it to be anytime soon. Hell... I don't even know if I want it to be."

"I understand, no expectations, just you and I living for today, because who knows what tomorrow will bring."

"Would more training be so bad? It would probably open up more doors, possibly into things you didn't even know existed."

"You're suggesting I take it."

"I'm suggesting you keep thinking about it. Do what's right for Chelle Saltarie and nobody else."

Chelle had given Steven a long kiss. As they slowly parted lips, she had whispered to him, "Thank you for being my friend. Let's just enjoy the present; I want it to last forever."

****

It had been good advice. Chelle's smile faded as she thought more about leaving for the extra training. Steven had been right. She didn't want to leave Washington, not now. Was it because of Senator Steven Westcott?

Probably, she admitted to herself. But that was silly. She wasn't a schoolgirl anymore. Yet she felt a schoolgirl crush; her life had never been more exciting and full. The decision still loomed.

Chelle stood. It was time to meet up with her new team at the FBI center. As she walked, another thought of that wonderful evening pricked at her mind over and over again.

Steven had said absentmindedly, "I couldn't think of anyplace or anyone I would rather be with before a mission."

"A mission?" she had asked.

"A trade mission, I mean."

Steven Westcott was a bad liar.

Chapter 11

Steven was alone in his hotel room, going over the psychological profile of Juan Guerrera Carlos, alias El Padrino, aka the Godfather.

Tepic was located halfway down the western coastline of Mexico and only an hour's drive from the waters of the Pacific Ocean. It was only about one hundred miles north of the tourist destination of Puerto Vallarta.

Its position made it a central spot for the distribution of drugs to the north. Unfortunately, it also made it one of the most dangerous cities on the earth, right alongside Detroit, St. Louis and Chicago.

El Padrino was married and considered himself religious, a Catholic. He was a father of three, ages eight, six and four. The oldest and youngest were girls. His wife, Anita, had kept her beauty. The picture Steven was looking at was marked 'Recent'.

He could have been any average businessperson, only he wasn't. He had worked his way up through a local gang. At first, drug running and graduating into smuggling. He had been caught with some raw cocaine paste and spent time in a Mexican jail. While in jail, he'd made some more serious connections, and when he was released, he became an enforcer for a much larger gang, collecting debts whether real or imagined.

The rest of the story was familiar. Known for his ruthlessness and effectiveness, he'd risen through the ranks, killed some of his bosses until he was boss and extended the organization. Aside from the business he was in, he would have been considered a success story.

El Padrino understood how to shift money from illegal operations into legal ones, and he was good at it. The dossier in front of Steven contained the names of many suspected fronts. That wasn't to say he didn't take risks in business; he had to. In order to enjoy his wealth, he was also taking risks in his private life. Those risks could be exploited.

Steven was curious as to how and when he had gained the moniker 'El Padrino'. He skipped ahead a few pages, flipped over the most recent photo of Juan Carlos and found what he was looking for. The Mexican authorities had infiltrated his organization and discovered that he was enamored with the Mafia.

Apparently, he had nicknamed himself after watching the Spanish-dubbed versions of the three Godfather movies, which the notes said were required viewing for all associates. El Padrino had learned much from his study of the Mafia. The fact was, El Padrino had been successful at mimicking the Italian mob's methods and had molded the Black Knights in that flawed image.

Steven went through the list of movies on demand in his hotel room. He wasn't particularly surprised when the 1972 original *The Godfather* was advertised. For twelve dollars US, he could watch it. Steven clicked it on; it had been years since he had last seen it.

"How do you know this plan will work?" Filipe asked the next morning.

"I don't. These guys kill people, often their own people, just to make a point. If El Padrino doesn't take our little demonstration as well as El Pequeño Diablo, the Little Devil and I will both be killed. If it comes to that, I'm hoping a red dot on his chest might be enough to settle him down so he can think about the situation."

Filipe and Steven were having a late breakfast in downtown Tepic. Both men were dressed casually in non-military clothes. Steven wore khaki pants and a light-blue polo shirt.

Steven sipped his coffee and was pleasantly surprised; his café Americano tasted, well, American. He went over the plan again.

"After tonight, we do not know each other. I'm staying at Hotel Fray Junipero Serra, room 505. I am expecting El Pequeño Diablo to contact me tomorrow. As soon as I know the when and where of our meeting, I'll get a message to you.

"It's critical that one hour into our meeting, the airstrikes begin.

By then, I will have told Juan Carlos what is about to happen. If at all possible, have your sniper in position to save my ass."

"El Cazador would be honored to save your American ass, if needed."

Steven left his friend and walked alone towards the Hotel Fray Junipero Serra. The early days of summer were just starting, the sun felt comfortable and Steven guessed that the high today would only be about eighty degrees Fahrenheit by mid-afternoon. The humidity was creeping up, not yet uncomfortable, but rain this afternoon was a good possibility. The mountains in the distance were starting to develop a cloud cover.

The main plaza, which was right next to the hotel, was occupied with people free to do nothing at all but enjoy the fountains of the plaza, the palm trees swaying and the perfect weather. This was Steven's first visit to Tepic. It was a modern, bustling city with a population somewhere north of three hundred thousand. The boulevard in front of his hotel was wide and modern even though, only a block away, taxis skirted around streets and tunnels so impossibly narrow he wondered how the drivers kept their side view mirrors attached to their cars.

Steven decided to scout out the area around the hotel. In particular, he wanted to see the roadway, which was on the same side of the hotel as his room. He was on the fifth floor, but he could exit a window onto the adjacent building if he had to. From there, he would need a way off the roof. A little reconnaissance would let him know if that was a possibility or not.

On the corner was a soft drink vendor. Steven paid for a bottle of Coca-Cola and started to walk away.

"Señor," the vendor chided as he pointed to a sign that said you had to drink it there or pay for the deposit on the bottle. Steven dug into his pockets for a few more pesos and paid the deposit.

He scouted the area as he walked down the street. His first partner, El Pequeño Diablo, had assured him that El Padrino wasn't arriving into town until late tonight. Tomorrow, sometime, they would meet. The pretext was that Steven was a new buyer for the stolen oil.

That was when Steven would introduce his true self. A demonstration of force would be arranged, and El Padrino would be offered the same deal as El Pequeño Diablo. Join or die. The plan sounded simple enough, but cartel bosses weren't known for their reasonable natures.

Steven sipped his coke and found the small alleyway alongside the hotel. A miniature delivery truck was blocking the far end. The driver was noisily stacking fruit containers onto a hand truck to be moved into the restaurant. Steven noticed two dumpsters jammed against the building. He looked up; maybe, if he had to, he could jump down to one of them. It would still be a two-story jump, but it looked possible. He looked into the dumpster and saw that it was half-filled with empty boxes and rotten fruit. If he had enough time during his escape, maybe he could do better.

Steven noticed the delivery man had gone silent; the truck was still there, but he was nowhere to be seen. He saw three men walk past the truck, jamming the far exit of the alley. They looked menacing; no doubt the deliveryman agreed and was hiding.

The wide, pedestrian-rich boulevard by the main plaza was his best bet for avoiding conflict. Steven wasn't against retreat when it seemed like the best option. He also wasn't against running as fast as he could. The three would have to be pretty quick to catch him before he made the plaza.

He didn't waste any time, running in the opposite direction. The three men immediately pursued. That was when a full-size, open-topped Hummer turned into the alley. This wasn't a random attack; it had been rehearsed. The men in the Hummer stood and aimed automatic rifles at him.

"We heard you want to meet El Padrino," a man sneered as Steven came to a stop.

The three men behind him had caught up, and they waited a respectful distance away with knives at the ready. Steven turned towards them, trying to assess his predicament and find an escape. He gripped the coke bottle by the neck and broke the bottom off it, creating a sharp edge.

"I was told we would meet tomorrow."

"El Padrino changed his mind. He wants to meet you now, on his terms, not yours."

"El Pequeño Diablo was to introduce me."

"He will; he is already on his way to meet El Padrino. If you don't cooperate, you will die right now, and El Pequeño Diablo will be killed for failing to make the introduction."

There was no decision to make anymore. Steven had wanted a meeting, and he could either die now or take his chances. He tossed the bottle to the side of the alley.

The men roughly bound his elbows behind him and also bound his hands with zip ties. Steven was searched and his cell phone was found straight away. The man searching him dropped it to the pavement and destroyed it under the heel of his boot. Steven's watch soon found the underside of the man's boot as well, but at least his wallet was handed to a man in the Hummer. He rifled through it, taking out the cash and putting it in his pocket. He stared at Steven's State of Massachusetts driver's license and the photo of Steven, carefully comparing the photo to the face in front of him.

He looked at the business cards, five of which were the same and advertised 'Anthony Miller', a petroleum exporter, but the ID was clearly a picture of the man they had captured, and it said 'Steven Westcott'. The man read the name aloud, heavily accented and in Spanish.

"Esteban Westcott".

He looked at Steven, knowing that at least one of the names was fictitious. That wasn't necessarily a bad thing; in this business, he didn't expect the man to use his real name. That would indeed be foolish.

The wallet and its contents would have to be given to El Padrino. With a silent nod, the leader motioned towards the Hummer, and Steven was pushed into it. At least this time he had his clothes on.

It seemed to Steven that he was being treated with a bit more respect than during his last ride. In this case, he reasoned that it was because he was being considered as a possible business partner. There seemed to be at least a little respect between thieves.

Steven was blindfolded, and his head was kept down as he lay on the floor of the large vehicle. The ride was smooth enough, and Steven sensed they were on a main road.

Eventually, he could sense the unmistakable smell of the ocean. Tepic was only about fifty kilometers from the coastal town of Miramar, and Steven was sure that was where he had been taken.

The Hummer came to a stop and, with his blindfold still on, he was strong-armed to a boat. The boat creaked as he was tossed to the deck, and the butt of a rifle against his back convinced him not to move.

At first, the ride was smooth, but after what he estimated to be about fifteen minutes, waves began pounding against the hull. They were out on the open ocean. Killing him at this point would be as easy as throwing him overboard. The sharks would take care of the evidence.

The ride was rough, and the men laughed more than a few times when Steven mistimed a wave and his head hit the floor. Eventually, the boat slowed, and Steven heard a slight thump as their boat was tied up to a second. Still blindfolded, he was lifted up onto a much more stable deck. Orders in Spanish said to take him below deck. Steven didn't recognize the voice; it belonged to a new player already on the bigger boat.

Steven realized the new boat was fairly big, because he was led down the stairs with a guard holding tightly to each of his tied arms. Once down below, he was set in a chair and tied down, his legs fastened to the front legs of the chair and his hands secured behind its back. Only then was the blindfold removed.

When Steven's eyes had adjusted, he discovered a bloody face across from him.

"Antonio, what happened to you?"

Through a swollen mouth, El Pequeño Diablo answered, "Did you think we were going to meet at the country club over drinks and a game of golf? You wanted an introduction, and El Padrino wanted to make sure I was certain about you. In this business, the wrong introductions kill people. I hope for our sakes that you have as good an offer ready for El Padrino as you had for me."

"I do."

Antonio winked to let Steven know the plan was still a go. Steven looked around the room. The furnishings were elaborate, they were obviously on a yacht, and an expensive one at that, to have a room the size they were sitting in. On an oversized and beautifully carved desk, Steven saw his wallet. It was sitting open.

A man walked into the large saloon, cutting chunks from a piece of cheese with a long knife. He slung one into his mouth.

"Gentlemen, I'm so sorry for the less than hospitable reception, but it can't be helped. You'd be surprised by how often these very precautions have saved my life."

El Padrino looked older than his thirty-five years. Apparently, drug smuggling was a stressful occupation. Not only that, but he looked shorter than his dossier suggested. Still, the way the man carried himself was enough to dispel any doubts. This was El Padrino.

"Antonio," he sighed, "you disappoint me."

By the look on El Pequeño Diablo's face, Steven could tell this was bad news.

"Your card says you are Anthony Miller, petroleum exporter, but..." El Padrino held out the driver's license. "*This* says you are Steven Westcott. I have heard of a Senator Steven Westcott. In fact, you look a lot like him."

Antonio looked up and whispered through cracked lips, "Listen to him; I wouldn't have brought him here if it wasn't important to you."

"You brought a United States senator into my company; that does not disappoint me, Antonio; it honors me. What disappoints me is that you didn't trust me enough to tell me the truth. Trust and truth are important to me, my friend. I must know that I can trust those around me."

Steven broke in, saying, "He didn't have a choice, just like you don't."

He thought he might as well begin the negotiations from a position of strength; after all, it was an all-or-nothing situation.

El Padrino held the long knife he had been using to slice his cheese up to Steven's neck.

"I don't have a choice? I see many choices. Tell me, Senator Westcott, are you here to kill me?"

"No, of course not, if my country wanted you dead, they wouldn't send a senator."

"Maybe this isn't about the United States; maybe it's about an ambitious senator." El Padrino waved his short arms around the beautiful room. "Maybe it is about money, lots of money. Why else would a US senator be a friend of El Pequeño Diablo?"

"I do want to make you a business proposition, but I can assure you it is with the approval of my government and yours."

"Ahh... you are here to make me an offer I can't refuse," El Padrino said, laughing at his own joke.

Even if he hadn't just watched *The Godfather*, Steven would have understood the reference.

Steven gave El Padrino a sly smile, saying, "Good, we understand each other."

"Am I to wake up to a horse head in my bed? You forget, *I* am El Padrino, not you."

"Tomorrow, you will lose two of your semi-tankers of oil."

"Oh, and how will I lose them? Are you going to just make them disappear?"

"As a matter of fact, that's exactly what I'm going to do."

"And you are telling me this now. Why? Why not wait until after you make them disappear?"

"Like I said, you have no choice. Telling you now will let you know that you are helpless to do anything about it."

El Padrino looked over at Antonio for his reaction to the American's bravado.

"Don't look at me, El Padrino. He blew up my mountaintop factory. And, like you, I was powerless to stop it."

"And so you bring him here? I am afraid, Antonio, you underestimate my forgiveness."

"And you underestimate how much I am trying to help you, not hurt you."

Steven interrupted, "I told you, he had no choice. He did you a huge favor. I was going to talk with you with his help or not. It was just that, with Antonio's help, we could do it in a much more civilized way."

"I tell you what. I think I will kill both of you now. If my trucks disappear tomorrow, I know who to blame, and the problem is taken care of. If not, I will be pleased to have stopped the theft of my tankers."

"El Padrino, if you kill us, you will die," said El Pequeño Diablo. "You know I wouldn't lie to you, my old friend."

"We are not friends." El Padrino cut off another piece of cheese as he thought, leaning against the arm of a plush, leather couch. "But you are right; you would not lie to me."

"Tell him, Señor Senator."

"He's telling the truth," said Steven. "Do you think I came here unprepared?"

"Yes. Yes, I do; that is why we picked you up a day early."

"Listen carefully, because this is the deal. If you cooperate with me, you will get to live, you will get to keep your money, and you will be able to keep your power. If you don't join me, you die. It's that simple."

"Join you? I don't work for anybody. I am El Padrino."

"Listen, Señor Carlos," Steven replied. "I've got an uncle who says otherwise."

"An uncle?" El Padrino laughed. "You have an uncle?"

"He's called Uncle Sam. Why do you think they sent a senator to negotiate?"

El Padrino's face showed that he instantly realized the gravity of the threat.

That was when a commotion broke out in another part of the yacht.

"El Padrino, El Padrino, something terrible has happened!" The men were so excited they ran into the large salon, ignoring the special guest. "Two of our tankers are gone."

El Padrino looked at Steven in anger, growling, "What do you mean? Gone?"

"They are gone; blown up, El Padrino! There is nothing left of them."

With terrible anger in his voice, El Padrino screamed, "Out of here you fool, out!" He shook the knife at Steven. "You! You said tomorrow."

Chapter 12

Why did you blow up my tankers? And why would you tell me you did it? Are you loco?"

"I guess my uncle got an itchy finger when I went missing. I think you should let me contact him before more things of yours start disappearing."

"El Padrino, listen to him," Antonio begged.

"You dare to come in here, onto my boat, and threaten me?"

El Padrino rushed towards Steven with the knife.

"Your family, think of your family," Steven shouted. "What will happen to them when you're dead? I'll tell you what. They will die. Your enemies will kill them, probably torture them."

"How dare you threaten my family?" El Padrino's rage kept building. "I will feed you bit by bit to the fishes while you are still alive to watch."

"I can protect you, I can protect them. But if you kill me, you will all die. Don't let that happen. Live, enjoy your wealth, your family. Join me and you have a chance at living wealthy and free."

"My life and freedom are at risk every day. I think it would be worth the risk to watch you die slowly."

"Think of your family, El Padrino," Antonio pleaded. "I wouldn't have brought him here if there was a choice. Think, El Padrino, think! You know I wouldn't do that. You have no choice, just like I didn't."

The long knife was pressed against Steven's throat.

"There are choices," El Padrino hissed, "there are always choices."

Steven glanced at Antonio with desperate eyes.

"Yes, Padrino, there are," insisted El Pequeño Diablo. "For all our sakes, make the right one. The Americans are tricky, with their technology and drones and satellites. You must believe me. If you kill him, they will know it, and then we're dead. This boat will disappear, just like your tankers."

Steven looked into El Padrino's eyes, trying to look confident even though he knew he could soon be dead or, worse, being slowly tortured.

Steven tried to reason one last time, saying, "Listen to him; you can keep your money. Your son and your daughters and your wife can live to spend it as you wish. No more hiding. The finest schools for your children."

"You are offering *me* protection? Me? I am El Padrino, *I* offer the protection, not you."

Steven saw Antonio slide a glace his way. The roll of Antonio's eyes told him that the message wasn't being received.

Steven hoped Colonel Tripp was listening, but regardless, it was time to prove his point or die trying.

"I tell you what. That small skiff, the boat that brought me here, set it adrift, you'll see I'm not bluffing."

The tactic had worked on Antonio, so maybe it would work again.

El Padrino moved the knife away from Steven's throat and used it to slice off another piece of cheese as he considered the offer.

"I tell you what, I will believe you if you blow up my small boat within the hour. Then, I will listen, but if it is still floating in one hour, you and I will have a different kind of discussion; one that will be slow and painful."

He moved away, shouting orders.

"No, you are making a mistake," El Pequeño Diablo protested as crewmembers came into the large saloon and lifted him from his chair, keeping his arms tied behind him.

"I think your friend Antonio should have a front-row seat. After all, without his help, we wouldn't be in this situation."

Antonio protested, but to no avail.

"El Padrino, I will not allow Antonio to be killed. After all, he is cooperating with me."

"Let me explain the situation to you. If the boat Antonio will soon be on is not destroyed within the hour, as you promised me, you will both die. You may be telling the truth, and I may have to let you live, but El Pequeño Diablo must be made an example of."

Antonio shot a pleading look back at Steven. Steven glanced back at Antonio, but he didn't have any immediate solution to their problem. El Padrino looked at his watch.

"In one hour, I shall return. When I do, I shall either make you comfortable as my honored guest or slowly make you dead."

Steven hoped the sensitive spy equipment hovering overhead could hear him as he said firmly, "The demonstration is off; I will not kill Antonio."

"That is your decision or your bluff. Either way, in an hour, he will be dead."

Steven was left alone in the saloon. He could hear the orders given to cast off the small boat. The men's laughter led him to believe that El Padrino was true to his word, and Antonio was on board.

"Do not sink the small boat," Steven said loudly. "Stand down, but be ready."

The plan was the same as the last mission. The small amount of radioactive material Steven had been exposed to would have been followed to the boat. The weather was well within operational guidelines for the Reaper drone to have been launched from the naval vessel off the coast. Colonel Tripp should be monitoring his every word using its sophisticated instruments.

However, the plan had been to use a show of force to coerce cooperation. After his abduction, somebody had made the call to blow up the tankers ahead of schedule. That somebody had probably been Filipe. The danger of his mission was that a show of force might not be enough. There was a clock on the wall; fifteen minutes had passed already.

Steven's bindings were holding fast. After another fifteen minutes of futilely trying to free himself, he realized he might have to sacrifice one drug lord in order to partner with one who was more powerful. That had also been the plan all along, if required. It didn't sit well with him, but if it came to killing a cartel leader or the end of his life and the mission, there was only one answer.

After another fifteen minutes of unsuccessful efforts to free himself, Steven shouted to the ceiling, "Fire at the small boat, sink it and all aboard."

Steven said a small prayer for El Pequeño Diablo. Yes, the man was responsible for probably thousands of deaths, but Steven had never been one to take a life easily. He had done what Steven had asked and would be rewarded with death. The only consolation Steven had was that the hellfire missile used to kill him would make it quick. Death by El Padrino wouldn't be so kind.

The next fifteen minutes went by so slowly that time seemed to stop. It was now past the hour allotment. Antonio was gone, but soon El Padrino would be down to see what the crazy American was proposing to him. He didn't have to wait long.

El Padrino and some of his soldiers came down the stairs.

"Retrieve the traitor El Pequeño Diablo," he yelled to his upper crew. Steven felt the engines kick in and the movement of the big yacht.

"So, you were bluffing," El Padrino said. "To what end; to gain another hour of life? I'm afraid your effort will cost you and El Pequeño Diablo another hour of suffering. So, Senator, do you like to fish?" El Padrino smiled wickedly. "Bring him upstairs. I want them both to see each other's pain as we use their flesh to catch dinner. And bring bandages, lots of bandages. I don't want them bleeding out all over my deck."

Steven's legs were unbound and two large sailors escorted him up the ornate staircase by nearly lifting him off his feet by his still bound arms. Outside, he was led to an aft deck. The yacht was slowing, making a large, open turn towards the small skiff floating in the distance.

"Set up my fishing equipment," El Padrino yelled to other sailors.

One of the men came running down from the upper bridge.

"El Padrino, our radar is picking up a small signature circling us, about two miles above. It looks like a small plane."

El Padrino stared at Steven for a moment before saying, "A drone, perhaps. Maybe even a Reaper, to be that big." He looked back towards the cabin they had just emerged from. "Sit my friend down," he commanded the two sailors guarding Steven. "Don't let him move a muscle, or *you* will be my fish bait."

El Padrino sat down in the plush fishing chair next to Steven.

"This boat serves many purposes," he said, "Sometimes, I use it to support my associates as they try to navigate away from surveillance planes. It is standard procedure for us to scan the skies when underway. The other thing you might find interesting is that the inside of my ship is hardened against electronic eavesdropping. I think your friends didn't get your message to destroy the small skiff. That makes me reconsider things."

He turned to one of his men. "Tell the captain to turn away from the skiff. I changed my mind." The man hurried off and El Padrino turned back to Steven.

"I will give you fifteen more minutes. Command your drone to blow up the skiff. If that doesn't happen, I will assume it is no more than another futile attempt to try to connect me to some illegal activities. In that case, your death may have to be postponed until it gets tired of watching us."

The yacht changed course away from the skiff, the shift in course momentarily unbalancing the two sailors guarding him.

Steven darted to his feet, shouldered the closest sailor and ran for the edge of the yacht. With all of the momentum he could muster, Steven jumped into the ocean. Now, he knew why the skiff was still afloat.

Working with El Padrino didn't appeal to him anymore. Steven thought of the old adage of working with the devil you know versus the one you don't. El Pequeño Diablo was starting to grow on him. If somebody had to die today, it would be El Padrino.

The momentum of the yacht took it away from him faster than El Padrino could organize his men to shoot. Steven kicked hard with his feet, praying that the small target his head presented, along with the rocking of the yacht, would keep him safe from the bullets.

Steven was able to tread water using only his feet, but he knew he couldn't keep it up for long. Taking one deep breath, he sank down into the water and curled his legs up as much as he possibly could. With all the effort he could muster, he brought his arms down his back, trying to work them under his legs.

It was a tight fit as he sunk deeper. The only way he could gain an inch or so more room would be to exhale, but his arms were stuck. It took a mighty thrust, but Steven was able to push his arms back again. With his arms still tied behind him, he kicked as hard as he could to get back to the surface. Steven's lungs were screaming for air. He could see the sunlight over the surface of the ocean, but it seemed impossibly far away. He kicked hard and broke the surface just in time to catch another breath.

The yacht was making a turn back towards him. Steven was too out of breath to yell to his friends in the sky. The yacht was bearing down directly on him. It took several more seconds before he could yell to the sky.

"Target the yacht. Target the yacht now!"

****

Back in Washington, Colonel Tripp was being relayed the visuals and audio from the drone. Nobody on the ship was authorized to act on the information collected, including the captain.

"Where is the senator?" Colonel Tripp yelled, louder than he had intended in his excitement. The near real-time transmission wasn't perfect, but only a moment ago, they had seen him on the aft deck of the ship. Now, the ship had moved, and Steven wasn't visible in the chair.

"Use the satellite, find the radiation signature."

"I have several signatures, sir; two still on the yacht and one on the skiff. And another... in the water, sir. I have a third in the water."

"Tag all the signatures until we can figure out who is who. Home in on them. I need audio, I need visual. Where is the senator?"

Over the open speaker system, Colonel Tripp heard Steven's voice shout.

"Target the yacht now!"

"Do it, do it!" Tripp ordered.

The radiowoman signaled the ship commanding the drone.

"It's turned around, the yacht is heading right toward him, sir. It's the senator in the water, Antonio Ortega is the man on the skiff."

"Tell them to fire! Shoot, damn it, shoot!"

"They're confirming the code now, sir," the radiowoman calmly updated the colonel.

Colonel Tripp sat slowly into his chair, realizing he was only a spectator at this point.

******

Steven took several deep breaths, oxygenating his blood. The ship was heading towards him. Apparently, El Padrino would be satisfied with cutting him into shreds with the powerful propellers.

One last time, Steven called to the sky, "Blow the goddamn yacht out of the water, now!"

Steven stopped his feet from treading water and let all the air out of his lungs, thrusting his legs tight into his chest. Because of the lack of air in his lungs, he sunk even faster than before. Steven pulled his arms under him once again. Slowly, he inched them under his legs.

From under the water, Steven saw a bright flash. A radar-guided Hellfire missile had found its target.

Steven felt his lungs begging to get a breath, even if that breath caused him to flood them with seawater. He fought the temptation and finally drew his arms in front of him. Steven kicked with all his might and used his tied arms to pull him up to the surface.

With a huge gulp, he sucked in air, realizing that the advancing but badly damaged yacht was moving towards him. However, the remaining crew were now more concerned with abandoning the burning ship than killing him.

"Amigo!" Steven heard from behind him. "I owe you a debt."

It was Antonio, and his bloody wrist indicated the difficulty he'd had freeing himself. But somehow, he had, and now he had control of the skiff and was coming to rescue him.

Antonio had grabbed El Padrino's cheese knife and cut Steven's bindings, helping him onto the skiff.

"I commend you on trading El Padrino's squalid life for my own."

Steven didn't think it necessary to correct El Pequeño Diablo's assumption; it was El Padrino's electronically hardened cabin that had saved him.

As they headed away, Steven looked back at the burning yacht that was now dead in the water.

"What now, amigo?" El Pequeño Diablo asked.

Steven examined his own sore and bleeding wrist.

"What say we do this without El Padrino?" he asked. He looked to the sky and shouted, "Finish it, sink it!"

Panting, he turned back to his ally, saying, "Let's get out of here.

There's going to be one hell of an explosion when the second missile hits."

That was when Steven saw El Padrino at the rear of the yacht. He was trying to help some people onto a small, inflatable launch.

"Shit!" Steven growled. "Turn us around."

"What?"

"Turn us around, his family is on the boat. I see a small girl and a boy. I recognize them."

"No, señor, they will be dead in another moment. You said so yourself."

Steven grabbed the tiller away from Antonio, and the skiff raced towards the yacht.

"They're just children, I'm not killing children."

It took precious minutes to race the skiff up to the stern of the yacht. Men were shouting at each other, trying to launch anything that could float. The fire that had been started by the missile was causing small explosions.

"You don't have time to launch it; tell your family to get into this boat!" Steven yelled as loud as he could over the chaos.

El Padrino saw the men he had threatened to torture and kill trying to save him and his family. He was suspicious of their intent and froze as he contemplated their offer.

"Damn it, Carlos, now! Another missile is coming."

El Padrino grabbed his youngest, a little girl. He threw her to Steven. It only took an instant more for him to take hold of his six-year-old son in one hand and eight-year-old daughter in the other. With a push, the older daughter fell into the skiff, and he threw his young son to Steven. With strength El Padrino hadn't known he had, he grabbed his wife by her hands and lowered her down.

Steven saw the vapor trail of the missile as it left the drone two miles above them.

"Jump, now! We're leaving."

El Padrino did jump, narrowly missing his wife. Steven gunned the motor, and the missile struck. Flaming debris rained down around them, but the small group escaped.

El Padrino was dirty and bleeding; he looked small and defeated.

"I think I will listen to your proposition after all," he said.

El Pequeño Diablo grinned at Steven. They both knew that another cartel leader had just been recruited, though neither El Pequeño Diablo nor El Padrino knew exactly what for, and Steven intended to keep it that way for now.

Chapter 13

Shannon Johnston knocked on the door of Senator Westcott's Washington office and walked in.

"Senator, you're running late. You promised Senator Collins that you would be there for the procedural vote."

Steven hung up the call he had just been on, saying, "Yes, Mother." He was kidding; she didn't look or act anything like his mother. In fact, she was twenty years younger than him.

"Don't 'yes, Mother' me; you told me to make sure you weren't late."

Steven stood and self-consciously tugged at the cufflinks of his white shirt. It was a recent habit he had developed to make sure the sleeves were out far enough to cover his still bruised wrists.

"Sorry, not your fault, but you know how I hate these things. First, I have to sit around for hours listening to a bunch of blowhards trying to get a sound bite on CNN. I already know what I'm going to do. I don't know why I can't just text my vote in or something."

"Because that would be too easy, and you need to learn how to get some sound bites too. The next election is just around the corner, and you do have some baggage you need to address."

"All right, all right, Mom, I'm out of here. What about tonight?"

"*This* you're going to like. Your dinner meeting with Mr. Ahlborn has been canceled. If I was you, I'd call Chelle up and see if she's free tonight."

"Shannon, you didn't?"

"I didn't, honest. She called me."

"Spill it."

"I guess it slipped out that your meeting with Ahlborn got canceled at the last minute. I told her you didn't even know it yet." Shannon could tell by the look on her boss's face that something was bothering him. "You've been avoiding her, and she knows it. Why don't *you* spill it?"

Steven hated the fact that Shannon and Chelle were both right. He had been avoiding Chelle for the last week. They had talked, several times, but he couldn't let Chelle see him. His body was bruised and cut, and that was something that wouldn't generally happen on a trade mission. Shannon could read him all too well.

"I have been avoiding her."

There was no use in lying. Shannon already knew the truth, and Chelle's intuition had told her the same thing.

Steven hated deceiving them, especially Chelle. In reality, he wanted to be with her in every way. That was the problem. Seeing her, being with her, how could he not take her home with him?

Steven realized that trying to escape from a power-crazy cartel leader seemed much easier to him than working his way out of this mess.

"I'm afraid we're moving too fast. We both have too many things on our plates to start a relationship."

"That is a load of bull! News flash, Senator; you've already started a relationship."

Without thinking, Steven subconsciously tugged on his sleeves again. In the office, he could cover his wounds, but in bed with Chelle, she wouldn't be able to help but notice. She would know he was lying about what he'd been doing the last few weeks, and there was no way he would be able to tell her the truth.

"Shannon, I'm late already. Could you please tell her I'm sorry but I just can't meet with her tonight? And tomorrow, I won't be in town, so maybe we can get together next week."

"Senator, I'll call her and tell her that you can't meet with her tonight, but I'm not going to do your dirty work for you. If you want to dump her, you'll have to do it yourself, and if you don't mind me saying, you'd be crazy to do that."

"Shannon, I don't want to dump her. I... I just can't meet with her right now. Could you please make up a believable excuse for me? You know I'm a terrible liar."

Shannon knew her boss was right. He *was* a terrible liar.

"OK, I will, but just this once," she agreed with a disgusted huff.

Steven left his office wondering why he had to be the only person in Washington who was a terrible liar *and* the only one who had to keep a secret for the country rather than for himself. Out on the street, the spring pollen started to tickle his nose towards a sneeze. He reached for the handkerchief that he kept in his back pocket and brought it up to his nose to catch the sneeze just in time.

He moved to put the handkerchief back when the monogram of his initials caught his eye. The white handkerchief was an innocent gift from Chelle. She had made a point of wrapping the small gift and handing it to him in person on the day of his birthday. It was a ploy to see him. The ploy had worked, and they had been seeing each other ever since.

Hours later, Steven walked out of the senate chambers. The vote had gone exactly as he'd thought it would, and he'd had a hard time not falling asleep during the long, repetitive dialog preceding it.

Steven walked down Senate Hall and looked at his watch. It was getting late, and he was famished. He had skipped lunch and thought he would just go down to the cafeteria, grab something and head straight home. Maybe he would still have time to call his daughter. Maybe he would even give Chelle a call, only later when they would both have an excuse for not talking long.

Steven looked up, and his heart stopped. Chelle was there, down the hall, and she wasn't smiling.

She stepped up to him, acting very formal in front of his colleagues.

"Senator Westcott," she said, "I was wondering if we could talk?"

She was dressed in an FBI-appropriate tan pantsuit. Steven excused himself from the small group he was walking with. Tentatively, he put his arm around Chelle's shoulders. She let him guide her down the hall.

Once they were in the privacy of a side hallway, Steven said, "I... I'm sorry, Chelle."

Chelle fought back her tears, saying, "What's happening? I don't understand, and I need to. I know we said we wouldn't hold each other to a relationship, but I didn't expect it to end like this."

"I was just going to get a bite; would you please be so kind as to join me?"

"I thought you couldn't. You have a splitting headache, or did you forget?"

Steven confessed, "I deserve that. I asked Shannon to make up a lie for why I couldn't meet with you tonight. I wish I could explain, but it has nothing to do with you or us."

"Senator, I haven't been in high school for a long time. The entire 'it's not you, it's me' thing isn't working."

"I didn't mean it that way." Steven found it difficult to look Chelle in the eye as he searched for the right words. "I missed you so much. I didn't want to lie to you. I just couldn't face you."

"This isn't helping, Steven."

"I know, oh hell, I know. Please, will you join me for dinner?"

"I don't know if that would be a good idea, under the circumstances."

Steven saw that Chelle was on the verge of tears. He reached out to hug her.

Chelle reached out also and grabbed his hands to stop him. That was when she felt his wrist. She had run her fingers up and down those strong wrists. Today, they were different; she could feel that they were swollen and welted.

Chelle looked up with questioning eyes. In an instant, Steven knew his secret was no more. Chelle looked down as she gently pulled his wrist away from the cufflinked sleeves. She held on to his hands gently as she examined them.

"Not here, not here," Steven whispered. "How about some Chinese? We can take it back to my place."

Chelle nodded silently. If she was about to get an explanation, the least she could do was wait for Steven to tell his story on his terms.

She waited for Steven in the parking garage under his building and rode up silently in the elevator with him. Steven carried a bag of Chinese takeout. He opened his apartment door and set it on the table.

Chelle watched Steven in silence. He knew she was waiting patiently. What would be the excuse? What would be the explanation? Those were the questions he was sure she was asking herself.

Steven didn't know where or how to begin. He couldn't divulge state secrets, even to an FBI agent. Even to his lover; especially to his lover. The president of the United States had sworn him to secrecy, yet he also couldn't lie. He knew he couldn't lie and that, even if he did, she would see right through him.

Steven took off his suit coat and slowly hung it over an unused chair. Out of habit, he loosened his tie. That was what he always did the moment he was home.

Chelle approached him, reaching up to undo his tie completely. Steven lifted his hands to object, but he couldn't force her hands away. She slid the tie out from around his neck and started to undo the buttons of his shirt.

Steven lifted his hands again and held her hands for a moment, freezing them in place. Chelle continued to unbutton, and Steven's hands fell away like lead weights, he was emotionally helpless to stop her. Chelle slowly opened his shirt. He could feel her warm hands through the undershirt that was covering his chest. He knew what she was doing and what she would see, and he felt embarrassed, but he couldn't stop her. His body would have to do his explaining for him.

Chelle opened the cufflinks and set them gently on the table. They locked eyes as she slid her hands gently under Steven's white dress shirt and let it drop to the floor. She moved her hands between the skin of his chest and the undershirt he was wearing. Her palms brushed against his nipples as she pushed the material up and over his head, and it too dropped to the floor.

Chelle bent forward and kissed the bruises that covered his body. Tenderly, she lifted the strong arms that were now putty in her hands. She brought the cut and welted wrists to her mouth and gently kissed the healing wounds.

"You can't tell me, can you?" she whispered.

Steven couldn't believe the love he felt in his heart as he gently shook his head.

She looked into his eyes with sympathy and forgiveness, murmuring, "Then don't. Let's go to bed."

Steven picked up Chelle in his arms as gently as he possibly could. He buried his head in her breast as she ran her fingers through his hair.

"I missed you so much," he whispered as he kissed her neck and carried her away.

"I know."

Chapter 14

With the directions he had been given, Steven eventually found the secluded elevator within the Eisenhower Executive Office. He waved an electronic keycard across the card reader, which was without markings of any kind. He only knew its function from previous escorted visits; today, he was alone. The word 'Accessing' appeared on a screen that had been completely blank and the door opened.

He stepped in and typed in a code. The door closed, and the elevator began its movement. Exactly what floor he was going to, he didn't know, because there were no floor indicators visible.

When the doors opened, he was greeted by two burly MPs. The two young military police escorted him the rest of the way down brightly lit hallways. On his walk, he had time to count the numerous cameras watching their every move.

Right on cue, Colonel Tripp stepped out of his office, saluting another officer who was apparently going to be escorted back to the elevator he had just come from.

"Senator Westcott, I would like you to meet Lieutenant Colonel Richard Pratt."

Steven immediately summed up the lieutenant colonel by looking at the badges on his uniform. He was an accomplished soldier, and by the wings with a shooting star, also an astronaut.

"My pleasure, Senator Westcott."

"The lieutenant colonel is helping me with one of my projects. Exciting; *very* exciting, but I'm sorry, Senator, even your clearance level doesn't permit me to discuss it."

"I was military, so I understand. It's my pleasure to meet you, Lieutenant Colonel."

The lieutenant colonel tipped his head and said goodbye, walking off with the two guards at his side.

Steven reached over and shook hands with Colonel Tripp, saying, "I have to admit, I had my doubts, but you and your team came through. You saved my ass down in Mexico, and I want to thank your staff as well."

Colonel Tripp's squat frame and flat face reminded Steven of a bulldog, though his haircut reminded him of the top of an aircraft carrier, as it was cut perfectly flat. The colonel's handshake was firm but deliberately unintimidating. Steven guessed his age at a very fit fifty; his flattop hair had a tinge of grey.

"Come into the control room and meet my team," he said. "I'm proud of these young people."

The colonel ushered Steven through several doors until they were looking through a glass wall at a dark room lit only by dozens of video monitors and computer screens.

"Before I introduce you to my team, let me say, you're the one who took all the risk meeting with those sons of bitches. I can't for the life of me fathom what the hell you're up to, but the president said to help you in any way we can, and that's good enough for me."

"Sorry I can't satisfy your curiosity. I can't divulge my mission; the mission I wasn't even on, and if you said I was, I'd deny it."

"Senator Westcott, I have been carrying out covert actions for a long time. No need to explain your mission, sir. It's none of my business. But I do know the president has an aircraft carrier group off the coast of Mexico doing war game simulations with the Mexicans. That happens to be pretty convenient for me in protecting your ass. Whatever you're up to, it must be damn important."

"The president believes our national security is at stake, and I agree with him. So yes, Colonel, what you are doing is important."

The colonel opened a wide, glass door and they entered the control area. Steven was surprised that the personnel ignored their entry and continued on with what they were doing.

Colonel Tripp continued, "This is where the magic happens. We don't dilly-dally on protocol, we just get the job done."

He pressed a button and Steven heard himself plain as day, rather loudly and angrily saying, "Finish it, sink it!" A moment later, "Let's get out of here. There's going to be one hell of an explosion when the second missile hits."

Steven took off his suit coat as he listened to his own voice.

"The drone's super-sensitive ears captured your conversation," Colonel Tripp continued. "The software is able to focus on your voice imprint over most background noise. There's a delay that can't be helped, anywhere from three to seven minutes. The drone relays to the ship, the ship to us, then we need to authenticate your voiceprint and send the message back to the ship. The captain verifies our message, and only after verification does he or she have the ship execute the command.

"In this case, it was almost fatal because, by the time we realized you were in harm's way, it was too late to stop the missile."

Colonel Tripp hit another button and played a video of El Padrino's yacht getting blown out of the water, a small craft speeding away just in time.

Steven rested both his hands on the back of the empty chair between him and the video console as he watched.

"Colonel, I assumed as much. It was my risk to take."

"Just letting you know some of the limitations, Senator. While you were inside the cabin of the yacht, we were out of communication. Our guess is that the boat had been electronically hardened."

"I can confirm that."

"Limitations, as I say, but the tagging system is working just as hoped. The two red dots represent your two targets so far. The low dose radiation is as individual to each of them as their DNA. The computer has memorized their signature, and a satellite tracks them and relocates them whenever it's in range. Anybody else that handled the ID is also tagged, but we know enough about who handled it when to filter them out."

The colonel pointed to one of the analysts on his team, and she zoomed in on a satellite map until a large dwelling came into view.

"We use other satellites in lower orbits to capture photo and video images. This is where target one is right now."

With a nod from her boss, the analyst zoomed in even further.

"It looks like he's in the upper room. In fact, this corner room right here. We can also get high-resolution satellite views of them anytime they skirt about in the open. However, we do have some limitations in that regard, the primary being that we need to have satellites in the right place at the right time. We have the drones, but the weather needs to be right for them. Also, the drone cannot be in the air twenty-four hours a day, so we dispatch it at strategic times."

"In other words, your best guess at when it will be needed."

"Precisely, and I have to remind you that, like any machine, it is subject to mechanical breakdown. The risk you take is real."

"Fair enough, no system is perfect."

"Senator, I also have to remind you that we obviously have the same capabilities on you. Be advised, Big Brother is tracking you too."

Colonel Tripp hit another button and a pulsing, blue dot was superimposed over the Eisenhower Building, which just so happened to be where Steven was at that very moment.

"We aren't following you with a drone or low-orbiting satellites while you're in Washington, but there will be a record of your radiation trail."

"I get it; don't go anywhere my mother wouldn't approve of. Thanks for the warning."

Colonel Tripp cracked the first smile Steven had seen on him.

"I understand you lost the ID in the sinking of El Padrino's yacht. We're preparing another for you on the assumption that you'll be needing it again. Don't forget, the wallet keeps the ID from tagging everyone you walk past. So, to actually tag somebody with any reliability, they must touch the ID itself. Carry your regular ID with you so that you don't tag everybody who needs to see one, like the good folks at TSA. The fewer people walking around with a radiation signature, the better."

"Got it, and there's one more thing that could be helpful to me. Let me explain."

****

Back in his office, Senator Westcott went through his appointments with Shannon Johnston. She read off her list, a copy of which she had just given the senator.

"Senators Michaels and Murphy want to meet with you at two

in regards to the farm bill. You are especially requested to be at the Subcommittee on Strategic Forces meeting at nine tomorrow. Also, the Subcommittee on Economic Policy is having a policy discussion over lunch tomorrow. I said you could be there.

"In light of the recent cyber-attacks, there's a special combined meeting between the Subcommittees on Consumer Protection, Product Safety, Insurance, and Data Security. They're meeting with the Subcommittee on Foreign Relations, specifically the Subcommittee on East Asia, the Pacific and International Cyber Security Policy. You're the only senator who's on both committees, and I think you need to be there."

"Sounds like a busy couple of days." Steven said as he scanned the document and sipped his coffee.

"Unfortunately, you're booked from hour to hour. A few meet-and-greets, constituents, fundraisers, supporters, that sort of thing. I'll do my best to keep things on schedule, but you have to work with me."

Shannon looked up from her carefully prepared timetable, and Steven leaned back in his chair and finished his coffee.

"Scolding me already; I haven't even done anything wrong yet."

Steven set down his empty Garfield the Cat coffee mug, a small gift from Chelle. On it, Garfield grinned widely with the saying, 'Never Trust a Smiling Cat' underneath. Steven appreciated the gentle warning from Chelle and Garfield; there were many smiling cats in Washington.

"Let's keep it that way, Senator." Shannon smiled. "I know you hate this kind of stuff, but it's what keeps the country moving and you in office. I promise I'll make it as painless as possible."

"I'm counting on that."

"I am, however, starting to get some flak on your Mexican Trade Mission meetings. Some senators are wondering why they haven't been included. Others, including the chairwoman on the Committee on Foreign Relations are wondering exactly what it's about, because they've seen no reports."

"Tell them that these are only preliminary, exploratory meetings at the request of the president and I've been doing them on weeks the senate isn't in session."

"I have, but they're not buying it."

"You mean *you're* not buying it," Steven said, picking up his Garfield mug and refilling it.

"No, Senator, I'm not. None of my business, but if I don't believe it, I can't expect anyone else to either."

Steven rubbed his hand through his hair; he'd known this day would come.

"Shannon, the truth is, a major manufacturer from Europe is considering a joint US and Mexico manufacturing partnership. They are acquaintances from when I was doing international finance with my private equity firm. The talks are extremely sensitive; mostly, they're afraid of their competition finding out.

"You can't tell a soul, but I don't want to keep it from you any longer, because the project still has a long way to go, and I will certainly be off to Mexico again. All I can tell you is that the discussions are on a very high level."

Steven didn't feel particularly bad about the lie. In a way, his mission was about trade with Mexico, and it certainly was on a very high level.

"Senator, you need to create a different smokescreen for a while. You can't keep calling it a trade mission."

Steven leaned against the counter that held the coffee maker as he sipped his freshly poured coffee.

"I see what you mean. But what? I can't conceal that I'm going to Mexico. If we lied about that, it would undoubtedly be found out, and that would make things even worse."

"Maybe, if we put our heads together, we can come up with something."

Shannon heard her phone ring just outside the door. As she walked out, she said, "Don't forget, farm bill, two o'clock."

Steven sat in his chair and rocked it backward. Shannon was right; he needed a better excuse, and he knew just the person to help.

****

Steven was on a commercial plane heading to Puerto Vallarta for a week's vacation while the senate was on its end of June break. A meeting with El Ángel had been arranged.

Apparently, he was gaining a reputation; both El Pequeño Diablo and El Padrino had vouched for him. El Pequeño Diablo had, reluctantly, confirmed to El Ángel his production losses and the penalty for not taking the American seriously. That was done solely at Steven's insistence. Antonio had reminded Steven of his reluctance to work with El Ángel, who had killed his father, the original El Diablo.

In contrast, El Padrino said that El Ángel was eager to meet with him, as his reputation as a man to be taken seriously preceded him. The loss of his yacht had become an unfortunately true myth within the cartel community. Like any other industry, the cartels were their own world, and news could travel fast. In this case, it gave El Padrino a certain amount of credibility.

Steven looked out of his cabin window and saw the plane crossing over the unmistakable Rio Grande. He was now back in Mexico, and the weight of the mission was becoming more real. He was also well aware of the adrenaline rush he was feeling, and he couldn't ignore the fact that he liked it. It energized him.

Shannon and he had agreed that a vacation in Mexico for the ten days the senate had off might be a bit suspicious to those following his routine, however it also made a plausible excuse. Steven had told Shannon to not be too secretive about his destination to anyone who might ask, because that would make it that much more transparent.

Steven had done his best to memorize the dossier on El Ángel. He closed his eyes to visualize it in his mind. El Ángel had wrested control of the smuggling routes along the West Coast of Mexico, including the Gulf of California and the Baja California, from two other cartel wannabes. They were now dead. He also controlled the Mexicali and Tijuana entryways into the US.

The file on Miguel Ángel Vega, aka El Ángel, had him ruthless to the point of sociopathy. However, his operation was well controlled. The dossier explained that his iron grip was absolute and his men loyal. Steven looked over the map of the area and concluded that, unfortunately, El Ángel was a necessary evil.

The shock and awe that Steven had used for his previous introductions hopefully wouldn't be needed. The where and when of his meeting with El Ángel would be cautiously set after he was in Mexico.

Steven handed his empty coffee cup to the flight attendant and folded up his tray table. He double-checked his seatbelt and, before he knew it, the plane was pulling up to the gate.

Steven had dressed the part of a beach-combing tourist. He had on a colorful silk shirt decorated with parrots and flowers. He wore an appropriate pair of shorts, not quite as colorful but something he wouldn't be caught dead in back home. He was waiting for his bag around the luggage carousel as pushy taxi drivers tried to drum up business.

"Taxi, taxi, I can take you anywhere. I give you special price!" an aggressive driver promised, taking Steven's case from him as soon as he had touched it.

"What hotel? I can take you there like the wind, my new friend. My car is right out the door."

Steven found it difficult to treat Filipe as a stranger, despite the disguise. The leader of his FES escort had said he would find him, and he had.

"What hotel, sir?" Filipe asked again.

"Fiesta Americana."

"Ahh, the Fiesta is a fine hotel. I know fastest way to get there."

Filipe had lied about the location of his cab. It wasn't right out the door; they had to cross several busy streets through a steady drizzle to reach it. Of course, none of the other cabbies' cars were just outside the door either, and they lied equally as well.

Once in the cab, Filipe said, "Fiesta Americana is a good choice, amigo. It's a big hotel, good security, lots of tourist. The men are already in place with various covers."

"Good to see you, Filipe. I've heard I'm gaining a reputation."

"'El Senador' is becoming a whispered name. Many think it is just a myth, a myth about an American trying to take over the cartels. This El Senador can blow things up just by pointing his finger at them."

Steven chuckled, saying, "Sometimes urban myths are real, I guess."

The cab pulled away down the modern streets of Puerto Vallarta, heading for what was known as Old Town. Filipe turned on his windshield wipers against the increasing rain.

"You are dealing with dangerous men, El Senador; please don't forget that. In many ways, it was easier to protect you in the jungle than here. In the Jalisco State, including Guadalajara and Puerto Vallarta, tourism is way down due to the violence.

"The cruise ships have stopped coming, and your own State Department warns tourists not to come here. Mexico takes its tourist safety very seriously. We cannot take the chance on any more bad publicity. Our orders are that, if it is between saving you and creating negative publicity, we are to stand down."

Filipe weaved his cab around stalled traffic and mostly kept it moving with generous help from its horn. Steven felt himself grip the tattered upholstery of the cab several times as it went into close quarters with other moving vehicles.

"Puerto Vallarta is gaining enough bad publicity on its own without our help, is that it?"

"Sí."

"Filipe, while I can't tell you the details of my job here. I can tell you that if my plan works, we can make all of Mexico safe again for its citizens *and* its guests."

"Amigo, it would help me greatly to know what your job here is. I understand secrecy, but at what cost? If you die, I assume the mission will have failed, so protecting your life is critical, and to do that, I need to know more."

"Filipe, I too was a soldier. I understand your concern, but I have to keep certain aspects of my mission a secret, even from you."

"I know you are trying to organize the cartels. To what end? I still think we should kill them when given the chance."

"I am trying to organize them, you're right about that. Please have faith in me for a little longer."

"I serve my president. She said to help you, so we will."

"I know you will. What next?"

"Just check into your hotel. I have no doubt that El Ángel has spies everywhere. He will find you when he wants to. Under the seat are a tracking device and a listening device. El Ángel will assume you are bugged and will find them and destroy them. That is OK, because at least we will know things are underway."

Steven slipped the pen into his colorful shirt pocket, where it became nearly invisible. A Mexican 50¢ coin that Steven assumed was the tracking device was slipped into the pocket of his shorts.

"This is going to be a fluid situation, and we will have little, if any, control over what happens after El Ángel contacts you. The best we can do is hope to follow you if you are taken somewhere. The good news is that El Cazador is here with us. I have your back, he has mine."

"If you lose contact with me, call this number," Steven said, handing Filipe a slip of paper. "Ask for Colonel Tripp and use the code words 'Grito de Dolores'. He might be able to help you."

"The 'Cry of Dolores', the speech that began Mexico's independence from Spain. I will have no problem remembering that, amigo. I will share this with El Cazador, if something should happen to me, he will be in command."

"Maybe we can free Mexico from the grip of the cartels. And maybe, I hope, El Senador's reputation will be sufficient to let me play it my way."

Filipe caught Steven's eye in the rearview mirror.

"Amigo, don't believe your own myth. El Ángel does not believe in fairytales, I can assure you. Now, here we are, the Fiesta Americana. It used to be one of the busier hotels."

"Let's hope we can make it that way again."

Steven paid Filipe in case anyone was watching, tipping him generously out of habit.

The lobby of the hotel was inviting. It was of an open-air design with waterfalls inside and out, and the stream they created meandered through the lobby. Steven's thoughts went to Chelle. Maybe, sometime soon, they could visit.

Checking in was simple and pleasant. The manager told him he had an ocean view suite with a deck and smiled with a knowing grin. Steven smiled back, wondering what the inside joke was. The next thing he knew, his suitcase was in the hands of the bellboy, who appeared to be about forty years old. He was guided to a lone elevator. It didn't take long for an elevator to appear, and he and the bellboy were lifted to the tenth floor.

Up at his room, his keycard flashed the indicator lights green and he opened the door. The bellboy carried the case inside and sat it down next to a bed. He smiled at Steven, not bashful about holding his palm out for a tip.

Steven slid a five dollar US bill into his hand. The man smiled widely. After he left, Steven carefully closed the door, making sure it locked. He turned and walked the few steps towards his suitcase and was about to toss it onto the kingsize bed when he saw another suitcase, already open. He looked around his room, thinking there must have been some sort of mistake.

His eye caught movement on the open balcony; it was a woman. She was wearing a lime-green two-piece bikini and see-through fuchsia cover-up, looking out over the ocean. The light wrap was blowing with the gentle sea breeze, but the overhang protected her from the rain. His heart jumped when the woman turned towards him and he recognized her hair and smiling face.

"Chelle!"

Steven rushed up to hug her.

"I... I hoped I would be welcomed," Chelle said, hugging back. "When Shannon told me you were going to Puerto Vallarta on vacation, I assumed you'd just forgotten to tell me to meet you here."

Steven gave Chelle a long kiss and a strong hug. Then, he took a step back and held her shoulders in his hands as he insisted, "You... you can't stay. Chelle, it's too dangerous. You don't understand. You have to leave immediately, you could be in danger."

"Not exactly the welcome I was hoping for, though I can't say it's a complete surprise."

"Chelle, I'm serious. I want to be with you, but not here, not now. Someday, we'll come back, I promise, but it's too dangerous for you right now."

"Hey, remember me? I saw your wrists and your bruised body. I know you aren't here on vacation *and* that whatever it is you're up to, it's dangerous. That's why I'm here; to help you and see to it you come back to me in one piece."

Steven started packing Chelle's things back into her suitcase.

"*No!* You cannot stay. You have to leave now. You're right, I'm dealing with dangerous people and you being here makes you a target. Pick out what you need to travel. I'm taking you back to the airport this instant."

Chelle put her hands on her suitcase and stopped Steven.

"I'm an adult, I will do as I want. I'll stay in a different room, but I'm not leaving until you do."

Steven stopped his panicked attack on her suitcase and hugged her again.

"Chelle, I won't be able to do my job if I'm worried about your safety."

"And do you think I can do mine as I worry about yours? I don't know what you've gotten yourself into, but I do know you're too stubborn to ask for help when you need it."

"No, Chelle." Steven didn't yell, but he was firm. "I do have people helping me. The best way *you* can help me is to go back home."

"Fine, I'll get my own room."

"Filipe, if you can hear me, get to room one zero four six immediately."

"You're bugged?"

"Yes, and being tracked. Chelle, I couldn't be more serious, you have to leave now."

"First, you have to tell me, tell me that you'll be safe and come back to me. Tell me that whatever you're up to is legal and almost over."

"Damn it, Chelle! Yes, it's legal, but it's dangerous. I'm working with the Mexican government." Steven thought he had better keep the president of the United States out of this lovers' squabble.

There was a knock on the door.

"Room Service."

"That's my friend, he'll take you safely to the airport," Steven said. He shouted to the door. "Be right there. I'm sorry, Chelle, but you do not have a choice in this. I'm pulling your passport. You're going home."

"You can't do that!" Chelle said angrily.

"Yes, I can!" Steven said as he walked over to let Filipe in.

That was when the door opened and five men, all with guns drawn, rushed into the room.

Chapter 15

Steven was caught off guard. Before he could react, the butt of a gun slammed against his head. When he woke, he reached up to feel the bruise, only to discover his hands were tied behind his back.

Through bleary eyes, he could see Chelle tied to a chair. He struggled to whisper her name as he slowly worked himself up into a sitting position from the couch on which he lay.

"Steve, Steven, are you all right?"

It took a while but, though his head was throbbing, his vision cleared and he felt more coherent.

"Yeah, I'm OK. How are you doing?" he asked, his voice weak.

"She is just fine, for now," said a man as he came out from the side room, where the balcony was. "What a beautiful view."

Steven's eyes had been locked on Chelle, but now he looked around and saw the five armed men and the man who was doing the talking. The apparent leader was puffing on a large cigar, and the smoke wafted through the room, slowly making its way out the doors of the open balcony to be washed out by the rain still coming down.

"Miguel, you are making a terrible mistake," Steven croaked, his throat coarse and dry.

El Ángel interrupted, "That is a nasty bump on your head, Senator. I think it is you who made a mistake. After all, you are the ones tied up."

"Let her go, she isn't part of this."

"Yes, I was listening as you tried to send her away. Unfortunately, you were too late, and now she *is* a part of this. Oh, and your friend, Filipe. You might be interested to know that the local police have detained him and his friends. It seems there has been a mix up in their authorization to operate in this city, and it appears that he was driving a taxi without a proper permit."

"Miguel, you do not understand what you're getting into," Steven said.

El Ángel nodded to one of the men and a large piece of tape was pressed against Chelle's mouth.

"Leave her alone, I'm warning you," Steven screamed.

El Ángel gave another nod, and Steven's mouth was covered with tape.

"Please, indulge me. As you can hear, my English is pretty good. I studied at some of your best schools. So, if you please, I will do the talking.

"I have heard all about El Senador from America." El Ángel made some shooting motions with his fingers. "He points at things and makes them blow up. So, let me be perfectly clear: I want to know more about you, and I do not have much time to listen."

El Ángel walked up to Chelle and took out a switchblade from his pocket; with a flick of his wrist and a snap, it opened and locked into place.

Steven tried to stand, but he was pushed back down by two burly men. He looked at Chelle, trying to comfort her. Chelle looked back at him, surprisingly calm and reassuring him with her eyes that she was OK.

"I hear you want to make me an offer to work with you. I am not the first, but it seems nobody knows exactly what you want. You see, that is going to change right now.

"In order to expedite things, I need you to know that I am serious. I ask the questions, you answer. If I don't like the answer or believe you are lying, there will be consequences."

El Ángel knelt down next to Chelle and cut the rope binding her left leg to the chair.

"Such a beautiful leg; you are indeed a beautiful woman, I would hate to change that."

El Ángel slipped off one of the sandals Chelle was wearing and lifted her leg up, holding her foot tenderly in his hand. Chelle tried to fight back, but El Ángel smiled and gave a nod to two of his men standing behind Chelle. They came around and took her foot, pressing it firmly against the wood floor. Another man approached Chelle and put his big arms on her shoulders, holding her tight against the chair back.

"So, Mr. Westcott, I need some answers, and I need them now."

Steven wanted to shout, he wanted to talk their way out of this, but the tape over his mouth forced him to control his breathing through his nose. Sadly, all he could do was watch. Now, he could see the fear in Chelle's eyes.

Without another word, El Ángel bent down. He pressed his knife against Chelle's little toe and, with one swift motion, it was off.

Chelle's screams were muffled by the tape. Steven had never felt such intense anger in his life, and he had never felt so utterly helpless.

He looked into Chelle's eyes, seeing that they were now wide with pain. He had seen that look before, and he knew that the pain was spiking her adrenaline level and her heart was now racing.

El Ángel took a few big puffs of his cigar. He blew the smoke out towards Steven and ground it into Chelle's wound, cauterizing it.

Chelle's head flopped as she struggled for air. Just before her head dropped to the side, Steven saw Chelle's eyes go white.

El Ángel stood, saying, "Now that you understand the rules, shall we begin? Oh, and Mr. Westcott, let's just have the answers to my questions. Any more threats and," El Ángel glanced at Chelle, "another demonstration will be in order."

Steven looked into the eyes of El Ángel with as much hate as he could muster. El Ángel ignored his glare and waited for a nod of understanding, wiping Chelle's blood from his knife with the bedspread.

"From what I have learned, you were responsible for the explosion of a mountaintop meth factory, a jeep taken out with a missile from nowhere, a boat at sea obliterated and fuel tankers destroyed. You are developing a reputation; a reputation I do not appreciate.

"It is also a reputation that tells me you are not working alone. In fact, I believe your partner is the United States government. That begs the question: what is the United States doing with its nose in Mexico's business?"

El Ángel gave one of his men a nod and the tape over Steven's mouth was ripped off. Steven took a few breaths.

"You bastard!" he shouted. "No, no! What have you done?"

The man who had taken the tape off Steven's mouth slapped him hard across the face, making his nose bleed.

Steven looked at Chelle, her body slumped over though still tied to the chair. Through gritted teeth, he said, "You just made a very big mistake. She isn't part of this, she's an innocent."

The man slapped him across the face again.

El Ángel puffed on his cigar until he had a mouthful of smoke. "Nobody is innocent."

He walked back towards Chelle and approached her from the back. His knife slipped down between her breasts and he slid it up between the cups of her swimming suit.

"I'll tell you the truth, just stop. Stop, before it's too late."

El Ángel pulled his knife up sharply, cutting through the thin, green cloth of the swimsuit. The top fell open, exposing her breasts.

"Too late for what, for who? I want answers, and I want them now. Or do I start carving up more delicate areas of her body? Of course, I will awaken her first so she doesn't miss out on the party. Again, what are you doing here?" he insisted calmly as he walked towards Steven, puffing on the very same cigar he had used to cauterize Chelle's wound.

"Look, I'll tell you, but don't hurt her anymore."

"That is up to you. Now, answer my questions, I am becoming impatient."

"My government, and yours, they're working together with a plan to shut down the cartels."

"And how do they think they will do that?"

"They want me to make a deal with the main cartels."

"What kind of deal?"

Steven looked toward Chelle, concerned for her welfare, and El Ángel slapped him.

"Look at me, not at her. What kind of deal?"

"Those that cooperate get to keep their lives and their money, and they will eventually get full amnesty."

El Ángel sounded suspicious as he asked, "And for such a gift, what do they have to give up?"

"The drug trade, human trafficking, theft of fuel, extortion, you name it. You all have to go legitimate over the next five years or die.

Think, Miguel. You can stop running. You just have to work with us and transition into legal businesses. If you don't, you'll be killed."

Steven hated the idea of offering life to the man in front of him, but he had to think of Chelle. It wasn't just his life anymore. Right now, it was imperative that he convinced El Ángel that it was he who was in danger if he hurt them more.

"I do have legal businesses," Miguel observed.

"Mostly to launder illegal money. If you want full amnesty, you must become one-hundred-percent legal by the end of the five years."

El Ángel puffed on his cigar some more, slowly enjoying its flavor; when he exhaled, he choked slightly on the smoke as he laughed heartily. He turned back towards Steven.

"How very generous, why me?"

"Not just you. As you know, there are others. El Pequeño Diablo and El Padrino are already on board, along with some other, smaller cartels."

"I don't believe you. You lie. They would never give up their territories. They have risked their lives to build them and control them. I told you, do not lie to me. I'm afraid that is going to cost your girlfriend one of her nipples. Maybe I will make you choose which one?"

"No, Miguel, wait. I'm telling you the truth. You hurt her more, and I won't be able to save you. But there is still time; you don't have to die."

"You sound very sure of yourself, but it is I who am holding the knife."

"You want to know why they agreed to cooperate. I'm telling you: so they could live. They saw what I could do to them. El Padrino's boat? I blew it up with a drone strike. El Pequeño Diablo's mountaintop factory? It was destroyed by a cruise missile from a US ship off the coast."

"So? These men play with danger every day. They have more than enough money to replace what you destroyed. Of course, they wouldn't do that until you were killed and a clear message sent to the United States to butt out of Mexico's business."

Steven looked at Chelle, desperately wishing that she hadn't followed her instincts this one time. The final bit of information was the last thing Steven wanted to share, but it was the only way to explain everyone's cooperative behavior.

"They can't run; I marked them. They're being electronically tracked night and day. If they don't cooperate, they'll be killed. They had no choice but to join me. Think, Miguel, think. Why wouldn't you join with us? They will be multi-millionaires and respected members of society. They and their families can enjoy their lives: their children can go to the finest schools, they can live anywhere they want. Now, you're at an advantage. You already know more than they do about the entire plan."

"You know where they are at all times?"

"Yes, people back in Washington are tracking them twenty-four seven."

El Ángel walked up to Chelle, who was still passed out from the pain, and held her left breast in his hand, hovering his knife around it with his right.

"Convince me, and do it quickly."

"My case, there are printouts in it. They show their locations. It only opens with my fingerprints; you'll have to untie me."

El Ángel nodded to the two men guarding Steven.

"Untie him, Sergio, hold your gun against his head," He walked around Chelle and held his knife against her neck. "One false move and I will slash her throat, you know I will."

Steven stood and turned his back to the man called Sergio. His bindings were cut, and he went up to the case on the bed and slid open the hidden lock, pressing his fingers against it in the correct order while under intense scrutiny. It was hard to ignore the rifle just inches from his head.

El Ángel gave the next instructions without moving his knife away from Chelle's neck.

"Tie him again. Now, tell us what to look for."

When Steven's arms were secured behind him once more, he was pushed back down onto the small couch. It was only then that El Ángel lifted his knife away from Chelle's throat and walked towards the case on the bed.

Chelle started to moan, slowly waking from her faint.

"There are maps, one for El Pequeño Diablo and one for El Padrino. Look closely, there are dates and times."

From across the room, he watched El Ángel examine the maps.

Steven watched his eyes travel over them. It appeared to Steven that El Ángel was looking for a specific place. After shuffling a few papers around in the briefcase, his eyes stopped and he fixated on something for over a minute.

El Ángel put the maps down outside the case and searched the briefcase for more information. Soon, he had something, and it was the file with his name on it. El Ángel paced the room as he read it.

"Whoever collects your information about me is hardly accurate. Some of it is flattering, some not so nice, but it is only opinions, and I should not get upset over mere opinions. The important thing is, I do believe you." El Ángel paced the room a bit as he thought. "And if I don't cooperate, like they say they are, I will die?"

Steven didn't want to anger the cartel leader, but he nodded.

"Yes, you and your men will die. You kill me, you will all die at the next opportunity. The rules have changed; no trial, you have already been sentenced to death. Your country and mine have declared war on the cartels."

El Ángel tossed the papers back into the case.

"I see a wallet and ID are inside this case. Could it be that this is how you marked your prey?"

Chelle moaned some more and lifted her body, slowly remembering where she was and what had happened.

"Chelle, Chelle," Stephen called.

Chelle's eyes lifted a bit, and she tried to focus on Steven.

"*Me*, you pay attention to *me* or I will make your friend pass out again," El Ángel said. "Are they listening to us right now?"

"Yes, they are."

El Ángel lifted up the pieces of a broken pen from his pocket.

"You mean through this?" he asked, smiling wickedly.

"No, that was just a decoy. We assumed you would find that. It was only there to make you feel secure after you found and destroyed it."

Steven could still hear the rain dripping from the balcony. He remembered Colonel Tripp's warning about keeping the drone flying in poor weather. He also knew that Filipe and his men wouldn't be coming to their rescue.

Having control of the local police was undoubtedly an operational necessity for El Ángel's success. If Steven was a betting man, he would have bet that the local police were detaining Filipe and his men just as he had said. The fact that El Ángel had their cooperation wasn't a surprise. He could pay them more in a year than the state could over their careers.

El Ángel walked to the window and stared out for a moment.

"Bring him here."

Steven was lifted to his feet by two of the biggest men and dragged to the window.

"I can tell that you can be most persuasive," El Ángel mused. "Perhaps you can persuade me also. But I am not a man of words, I am a man of action. Perhaps you do have the power you claim, but do you have the resolve to wield it? I will make you a deal. If you blow up the hotel on that corner down there, I will not cut into your girlfriend's breast." El Ángel pointed down the street. "Talk to your friends right now. Tell them to blow up that hotel. Because if that hotel doesn't go down, you will die, and your girlfriend shall become my new plaything. And my playthings don't last very long."

Steven looked toward Chelle. He didn't care about his life and would gladly rain holy hell down on his own hotel room if it meant killing El Ángel, but to take innocent lives just to prove a point was something he couldn't do. Chelle started to shake her head to indicate that she did not want to be the cause of the death of so many people either.

"She is such a brave woman. But she does not yet know how much pain she will have to suffer before she finally dies."

"See that empty soccer field, two blocks down." Steven nodded in the general direction of the field. "That will do. My people will not blow up a hotel full of innocent people. Not unless you're in it too."

El Ángel turned his gaze to the empty field.

"Target the soccer field two blocks west of my position," Steven said loudly, not giving El Ángel time to argue the point.

Chapter 16

Within the Eisenhower Building, Colonel Tripp was jumping from one computer board to the next. Each screen he looked at just increased his anxiety.

"What soccer field? Shit! Mitchell! What the hell is going on?"

"Sir, I have a solid lock on Senator Westcott's position, but the cloud deck is just too low for a visual, and the ship says the drone can't go lower."

"Tell them to keep it circling; maybe the clouds will lift. But whatever you do, don't lose the audio. If we don't blow up that soccer field soon, Westcott will be dead. Lieutenant Kastner, can you confirm the identity of the woman they're talking about and what she's doing in Mexico?"

"Yes, sir. The veranda door must have been open, because I have their initial conversation. I was able to enhance it, sir, and match it against a voice print I had from his last Washington visit."

Colonel Tripp said, "Are you telling me it's that FBI agent he's been seeing?"

"Yes, sir, it's her," said Lieutenant Kastner.

"Now we have an FBI agent involved, dammit!"

"From their earlier conversation, the senator didn't know she was going to be there," Lieutenant Kastner volunteered. "He was trying to make her leave when they were ambushed." She furiously worked her keyboard, saying, "I have a stored satellite image coming up, sir. It's from a week ago. I think I have the soccer field in question on the screen now."

Colonel Tripp ran over to Kastner's bank of computers.

"There, sir," she said, pointing, "and here's where the senator is right now. That has to be the field he wants us to hit."

"Mitchell, we need to blow up that soccer field, now."

"Sir, the drone still doesn't have a visual. It just can't go lower. There are numerous mountains and towers and buildings in the area. I'm sorry, sir. We're looking for a break in the clouds, but no luck yet, and the missile needs to be guided visually to the target."

Lieutenant Kastner broke in, "Sir, none of the other voices we hear are from any of our other tags; the other cartel members are not at this meeting."

"That would make sense, it's Miguel Ángel Vega and his men. Steven hasn't been able to tag him yet. Do we know how many men?"

"I can't get voice prints; nobody but Miguel Vega is talking."

"Full audio, I need to hear every word. And where is his ground support? Don't tell me the FES bailed on him."

****

"How long?" El Ángel asked.

"I don't know, it varies. There are protocols to follow, the navy needs to decide how they'll do it; they have a few options to choose from.

"Look, Miguel, join us. Keep your money, keep your soldiers. All you have to do is stop any other organization from shipping drugs through your territory into the US. That's nothing more than you're doing now!"

"And I can continue to sell my drugs without interference from the federales?"

"No, of course not. But, as you wind down your smuggling operations, the federales will wind down their manhunt for you. You will get a full pardon if, after five years, you have stopped all illegal trafficking from flowing across the border in your area. We will even help you start legal companies.

"As you and the other cartels share information about their illegal operations, the federales will be able to stabilize the areas. Eventually, they will be able to maintain law and order without your help. Think of it as phasing out of one business and into another."

"Would I get it in writing, a letter from my government and yours that I am pardoned?"

"Nothing can be in writing, at least not yet. If people find out the government is cutting a deal with the cartels, the whole thing could fall apart, and you don't want that."

Steven was getting nervous. Without the conviction that he would die if he didn't cooperate, Steven was sure El Ángel wouldn't be persuaded. Steven needed the missile strike soon. Very, very soon.

"Do not presume to know what I want, Mr. Senator. That could be bad for your health."

****

Colonel Tripp's jaw dropped. The room had become extremely quiet as he and his team listened in real time to what Steven had said. He couldn't believe what he was hearing. He was actually helping ruthless murderers and torturers to go free. Still, it wasn't his job to question the mission, and he prayed the president knew what he was doing.

"Mitchell, any clearing?"

"Sorry, sir, nothing. It's solid overcast."

"Remember that practice simulation you flew last week?"

"Yes, sir?" Mitchell wasn't sure where the question was going.

"How realistic was it?"

"Couldn't be more realistic, sir. The satellite imagery it uses is top notch."

"Lieutenant, can you superimpose the simulation over Mitchell's real-world GPS position?"

Lieutenant Kastner thought for a moment.

"If I override the simulators tracking input with Mitchell's real-world GPS output, it might work. But flying in simulator mode is completely different than flying in the real world. I'm afraid that Mitchell might lose communications, and if that happens, he could lose control of it all together. And the drone is one thing, but if I'm thinking what you're thinking, visually guiding a missile to a real location using a simulation program has never been done."

"Set it up. This little experiment is on me."

****

"And why would the government give me a pardon?"

El Ángel was watching Steven with one eye and the soccer field with another.

"Because they have been trying to shut down the drug and human smuggling trade for years. Every time they kill one cartel leader, two more pop up in their place.

"The thinking is that we want the cartels to patrol and control their areas as they are now. Nobody new sets up shop or gains access routes but, over the next five years, the cartels slowly give up territory to the federales to control. While doing this, you grow your legal businesses and hire legal employees. Once you are completely legal, you get your pardon. Hell, everybody wins."

"Not everybody, amigo. Many, many people, powerful people, would disagree with you."

Chapter 17

Colonel Tripp was watching the computer screens in front of him. To him, it looked like the Reaper drone flying over the seaside resort of Puerto Vallarta had suddenly broken into clear air. He watched to computer screen as he called the captain of the ship off the coast of Mexico.

"Captain, we are certain it will work. Lives are at stake. The drone thinks it's in clear air. It has a lock on the soccer field. You needed a visual to guide the missile, now you have a visual," he argued. "Yes, sir, I understand it's against protocol. We don't have time to debate this, Captain. Turn over control of the drone to us, sir. I will take the responsibility."

The reply came, grave and noncommittal, and Colonel Tripp nodded.

"I do understand, Captain. Yes, I do have authority. You have already seen it. It comes directly from your commander-in-chief, the president. Please, sir, we are running out of time." Colonel Tripp muted the phone in his hand. "Lieutenant, are you sure this will work? If it lands anywhere but the soccer field, we will kill many innocent people."

Lieutenant Kastner didn't stop working her keyboard and didn't stop to think before answering.

"The Reaper knows exactly where it is and thinks it's in clear air. It believes it sees the target. Yes, sir, it will work. I'm sure of it."

Colonel Tripp unmuted his phone, saying, "Sir, I need control now. My ass, sir."

Over the phone, he heard the captain order, "Release the drone to backup control in Washington."

"Thank you, Captain." Hanging up the phone, he said to his team,

"Let's pray to God that this works and that nobody is on that field. Despite what the screen looks like, we are shooting blind. Let's hope the senator knows what he's doing."

****

El Ángel was peering out the window, looking at the soccer field.

"You are running out of time, Senator."

Steven was still tied down and flanked on both sides by the big men. He agreed; time was indeed running out for everybody. He watched cars starting to park in the immediate neighborhood. Children were starting to gather, already practicing with their soccer balls bouncing off their knees.

"Shoot, dammit! Shoot! There are people starting to go towards the field!" Steven cried to the sky.

El Ángel looked toward the overcast sky, trying to see who or what the senator was talking to.

"That's your plan? Just like that, you expect me to quit and shut down what has taken me a lifetime to build? In case you haven't been paying attention, Mexico is a poor country. What are all these legal businesses we are all supposed to build? For who? Factories for what?"

Steven wasn't paying attention to El Ángel. Instead, he was focused on the children and their parents gathering at the outskirts of the soccer field.

There was a streak in the sky, a loud explosion and a cloud of dust. Debris flew skyward.

El Ángel stood motionless, his mouth agape. He couldn't take his eyes off the scene in front of him. El Senador had shouted to the sky, and now a soccer field had a huge hole smack dab in the center of it.

Men, women and children were all running as fast as they could away from the cloud of dust and smoke. All seemed unharmed to Steven. He hoped that they would blame the explosion on the cartels and another turf war.

El Ángel collected himself and pointed a pistol at Steven's head, saying, "Not a word. Not a fucking word."

El Ángel motioned to his men to get the tape. After Steven's mouth was covered, he was hogtied and tossed to the floor.

"Grab the girl, leave him," El Ángel ordered. He bent down and talked to Steven softly. "I will not kill you today, but you must leave Mexico immediately. Your pretty friend will be my toy until I hear you are back in the states. Then, maybe then, I will let her go. Not unharmed, of course, but still alive."

Every vein in Steven's body was near bursting with the strain to escape and strangle the man in front of him.

El Ángel stood and told his men, "After we get to the cars, scatter and get lost in traffic. Don't go to the rendezvous until tomorrow. And, for God's sake, make sure you aren't followed, or I will kill you myself."

Steven managed to catch Chelle's eye one last time as she was lifted to her feet and dragged off. The door closed, and Steven was alone, hearing only the commotion and sirens blaring a few blocks away.

****

"I need to talk with la presidenta."

Colonel Tripp had dialed the special number he had been given for emergencies. While on hold, he hollered to Lieutenant Kastner, "Get me the president!"

"Gracia, la presidenta. Yes, I know, again, I thank you for taking my call. I was instructed to tell you, 'Grito de Dolores'." There was a moment of hesitation before Colonel Tripp confirmed, "Yes, I work directly for the president of the United States, and I need your help.

"It appears that Senator Westcott has been compromised. We haven't heard from him for an hour, and we believe an associate of his has been abducted by a cartel leader known as El Ángel. They are in Puerto Vallarta, and the team from your country that was supposed to be backing him up were apparently taken into custody by the local police on El Ángel's orders."

Suddenly and without warning, he heard his phone click and he was put on hold. Several minutes later, President Alejandra Espinoza Torres was back on the phone with a question for the colonel.

"Yes, I'm afraid the bomb that went off in Puerto Vallarta was ours," Colonel Tripp answered, sounding contrite. "Was anybody hurt?"

The president replied and he sagged with relief.

"Thank goodness, of course we had no choice. The mission was in jeopardy, and it was ordered by the senator. I assume full responsibility. "Thank you, la presidenta. Yes, I will keep you updated. And I assure you that, as soon as possible, I will explain the situation to President Walker. I'm sure he will contact you also. Yes, ma'am, that would be appreciated. We sure could use their help."

Colonel Tripp reached for a full cup of coffee that had been sitting cold for a long time already. Before he walked to empty it, he said to his team, "The Mexican president said she will find the people who arrested the team and have them horsewhipped. I think she meant it. I'm going into my office to make up some sort of explanation for this mess. If anything happens, anything at all, patch me in."

****

It was a long two hours later when Colonel Tripp got a call from Mexico. Filipe was climbing into his jeep when he used the code word and number supplied by Senator Westcott to call Colonel Tripp.

"Commander Vasquez, thank God. We haven't heard from the senator for hours. We believe a friend of his was tortured and kidnapped by Miguel Ángel Vega. We don't have any idea where she or they might be."

Filipe answered, "We were detained by the local police; that was a mistake that has been rectified. We are on our way to the hotel now, and we expect to be there in fifteen minutes. I will call you back as soon as I know what happened to El Senador."

"Thank you, Commander. We will be standing by."

Fifteen minutes later, with one solid kick, El Cazador barged down the hotel door to Steven's room. He stood to the side, guarding the hall, as Filipe and the team stormed in.

"Amigo!" Filipe called out when he saw Steven on the floor, his eyes pleading for help.

While Filipe took off the tape around his mouth, another soldier cut off the bindings around his feet and hands.

"What happened?"

"Water," Steven gasped as he got to his feet. After a short drink, he continued, "They took Chelle, my girlfriend. She wanted to surprise me on my vacation. The bastard cut off her toe to make me talk."

Filipe did a quick inspection of Steven and surmised he was mostly OK. He surveyed the room and saw the blood on the floor and the severed toe.

Steven said, "They took my briefcase and my phone. Filipe, I need to borrow your phone. I know someone in Washington who might be able to help us find Chelle."

It didn't take long before Colonel Tripp was on the line.

"Colonel, my wallet, my special ID, it was in my case. Can you track it? What do you mean 'eventually'?"

Steven hung up without saying a word and sat himself down on a wooden chair by a small desk.

He said to Filipe, "The colonel said that Mexico's a big place. Right now, they don't have any idea where to tell the satellite to look. Filipe, we have to find her. They're going to torture her. El Ángel said that if I don't leave for the US immediately, they'll kill her."

Steven stared at the blood on the floor in disbelief. Filipe approached him from behind and placed a comforting hand on his shoulder.

"We will start by interviewing the police captain. The local police just found out what happens when you mess with the FES. I think we will find them a bit more cooperative from now on."

Looking determined, Steven turned towards Filipe and insisted, "I'll interview him, and I guarantee you he will tell us everything he knows."

"I think it best if you do as El Ángel said and go back to the US; it might give us more time. Though, I must be honest, I doubt very much El Ángel will let her live. I could give you many reasons, and he needs none."

"I'm not going back without Chelle. Let's go. I want a few cracks at the police captain. We know he's on El Ángel's payroll."

"No, amigo, I insist. You must have faith in my communication skills."

"Filipe, Chelle's special. She came down to help me because she thought I was in some sort of trouble. I should have told her the truth. I shouldn't have lied to her; she wouldn't be in this predicament if I had just told her the truth. If anything happens to her, I'll never forgive myself."

"I do not need any more incentive to aggressively question the captain," Filipe promised. "Rest assured, I will find out what he knows, but that doesn't mean it will help us. Time is our only ally. You must buy us that time by going back home."

El Cazador stepped into the room as two of the other men took position in the hallway.

"The commander is right," he said. "El Ángel does not make empty threats"

Steven angrily replied, "Neither do I. I promise you, El Ángel is a dead man."

"Please, señor, let us do our job. We need you to buy us the time to do it."

"Please, amigo," Filipe pleaded. "We must let El Ángel think he has won this battle."

Steven sat down and rested his throbbing head in his hands.

"If I leave Chelle behind, he has."

Chapter 18

S o, Senator Westcott, I want to thank you for being here today," said the pretty news announcer. Steven smiled into the television cameras and assured everybody he was the one thankful for being booked on the show at the last minute.

"As you know, I was scheduled for a wonderful vacation down in Mexico, but when this issue came up, I felt compelled to address the American people in person."

"Well, Washington is glad to have you, and it's always a pleasure to have you on our show, Senator. Please, tell us more."

"The North American Trade Agreement is crucial, and I support the president..."

Eventually, with the interview done, Steven was in the back of the studio where he cleaned off the makeup that covered his face. He wondered why he bothered. Shannon had done an amazing job of getting him booked on all of the networks in such a short time. By the end of the day, his face would be raw from rubbing makeup off, but it was the only way to convince El Ángel that he was back in the states.

****

Chelle lifted herself from the soiled mattress and propped herself up against the cold, brick wall. She looked around at her reality. The mattress was blood-soaked, undoubtedly from other visitors to the room. The only other things in the room were the blanket she had wrapped her naked body in and a worse than filthy plastic bucket in the corner that she had been forced to use over the last few days to relieve herself.

She stared at her throbbing, bandaged foot. At least the man the others called 'Miguel' had sent in a doctor to look at it. Chelle didn't believe for one second that he was a real doctor – though that was what he called himself – but he had cleaned her wound and bandaged it. He had also given her some pills he claimed were antibiotics. Chelle didn't feel she had much choice but to believe him, so she had taken them.

She heard a key turn, and then the door to her cell opened slowly. A man with a gun remained in the doorway, not too worried about a small woman with a bandaged foot rushing him.

He opened the door further, and a young, very pretty woman with long, jet-black hair stepped past him and into the room. She had some food on a tray. The young woman was dressed in a transparent white top and a long, flowery dress. Her feet were bare on the concrete floor, though her nails were painted pink.

In Spanish, she said, "I was told I could bring you some food. And I brought you some dry, clean bandages."

Chelle was famished, and she welcomed the food.

"Gracias," she replied. "I think I have been down here for days with nothing but water, and not much of that."

"Sí, Miguel and his men brought you four days ago."

Chelle saw the visible shaking of the woman's hands as she bent down and placed the food in front of her. Chelle took the paper cup of water first and drank. Water had never tasted so good to her before. There were four pills on the tray. She picked one up and read the lettering on its side: 'Advil'.

Chelle looked up at the girl and said, "Muchas gracias".

She flipped all four pills into her mouth and downed them with another drink.

Chelle ate some of the fruit on the tray. Looking up at the young woman, she asked in Spanish, "Are you Miguel's daughter?"

The girl averted her eyes and shook her head.

"He took me from my village. He said I was too pretty to stay in such a remote village, and he made me his girlfriend."

"You *are* pretty, Miguel is right about that."

"It is a curse."

"What is your name?" Chelle asked.

"Adriana." The girl's eyes started tearing up. "Adriana Romero Reyes."

"What's the matter, Adriana?"

Adriana looked back towards the locked door.

"I'm so sorry for what Miguel did to you. I heard the men talking, they all laughed about it." Adriana looked back at the door again and whispered, "I hate them, I hate them all."

Chelle ate some more of the fruit. There was also a tortilla with a slice of some sort of meat on it.

The young girl was trying to dry her tears when she offered some clothes to Chelle, saying, "I picked out a dress for you."

Chelle got to her feet painfully and accepted the dress, asking, "Is it one of yours?"

"No, it belonged to one of Miguel's other girls. She is gone now. The blouse was hers too. Miguel said I couldn't give you a bra though." Adriana looked down at her sheer, white blouse, knowing her breasts were clearly visible through the material. "Miguel doesn't permit them."

"Why are you here? I mean with Miguel, if you don't like him? Why don't you run away?"

"I spit on him. When he stole me from my village, he killed my papa, mama, little sister and brother. He said I was so beautiful, he wanted me to go with him and he didn't want me longing for my family."

Chelle dropped the dirty blanket covering her and slipped the dress on over her head.

Adriana once again diverted her eyes, saying, "But I know what will happen when he is sick of me. I will be killed too, just like the girl whose cloths you wear. For now, I keep him happy as much as I can."

"Who is this Miguel. What does he do?"

"He runs the biggest cartel in all of Mexico. He is cruel beyond belief."

"Can we escape?" Chelle whispered.

"Please sit and I will tend to your wound."

Chelle carefully sat back down. Adriana started to unwrap Chelle's bandage, shaking her head.

"You cannot escape, señora, Miguel has guards everywhere."

Chelle held Adriana's hand in hers, whispering, "Maybe there is a way, if we think hard."

Still with tears in her eyes, Adriana said, "There is none. Even trying to escape, he will do terrible things to us. He has made me watch him hurt people and kill them. It is a terrible thing he does. And the guards watch me everywhere I go."

Adriana took the new bandage and rewrapped Chelle's foot.

That was when the key was turned and the door opened. The guard motioned Adriana to come out and he checked to make sure that everything she had brought in also left, including the now empty paper cup of water.

Chelle was left alone again to ponder what Senator Steven Westcott was doing meeting up with the leader of one of the biggest cartels in Mexico.

It was about an hour later when two guards rushed into her room and roughly dragged her up narrow stairs to the main living area.

From there, she was guided to a huge, cantilevered deck over-looking the Gulf of California. Chelle had on the white dress Adriana had given her and a red, silk blouse with blue, tropical flowers. They fit surprisingly well. Her breasts were bare inside the blouse, which wasn't quite as transparent as Adriana's had been. Just the same, it left little to the imagination.

She was left standing just outside the main room of the mil-lion-dollar home, which was built on a high, rocky cliff. The rounded glass wall of the structure was just behind her, but when Miguel stepped up to the deck, all she could focus on was the round, puffy face smoking the big cigar. The anger in her swelled at the sight of him.

"Please, sit," he said. "I'm sure your foot is still in much pain. It's a shame you had that nasty accident and lost you toe."

Chelle's foot was hurting her and standing was making it worse, so she hobbled to the nearest chair and sat.

"Look, buddy; whoever you are, you have no idea the kind of trouble you're in."

"That's right, we have not been formally introduced! I am Miguel Vega. I am your host for the time being. I, of course, have had time to learn exactly who you are. So, if you are referring to kidnapping an FBI agent, then yes, I do. And I have learned that you and Senator Westcott have a history together. Are you aware of the fact that your boyfriend wants to do business with me?"

"I know nothing. I just came down to Mexico to join him on vacation."

"Maybe, maybe not." El Ángel took another slow puff of his cigar as he stared at his prize for a long moment. He let a big breath of smoke escape his mouth. "They say smoking is bad for your health, in fact it could kill you." He took another puff and said, "Your threats mean little to me. Every day I live is a gift, especially in my line of work. The least of my worries is the negative consequences of smoking. I assume I will be dead, probably violently murdered, well before smoke could kill me. So, you see, smoking is something I do without guilt. To look at life that way is..." El Ángel took another slow puff and smoke escaped through his lips as he contemplated. "I guess the right word would be 'liberating'. So, Chelle, why don't you tell me what you know? You might also find it liberating."

"I only know what I heard before you cut off my toe. But, if Steven wants you to work with him, I would highly recommend it."

"Haha! You are confident of your boyfriend's threats. Maybe you shouldn't be; besides, I don't know that I want to. I kind of like my life just the way it is. It may be short, but," El Ángel floated his hand with the cigar in it over the ocean below, "as you can see, I am living in luxury. It is beautiful, isn't it?"

Miguel stared at the horizon as he continued.

"You were passed out when your boyfriend and I had an interesting talk. He wants much more than to just work with me. However, the consequences could be much, much worse than he and our presidents anticipate. Perhaps they haven't thought this through far enough. You do pose a dilemma I hadn't counted on, though. What do I do with an FBI agent on vacation in Mexico?"

"You let her go, and then you run like hell in the other direction."

"Ha! You make me smile. I have something I would like you to see." El Ángel took a remote control off the glass-top table and flicked it at a television protruding from the wall. "I recorded this earlier today, and I thought you might find it interesting.

Senator Westcott was on the television earlier. In fact, he was on several of the news shows today. He has been busy back in Washington. It doesn't appear to me that he is all that concerned about you."

Chelle saw Steven being interviewed, the date and time were stamped in the corner of the screen.

"What did you expect? I heard you threaten him with my life; he's protecting me."

"From two thousand miles away?"

El Ángel took another puff of his cigar as he turned away from the spectacular view and paced slowly in front of Chelle.

"What do I do with you? I mean eventually. I do not see many options for you, I'm afraid."

"You're going to kill me regardless of what Steven does, aren't you?"

"Yes, you are right of course. But that is my dilemma. Killing you is so permanent, and it very well could be my undoing. It might take years, but your special forces or Mexico's would break many laws to take revenge for one of their own. However, if I let you go, maybe that gesture would be taken as a sign that Miguel Vega is somebody who can be taken advantage of. A proper dilemma."

El Ángel walked over to the glass railing and took a final puff of his cigar before tossing it over the railing and watching it disappear into the abyss of the waiting ocean.

"It would be so easy to dispose of my problem over this railing. Death would be quick; if you missed the rock outcroppings, you would hit the ocean below like it was solid concrete.

"I do worry about your senator friend. The governments might forgive me, but I don't think he will. He might not be able to protect you, but that doesn't mean he won't try to avenge your death. So, what do I do?"

"The answer is obvious. Let me go."

"As I mentioned, I can't let that happen either. But I believe I have come up with a creative solution. I doubt you will approve, but let me introduce you to another guest. I believe you know him." El Ángel walked to an intercom and said, "Bring him."

Two big men escorted a man to the deck. He wore long, khaki pants and a tropical shirt that made him look like a typical tourist. Chelle stared at the man, who she thought had a remarkable resemblance to Steven. The several days' worth of stubble confused her for a moment, then she said, "Ernie?"

"Hi, Chelle. We only met briefly; I'm surprised you remember."

"What are you doing here?"

"Let me explain," El Ángel said as he lit another cigar. "Mr. Westcott, would you care for a cigar, my friend?"

There was no mistaking that Ernie and Steven were brothers.

Ernie had the same square shoulders and muscular build; even his height was about the same. One difference from the last time Chelle had seen him was his brown hair. Today, it was long and tied in a short ponytail.

"No thank you, Mr. Vega."

El Ángel continued, "Mr. Westcott, I mean *this* Mr. Westcott, the brother to *your* Mr. Westcott, is also a talented man. He has exceptional management skills. It hasn't taken him long at all to prove himself over the last year."

Chelle felt a twinge of hope. Maybe Ernie would help her. Steven had said he was close to his brother and that he hadn't been able to believe it when he broke parole and disappeared.

"At any rate, Ernie has proven himself valuable to our organization. So, I'm thinking about my dilemma, and I think I have a card up my sleeve that Senator Westcott doesn't know I have.

"Ernie, I have a proposition for you. If you kill your brother, I will let this woman live. I'm thinking he is wary of people trying to harm him. But you, his only brother; I'm sure you can find a way to get close to him. When you are successful, this woman is yours to do with as you wish."

Ernie looked at Chelle and at her bandaged foot.

"She is damaged, why do you think I would want her?"

El Ángel took a slow inhale of his cigar as if contemplating the question over the volume of smoke.

"Because she was your brother's."

Ernie laughed, then he said, "Maybe I will have a cigar, Mr. Vega. It seems we have a lot to talk about."

"Please, call me 'Miguel'. You said your brother was always the lucky one, he was the one born with a silver spoon in his mouth and you, well, you got the shitty end of the stick. Could be that your luck is changing. I know of another home overlooking the ocean, not far from here. Consider it a wedding gift for you and your new bride after you have been successful."

Miguel handed Ernie a cigar and the razor-sharp cigar cutter. Ernie placed the end of the cigar through the cutter and easily cut off the end. He handed the cutter back to Miguel, trading it for the cigar lighter.

"My luck started changing a year ago, Miguel, and I thank you for that."

"Why, Ernie? Why?" Chelle asked.

Ernie ignored Chelle while he lit the cigar and enjoyed a few mouthfuls of smoke. "Excellent, Miguel, just excellent."

Ernie turned to Chelle, asking, "You want to know 'why'? One mistake, one, and I end up in prison for five years. Five years, for nothing. I never hurt nobody."

"You threatened a shopkeeper with a gun, you were high on heroin."

Ernie looked at El Ángel and added, "I haven't done anything since prison, honest."

"I know you haven't. You wouldn't be here if you had."

Ernie turned back towards Chelle, snarling, "I tried going straight! Got a job and everything. Yep, even a tiny little apartment. But hey, it was bigger than a cell. I could come and go as I wanted. But to where, with who?

"I was a con, and because of my big-shot brother and his campaigns, there wasn't anybody in the country who didn't know it. I was talked about on national TV. Mr. Senator's loser brother. How wonderful he was to put up with me.

"Can you believe it? I'm sitting in prison, minding my own business watching TV in the common room, and boom: there's my brother, talking and laughing with celebrities. Talking about *me!* The guys thought that was pretty funny.

"But did he help me? He could have got me off early. Did he? No. He said I had to do my time like anybody else. He didn't have to stare at the same three walls and a row of bars for five fucking years, eating the same slop day after day like a caged animal."

"Steven loves you," Chelle replied. "He'd do anything for you. He's told me so much about you growing up together."

"I hope you're right. I mean, about him doing anything for me, because I'm going to ask him to die for both of us. How's that? And when I come back, you and I are going to party. And you are going to like it."

"I have an idea," said Miguel. "Let's take some photos of the happy couple. We can post them on the internet and show the world how happy the senator's brother is with his new girlfriend."

Ernie looked up, surprised.

"You want to show the world where Chelle is?"

"Not where she is, but that she is happy with the brother of Steven Westcott. What better way to show the world that Miguel Vega did not harm her in any way? And, if El Senador says otherwise, it is only... how do you say it? 'Sour grapes' because she chose his brother over him."

Chelle's mouth was agape.

"You're out of your mind. Nobody would believe that."

Ernie raised his eyebrows in indignation.

"Are you insinuating you would never choose me over my brother?"

"Not even close. I assure you, you are not your brother."

Ernie chuckled at Chelle's bluster. Understanding crossed his face as he looked back at Miguel.

"We show Chelle having a good old time and not missing her beloved Steven; I like it. It clears your name in her disappearance and limits how he's able to respond."

"Precisely, she merely ran off with her boyfriend's brother. Who wouldn't understand that? Would you care for a drink, my friend? We can celebrate your new romance."

"I would be honored, Miguel."

"Bring my friend a drink," El Ángel said to one of the men who had escorted Ernie. Miguel edged up to the wall close to Chelle and pressed a button on the intercom. "Have Adriana come here immediately."

Chelle caught Adriana's eye as she walked onto the deck, properly subservient to Miguel. She was dressed immodestly, just as she had been when she visited the basement room.

To Ernie, Miguel said, "Meet Adriana. She is a beautiful flower that I found in the desert. Such a prize. You may have yours, and I have mine."

"How do you do, señorita?" Ernie bowed his head slightly.

Miguel walked up to her and gently ran the back of his hand over her cheek.

"Have you ever seen skin like this? On a baby, maybe; it is so soft and perfect in every way. I can assure you that the rest of her skin is equally as fine. Would you like to see for yourself?"

Chelle was watching the poor girl closely. It was clear that she wasn't flattered in the least, but she didn't move away either. The fear was evident in her eyes as she glanced at Chelle, embarrassed. Chelle had guessed that the girl was no more than eighteen, if that, and she wanted to protect her. At that moment, though, it was impossible.

"As you wish, Miguel, I am your guest. However, I certainly will be more than happy to take your word for it. As you say, she is your flower and needn't be shared."

Chelle didn't know if Ernie was being chivalrous to the girl or patronizing to his boss.

"Such a diplomat, Mr. Westcott. That is why I like you so. Adriana, I want you to find a selection of clothes for Miss Saltarie. Swim suits, camisoles, dresses, tops. Bring Mr. Westcott a selection of shirts and a swimsuit or two."

Chelle saw Miguel's hand descend to the girl's backside, and he rubbed it gently before giving it a not-so-gentle slap.

"Now, be quick, you do not want to disappoint me, do you? And bring my camera." Miguel looked at Chelle and bragged, "I am not a bad photographer, you will see."

Chapter 19

W"hat makes you think I'm going to cooperate?" Chelle asked.
Miguel puffed on his cigar, held up the razor-sharp cigar cutter and smiled at Ernie.

"Fingers and toes cut almost as easily as a cigar. I have done it before with this same cutter. There is no reason to have your feet show in the photos. So, if convincing you that you are having a wonderful time takes the removal of another toe or two, that can be arranged. But, I assure you, you *will* smile when I tell you to."

Adriana came back with a selection of women's clothes. Miguel approved of the items and sent her away for a few more.

"What say we start with some pool shots? It is your choice, señora. With or without a swimsuit doesn't matter to me, but you *are* going into the water, and you *are* going to look like you're having the time of your life."

Chelle realized she didn't have a choice. El Ángel had already proved to her that he wouldn't think twice about taking another toe.

She stood, picked up a skimpy two-piece suit and asked, "Where do I go to get changed?"

"Go? You are already there. Let's not be so modest; we are all friends here."

Chelle looked at Ernie, but he didn't even pretend to avert his eyes and nor did Miguel. She dropped her bottoms while staring at both of them in defiance. She did the same with her top and stepped into the bottoms awkwardly, thanks to her bandaged foot. She turned away as she snapped on the top.

When Adriana came back out, she caught Chelle's eye and suffered her embarrassment with her.

"The pool is this way. I have a fine photographer's eye, Miss Saltarie; my lens had better see a pleasant face."

Miguel and Adriana guided Chelle down the stairs to the pool. Adriana tried to help Chelle navigate the stairs with her painful, bandaged foot.

****

Miguel was sipping another drink and smoking another cigar on the deck. He was seated at a large, glass table with photos scattered all about.

"The pictures turned out very nice. Don't you agree, Señor Westcott?"

Ernie was standing next to Miguel, examining the photos scattered on the glass tabletop, and said, "Miguel, you were right; you do have a photographer's eye."

As usual, they weren't alone. Two bodyguards stood patiently by, close enough for immediate action if their boss so much as winked at them. They had escorted Chelle back to the small room in the basement hours ago.

Miguel stood and went to the glass railing, looking out over the ocean. The sun was setting, an orange ball sinking into the sea.

"We have much to discuss. I have some ideas for you."

Ernie left the scattered pictures and walked to where his boss was enjoying the ocean view. Ernie leaned over the railing, looking over the expanse of ocean as the last of the sun disappeared.

"I'm all ears."

"I confiscated your brother's briefcase. Inside of it were many things of interest. Two were his wallet and passport. I must say, you have a remarkable resemblance to your brother, they should come in handy on your trip north of the border."

"I can't go in legally, his passport *and* mine are probably flagged."

"Amigo, we have many ways to get you into the US without any government knowing, but your brother's ID should come in handy once you are inside the border."

"I'm sure it will, I'm sure it will."

Ernie finished his drink, the ice clinking in the bottom of his glass.

"Another, my friend?"

"If you're offering, I will. Like you said, we have much to talk about."

****

Steven was huddled with Colonel Tripp in his Washington office. He had just come back from a meeting with the president. They had agreed that the mission should be temporarily suspended until Chelle was found.

Steven was pacing back and forth. He asked again, "You still haven't heard from Filipe? What about a radiation signature? There has to be one by now."

"Not if he hasn't pulled your ID out of the wallet, and if he left it inside your briefcase, that could serve as an additional radiation block. It was special too. I'm sorry, Steven. I know this last week has been difficult on you, but we'll find her."

"Difficult on *me? She* might be dying from pain right now. God knows what that monster has done to her. When I find him, I'm going to slice him into little pieces, I swear."

****

Chelle was lying on the bloody mattress with her leg propped up on the single blanket. Keeping her leg elevated seemed to help the swelling.

The photo shoot had been the epitome of embarrassment. Miguel had insisted she show more and more skin as the day went on. He even insisted that Ernie take off his suit in some of the shots.

Chelle was angry with herself for being such a well-behaved model, but the choice was between smiling or losing another part of her body to the monster. She accepted she'd had no choice, but it didn't make it easier to acknowledge what she had done.

There was no doubt in her mind that anybody seeing those photos would see a couple madly in love and enjoying a carefree day in the sun and opulence. Chelle hoped for another visit from Adriana. Maybe they could both take solace in each other's company. Despite her own predicament, Chelle felt sorry for her; nobody, especially such a young girl, deserved what she went through on a daily basis.

****

Ernie was standing in the security line at Los Angeles International Airport. He was clean-shaven and had on a well-tailored suit. Ernie admired the gold cufflinks that stood out against his white shirt. Insertion into the US had gone without a hitch.

The cufflinks, as well as the suit, had been a gift from El Ángel. He had said, 'If you are going to pretend you are Senator Westcott, you should look the part.' He had also given Ernie some pointed advice. 'Failure to kill your brother is not an option. I would be very disappointed in you.'

Two of El Ángel's most trusted men – Marquez and Ronaldo – were shadowing Ernie, though they traveled apart. Ernie assumed their job was to make sure Ernie did not disappoint El Ángel.

Hours ago, in Tijuana, he had emerged from a house with a smuggling tunnel in its basement. Outside, a ride had been waiting. He had kept his suit well wrapped to protect it from the mud and filth of the tunnel. They had stopped at a McDonalds on the outskirts of LA, and he had changed clothes. From there on, he was Senator Steven Westcott.

"Senator," the TSA agent said, respectfully nodded a greeting as he compared the photo ID to the name on the first-class ticket to Washington, DC. "Heading back to the Capitol?"

"Yes, time to get back to work for the people of Massachusetts." Ernie smiled easily. He realized that he should be nervous about being caught, but the truth was, he wasn't. As long as he believed he was Senator Westcott, he would be. A simple comparison of his face to the face on the ID would not be questioned. Nervousness at going through security would.

"You have a safe flight to Washington, sir." The agent handed back his photo ID and ticket. Ernie tucked the ID back into his brother's wallet.

****

Back in his Washington office, Steven was frantic.

"I know, Filipe, I'm sure you're doing everything you can. I understand, these guys are good at hiding, that's what they do, but *dammit*, Filipe, we have to find her. I'm going nuts here! I keep doing things to keep myself in the papers or on television for Chelle's sake. I just pray that she's still alive."

Filipe's reply brought little comfort.

"OK, sure," Steven sighed. "Talk with you tomorrow. Sooner, I hope."

Steven hung up. A week and a half had gone by since Chelle's abduction. Steven knew that, in situations like these, time was critical.

Chelle was a person of high value. Steven hoped that meant he would be contacted with a ransom demand, but in his heart, he knew that Miguel didn't want ransom money. He wanted Chelle, if for no other reason than to keep Steven from completing his plan.

Steven's cell phone rang. He answered it, wondering who it might be, as he didn't recognize the number.

"Hey, bro?"

"Ernie? Where the hell are you? Are you all right?"

"Yeah, I'm good, and I want to stay that way."

"Shit, Ernie, you shouldn't have run. You're in deep trouble now."

"I know. That's why I'm calling. I want to give myself up to you. I figure that the least I can do is let you turn me in to the police. You know, senator upholding the law, even if it means turning in his own brother."

"Ernie, I don't think that's a good idea. I mean me taking you in. Let me call a lawyer. I can get Teddy Johnston, he's good."

"Not good enough for me. Look, I get it. I'm going back to jail for a long time. I'm tired of running, but I'll only give myself up to you. I don't trust the cops, but if you take me in yourself, they won't mess with me. They can't."

"Ernie, I just don't think this is a good idea."

"Listen, bro, you know I trust you like nobody else in the world. This is the only way I'm going to do it."

"OK, where do you want me to meet you?"

"Come alone, Steven. I mean it. I can smell a cop a mile away."

"I promise, I'll be alone."

"I'm across the river in Arlington. Take Three Ninety-Five until King Street North. In fifteen minutes, call me. I'll give you further directions. And don't call that cute little FBI friend of yours either. I will run like a rabbit if I smell a rat. Steven, I'm timing this, so you had better get a move on."

Steven slipped his phone back into his pocket, rushing over to his desk, where he had his gun locked in a drawer. He put it in his hand and slipped it into his back holster, under his suit coat. Since he had started his Mexican assignment, he hardly ever went anywhere without it.

He was about to leave when he thought about the potential consequences if he took Ernie to a police station and had a gun on him. Thinking again, he locked it back in the drawer.

****

Ernie slipped the burner phone back into his pocket. It would be the first thing he would ditch after killing his brother. His two partners had listened to his conversation and were convinced things were going as planned. The three of them grinned at each other.

Marquez took out a handgun and handed it to Ernie. Ernie checked the action and made sure the magazine was fully loaded. While he did that, Marquez and Ronaldo checked their own weapons. There was an undeniable air of excitement; all three would be rewarded handsomely for killing the senator.

Ronaldo used his cell phone to make a call to Mexico.

"Yes, that is right, Miguel, he should be here in thirty minutes. Everything is going as planned."

Ronaldo turned off his phone, took the battery out, tossed it to the ground and stomped on it.

"El Ángel does not want us to communicate with him any longer. He will find out what he needs to through the news."

Ernie looked up and down the alleyway they were hiding in as he checked his gun some more and said, "I hope he has some patience. I intend on being back in Mexico by the time they find the body." Ronaldo and Marquez both agreed with a grin, and Ernie added, "You two can go by air; I'll have to make other arrangements. It wouldn't do for the authorities to see a dead senator traveled to Mexico."

Both of his partners murmured in agreement as they tucked their guns under their light jackets.

"So, here's the plan; I flag my brother over, and you two stay out of sight. I'll get in the front. Give me thirty seconds, no more, no less. By that time, I'll have my gun on him. You two climb in the back. We'll make him drive to a spot I know. It's secluded; he won't be found for days, maybe longer."

Both men agreed to the plan with a simple nod.

They didn't have to wait long. Soon, Ernie was on the phone again, talking Steven to them.

"That's right, turn left now on Lucky Avenue. No, I'm not kidding, bro. I figured I needed all the luck I could get. Drive slow down the alley. No tricks, I can see into your car from my position. There had better not be anybody besides you in it."

Ernie watched Steven slowly drive past him. Ernie was standing on the edge of a fire escape and, indeed, could see into the car.

"OK, Stevee, stop there."

Ernie dropped to the ground, ran up to the car and jumped into the front seat.

"Thanks, Steven. I knew you wouldn't let me down."

Steven was reaching over to give his brother a hug around the neck when he spotted the gun aimed at him.

"What are you doing?"

"Sorry, bro. All I can tell you is that Chelle is OK and will stay that way if I kill you."

Chapter 20

Steven was just about to ask Ernie how he could possibly know about Chelle when another gun was aimed at him from outside the car.

Steven's door opened. In a thick Spanish accent, the gunman said, "Get out, now."

Ernie's door opened and a gun was pointed at him.

"Move over, you're driving."

"What are you guys doing? This isn't the plan."

"Yes, it is; it's Miguel's plan. Do you think he was going to trust you to kill your own brother?" asked Marquez.

"I told him, and I'll tell you: the piece of shit means nothing to me."

"You will have your chance to prove your loyalties. But, for now, I will take your gun."

Ernie handed the gun over and slid over into the driver's seat.

Marquez slipped Ernie's gun into the holster inside his jacket. He stuck his gun in Steven's side and ushered him into the back seat.

When Steven tried to put on his seatbelt, Marquez stopped him though he was sure to strap himself in, all the while his gun and his eyes on their hostage.

"Don't get any crazy ideas like crashing the car," Marquez said from the back seat. "Your brother will be the first to fly through the windshield if you do."

Ernie saw that both men now wore gloves and moved with precision. Somebody had coached them, and it hadn't been him.

As Ernie drove away, Steven asked, "How do you know about Chelle, and who are these guys?"

"Pretty simple. These guys work for El Ángel, and as you might have guessed, so do I, and I have for the last year. Pays well too; a whole lot better than that gravel pit in Peabody, Massachusetts. People look up to me in his organization. Back in Peabody, I'm nothing but an ex-con, and that's all I'll ever be. And Chelle, well, if I kill you, I get to have her too. Not a bad deal there either."

"So Chelle is all right? Where is she?"

"Stop talking," Ronaldo said. "Head out of town."

"I told you, I know just the spot," Ernie said.

"Ernie, you're just making things worse for yourself," Steven said.

"He said shut up."

Ernie saw Marquez take the hilt of his gun and hit Steven over the head. Steven slumped over, out cold. Ronaldo looked towards the back seat disgustedly.

"What?" Marquez asked. "We are going to kill him anyway."

"You idiot," Ernie said. "Roll him to the floor so nobody sees him slumped over like that, and throw your jacket over him."

****

El Ángel was sitting by his pool, enjoying watching Adriana sun herself in the late-morning sun. She was nude, of course. He wouldn't have had it any other way. The thought crossed his mind that having two beauties to look at would be even nicer. The American FBI agent locked in the basement would perhaps appreciate some sun too. Then, he thought better of it. She would have to be carefully guarded. He didn't underestimate her as an FBI agent. No, he thought to himself, they were all better off with her locked away.

One of his bodyguards brought him another drink. Miguel glanced over at Adriana as he pulled a phone out of a bag full of burners he had near his chair. She had just turned from sunning her pretty backside to her front. After this call, it would be his duty to rub more suntan lotion on her.

"Juan, it is a shame that I can't offer you the courtesy of thanking you in person for the valuable information you have given me."

"You are welcome just the same, Miguel," El Padrino said.

"Are you sure that the radiation of the ID is contained inside the special wallet?"

"That is what I was told. In order to not mark everyone he came in contact with, the ID only contaminated those who touch it. Only after it is touched can the US government track them. Unfortunately, I was one such man."

"I now understand your cooperation with the senator. I am hoping that, soon, he will cease to be a problem. I believe that his jealous brother will be killing him shortly. In fact, he is using the senator's ID to do it. Unfortunately for him, he doesn't know that he can't escape back to Mexico, because he is now tagged by the same technology used against you."

"Love triangles can be so dangerous," El Padrino said. "The pictures you sent me of the FBI agent and the senator's brother will soon be online for all to see. It will be apparent that they are lovers. Sometime after that, I assume the pretty FBI agent will kill herself in her grief of losing both lovers?"

"You are a wise man, El Padrino. Yes, her body will be conveniently found, and her suicide will coincide with the discovery that her new lover was arrested in the murder of his brother. Perhaps she will even overdose; a fitting end to a tawdry story.

"And I owe it all to you. Because of your warning, I never touched the ID, and nor did any of my men. We are not marked, and neither is the girlfriend.

"Soon, it will again be safe for us to meet in person. I am anxious to show my appreciation. How about a new yacht to replace the one El Senador blew up?"

****

Lieutenant Kastner was doing her usual; scanning all the persons of interest that the computer was picking out from the millions and millions of people on the planet. Their hope was that one of the cartel leaders would be careless and lead them to El Ángel.

She time-stamped everyone's position so she could compare it to other known intelligence of the area. Senator Westcott was a blinking blue light in Arlington, so she pressed delete; recording his location inside the United States wasn't part of her assignment.

Strange...

She looked at the continued flashing of his blue dot, only it wasn't blue anymore. It was marked as 'Unidentified'. Lieutenant Kastner double-checked the readout and added back the senator's tag. There was no doubt. The computer was registering two separate tags. Somebody was with the senator, and they had touched his ID. The lieutenant's heart skipped a beat.

The senator doesn't have the ID, the cartel does!

One second later, she pressed the intercom button.

"Colonel, you had better come out here at once. I think the cartel found Senator Westcott."

****

"How far until we're out of town?" Ronaldo asked.

"As you can see, this area is pretty well populated, but in another half-hour, we can turn off the highway. There's a wooded spot where I used to hunt off an old logging road. We can disappear from view."

"But we want the body found immediately."

"Really? I didn't know that. Why?"

Ronaldo realized he had misspoken and tried to recover.

"To send a clear message not to interfere in cartel business."

Ronaldo wasn't a good liar, but Ernie accepted the explanation.

"I get it. Cartel politics, huh? I'll leave his car abandoned somewhere not too far from here. Say, two miles away. It'll take a while to find the car. They'll bring dogs in and have the body immediately, but we should be safely back in Mexico at that time."

Ernie hadn't imagined it: he had caught a sly grin on Marquez's face in the rearview mirror. Marquez knew something he didn't. Well, it didn't matter; Ernie had his own plan too.

Within half an hour, as promised, the car sped through a deserted section of farmland. The only things between the scattered farms were small sections of woodland and a few tall poles carrying electricity.

Ernie looked over at Ronaldo in the front seat and gunned the engine.

"Don't speed, amigo. There is no need to take chances."

It only took seconds for Steven's sedan to hit sixty miles an hour.

Ernie smiled at Ronaldo, who looked back at him with utter

confusion. That look of confusion soon turned into a look of fright as the power poles began buzzing by them, dangerously close.

"Slow down or I will shoot you."

Ernie smiled, saying, "If you do, we'll crash."

Ronaldo's fingers were turning white on the dash.

"Slow down, now!" he screamed.

Ernie just smiled at him, glanced back at the road and jerked the steering wheel hard to the right.

Ronaldo braced for impact as he saw them heading straight for a power pole. As he did so, he didn't see Ernie reach across and unhook his seatbelt at the last possible moment.

The car jumped as it left the road. Nobody stayed conscious long enough to hear the terrible sound of steel and plastic crumpling as it came to an immediate halt.

****

"I'm sorry, Waters, I must talk to the president directly."

Colonel Tripp was exasperated; he held the phone receiver away from his ear as the chief of staff argued back loudly. The president's chief of staff, Mitchel Waters, was roadblocking him again.

"Look, Waters, we've been through this. I report directly to the president. I was there in person when he told you so himself. Yes, I know his time is valuable. No, that is not good enough. I was ordered by my commander-in-chief to report directly to him. That is what I am trying to do. I would suggest you do not obstruct me, because he will hear about it."

Without a response, the phone clicked silent. Colonel Tripp waited and hoped that the chief of staff had capitulated. Eventually, the phone clicked back on.

"Yes, Mr. President," Colonel Tripp said, relieved. "We had two tags, one being Senator Westcott's. They were moving at a high rate of speed, but they both stopped suddenly. No, sir, I believe it was a car and it crashed.

"Sir, the second unidentified tag could only have come from the cartels; they have taken possession of the ID. I believe that Senator Westcott crashed his car and may have even done it on purpose.

"One way or another, Senator Westcott is in trouble, and he needs immediate assistance. If you are trying to keep the senator's involvement with the cartels a secret, you have a big problem on your hands. Yes, Mr. President. We'll stand by and keep monitoring the situation with the satellite."

****

Ernie opened his eyes. He couldn't see anything but white smoke billowing around him, and there was a terrible smell in the air. There was warm liquid running down his forehead and into his eyes. His first thought was that the car was on fire.

The sudden stop had disoriented him, but the white smoke had started to dissipate. Ernie realized it was just dust from the explosion of the airbag and that the terrible smell was the propellant. Groggily, he looked to his right and saw that the airbag hadn't been as kind to Ronaldo. Without the seatbelt, his head had found the windscreen and a wide gash was spewing blood.

Ernie's eyes widened suddenly. He remembered everything. The gun! He needed to find Ronaldo's gun.

Ernie unfastened his seatbelt; the cops would be here soon, but he had unfinished business he was sure they wouldn't approve of. Lifting Ronaldo's slumped body, he searched for the gun he assumed was somewhere underneath.

Groaning came from the back seat. Marquez was beginning to stir. Unfortunately, his seatbelt had saved him.

Ernie was starting to panic. He couldn't find the gun under the big man's body. It was possible it had flown out of the car. He heard the click of a safety and turned around to see a gun pointing at him.

"Thank God, Marquez, you're all right. We have to get out of here. The police will be here soon."

"Do not move a muscle, amigo."

"Marquez, we need to get out of here now. We can still get out of here unseen!"

"You tried to kill us." Marquez's eyes went to Ronaldo's body. "It looks like you were successful with Ronaldo. Get out slowly, one wrong move and I will shoot you."

Ernie stepped out of the crinkled car. Marquez kept his gun trained on him.

"Over here," Marquez said. "Get in the back seat; we don't leave until you complete your assignment. And if you don't do it, I will, after I kill you."

"Marquez, we don't have time for this. He's probably already dead from the crash."

Steven let out a small groan.

Ernie sat in the back seat and looked down at his brother, who was curled up on the floor between the passenger's front seat and the rear seat. Just as he had hoped, the front seat had protected his brother's prone body. It looked like he had survived the crash and was slowly coming to.

Marquez pointed his gun at Ernie, saying, "It appears he is still alive. Do your job, or I will kill you." He reached into his jacket and pulled out Ernie's gun. "It is time to prove your loyalty. Kill your brother now. Like you said, we don't have much time."

Ernie took the gun in his hand, flicked off the safety and pointed it at Steven. With the gun still pointed at Steven, Ernie turned his head towards Marquez. "Something isn't right here. That's why I crashed the car. Tell me what the plan is, or I won't shoot him."

"You have two choices. One, shoot your brother and take your chances on running from the police for his murder. Two, I shoot you dead now and make it look like you and your brother had a standoff."

"So that's it. El Ángel wants me caught."

"Two brothers die over a lovers' quarrel. Brilliant, no? Back in Mexico, the girl kills herself out of grief for the brother that didn't return to her, and none of it traced back to El Ángel.

"Hurry, now, make a decision. Kill your brother and I will let you live to run from the police. Or?" Marquez took aim at Ernie. "There is only one bullet in your gun. Make the right choice, *now!*"

There was a shot. Marquez's body twisted away from car. By the time he landed on the pavement, he was dead.

"Steven, you're OK!"

Steven twisted the gun out of Ernie's hand and gestured with his own.

"Out slowly, Ernie. Don't make me shoot you. You know I will."

Ernie did as he was told, and Steven kept his gun on Ernie as he lifted himself off the floor and slid out of the car.

"You won't shoot me."

"You don't know that," Steven said.

"Yes, I do; you couldn't shoot me any more than I could shoot you."

"It sure didn't look that way a moment ago."

"Why do you think I crashed the car? Maybe you didn't see it from the floor, but I ran into the pole on purpose. I didn't see any other way to save both of us. I was just about to take a chance on shooting Marquez with the one bullet he gave me, but you saved me the trouble."

Ernie could see by the look in Steven's eye that he wasn't convinced, but his brother flicked his safety on and slipped the gun into the small of his back.

"What about Chelle?"

"She's OK, for the moment."

"Do you think it's true what Ronaldo said? I mean about Chelle killing herself over us."

"Yeah, I'm sure that was the plan all along. El Ángel wanted you out of the way and didn't want a government vendetta against him for killing you or Chelle, so it would make sense. No doubt they would make her death look like a suicide. But he won't do it until he knows that you're dead and I'm on the run."

Steven looked at the crumpled car, bent power pole and two dead bodies.

"There's no way we're going to keep this out of the news. This will spread like a wildfire. El Ángel will soon know the truth."

Ernie and Steven leaned back against the crumpled car, unsure of their next move.

They were about to start a long walk when a helicopter scooted over the tree line and four rifle-toting men in dress suits rappelled down on ropes. Two more men in black suits still on the helicopter pointed rifles at them.

Ernie and Steven put their hands up.

"Looks like the cavalry is here," Steven said.

"Late as usual." Ernie grinned at Steven. "Friends of yours?"

"I hope so. And you still have a lot of explaining to do."

Chapter 21

At Joint Base Andrews, Maryland, Ernie and Steven had just finished pulling on their flight suits. They walked together, their pilots just in front of them. Soon, they would be flying inside two F16s, heading back to Mexico.

"Ernie, you're sure you know where El Ángel has Chelle?"

"I was taken there blindfolded, but I can find the place again, I'm sure of it."

"My team in Mexico is standing by. At eight hundred knots, we should do the two thousand miles to Puerto Vallarta in just over two hours."

"Boy, it pays to be buddies with the president."

"We are not 'buddies'."

"His CIA guys sure took care of the local police and the bodies of El Ángel's men fast enough. You must be something to him."

"Let's just say he owed me a favor."

Ernie patted Steven on the back.

"It must be a pretty big favor to get him to loan us a couple of F16s."

****

"Filipe, are the men ready to roll?" Steven asked as he walked down the Puerto Vallarta tarmac, stripping off his flight suit.

"Sí. We won't let you down this time."

"It's not your fault the local police were working for El Ángel."

Steven caught the suspicion in Filipe's eyes as he watched Ernie approach.

"Filipe, this is my brother, Ernie. He's going to take us to where El Ángel is holding Chelle."

"He may look a bit like you, but that is where the resemblance ends, I'm sure."

Ernie handed a shiny, oversized, hardcover briefcase to Steven and shook Filipe's hand.

"Steven says you guys are the best."

"Thank you, maybe you would like to ride with me? We could get to know each other better."

"I know the way, so I'll ride in the first truck," Ernie suggested.

Steven motioned to the second vehicle, saying, "Filipe, we need to get caught up. You two can become friends after we save Chelle."

Steven and Filipe continued to walk to the second truck in line while Ernie headed for the first.

Once alone, Filipe asked Steven, "How would your brother know such a secret?"

"Long story, I'll tell you in the truck. Now, let's roll, I'm a bit in a hurry." Steven carefully placed the case on the back seat.

Filipe updated Steven, "We studied the satellite photos of the terrain around the home that Colonel Tripp sent. With the little time we had, we also practiced storming the house using the diagram you supplied. Hopefully, Chelle is still in the basement cell. That should keep her out of harm's way until we can free her. But I need to know how you know so much about this place, even down to where the girl is held."

They both turned and looked over their shoulders when they heard a thundering noise. The two F16s took off, heading back to the US. *Just like they were never here,* Steven thought.

As they climbed into the back of the truck, Steven said, "It's a long story, my friend, a story I didn't know myself a few hours ago. In fact, a few hours ago, I was afraid my brother was about to kill me."

Filipe lay his gun across his lap, saying, "I have nothing better to do, amigo. I would enjoy a long story."

"My brother spent some time in prison." Filipe's face didn't betray his emotions, so Steven continued, "High on heroin, Ernie robbed a store. Anyhow, he made some friends of the wrong kind in prison, and, apparently, he developed a reputation of his own.

"He ran from his probation and ended up in Mexico, working for El Ángel. El Ángel tried to use Ernie to kill me. That's why Ernie knows the home's location and floor plan. He was at the house and saw Chelle."

Filipe turned his head away from Steven, watching the urban setting change rather abruptly to heavy woodland.

Steven continued, "Somehow, El Ángel knew not to touch my ID. Somebody must have told him it was radioactive. Instead, he made sure that Ernie used it, so he'd be found after killing me.

"We now know that as soon as El Ángel can confirm my death and Ernie's arrest, he's going to kill Chelle, making it seem like she killed herself in grief because she was in love with Ernie. Why he thought that would sell is beyond me."

Filipe looked back at Steven with a blank expression, saying, "How do you know you can trust your brother?"

"Ernie? Hell, he would never hurt me. But the only way out of the mess we were in was to crash a car and hope for the best. What? Why are you looking at me like that?"

Filipe looked straight ahead for a moment.

"How can you be so sure about your brother?"

"He's my brother. I visited him in prison all the time."

"Maybe you do not know your brother as well as you think. I might know why El Ángel thought people would believe your brother and the girl were in love."

"What... what the hell are you talking about?"

"Maybe they *were* in love."

Steven laughed, replying, "I don't think so. She came down to Mexico to be with me."

"I saw pictures of them kissing. They were in a pool. She didn't have any clothes on. Having fun, drinking, eating tropical fruit; there were many pictures."

"Are you sure?"

"Positive. We monitor the internet for suspicious activities. It was posted on your brother's account from a masked IP address, but that could have just been to hide his exact location. We were watching your brother closely. At the time, we didn't know who he was, we just knew an American was gaining influence in El Ángel's organization.

"We thought he might someday lead us to El Ángel, only we didn't know his true identity until we saw the pictures. At first, we thought the photos were of you and her. It didn't take long for us to realize that wasn't the case. I have some of them with me."

Filipe took the folded papers out of his leg pocket and handed them to Steven.

"This doesn't make sense," Steven said, unfolding them. "When were these taken?"

"That, we do not know. The post was recent, but the pictures could have been taken anytime or anywhere."

Steven couldn't take his eyes off the photos. There was no doubt about the playfulness between the scantily clad couple.

"Filipe, stop the trucks; I need to talk to my brother. It doesn't make sense"

Filipe picked up his radio and ordered the convoy to come to a stop. Steven rushed to the front truck and ripped Ernie out of his seat.

As Steven gripped his shirt and pressed him up against the truck, he said angrily, "You have a lot more explaining to do,"

"Oh, shit, you found out about the pictures, didn't you?" Ernie clenched his teeth and grimaced.

Steven couldn't contain himself. He punched Ernie in the stomach, hard.

"*Ohhh...* that was a good one, bro."

Ernie doubled over, but he didn't try to fight back or defend himself against another blow.

"When were they taken?" Steven demanded.

Ernie struggled to catch his breath and stood up as straight as he could, saying, "Listen, please listen for a minute. It was Miguel's idea. He told me I had to, and he threatened to cut off more of her toes if she didn't cooperate. We had no choice.

"Those pictures were meant to convince everyone there was a love triangle going on. Not a bad plan, if you think about it. Only, he didn't tell me about the part where I'd be arrested for killing you."

Steven relaxed his grip on Ernie just a bit as Ernie took a few deep breaths to continue, "Her bandaged foot was kept out of the pictures. Miguel directed and took all the photos himself. All the while, he was threatening Chelle to smile and such. I didn't have a choice either; I had to play along. If I didn't look like I was all in, both of our lives would have been in jeopardy right then and there. The pictures were all taken at his place on the ocean about two weeks ago; the same place we're headed. Think about it: why would we hire a photographer to follow us around as we made out in a pool?"

"Why didn't you tell me?"

"There wasn't time! And I didn't think it would be important."

Steven swung Ernie to the side and pushed him away.

"*Not important?*"

"To saving her. That's what we're here for, ain't it? I did what I had to do to keep her alive. Look... I knew you'd get pissed off, why go there if I didn't have to? I thought that after we saved Chelle, she could explain it to you, though I don't know if it would have sounded any better coming from her."

Steven walked back towards his truck but brushed past Ernie, swinging his shoulder hard into his brother. It did all make sense, but that didn't mean he liked it.

Filipe had heard Ernie's explanation too and climbed back into the truck along with Steven. Steven slammed the door closed. Nobody talked for the next half-hour.

Steven broke the silence, "Filipe, if Ernie does something suspicious, shoot him and ask questions later."

Filipe nodded, saying, "Brothers are not always what we wish them to be."

Ernie's voice came over the radio.

"Here's where it gets tricky. This road through the jungle is windy and all uphill; perfect for an ambush anywhere. Miguel also has land-mines and vibration sensors. We go the rest of the way on foot, very, very slowly."

Both trucks pulled over into the jungle and the men got out.

Steven got on his own radio and asked, "What are the infrared sensors showing?"

Lieutenant Kastner's voice came back over the radio. "We are picking up numerous heat signatures. Stand by, I'm trying to hook you up with a live feed."

"You have a drone overhead?" Filipe asked, surprised.

"No, of course not. This is sovereign territory. The United States isn't here and neither am I, but you might want to see this just the same."

Steven went to his case and took out something that looked like the military version of an iPad.

Filipe and Ernie flanked Steven as they conferred for a bit, studying the movement of the inferred figures guarding the villa.

Ernie pressed his arm around Steven's shoulders, saying, "Don't worry, bro, we'll get her. He has to be waiting to hear about your death on the news." Ernie looked at his watch. "Only eight hours have gone by since he got the call you were going to be dead soon. To make her suicide look real, her death needs to correspond to my capture. He won't risk it until then. Trust me, she's still OK."

Steven looked up the hill.

"After we have Chelle, El Ángel is mine. I owe that bastard."

Filipe and Ernie caught each other's eyes and nodded in agreement.

The team slowly and carefully made their way up the mountainside. It took an hour to get within viewing range of El Ángel's home.

El Cazador positioned himself on the edge of the cliff. He had a clear shot to one side of the large balcony jutting out over the cliff. Snipes was back with the team and had the other side of the balcony covered.

Steven and Filipe monitored the live infrared feed coming from the drone.

"Everyone is in position," Filipe said softly. "When I give the word, Snipes and El Cazador, take your two men out. At the same time, the front team attacks. Kill silently for as long as possible. Remember, there are two non-targets, both are women.

"Get ready. One, two, three, now!"

Steven realized that, despite the eerie silence, the attack had begun. Silencers and knives were used as pairs of soldiers attacked each known target. Prisoners were not expected.

Snipes and El Cazador reported that the two rear guards were neutralized. Team One reported that the front exterior of the home was also secure.

Steven and Filipe studied the infrared signals again. All known exterior threats had been taken down. Steven and Filipe rushed up the hillside for the main assault on the home's interior.

Flash grenades would be used for the simultaneous assault. The grenades would give off a blinding flash and an extremely loud bang. The hope was that the resulting disorientation would give the team time to neutralize any threat without permanently harming any innocents.

Filipe gave the command, and all hell broke loose. Doors and windows crashed open, and the rapid explosions of the grenades followed. There was sporadic gunfire, then a room-to-room search was conducted. Steven and Filipe were inside the main room when the 'all clear' was sounded.

Ernie rushed past Steven and Filipe and said, "Something's not right; this was way too easy. The lower level is this way."

Ernie led the way, his gun drawn and ready to fire. Steven was next, and Filipe covered them from the back.

At the bottom floor, Ernie twisted around the steps to check for an ambush. Steven rushed towards the holding room. Expecting an attack from inside the room, Steven pressed his body against the wall next to the door.

"Chelle? Chelle, can you hear me? It's Steven."

There was no answer. Slowly, he reached over to check the door handle. It was unlocked. He pushed the door open and swung around with his gun, ready to shoot anybody but Chelle.

The room was empty. Steven saw a used and bloody bandage on the old mattress. His heart pounded in his chest as he realized that they were too late.

Filipe and Ernie stood outside the room, letting Steven collect himself. Through his earset, Filipe heard a report and repeated it for Steven and Ernie.

"Eight men, all dead, none of them El Ángel. The hostages are also not here."

"Son of a bitch," Ernie cursed. "That's why it was so easy; he's gone to who knows where and taken Chelle with him. The men left here were basically just badly paid house sitters."

Steven searched the empty room hoping to find something, anything, but he found nothing else. The bloody bandage was all he had. Steven pressed the dry but bloody cloth to his cheek. It was all he had of Chelle right now. A fit of anger overcame him, and he pointed his gun at Ernie's head.

"If you know anything, anything at all, now would be a good time to tell me, because I think he was tipped off."

"Bro, look, maybe he was, but it wasn't by me," Ernie insisted, glancing toward Filipe.

"You want me to believe that Filipe undermined his own raid?" asked Steven.

"Others within the FES knew of the raid as well," Filipe admitted. "It was cleared by higher ups. Mexico has many ears and many lips. Remember, I was with you nearly the whole time."

"Damn it, Ernie. Where did he take her? You know his organization."

Filipe found a chair and sat down, his gun pointed at Ernie.

"It seems you two need to work some things out. Please, don't let me stop your discussion."

"These guys move around constantly," Ernie argued, "that's how they stay alive. He was here a couple of weeks and might have thought it compromised. Filipe, tell him. You know I'm right."

"Sí," Filipe said, lowering his gun. "Your brother is right."

Chapter 22

After a two-hour flight, the plane taxied into a large hanger. Chelle looked out of the tiny window by her seat, but nobody moved from the plane, not even the four bodyguards, until the huge hangar door closed.

Her hands were tied behind her back and had been since that morning, when El Ángel had suddenly decided to leave his clifftop home. Her foot was feeling much better, and she could now wear the sandals that Adriana had found for her.

Now, Chelle was ushered out of the plane and had only taken four steps before she was inside a black, dark-windowed, heavy duty SUV. Inside the car, two armed guards sat on each side of her, not bashful about pressing her tightly between them.

El Ángel kindly helped Adriana into the middle front seat and sat down next to her by the passenger window. The driver sat in his seat and started the engine.

"You will like Acapulco, my dear. It doesn't have the tourist draw it did years ago, but that only makes it better for us. Unfortunately, it has earned the designation of the second most dangerous city in the world, but don't you fret your beautiful face any. You are with me and are as safe as in your mother's arms."

"You killed my mother."

"And I am sorry for that. But living in that small village, you would never have seen such wonders or luxuries as I have shown you."

Adriana tried to ignore Miguel as he wrapped his arms around her and kissed her neck.

A garage door opened, and Miguel's SUV crept out of the hangar. It was followed by an identical SUV filled with men holding high-powered rifles.

Once El Ángel sensed they were safely on their way, he turned toward the back seat and said to Chelle, "Your boyfriend, the senator, is correct, of course. In order for Mexico to prosper, the violence must stop. Do you know that there are over forty different gangs operating right here in Acapulco? They will happily kill a street vendor if not paid two dollars a day.

"But that keeps the police busy protecting the tourists, and that is good for me. I think you will like my home here. It is as nice as the one in Puerto Vallarta and, as you will see, it is equally as secluded. I am fortunate that homes in these areas are being sold very, very cheaply.

"Driver!" El Ángel said loudly. "Turn on the news, US news. I want to hear if there is any word of a senator being killed by his brother."

Chelle shot a sharp glare at Miguel.

"You didn't think those photos were for a tourist magazine, did you? I sent your new boyfriend on a little mission to prove his loyalty to me. I told him to kill his brother; in an act of jealous rage, of course. I mean, you and Ernie are such a happy couple, he can't afford to have his brother alive to steal you away from him.

"With the pictures of you and Brother Ernie having such a wonderful time posted on the internet, anyone who cares to know will believe a lovers' triangle had developed and Ernie, a felon, an escaped con, decided to end it."

Chelle thought for just a moment before shouting, "It'll never work, nobody will believe it."

"They won't have to, all that is necessary is that they can't prove it didn't happen that way."

Chelle's heart sunk; Her captor had set a perfect trap. If Ernie was successful in killing Steven and was killed himself, it would look like a love triangle gone bad, and that would mean the FBI wouldn't come looking for her either.

Chelle prayed that the news wouldn't announce the death of either brother.

****

Steven was on the huge expanse of the deck of El Ángel's Puerto Vallarta home, pacing back and forth. The ocean pounding on the rocks below and the setting sun were anything but relaxing to him.

Steven considered Ernie's words. After Lucille's betrayal, he had found it hard to trust anyone. Chelle's love had won him over as he learned to trust once again. Now, Ernie had reminded him that trust was a commodity he couldn't afford. Ernie had been right; there were many players in this game, and his trust had been too easily given. That especially applied to Ernie.

"I thought you were monitoring the house, Colonel?" Steven demanded of his satellite phone.

"We were, but by the time we found it per your brother's description, it must have been too late. We never saw any vehicles leave the compound."

"OK, but we must be able to narrow it down a bit. At least we know the time when they were already gone."

"Steven, it could have been anytime after Ernie's visit. Anytime! Hell, he could have left that afternoon. I'm sorry, Steven, we have nothing."

Steven hung up and kicked at a chair. It crashed against another, and the phone in his hands also almost went sailing over the railing to shatter on the cliffs below. Steven held the phone tight and let his arms settle at his sides. He realized that his tantrum wasn't helping anybody, especially Chelle.

The sun was dropping into the sea and would soon set. Ernie had been escorted back to the vehicles and was under guard. He had been of no help; the cartel was fragmented, he had explained, with El Ángel doling out just enough information for his employees to do their jobs, no more.

They had searched the house for clues and had found nothing; only a pile of burner phones at the bottom of the pool. Steven looked at the rocks out past the deck and saw another of Miguel's cigar remnants. That was about the only thing left behind, Steven mused. Some of them would be checked for DNA, but for now, that wouldn't help them.

Steven looked at the stub lying on the ground. Maybe forensics could tell them the last time it had been smoked. That could help set the day of departure. Steven stared at it some more, then he ran into the house to the men sifting through the garbage.

"The cigar butts, every one of them, I want to see them."

The men looked at Filipe as if the American had just gone loco, but Filipe nodded his approval. Soon, every cigar butt that could be found outside or inside was lying on the kitchen counter.

"Look, Filipe, don't you see?"

"I see, all right. I see a filthy, stinking mess on the counter."

"They're all the same. Not a one is different. He only smokes one kind of cigar. Here, look at the label."

"Sí. They are all the same brand."

"A familiar one too, or at least I hope so. I might know somebody who knows it."

Steven laid out a few of the cigars in a row and took a picture of them with his phone. He carefully took a close-up of the golden band.

Steven prepared a short text and sent it off with the pictures attached. It was only two minutes later that he got back a picture of an identical band. Only, it was still wrapped around an un-smoked cigar.

Steven immediately knew that the photo had been taken in a spot few people on the planet would know. The cigar was on top of the Resolute Desk. It was the president of the United States' desk. There was only one like it on the planet; a gift from the British built from the timbers of the HMS *Resolute*. Along with the photo was a text.

'I know the cigar brand, and so do you. It is very special indeed. This is my last one. If you remember, it was a gift from the president of Nicaragua.'

Steven texted back, 'I need to know everything you can tell me about it.'

'I'll do better than that; I'll have the FBI research it for you.'

'Specifically, I need to know where I can get them in Mexico.'

Filipe was standing over Steven's shoulder.

"Did you just ask the president of the United States if he smoked this kind of cigar?"

"I did. That is the top of the desk in the Oval Office."

Filipe stood tall and smiled, saying, "My friend knows the president. Now *that* is a good thing to know."

"I'm hoping we can find out who distributes these cigars in Mexico. If and when we do, let's hope El Ángel runs out soon."

****

True to El Ángel's word, the home they drove to was secluded. They drove up a long, gravel road and, finally, the home came into view. It was the only home Chelle had seen since they left the main road a half-hour ago.

She was hastily ushered into the home. Apparently, there wasn't a basement cell here, because her hands were cut free and she was locked in a bedroom on the main floor. One man was guarding her door and another was posted outside the only window. He wasn't bashful about spying on everything she did.

Chelle looked around at her new surrounding and, though the room was sparsely furnished, at least it had a bed and clean mattress. Hours later, a guard opened the bedroom door cautiously, gun drawn and ready. Once satisfied, he let Adriana through the doorway.

"I brought a change of clothes for you and a fresh bandage. Miguel agreed to let you shower and change."

Chelle looked at the skimpy dress, saying, "I might as well be naked."

"I am sorry, but Miguel picked this out himself."

"I'm afraid that the guards will be watching you at all times, you are not to be let out of sight. I am sorry."

"I'll bet they're not," Chelle said, nodding to the guard watching them through the window.

Adriana looked away, ashamed that she could not help her new and only friend.

"Señora," she whispered, "I must tell you; I overheard Miguel talking to a man on his phone. They intend to kill you and make it look like a suicide."

"Doesn't surprise me, that fits into the plan they have for Steven and Ernie. Do you know who he was talking to?"

"I couldn't hear, I was in another room and listened through an open door."

Adriana stared at the wall, contemplating whether she should share her next thought.

"Señora, I am afraid. I feel Miguel is growing tired of me. It is getting harder and harder for me to please him. I am just a plaything; when he is done with me, I will be killed, just like the girl before me."

Chelle took her hand. She could sense the girl's fear, though she was trying to be brave.

"Keep doing the best you can," she suggested. "I don't know how yet, but we will get out of here. I have friends looking for me, and I haven't given up on them. You shouldn't either."

"I will do my best."

"But we must also help ourselves. Can you sneak a knife to me?"

"That would be impossible. Besides, if I am caught, Miguel will do terrible things to me. I have seen some of what he is capable of. He made me watch. Nobody should see such things. I am sorry, señora; I cannot help you."

****

Steven and Filipe were at the military barracks at the south end of Licenciado Gustavo Díaz Ordaz International Airport, Puerto Vallarta. They were having a meeting; one from which Ernie was noticeably missing. Steven didn't trust his brother, and Filipe didn't disagree.

"I think it's time to move on with the next phase," Steven said.

"But what of our hunt for El Ángel?"

"We can't postpone our plan any longer, that's exactly what he wants."

"But when he finds out you are not dead, he will kill Chelle."

"He might, but it will only be days until he knows that his plan wasn't successful anyway. I'm hoping, and betting Chelle's life, that until I'm dead, he'll see her as his trump card. We go with plan B, and we make sure he knows just how alive I am."

****

"Yes sir, thank you for your help." Steven hung up with the president. He had been pacing the floor, but now he slumped down into a chair.

There was a rap on his door and he called, "Come in."

"Are you going to punch me again?" Ernie asked, stepping in.

"Only if you give me reason to again. The truth is, I don't know who you are anymore. I'm not even sure you're my brother. How could you work for the cartels? They're killing tens of thousands of people a year, and that's just in the US."

"What about you? What the hell is a US senator doing down here in the middle of Mexico, deal-making with the cartels?"

"I have my reasons."

"Yeah, well, maybe I have my reasons too."

Ernie grabbed the chair across from Steven and swung his leg over the seat, sitting on it backwards and resting his arms across the back.

"Come on, Stevee, it's still me. It's not what it seems, but I couldn't go back to jail. You don't know what it's like. I *couldn't* go back, not for one more year, month, week, or one more fucking hour. Wasn't going to happen. But I do want to help you find Chelle. Did you look at the pictures?"

"Are you sure you want to go there?"

"Did you look at them?"

"Yeah, I had to see her," Steven admitted. His eyes welled up and were beginning to turn red.

"She was in pain, but still she smiled for the camera. I want you to know, she was brave. Do you realize how hard it was for her not to tell El Ángel to go fuck himself?"

Steven managed to chuckle a bit.

"Actually, yes, I would imagine it was near impossible."

"She's a fighter. But I suspect you already know that."

Steven thought about Chelle and the danger she was in, then he said, "After what Lucille did to me, I didn't think I would ever love somebody again. But Chelle... she didn't push, she just let me work it out in my own time. I never expected her to still be around by the time I got my act together, but she was, and she still never demanded anything of me."

"Steven, she believes in you. You know those smiling pictures of us? She was in terrible pain. Her foot was bleeding as the photos were being taken. You know the photos of us drinking those tropical cocktails? Where we were smiling and kissing and having fun in the sun? The truth is, the concrete leading to the table was smeared with blood, her blood. Steven, she was buying time, time for you to save her. Let me help, I know people; I might be able to make people talk. I am not a senator or a cop. I can play by their rules."

Steven walked to a small refrigerator and took out two beers. He twisted the top off one and it hissed open. He handed it to Ernie and then twisted open a second beer, taking a deep gulp. Steven had made a decision; Ernie was right, he *did* need his brother's help. The beers were a symbolic declaration: 'truce'. At least for the time being.

"I just talked to the president," he said. "He says the FBI have located the distributer of the cigars. They're a Nicaraguan special blend. The good news is that they can't be mail-ordered. Our FBI is working with the Mexican PFM, trying to track the movement of the cigars. Did you say you were learning El Ángel's organization?"

"I was trying to work my way up the chain of command. I guess I wasn't content to be just one of his grunts. He liked the way I ran one of his factories."

"Could your run his organization if you had to?"

"Are you kidding me?"

Steven took his chair and swung it around. Resting his arms on the back of it, he sat and sipped his beer.

"Could you?"

"Steven, I made a mistake, a big one. It seems I excel at making mistakes. I thought being a bigshot in a cartel was a good plan. It's not. They don't operate like any of the Fortune 500. Once they think you know too much, you're expendable, and they don't give you a severance check and send you on your way. If you're lucky, you just get a bullet in the head."

"But could you?"

"Why would you want me to?"

"It's simple."

"What's so simple about it?"

"Somebody has to, and the devil you know is better than the devil you don't."

"You're serious?"

"Perfectly."

Ernie stood and paced the floor in thought.

"You're 'El Senador'! Of course, how could I have been so blind? I can't believe the rumors were true. Why?"

"You're in no position to ask me anything."

"I am if you want me to help you."

"You don't have a fucking choice. I can have you back in prison with one call."

Ernie took a long drink of his beer and sat down again.

"Yeah, one call to your buddy the president. You know what I think? I think you're in cahoots with the president to fill his election coffers with illegal cash. Shit, Stevee, shit." Ernie shook his head in disgust. "I know why I'm mixed up with these devils. Hell, I had no choice. But you, Senator Steven Westcott, of all people, mixed up with the drug trade? I have to admit, nobody would believe it. It's the president, isn't it? He saved your ass last year and now you owe him.

"You can believe whatever you want, but you *will* work for me."

"You want me to run a cartel for you so you can make a damn political payback?"

"Sorry, Ernie, you're the one with no choice. And since when did you decide to take the moral high ground? Better me than El Ángel."

"What was it you said? The devil I know is better than the devil I don't? And if I don't obey..."

"Exactly. Don't forget I have the president on my side."

"You're an asshole, you know that Stevee? If I cooperate, do I get some sort of presidential pardon?"

"In time, maybe. But for now, if you're arrested for any reason, we can't help you."

"Yeah, because what you're doing is illegal as hell. What if I say no?"

"After we find Chelle, you're going to prison again."

"If you send me back to prison, I'll spill the beans on all of you."

"I wouldn't recommend that. The guys I'm working with make the cartels look like playground monitors."

Ernie stood and tossed his bottle across the room. It crashed into a garbage can.

"See you later, Stevee. Thanks for nothing."

Ernie stormed out of the small apartment and headed to his own barracks, contemplating his next move. What his brother didn't know was that their lives were on a collision course. Steven wasn't the only one with a hidden agenda.

Ernie was nothing if not pragmatic, and he had seen a lot of bad over the last year. They were both warriors; up against each other, only one of them would survive. He wondered who it would be. Ernie resolved to leave during the night. He had to contact his superiors, and he couldn't do it from here.

Chapter 23

Today was Chelle's third day in the small room, and it seemed boredom was her greatest enemy. Adriana had been allowed to visit her with a small tray of food once a day, often nothing more than fruit.

With her fingernail, Chelle scratched a third mark in the bed frame. She had no idea how long she would be in the small room, and instinct told her it was critical to her sanity to know exactly how many days had passed.

Chelle heard some noise on the other side of the door, so she decided to test an idea. She rushed to the door. When the guard cautiously opened it, there was a great commotion as soon as he saw her.

The guard outside the open window immediately had his weapon pointed at Chelle. The guard by the door hit her hard in the stomach with the butt of his rifle.

"On the bed, now," he said in excited Spanish.

Chelle was doubled over, so he pushed her roughly until she tripped on the bed frame and fell onto the mattress. When she looked up, his gun was pointed at her head. Slowly, he backed up, leaving Adriana standing in shock. The lock clicked.

Adriana rushed to Chelle and held her head for a while until Chelle could sit up.

"I guess they don't like it if I'm by the door when they open it," Chelle said, smiling weakly.

"Please eat, señora, you need your strength."

Chelle forced a few pieces of pineapple into her sore stomach.

"I'll be fine," Chelle comforted the young woman. Slowly, she stood to stretch out the pain.

With the excitement over, the guard on the other side of the window decided the view of the ocean was more important. "A man they call 'the doctor' gave me some salve for your wound. He said it would help with the healing."

Chelle took the tube and looked at the label. It was an antibiotic-laced cream, and she decided it couldn't hurt. Adriana tentatively helped her remove the old bandage.

Luckily, the wound seemed to be healing. The crude cauterization with Miguel's cigar seemed to have worked. Chelle gently massaged the cream into the wound and bandaged it.

"Is he a real doctor?"

"No, señora. He is a man who knows some medicine. Miguel has him keep people he tortures alive for as long as possible."

"That's comforting."

Chelle had a few more pieces of fruit, and soon the plate was clean. Finishing the last piece, Chelle said, "Adriana, I need you to tell Miguel that I have to talk to him."

"No, señora, no. You have seen what he is capable of; you do not want him here."

"You're right, I don't want him here, but I do need to talk to him. In fact, I demand to talk to him. You tell him *that*."

The door clicked and opened. The guard was prepared for another challenge, his gun at the ready.

"Out, now!" he ordered gruffly.

"Tell him, Adriana."

****

The next day, the lock clicked open. Chelle stayed on the bed, sure her next warning wouldn't be as pleasant as the first.

A guard with the usual small tray of food entered, and Adriana came in behind him.

"Adriana, what happened?"

The dark bruise on her cheek was impossible to miss. The guard cracked a smile as he left, locking the door behind him.

"Tell me, what happened?"

Adriana looked away sheepishly.

"I told Miguel that you demanded to see him. He immediately got angry."

"Oh, Adriana, I'm so sorry. I didn't mean for you to get hurt."

"I told you, you do not want him near you. If he stays away, you are lucky."

The door clicked open again, and both women looked up as the guard walked into the room with his gun pointed at Chelle. Miguel followed.

"So, you wanted to see me, I heard," Miguel said, glancing at Adriana, who promptly stared at the floor.

"What I have to say is between you and me," Chelle said, standing defiantly.

Miguel pulled out his pistol from a holster on the small of his back.

"Go!" he said to Adriana.

Without looking up, Adriana sped out of the room.

"Them too," Chelle said, eying the guards.

With a click of his tongue, the guard in the room and the one outside the window disappeared.

"If this is not important, you will suffer. Certainly, you know that."

"I want a change of clothes and better food, twice a day."

"You *want?*" Miguel laughed heartily. "You are alive. What more could you *want* from me?"

"Decent cloths, more food. I am on starvation rations. Thank you for the medication and bandages though."

"You are in no position to demand anything of me."

Chelle took one step towards Miguel. Miguel took a step back, and the muscles on his hand clenched around the pistol.

"If you wanted me dead," she said, "I would be dead already. You are keeping me alive and healthy for a reason. If I don't get more food, I will not stay healthy. After all, if you want to fake my suicide, it wouldn't do to have me starved to death."

Miguel pulled back the hammer of his gun. Chelle knew that it was now on a hair trigger. Miguel pointed the gun at Chelle's head from only inches away. The slightest movement of his finger and the gun would go off.

"You do not like the clothes I picked out for you?"

Miguel took his other hand and gripped at the low-cut material between Chelle's breasts. With a mighty tug, the flimsy material tore. The thin shoulder straps dug into her skin before they split off.

Chelle stood firm, staring at the gun an inch from her eyes. Miguel tore at the dress one more time and it fell to shreds.

He backed slowly away from Chelle, keeping the gun aimed squarely at her head.

"If you do not like it, I will take it with me. Besides, I think I like you better this way. Open the door!"

The door opened cautiously, and the guard pointed his gun at the naked Chelle. Miguel uncocked his gun and backed out of the room, never taking his eyes off her.

"Maybe, from now on, you will think twice before telling me what I must do?"

The guard smirked at Chelle as he took an extra-long look at her before locking the door again.

****

"I'm sorry I had to be the one to show you this, Senator." Shannon was drying her tears with a fresh Kleenex. "Doesn't the press have any sense of morals? They didn't have to print these pictures."

Steven couldn't tell Shannon that he had already seen the pictures that were now on the front page of the Washington Post. He had known it was only a matter of time before the photos found their way to the press.

The funny thing was, he liked the photos. Not what they implied, of course, but for him, right now, though they were separated by thousands of miles, the photos seemed to be his best connection to her. In fact, he didn't even see Ernie in them; he could only see his Chelle.

Steven also couldn't tell Shannon that the romance between her and his brother was fictitious. He didn't have to try very hard to act heartbroken over the exposed news. The fact was, he *was* heartbroken and worried sick that the worst had already happened to Chelle. The only reason he was back in Washington was to protect her with his own conspicuousness.

"I just can't believe it, Senator. I talked with Chelle before you left for your vacation in Mexico. She was terribly upset because she wanted to see you and you weren't responding. She loved you, I know she did." Shannon was crying over the pain she knew her boss must be in.

Steven put down the papers and tried to act stoic, saying, "I can't say that I understand it myself. I think I know where she is. After I make a few appearances to promote the president's new trade initiative, I need to go to Mexico again to talk some sense into her."

"It just doesn't make any sense to me. She's a cop, an FBI agent! Your brother is an escaped con, on the run in Mexico. Why dump you for him? And her career, her career is finished. Everybody in the world knows what she did." Through sobs and a bundle of fresh tissue, she approached Steven and gave him a hug. "I can't imagine what you're going through."

Steven gently hugged her back, "I know, Shannon, and I appreciate your concern for me. Please book me on a flight to Oaxaca, Mexico. And Shannon, don't worry about me; I'll be all right. I just have to find her and get some closure."

"At least this will mollify those vultures who were so suspicious of your trips to Mexico."

He had to admit that Shannon's hug, though for the wrong reason, was welcome, but it also nearly caused him to break down from his steely façade. Steven clung on to his hope that Chelle was still OK and that his plan to rescue her would work.

****

It was later that night when he got a call from the president at his small apartment.

"Steven, it looks like your hunch paid off. The FBI got a hit on the cigars you were wondering about. First, I was right: they can't be bought over the internet. We've been working with Mexico's PFM, and they found three places that handle them. There are two in Mexico City and one store in Acapulco. Apparently, there are still enough VIP's going to Acapulco to make it pay."

"Or one important customer who happens to be a top cartel chieftain."

"Steven, I'm sure you'd like to go to Acapulco and shake down the store owner, but please listen; that will accomplish nothing. The PFM are going to monitor the store. They will follow anyone who buys those particular cigars.

"You and I both know this is a long shot and always has been. Let them do their job, and you do yours. You might have a lot better chance at finding El Ángel from Oaxaca than trying to follow a hunch in Acapulco."

Steven knew the president was right. It took a moment or two for him to think it through, since his heart said to go to Chelle in Acapulco.

"Mr. President, I truly appreciate your efforts and those of the Mexican authorities. You're right, it is a long shot. Besides, Oaxaca is only about an hour from Acapulco by air."

"Trust me, Steven, I am in direct communication with the Mexican president, and she is pressing her people pretty hard. I promise I will let you know as soon as anything of interest happens."

"Yes, sir. Does the FBI understand they are looking for one of their own?"

"Not exactly; they were doing a special favor for their president. Officially, she's AWOL, with her picture plastered all over the internet, frolicking in a pool with an escaped con. Things aren't looking good for her right now, and I can't tell them otherwise, at least not yet."

"I understand, sir. All the more important that we find her, and soon."

"I couldn't agree more, but are you sure it's time to continue on with the mission?"

"El Ángel has Chelle, and he doesn't want me to have this meeting. I think using myself as bait might be the only way to draw him out. If Chelle's still alive, maybe I can negotiate. If not, I'll deal with him in my own way."

"Call me from Mexico on your sat phone anytime you want. I'll call you the instant I learn anything."

"Yes, sir. Thank you, sir. Goodnight."

"Goodnight and good luck, Steven."

Steven walked over to the window that looked out over the lights of Washington. He swirled the ice in his glass of scotch while he looked over the city that seemed so small and unimportant right now.

After the failed raid on El Ángel's home, Steven's plan had been to keep himself as visible as possible on any news shows he could win an interview on. His hope was that it would somehow help Chelle if El Ángel saw him in DC and not in Mexico. Now, Steven sensed a stalemate, and time wasn't on Chelle's side. Soon, he would be raising the stakes. He poured the nearly full glass of scotch down his throat.

Tonight, he would try again to get a good night's sleep, hoping the recurring nightmare of watching El Ángel cutting away at Chelle didn't haunt him again.

Chapter 24

Chelle scratched another notch into the bed frame. A day had passed since Miguel's visit. It was morning, and Chelle was still naked and hungrier than ever. She wrapped herself in the blankets, wanting to cry in the worst way, but stubbornness forced her to not give that satisfaction to the guard constantly watching over her.

The lock on the door clicked and, after checking on Chelle's position, the guard let Adriana in. The plate she held was full of food and even a hot cup of coffee. As she smiled at Chelle, it didn't look like she had been beaten any further.

"Miguel said to bring a meal to you twice a day with good portions. I made you a meat tortilla."

Adriana held the tray on her lap as Chelle tightened the blanket around her and savored a taste of the coffee and tortilla.

"I will ask every day for clothes; Miguel will tire of my asking and will eventually agree."

Chelle looked up from her food and said, "No, please don't, I don't want him to beat you."

Adriana looked into Chelle's eyes sheepishly, saying, "I wish I was strong like you. You make Miguel respect you. I know you made him give you more food."

Chelle motioned for Adriana to sit next to her, then she whispered, "I didn't make Miguel do anything. I convinced him that, if he wanted my death to look like a suicide, he had better not starve me to death first." Chelle pointed at the food she was still eating. "This doesn't look encouraging, and the price I had to pay was losing my clothes, what little they were."

"Still, you stood up to Miguel. I think he is afraid of you."

"Not afraid of me, but of what trouble killing me might bring. Make no mistake, we are both in grave danger." Whispering, Chelle continued, "If you help me, I think I know a way to escape. We're probably both dead if we don't. You know that, don't you?"

"Miguel is acting strangely. He is smoking more cigars than ever, and he is very nervous. I'm afraid we will be moving again soon."

"He might decide that we're not worth taking with him as he runs from place to place. We need to act soon." Chelle reached over and took Adriana's hand. "I can't do this without your help."

"I am not brave like you; I am frightened of what Miguel will do to me."

"I understand, but, if we do nothing, we will still die."

The door creaked and the guard entered, pointing his rifle at Chelle.

"Time," he said as Adriana got up with the empty tray.

"I will see you again today, unless Miguel changes his mind."

Chelle didn't blame the young woman for being afraid. Chelle was plenty afraid for both of them, but she needed to convince Adriana that the risk would be worth it if they were to have a chance at life.

Apparently, Steven's death hadn't been reported yet. At least, that was what Chelle hoped. Chelle guessed Miguel's plan hadn't gone off like clockwork, as he'd assumed. Hopefully, that meant Ernie hadn't been successful and that Steven was still alive.

****

The commercial passenger jet touched down on the single runway of the Oaxaca airport with a screech of its tires and a puff of smoke. Once off the plane, it didn't take long for Filipe to find Steven.

"Amigo, welcome to Oaxaca, the center of civilization for ten thousand years."

"You would think that, in ten thousand years, they could have made a longer runway."

"The planes mostly always stop on time," Filipe chuckled.

"That's comforting. What about Chelle?"

"Sorry, amigo, no word. Let me take you to your hotel. After I drop you off, I will make another call."

On the ride to Hotel Marqués del Valle, Steven could tell that the city of Oaxaca was typical of the contradictions of Mexico. With a population of about two hundred and fifty thousand, it was both modern and primitive at the same time. They drove past a small Penny's department store and a Pizza Hut with a donkey and wagon parked in front. A long line of workers were using picks and shovels to dig a trench that would have been done in an hour or two by one man and a backhoe in the States, yet nearly everyone walked around with a cell phone to their ear.

The main road from the airport was modern and paved, but nearly all the roads leading away from it were gravel and mud with large ruts in them. Less than an hour later, they were at the hotel. Steven had chosen the Hotel Marqués del Valle specifically because it overlooked the 'zocalo' or main square.

Oaxaca was the capital city of the Mexican state of the same name. An inland city, it rested at the base of the Sierra Madre mountains at about five thousand feet. It was about six hours by car southeast of Mexico City and about two hundred miles as the crow flies, straight east from another tourist destination, Acapulco.

Steven admired the mid-twentieth-century architecture of the Hotel Marqués del Valle for a moment before he walked through its open twin glass doors. In the large lobby, he was treated to marble columns and beautiful wood moldings that framed even more marble. And where there wasn't framed marble, there were framed mirrors, making the lobby feel even bigger than it was.

The hotel manager spoke in easy English when he looked at Steven's passport, even though Steven had greeted him in Spanish. His reservation was found and a modern electronic key was given to him. A busboy carried his luggage past a wide, white-marble staircase that ascended to the next floor and led him to a three-person elevator that felt claustrophobic after the small door closed.

After the creaky old elevator opened its doors, he was led to his room. Inside, the air was fresh and the room airy and large. The double doors of his veranda were open, and Steven could hear the sounds of the numerous vendors jostling for space and setting up their tents along the side streets of the zocalo. The sounds drew him out onto the veranda, and he looked down on the organized commotion from his fifth-floor room.

With a tip, the busboy departed, and Steven walked to the open veranda and scanned the zocalo below. It was the designated meeting place for the people of the city and was nearly five hundred years old; as old as the city itself. It was roughly the size of two football fields, and gigantic, ancient shade trees graced its sides. More importantly to him was that it was where many of the festivities would take place for the coming festival of the Guelaguetza.

During the Guelaguetza, the population of the city of Oaxaca would grow from two hundred and fifty thousand to nearly two hundred and eighty. The added vendors, performers, local visitors and tourists made it a busy place.

Steven's thoughts wandered to his brother Ernie. He was sure Ernie was still in Mexico someplace, though exactly where, he had no idea. The morning after Steven had approached Ernie about helping him with the cartels, he had disappeared. Steven couldn't help but wonder if he had gone back to the cartels; back to El Ángel. He had already concluded that an insider was keeping El Ángel one step ahead of them, and now he acknowledged to himself that it could be Ernie.

His satellite phone rang, and he went inside to answer it. He clicked the answer button and walked back out to the small veranda.

"I can see you. You look well, my friend," Filipe said.

"Any word on Chelle?"

"Sorry, amigo, I am pressing all of my contacts."

"I know you are, and don't let up. I've contacted the other leaders. They all claim to know nothing, but somebody does. Somebody tipped El Ángel off not to touch my ID."

"I agree, he must have someone feeding him information, which will play well for your plan. I have to believe that El Ángel will learn of the meeting of all the cartel leaders; an important meeting to which he is not invited."

"I think the bait will be impossible for him to ignore. He'll want to know what's happening and won't be able to resist finding out in person. After all, the prospect of a major change in cartel operations can't sit well with him as the odd man out. Make sure your men are ready. We'll probably have one chance to catch him, and it can't be wasted."

Steven looked down at the large, wooded square below him. There was a lot of activity as all the vendors set up their small pavilions for selling food, arts and craft, hats and t-shirts.

"To bring together so many major players in the cartels of Mexico... You have done the impossible," Filipe said.

"*We* have done it, Filipe. All the risks we took up to now have been for this meeting. Now, I need to convince them all that it's my way or the highway to hell."

"My friend, you have risked much to get this far, but do not assume you are out of danger yet. There is much hatred out there towards you for what you are forcing them to do."

"I don't underestimate the danger, and I welcome you as my guardian angel."

"Be advised that our instructions are to protect and defend the patrons of the Guelaguetza. This festival is important to the people of this region. Make no mistake, even you and your mission are of secondary importance to protecting them from violence."

"That's exactly what the leaders of the cartels are counting on. They would only agree to a meeting where El Senador wouldn't dare use his missiles against them. They view this festival as a way to create a neutral territory for our discussions."

"They are correct; we cannot fire into the crowd. Where is the meeting to be held?"

"I believe I've found the perfect spot to calm their fears. On the ground floor of this hotel is an open-air meeting room. It is exposed to the zocalo and will be public, but with a little careful planning, we can make sure we create a buffer zone between us and the crowds. Our discussions will be private even though the festival is going on only meters away."

"Be careful, El Senador; Snipes just reported that I am not the only one who sees you, and soon there will be many more eyes on you."

"They're all concerned that I'm setting up a trap, but I don't blame them for being cautious. I'm safe enough from most of them; they know that if I die, they die. It's El Ángel I'm most afraid of and also the most anxious to see. Call me immediately if anybody spots him or his men."

"Will do, amigo."

Steven felt hungry and decided to eat at the small café on the first floor of the hotel. He'd been told that the local specialty was mole, and he was anxious to try it.

Steven looked out at the preparations going on just past the open-air café. The Guelaguetza was a celebration of giving that included the seven closest regions to Oaxaca. It was a colorful festival of song and dance with traditional garments worn by the participants.

The meeting was scheduled for the second day of the festival; it would most likely be the busiest. That would be in two days from now, after thousands and thousands of tourists and Mexican citizens had descended on the city to visit the zocalo and watch the pageant inside the open-air auditorium, which was high on a hill overlooking the city.

Steven nodded a thank you to the waiter as he served a dish of chocolate mole over a generous helping of shredded chicken. The interesting thing about mole sauce was that it was meant to go with anything and everything. In fact, the mole was often considered the specialty regardless of what it was served over. Alongside the chicken was a soft-rolled tortilla to soak up the generous helping of mole.

Steven tried his best to enjoy his dinner, though he couldn't stop thinking of Chelle. He prayed she was still alive. Tomorrow was the official start of the Guelaguetza. The first show at the amphitheater would be tomorrow night. Steven thought maybe there would be a way to draw out El Ángel before the cartel leaders gathered.

He took the rolled-up tortilla and twisted it in the mole sauce, biting off a piece. The mole was everything he had been promised. Steven took the remaining tortilla and swirled it in the sauce as he thought about his plan. It would be better to deal with El Ángel on his terms than wait for an ambush. He was sure Filipe wouldn't like his plan, but it was a risk he had to take, for Chelle's sake.

Chapter 25

Chelle had just finished scratching in another mark on her bed frame. The sun had been up for a couple of hours, and she was getting hungry. A week had now passed, and Chelle guessed that Miguel would soon need to be on the move. Without looking, Chelle knew the guard outside the small window was still there. She could hear the pacing and the creaking of the small deck. It was one of the few sounds she had heard during the last week, so she had the noise of every board memorized.

Even though she didn't have any way to tell the exact time, Chelle's stomach told her that Adriana would soon appear with breakfast. Over the last week, Adriana and Chelle had become close. Even though Adriana was free to roam the home, Adriana was as much a prisoner here as she, and the two kindred spirits had forged a bond.

Through conversation, Chelle had learned that Adriana was only seventeen. Since she had been captured, Adriana had been all alone in a surreal world created by a sadistic monster. Whatever dreams the young girl had once treasured, they had died the day Miguel killed her parents and kidnapped her.

Chelle heard another familiar sound as the lock on the door clicked. The guard let in Adriana, who was dressed in a skimpy, nearly sheer, blue-patterned dress that must have been what Miguel had picked for her to wear today. Adriana walked on matching blue high heels. Her gate was practiced and steady. The shoes were hardly practical, but Chelle assumed Miguel also insisted on them. Chelle had to admit that Adriana posed a striking figure, her long, shapely legs accented by the heels.

The door locked closed again as Adriana approached Chelle, who was sitting on the bed. At first, the women didn't say anything to each other. Adriana sat a tray of food down on the side of the bed as she caught the eye of the outside guard, who was undoubtedly trying to listen to their conversation.

"How are you today, señora?" she asked.

"Considering everything, I'm doing fine, thanks to your help. At least I have a bed to sleep on, and some clothes to wear again, if you can call these skimpy garments 'clothes'." Chelle held up the hem of the sheer, white dress that pressed tightly against her naked breasts. She lifted up her bare feet and said, "I guess I don't have much use for shoes; I only get to go from here to the bathroom."

"I don't think we have much time," Adriana whispered as the outside guard turned away in boredom. "Something is wrong; Miguel is nervous. I'm sure we will be moving soon." In an even quieter tone, she said, "I have the knife."

Chelle looked confused.

"Where?" she whispered back.

Adriana was reticent and gave Chelle a look of resignation.

Chelle gave a slight nod that she understood, assuming it was in the only place it could possibly be hidden from the guards.

She made sure the outside guard was watching when she took a piece of fruit and whispered to Adriana, "Play along."

Adriana's discomfort was obvious as she opened her mouth and accepted the fruit. Chelle delicately slipped it into her mouth and smiled.

Chelle reached over for a strawberry and made a point of biting off a small piece. She offered the rest to Adriana, who nibbled on it little by little as Chelle held it. Out of the slightest corner of her eye, Chelle could see the guard glued to the window.

Chelle ran the back of her fingers across the side of Adriana's cheek slowly and softly. She picked up a small piece of pineapple and sensuously fed it to the younger woman.

Adriana was becoming more comfortable with Chelle's attempt to seduce her and started to act more invitingly. She took a strawberry and returned the favor by nibbling on the fruit close to Chelle's mouth before offering what was left to Chelle.

Adriana could see the effect their advances were having on the guard. He was frozen in place, his mouth agape.

Chelle took Adriana's face gently between her hands and gave her a kiss. Adriana slid her hands around Chelle's shoulder and pulled her towards her as they kissed longer.

"No, no, señora and señorita, do not do that," the guard whispered as loud as he dared. "Miguel will kill us all, you for kissing and me for letting you."

Chelle seemed to ignore the guard, reaching between Adriana's legs.

"No, no, señora, don't!"

Chelle looked back at the guard with a wicked smile and said seductively, "Are you going to stop us? Why don't you come in and play for a while?"

The women fell back on the bed in a lovers' embrace.

"No! Señora, I beg of you. Señorita, you know what Miguel is capable of!"

All the guard heard were lovers making the sounds lovers make.

"No, you must stop now."

The guard, determined, heaved his legs through the open window one at a time, pulling himself into the room.

With his gun strapped around his neck, he tried to separate the two women. That was when Chelle swung around and stabbed the guard in the throat. He reached up to pull out the knife, but he didn't have to; Chelle did it for him as she twisted it out.

The guard's eyes bulged; his throat gurgled, but that was the only sound anyone heard, despite the fact he was trying to scream for help.

The women pulled him to the bed and held him down for a long minute. Soon, the struggle was over. Chelle wiped the bloodied knife off on the already blood-soaked sheets and tucked it into her side, under the cloth of her dress. She lifted the gun off the bed and checked it for a chambered bullet.

Chelle held her finger to her lips and pointed to the window. Adriana slipped off her shoes and hooked the straps through her fingers as she climbed out. Thirty seconds later, both women were outside and running towards the jungle.

"Where to now?" Chelle asked as they ran.

"We can't run through the jungle, it's too thick. There's a small path down to the beach."

Chelle and Adriana ran towards the cliffside.

"Are you sure it's on this side of the house?"

"Sí." Adriana started crying. "Miguel, he will do such terrible things when he catches us."

"There, there, up ahead, is that it?"

Adriana wiped her tears away with her forearm, saying, "I can't be sure."

"It's the path, we'll make it. Come on. We'll run to the ocean and the sea will cover out tracks."

Chelle guessed only a couple of minutes had passed since they'd left the house. She'd estimated that the guard usually gave them about fifteen minutes together. Unless the outside guard was missed sooner, that would be when all hell would break loose.

The path led down the steep cliff. It didn't look like it was used often and was steep and rough, though the thickest of the vegetation had been beaten back.

"Adriana, hurry. We can do this, but we only have about fifteen minutes to get a head start on them. We'll run down the shore until we find another home or another path that leads to a road."

Adriana fought back her tears.

"I am afraid, señora, very afraid."

"That's OK, I'm afraid too, but we can do this."

****

Steven swung his feet over the edge of his bed, dressed in nothing but his boxer shorts. His room was starting to warm from the sun that had risen several hours ago. The recent travel had tired him, but now he felt rested.

The small luxury of a personal coffee maker wasn't lost on him as he poured some bottled water into it and pressed the heat button. His coffee would be ready when he finished his shower. He had just turned on the water when his satellite phone began buzzing. He looked at the digital display and saw it was the president's number. He turned the water back off and sat on the side of the bed with the phone.

"Sir, do you have word on Chelle?"

"I do; your hunch on the cigars was right. They followed a runner, and he led them to a home in Acapulco that they believe is where El Ángel is holed up. There's a good chance Chelle is also there."

Steven looked at his watch and then out the open doors of his veranda at the rising sun.

"I can be there in an hour. Two, tops."

"Steven, these guys are as good as ours, professionals. You know what I'm getting at. They know time is of the essence, but the raid can't be botched. They're planning an early morning raid for tomorrow. They wouldn't be ready before that anyway. Shock and awe, you know the drill, but it takes planning, and planning takes time. We all want Chelle back, but we want her alive. Trust me, Steven, these guys are well trained. If they can't do it, nobody can. Not even you.

"If he's there, they'll get him. And if Chelle is there, they'll rescue her. Steven, I know how helpless you must feel, but I'm afraid you have no choice but to sit this one out. I'll call as soon as I hear anything at all."

In a dejected voice, Steven agreed, "Yes, sir, but if you hear anything or need anything, let me know. By air, I can be there pretty fast."

"Will do, bye for now."

Steven headed back to the shower; he knew the next twenty-four hours would be the longest of his life.

Chapter 26

The guard outside the door was becoming impatient. Miguel had never given him an absolute maximum time that Adriana could visit with the prisoner, and it seemed to him that her visits had become longer and longer. He checked his watch impatiently again. It was time. Miguel would understand, even if it did upset Adriana.

He prepared his gun and opened the door, leading with his weapon. He saw the open window but not the guard. There was no movement in the room, and the bed was empty. Suddenly, he realized the bed *wasn't* empty. He rushed out of the room and sounded the alarm.

Miguel ran down the stairs from the veranda, his breakfast unfinished. He broke into the room and saw the blood. It was too bad the guard was dead; Miguel wanted to torture and kill him himself.

"Get everyone! I mean *everyone*, even the cook!" Miguel screamed. "They have to have gone north, to the beach. The approach to the house was too well guarded. We'll find the bitches. One thousand pesos to the person who brings them to me. And I want them alive."

Miguel went back upstairs to the deck overlooking the ocean and grabbed a pair of binoculars. The beach was partially obscured by brush and trees, but he scanned it slowly, trying not to miss any exposed areas. In the distance, he saw them running along the surf. It was only a glance, but he knew it was them. They had a fair head start, but it was nothing his speedboat couldn't overcome.

Miguel smiled; he had been growing tired of Adriana anyways. One last, long, pleasurable night was all they would have together now. But what a night it would be, he dreamed. He could do all the things he hadn't dared do before, not while he'd wanted her alive.

Miguel picked up his phone and made a call. Soon, a helicopter out of Acapulco would be at his disposal, and he could organize the search and capture operation from the air.

Chelle and Adriana continued running along the surf. The sand was the hardest there and provided the best surface for running. On top of that, it erased their footprints almost immediately.

Chelle stopped to catch her breath and looked back from where they had come. The surf was crashing onto the beach with a dull but constant roar. The waves washed up the shore and cooled her feet.

In between big gulps of air, she said, "I can't see the house anymore. Let's go down a few more coves along the ocean. After that, we can look for a route into the jungle."

Equally out of breath, Adriana said, "Maybe somebody with a boat will see us and come to shore."

"We can't take that chance, it could be Miguel looking for us."

Adriana's face fell as she realized that Chelle was right.

"The jungle and the mountains are dangerous. How will we survive?"

"We'll find a trail; there have to be more homes along the ocean. If we can find a trail, we will find a road. Eventually, we will get a ride to safety."

Chelle knew she was making it sound much easier than it would be, but going back was not an option.

Adriana looked down the beach towards Miguel's house.

"Maybe Miguel will forgive us if we go back now."

Chelle took the moment's rest to examine the rifle she was carrying. She ejected the clip and confirmed that it was full, then she clicked it back in and made sure the chamber was loaded and the safety was on.

Between long breaths, she said, "We have a gun, and I know how to use it. Do you believe Miguel will forgive us for killing a guard?"

Adriana took the back of her hand and wiped away some tears.

"No, but I can't go on, I am too afraid."

Chelle took Adriana's high heels from her and pounded one against a rock until the heel broke off. Handing it back to Adriana, she did the other.

"Here, this will help, you can wear them now. You do trust me, don't you?" Chelle asked, taking Adriana by the hand.

"Sí, señora," Adriana said, trying to sound brave.

"We can't go back; Miguel and his men will kill us. We have to keep moving. Keep your eye open for a trail," Chelle said as she half-pulled Adriana after her.

****

Chelle was happy with their progress. She could only guess that about an hour had passed. Miguel's home was well behind them, down numerous ocean-carved coves. They had run up another cove and rounded another bend when Chelle noticed a small stream that had found its way from the jungle and through the beach into the ocean.

The women stopped at the small waterway and caught their breath.

"Let's follow the stream, maybe it will lead us to a way up the jungle."

A low-pitched sound came from around the bend in the shoreline. Chelle and Adriana heard it at the same time.

"Run, *run!*" Chelle shouted as she pushed Adriana towards the jungle. A helicopter came around the bend and swooped down towards them.

Chelle looked back just as they entered the heavy foliage of the forest. The helicopter did a circling maneuver; there was no doubt they had been spotted.

She realized immediately that it had to be Miguel. Luckily, the beach nearest them was too narrow for the beating blades. Chelle and Adriana scrambled up the creek bed. The sound of the blades was slowing, so Chelle risked a look back, hidden by the foliage.

Down the beach, she could see four men get out of the helicopter, all with guns. One of the men was Miguel, and he was talking into a radio. A boat with more men was just off the shore. The surf was too shallow for them to get closer, but eventually even more men would soon be on their trail.

They had a head start, but not much of one. The helicopter had taken away their lead.

"Follow the stream, and don't stop."

Adriana didn't look back; Chelle could see that her fear of Miguel had erased any qualms she had about going into the jungle.

Adriana and Chelle clawed their way up the streambed, slipping often on loose rocks polished smooth by the running water.

"The foliage is getting thicker. We must find a place where we can leave the stream and hide in the jungle, but we must be careful to find a place where our tracks will not be seen."

Chelle started to lead the way. The sound of the men below them wasn't far away. As they proceeded up the streambed, Chelle carefully studied its banks. They needed a place free of mud, preferably with fine gravel stones in which their departure wouldn't be noticed.

A call rang through the air. Both women froze in their tracks to listen. It was Miguel's voice.

"Adriana, come to me! I will not hurt you. I know that the American has poisoned your mind. Please, come back to me and I will not harm you."

Chelle saw in the stillness of Adriana's eyes that she was considering the offer.

"You know that isn't true. You know that, don't you?"

Adriana looked up the stream and nodded, saying, "Yes, but either way, I am dead. It might be better for me to die returning to him than be caught running away."

Chelle made a point of gripping the rifle in front of Adriana.

"We're not dead yet, and I sure as hell am not giving up without a fight. Be brave with me Adriana, I need you."

Miguel called out again, offering the same bargain.

Adriana looked down the streambed and up past Chelle.

"Look," she said. "I think we could enter the jungle there."

"That is the perfect spot," Chelle agreed. "Now, be careful and do exactly as I say. We mustn't leave any evidence that this is where we went into the jungle."

Chelle led the way and cautiously kept her weight evenly distributed over the ground, making sure they disturbed the surrounding brush as little as possible.

Adriana followed and Chelle assisted her. Their instincts told them to run, to flee as fast as possible, but Chelle fought off that impulse and, silently, she forced both of them to do the opposite. They moved painfully slowly into the brush.

Chelle looked over their tracks and, with a stick, moved back any leaves and brush to cover wherever they were forced to leave foot-prints. The voices and sounds of the men climbing the creek bed were coming closer.

Chelle pointed into the jungle and held her finger to her lips to signal that they had to move quietly. Again, they fought the instinct to run, and instead they moved deliberately, trying to disturb as little of the jungle as possible.

The sound of the men soon came impossibly close. Chelle signaled to Adriana to squat down as far as possible and aimed the rifle toward the stream. Through the brush in front of them, they could see the boots and pants of the men as they probed their way up the streambed.

"Dogs, we should have dogs," one of the men shouted.

"Shut up, you fool, I'm trying to listen." It was Miguel's voice. "When we catch those bitches, they are going to pay for this. I've had it with the American, and Adriana can suffer the consequences too."

The men continued up the streambed, walking away from the hiding women.

Tucked in the foliage of the jungle without the benefit of the sea breeze, the heat and humidity engulfed them. The strong smell of the earth was just inches from their faces.

Chelle again signaled to Adriana to be quiet and not to move. That was when a large snake that had been enjoying the fresh water of the stream slithered across Adriana's ankles.

Chelle raised her hand over Adriana's mouth as a warning that her silence was critical. The snake stopped right on top of Adriana's ankle, sensing danger. It lifted its head and tasted the air with its split tongue.

Then they heard, "Look carefully, they could have headed back into the jungle anywhere. I'll double the reward for the man who brings them to me."

Adriana stared at the snake as it started to slide across her legs again. The panic in her eyes was unmistakable. She was fighting the urge to scream as the red-, yellow- and black-ringed snake continued to slither up her legs, closer to her midsection.

"I think they went this way!" a man shouted.

Boots started to break through the brush in their direction.

Chelle took the gun and laid it carefully over Adriana's hip, point-ing it in the direction of the sound.

The snake continued on its slow crawl, moving up the bare skin of Adriana's legs and towards her bare thigh.

Chelle unclicked the safety.

"Miguel, I saw a broken branch down this way," the closest of the voices said.

The snake stopped its slithering for a moment as it tasted the air once more.

From a distance, Miguel called back, "A broken branch?"

"Sí, it is in from the stream, and it is fresh."

"Wait there."

The snake continued its journey up Adriana's prone body. It wiggled itself over the barrel of the gun, just inches away from Chelle's hand.

"Wait! Quiet, you fools," Miguel cried out. "I can hear a sound coming from above me. Ricardo, up here, now!"

The boot steps moved away from them.

The snake seemed to look Adriana in the eye, then it turned towards Chelle and slunk around the barrel of the rifle towards her trigger finger.

Chelle flipped onto her back and flung the barrel of the gun toward the sky and an opening in the brush. The snake flew away from them.

Both women lay still, breathing hard for a long moment. Chelle motioned for Adriana to follow her deeper into the brush.

They heard a growl, then a gunshot.

"Did you get it?"

Miguel's voice answered back, "I don't know."

"What was it?"

"It was a fucking jaguar. Not more than ten fucking feet from me. Get those bitches. They nearly had me mauled to death."

Chelle and Adriana moved cautiously away from the sound of the men's voices.

"Señora!" Adriana said quietly but excitedly enough to get Chelle's attention. "Your feet are bleeding."

Chelle looked down at where she had walked and saw a clear trail of blood. Her bare feet were bleeding, and there was no way not to leave a trail.

"We have to keep moving," she whispered back.

They proceeded deeper into the jungle at a slow pace, choosing not to go up the steep cliff but rather to traverse it away from the stream. The thick humidity held on to the scents of the jungle, combining the smells of fresh orchids with rotting leaves and wet ground.

"We're small; as long as we stay under the cover of the foliage, they would have to step on us to find us," Chelle said confidently.

Adriana seemed to be gaining some courage, and the slow but constant pace strengthened them. Now, the sounds of the men seemed far away.

Above them, the jungle thinned into a rocky climb to the ridgeline.

Chelle whispered, "We can rest here for a while, then we must slowly make our way up. We need to be on the top of the ridge by nightfall. We can rest through the night. I'm sure that Miguel will not be willing to sleep in the jungle tonight, and they won't get back here until dawn."

As they rested, Adriana plucked a series of wide leaves off of a particular plant near them.

"You are brave, señora," she said as she took the leaves and pressed them around the bottom of Chelle's feet. "The leaves will cool your feet."

Chelle lay back, sighing, "You're right, that feels wonderful."

Adriana looked up the hillside and said, "It will be a hard climb."

"Yes, but we can do it."

"You make me feel brave, señora."

"Please, call me 'Chelle'. And you *are* brave, *very* brave. Not many people, including Miguel, would have been able to stay still and quiet as a poisonous snake crawled up them."

"I never saw a flying snake before! You were very brave too. As you can see, there are many ways to die in the jungle; Miguel is only one of them," Adriana reminded the American.

"We'll be OK; it's warm and we have a gun to protect ourselves. Besides, I would rather die a hundred different ways than give Miguel the chance to kill me."

Adriana pressed some new leaves against Chelle's feet. She lifted the sore and swollen feet and let them rest on her lap.

"Papa taught me some ways to be safe in the jungle; I wish I had listened better to what he taught me."

"Don't we all." Chelle smiled back. "You must remember some of it; you're making my feet feel better. I'm sure it will come back to you."

There was a gunshot and a loud shout echoed over the cliffs.

"Listen, my sweet Adriana. Unfortunately, I must abandon your rescue. I have been called away on business. But do not fret. My men will find you. And when I return, you and I and the American, we will have a wonderful time in my playroom. Rest well tonight."

There was loud, wicked laughter.

"He knows that they can't find us if we stay put and quiet," Chelle assured her.

Adriana looked even more scared than before, but Chelle wrapped her arm around Adriana's shoulders and pulled her towards her.

"We'll be OK, I know it."

Tortuously slow, the women worked their way up the mountain-side, making sure they took the most protected route, if not the easiest. Eventually, they saw the helicopter leave.

"We can be sure Miguel is on the helicopter, because it would not leave without him," Chelle said. "But that doesn't mean he didn't leave some men behind. The good news is they won't gun us down; he wants us alive."

"Nightfall is not far off. We must prepare," Adriana warned.

"Prepare? Prepare for what?"

"If the jaguar smells your blood, he will follow the trail. And if he does not find us, the bugs and mosquitoes will. They will eat us alive."

"I was more worried about bears or wolves or coyotes."

"They are concerns, but first the mosquitoes. We must find the stream back to find mud to coat our bodies in."

"You're kidding?" Chelle said as she slapped a mosquito away.

"They will get worse, much worse, when the sun goes down."

Chapter 27

The women were exhausted by the time they reached the top of the ridge. Adriana had been right; the mosquitoes had been relentless for the last half an hour. Trying to swat at them had become such a full-time job that, eventually, the women succumbed to the biting as unavoidable.

Adriana dug through a ground cover of decaying leaves and found some moist ground. She asked for the knife Chelle was carrying and used it to work up the wet ground.

"Rub this on, as thick as you can. It will protect us from the mosquitoes and hide our smell from the other predators."

Chelle did as she was told.

"You believe Miguel left some of his men behind?" Adriana asked as she covered herself with mud.

"I saw him talking on a radio. He knows we're not on the beach and that we were climbing back up the ridge. I'm betting there are men waiting for us on top, yes. They would want us to make a mistake like light a fire or make a loud enough sound for them to hear.

"We're fine for tonight, and we can go days without food if we have to. But tomorrow, we need to find some water. Trust me, Adriana; if we're slow and careful, we can get far enough away that we can find safety."

"You are a strong woman, señora. Your feet must be in terrible pain, yet you don't complain. I could not be doing this without you."

"Let's get some sleep if we can. Tomorrow will come soon enough."

Eventually, somehow, despite the constant buzzing of the mosquitoes, Adriana fell asleep. Chelle felt compelled to watch over the young woman and, though her eyes closed on her several times, she pushed the sleep away.

Adriana was right; if the jaguar caught the scent of fresh blood, there was no doubt the trail would lead it right to them. In the moonlight, Chelle saw another mosquito land on her. She was too tired to swat at it and watched as it tried to find its way through the mud to her skin.

She heard a sound. Chelle realized that she must have dozed off despite her best efforts to stay awake. She listened intently and could only hear the soft sounds of Adriana sleeping.

Chelle had nearly dozed off again when she heard the crack of a small branch. She knew it wasn't her imagination when she heard a sound again; it was faint, but it was real. Chelle flicked off the safety on the rifle.

In the moonlight, the jaguar's head came into view. It locked eyes with Chelle. Neither moved, then it gave a small growl.

Adriana was instantly awake, and she turned slowly toward Chelle.

"Don't move," Chelle said. "The jaguar found us. If I shoot it, it will give our position away."

Adriana froze with fear and didn't say a word.

The jaguar growled a bit louder and took a cautious step towards them.

"Shoo, go away," Chelle whispered.

She was answered with another growl, only louder.

"I don't want to shoot you, but I will."

Chelle pointed the gun at the animal, hoping the warning might make some sense to it.

The animal's muscles tensed around its shoulders.

Chelle fired. The big cat dropped dead.

Instantly, men were shouting. The hunt for them was on again. There would be no more sleeping tonight.

"Let's move along the ridgeline. If we have to, we can retreat back to the beach and the ocean."

In the darkness, the women's movement was slow, though the full moon provided some help in finding their way. They inched along as quietly as they could, feeling their way through the thick edges of the jungle near the ridge. They hoped the sound of the ocean waves crashing below them would mask any noise they did make.

Since the killing of the jaguar, the jungle had become eerily quiet. Chelle and Adriana didn't talk, but they were both listening intently. Unfortunately, the full moon would also be helping those trying to track them.

An hour had passed, and Chelle stopped to rest. She sat up as Adriana caught up to her.

"At least we're not where they heard my gunshot come from," Chelle whispered. "I think we should start heading more inland and wait for morning."

"Sí," Adriana tiredly agreed. "Maybe we can find a stream to drink from."

"Amen to that, I'm thirsty too."

That was when they both heard the unmistakable click of a gun being readied.

"You two aren't going anywhere."

Chelle moved to aim at the vague figure pointing a rifle at them, hoping the darkness would hide her slow movements. He was standing about ten feet away from them, the moon clearly outlining his silhouette.

She heard another gun being cocked.

"I wouldn't do that, señora," came a voice from the other side of them. "Miguel wants you alive; that's the only reason I don't shoot you right now."

Adriana cried, "Don't shoot. I will go back to Miguel."

Chelle eyed the cliffside below them. It would be a suicide leap, but probably a better choice than going back.

"Stand up, both of you, slowly," the man to her left said.

Adriana stood first. Chelle realized that Adriana now blocked the view of the man from the right. Chelle wasn't going without a fight; she dropped flat and took a shot at the man to her left.

His rifle flashed and, simultaneously, a bullet whizzed past her head and pounded the ground.

"You bitch!" he cursed as his silhouette dropped to the ground. "Marco, I'm hit, kill the bitches!"

The man to their right pounced upon Adriana and shoved her down to the floor of the jungle. As he held his rifle high, with the butt of it aimed at Chelle's head, she heard another shot come from the jungle. That meant there was a third man after them.

Chelle didn't have time to worry about the third shooter. The man over her was ready to bash her head in and her rifle was pointed in the wrong direction.

Adriana saw what he was going to do to Chelle. She coiled both her legs and kicked the man as hard as she could.

With a scream, he tumbled over the edge.

Chelle flung her arm around Adriana and pressed her flat to the ground. As rapidly as she could, she twisted her body and pointed the rifle towards the jungle, scanning it for any movement. Now, it was a matter of which of them saw the other first. She could only hope that she spotted the shooters before they saw her.

They both listened for the slightest sound.

"Chelle, Chelle," came a voice. It wasn't shouted, but it wasn't whispered either. Chelle couldn't believe it. The voice; it sounded like Steven had come for her. Still, she stayed quiet.

"Chelle, can you hear me?" It was Steven's voice, she was sure of it.

"We're here," Chelle answered, though she was prepared to shoot at whoever came towards them if it was a trap of some sort.

"Keep your voice down in case there are more listening."

"Ernie? Is that you?"

"Yes, start a count, but do it softly, I'm getting closer."

Chelle started the count. Soon, the brush in front of them parted.

"I got one of them when I saw his muzzle flash."

"The other fell," Chelle whispered as she tried to catch her breath.

"I heard his scream. Good job."

"I didn't do it, she did." Chelle looked towards Adriana still on the ground.

"I've been tracking them, there were only the two."

Chelle stood and didn't click the safety back on as she pointed her rifle at Ernie.

"Considering I spent the last two days in the jungle trying to figure out how to rescue you, I was hoping for a bit more of a welcome."

"How did you know we were here? How did you find us?"

Ernie whispered back, "I was watching the house when you two escaped. I was trying to figure out how to rescue you from El Ángel. "

"Who?"

"Miguel, Your host for the last few weeks, he is also known as 'El

Ángel'. Trust me, it's not a compliment. We gotta get out of here. The gunshots were definitely heard."

A handheld radio lying on the ground squawked, "Ricardo? Ricardo, can you hear me? We heard gunshots, where are you?"

Ernie found the radio and turned it off.

"We need to be up to my jeep by dawn. Come morning, this place is going to be crawling with El Ángel's men."

With the gun still aimed at Ernie, Chelle said, "You *are* one of El Ángel's men."

"No, I'm not. Not anymore. Please listen. I don't blame you for being mad at me, but I had to do what I did so that neither of us would be killed. What Miguel had me do with you wasn't a request. I was just as powerless as you, just threatened more politely."

"How do I know you're telling the truth?"

"Do you think I could have said no to him? We don't have time for this right now. I'll fill you in later, we have to go."

Chelle gripped the gun solidly, keeping it pointed at Ernie.

"Tell me now."

"I knew where El Ángel's Puerto Vallarta home was, so I led them on the raid to save you."

"*Who* did you lead on a raid?"

"Steven and the FES guys. After a bit of a firefight, we realized you weren't there. Steven was heartbroken when all we found was a bloody bandage in a basement cell.

"Anyway, I took off on my own and used my powers of persuasion with some of my contacts to find out where he took you. After a day of watching the house, I was sure I had the right place, but I had no way of contacting Steven to tell him."

"Where is Steven?"

"He went back to Washington to prove to El Ángel that he was in the states and still alive. His hope was that, as long as El Ángel knew he was still alive, you would be safe. Last I heard, he was all over the airwaves promoting himself. By now, El Ángel must suspect his plan didn't go as smoothly as he had hoped."

"Why should I believe any of this?"

"If I had killed Steven, I wouldn't have to be sneaking around in the woods with you now, would I? We would be consummating our marriage."

Chelle wasn't impressed and didn't lower the rifle.

Ernie added, "As you know, to prove my loyalty to El Ángel I was supposed to kill Steven. If I refused to kill Steven, I was dead, and they would have killed him anyway. I went back to the States to somehow warn Steven, not to kill him. I was being watched by two of El Ángel's best, but we managed to kill his men before they could kill us. That's when we rushed down to Puerto Vallarta to save you before El Ángel could find out I turned traitor on him, but you and El Ángel were already gone."

Chelle lowered the gun, and Ernie reminded her, "We have to go."

"How can we? It's so dark, you can't see through the brush."

"Same way I found you; I have night vision glasses. The moon is supplying plenty of light. I'll lead you, just stay very, very close."

Chelle didn't trust Ernie just yet, but she couldn't hold the gun on him all night either. She lowered it and clicked on the safety, declaring a truce for now.

"We've been running all day. We're tired and hungry and thirsty."

"I know, I watched your escape down the beach. I have some water." Ernie opened up his canteen and handed it to the women. He quietly dug through his backpack and produced two energy bars.

Whispering, he said, "This will have to do for now. In five minutes, we go, and for God's sake, be quiet. Sound travels at night. Now, you need to tell me something. What the hell is Steven up to down here? He's going to get himself and others killed. He has no idea what these guys are capable of."

"I don't know, but even if I did, I don't know that it's any of your business."

"Really, you don't know either? Then what are you doing down here?"

"Look, I knew Steven was into something dangerous and that's all. I came down to help him. He was frantic that I go back home, and that was when your El Ángel showed up and cut off my toe to pressure Steven. I passed out. All I know is, when I woke up, my toe was gone and Steven was ordering a missile strike on a soccer field."

"A missile strike?" Ernie was silent for a minute as he listened to the sounds of the jungle. Not hearing other voices, he added, "There are rumors of a man called 'El Senador' who blows things up. Steven is El Senador."

"El Senador? What are you talking about?"

"It's a cartel myth, or at least I thought it was. It sounded too far-fetched to be true."

"What's so far-fetched?"

"Let's go, I'll tell you next break. But you won't like it."

"First, why are you here?"

"I figured I owed it to Steven. It's clear he cares about you, and let's say I owe him a favor or two. He's always looked after me, or at least tried to. Enough talk, take some more water and then we're out of here."

Chapter 28

Tired, hungry and thirsty, Ernie and the two women had managed to avoid El Ángel's men. Through the night, they had cautiously circled around and had now finally found their way back to Ernie's jeep, but Ernie motioned for the two women to keep their heads down.

"They found it," he whispered.

Adriana and Chelle peered through the thick leaves. The rising sun showed four armed men standing in the morning mist, guarding the jeep.

After ten minutes assessing the situation, Ernie whispered, "It's no good; we need the jeep. We can't get out of here without it. But if we get in a shootout with those guys, we might not win, and it won't take long for others to close in."

"So, what do we do?" Adriana whispered the obvious question.

"Until we come up with a workable plan, nothing. Maybe they'll leave to help in the search. Until then, we fall back some more. One of us can keep watch on the jeep at all times, and, if needed, the others will provide cover for an escape."

It was agreed that Adriana would take the first watch, and Chelle and Ernie would stay back with rifles ready.

"Listen, Adriana, this is important," said Ernie, and Adriana nodded that she was listening. "If the shit hits the fan, you run as fast as you can through here. Chelle and I will split up, and the hope is that we can catch whoever is chasing you in our crossfire before they can harm you. Don't look back. Just keep running. Find your way back to the road and wait. If you see us coming in the jeep, jump out. If it's not us, good luck, because we will probably be dead."

With a scared look in her eyes, she nodded that she understood and crawled slowly ahead.

Chelle said, "Looks like we have time for that story. Tell me about El Senador."

"There has been talk that a powerful man from the United States is trying to organize the cartels. They call him 'El Senador', but I never imagined the name was intended so literally. Then again, I never believed it was true at all. I mean, they claim he can destroy a mountain by shouting at it! It's said that the fiercest of the cartel lords are deathly afraid of him and will do whatever this man says."

"And you think this man is Steven?" Chelle asked, sounding shocked at such an accusation."

"I know it's him. And that would explain why El Ángel wants him dead so bad."

And that was when they all heard the crackle of a handheld radio.

****

It was early morning in Oaxaca and still dark out. Steven was lying in bed, his eyes wide open. It was possible that he had gotten a couple of hours of sleep, though he was fairly certain that he had lain with his eyes and mind wide awake all night. The thought of Chelle being at El Ángel's mercy haunted him.

He looked at his watch; the hour hand had crawled unmercifully slowly toward five. He knew the hostage rescue team must be in place by now. Steven stared at the ceiling, hoping for a bit of sleep before dawn.

The phone rang. Steven fumbled in the darkness to answer it.

"Steven, they will be storming the house at the crack of dawn."

"Yes, sir, thank you."

"In an hour, hour and a half max, I'll call you back. Sorry to keep you hanging."

He swung his feet over the edge of the bed. Whatever sleep had already escaped him wasn't going to be won back.

****

Two hours had gone by since the president had called Steven about the planned rescue attempt. He was nearly crushing the phone in his hand as he waited for the call. Finally, it rang.

"Steven, good news, I think. The raid on Miguel Vega's home went like clockwork for the most part. One of the FES soldiers on the raid was injured, but it sounds like he'll survive. They captured a couple of Miguel's bodyguards alive, six didn't make it."

"Chelle, sir, what about Chelle?"

"She wasn't there, nor was Miguel. But, Steven, listen: what I was getting to was that the men that survived got in a talkative mood with a bit of Mexican persuasion. They said she escaped by killing her guard and taking his weapon. The guard's body was found with a fatal knife wound to the throat.

"Apparently, she escaped into the jungle along with Miguel's seventeen-year-old girlfriend. Her name is Adriana Romero Reyes. She was more slave than girlfriend. Anyhow, they escaped yesterday, and the search team Miguel sent after them came back empty.

"What we know for sure, at this time, is that Miguel left last night without the women. That means they're still out there in the jungle somewhere. As soon as the house is secure, some of the team will go search for them. I'm sure they're terrified of Miguel and his men and won't easily show themselves, but the FES will find them, I promise you."

"Yes, sir. Thank you, sir. That's good news. What about Miguel?"

"It seems like nobody knows where he went, and we don't expect them to; it's unlikely he divulged his whereabouts to anyone who was staying behind. However, they did say he was leading the search for the missing women when he was suddenly called away."

"The meeting in Oaxaca," Steven whispered to himself.

"That would be my guess too. It would be the only thing I can think of to make him move out so fast."

"Sir, I need to warn my men that he's most likely here already. Please, call me with any news on Chelle."

"Steven, I'm leaving for the international trade talks in Sydney. Privacy will be hard to find, and I won't be able to communicate with you once I board Air Force One. This phone won't work, and all my calls on Air Force One are logged. It's imperative that nobody knows of my involvement in Mexican affairs.

"Colonel Tripp has instructions to help you in any way he can, and your man Filipe is going to be in direct contact with the FES in Acapulco. I'm sure he will contact you as soon as he hears anything."

"Yes, sir, thank you. Goodbye for now."

"Bye, Steven, and good luck with your little get-together."

Stephen felt positively buoyant. Chelle was alive! He shook his head with a wide grin. She had escaped, saving a young woman in the process!

"And I was worried about you?" Steven laughed to himself. He walked to the shower feeling sorry for any dangerous man or animal that crossed her path.

****

Chelle, Ernie and Adriana stood motionless as they strained to listen to the report coming over the radio.

"We are under attack, everybody report to the hacienda immediately."

Instantly, there was shouting and frantic running in what seemed all directions. A group of men jumped into a truck not far from Ernie's jeep.

Ernie looked at Chelle and said, "Looks like our lucky day. As soon as they're gone, we jump in my jeep and get the hell out of here."

The truck was turning around, ready to go down the dirt road, when one of the men shouted an order and two men riding in the back blasted Ernie's jeep with automatic rifles. In a moment, the engine was all shot up, and all four tires were flattened. The truck took off down the road.

"You were saying," Chelle said, feeling like someone had just punched her in the stomach.

When the truck was well down the rutted lane, the three came out of hiding. Ernie kept his gun in his hands, ready for anything. When he was convinced that there were no stragglers, he let the rifle hang on its sling across his shoulders. Ernie examined the truck, kicked angrily at a flat tire and pounded on the shot-up hood with both hands.

"Shit!"

"Now what do we do?" Adriana asked dejectedly.

Ernie looked down the rutted path that passed for a road.

"I guess we walk until something better comes along."

"Don't you have a phone, can't we call somebody?" Chelle asked.

"After not killing Steven and beating the hell out of a few of my contacts to find you, I don't have a lot of friends to call. And no, I don't have a phone. It's a good way to get yourself killed when El Ángel is looking for you."

Ernie opened up the back of his jeep and sorted through those supplies that hadn't been shot to pieces. He found some food and some bottled waters, filling up his backpack and slinging it over his shoulder.

"Maybe we can find a main road and hitchhike?" Chelle suggested, but Ernie started to laugh.

"I can't imagine who would stop to pick us up with you two looking like that."

Chelle frowned, not understanding until she looked to Adriana. In an instant, she realized that their bodies and clothes were smeared with mud from the night before.

Ernie pulled out the visor mirror from the shot-up jeep and gave it to Chelle. Chelle examined her filthy face.

"Yes, that could be a problem."

"Grab as much water as you can. We'll get down the road some and away from here. Let's get a couple of miles from here, we can find a spot where you two can wash up."

Ernie picked up his rifle and started to walk, and, keeping her rifle in her hand, Chelle followed at a short distance.

****

After his shower, Steven called Filipe once again.

"Sorry, no word on Chelle yet, amigo."

"I know, I'm being ridiculous. I'm sure they'll find her before nightfall. Let's talk about tomorrow morning's meeting at the hotel."

"Sí. I have set up stations. We will have two snipers protecting you, Snipes and El Cazador. It is close quarters, so very dangerous. The good news is that most traffic is already blocked from the square because of the festival. The only vehicles allowed through the checkpoint are delivery vehicles, but none will be allowed through until thoroughly searched."

Steven understood that, as a practical matter, only so much could be done to protect them.

"El Ángel isn't going to take this lightly, trust me; he *will* think of something."

"I agree, but there isn't much we can do until he strikes. We just have to hope we're ready for him."

Steven had a thought: maybe he could draw out El Ángel. It would be dangerous to use himself as bait, but, he reasoned, it could be far easier and better to try and draw him out and catch him today than to wait and meet on El Ángel's terms.

"What if we don't have to wait for him?" Steven asked, hatching a plan.

"Amigo, I already don't like the sound of this."

"I have an idea."

Steven explained his plan to Filipe, who knew better than to dissuade his friend.

Steven closed the shutters on his room and sat on the chair facing his bed. He poured himself a shot of mezcal, the local alcoholic specialty. Steven picked up the bamboo shot glass and poured the drink down his throat.

Life was a gamble, and tomorrow's meeting meant going all in. If El Ángel disrupted the meeting, it would make him look weak. On the other hand, capturing or killing El Ángel tonight would cement the deal. El Senador would never be questioned again. Steven made up his mind: a trap had to be set, and he would be the bait.

The morning air was cool and refreshing, and Steven enjoyed a leisurely breakfast as he worked on the details of how he might draw out El Ángel.

It was mid-morning when he met with the hotel staff about the arrangements for tomorrow's meeting. The open-air salon was on the first floor of the hotel but secluded from the main lobby. Besides the one common wall with the interior of the hotel, it was surrounded on three sides by a waist-high brick wall. The effect was to keep things private from passersby, but the participants could all see what was going on around them.

Stepping outside, Steven stared for a moment over the short wall at the tourist activity in the zocalo just meters away. His guests were a rightfully suspicious lot. He hoped the open-air room and the closeness of an escape route would make them feel comfortable enough to listen to his message.

Steven walked out of the ground floor of Hotel Marqués del Valle, and the shade of the huge Indian Laurel trees greeted him. They lined the interior of the zocalo and provided shade over large areas of the plaza. Music from the central gazebo stage drifted through them, many hundreds of years old.

It's time to set the trap and dangle the bait, Steven thought. The odds were that many eyes were on him. Filipe's men had their stations, of course, but any one or all of the cartel bosses might be scouting out the turf before tomorrow's meeting.

Chapter 29

Steven was well aware that the game they were all playing meant that nobody could afford to trust anybody else. It was a game where the participants knew their lives were on the line. However, there was only one major player who wasn't tagged by radiation and that made El Ángel particularly dangerous. El Ángel could still travel undetected, and that made him the one player who wasn't afraid of immediate death if El Senador suddenly died.

Steven slipped on a pair of sunglasses as he started his tour of the zocalo. He wore khaki slacks and a flowery shirt that covered a Kevlar vest. If he was being watched, he wanted to give whoever was watching him ample time to discover he had left his room. It was time for Steven to enjoy the sights, sounds and flavors of the Guelaguetza.

The vendors were all set up and ready. Today was Monday and the official first day of the Guelaguetza. A lady walked by carrying so many colorful, helium-filled balloons that you would have thought she would float away. The smell of some sort of cinnamon-flavored cake seemed to be all around him.

Steven stopped to admire a man who was making cowboy hats.

"You want hat, you like Indiana Jones?" the man called. "I make you hat like Indiana Jones."

With that, he pulled down the brim of a hat, creased it in several places and put it on his head.

Steven had to admit, it did mimic the hat worn in the popular movie series. He replied in perfect Spanish, "No, thank you."

In the next booth, a woman was selling bouquets of some of the most beautiful flowers and orchids Steven had ever seen. That made him think of how badly he would have loved to buy Chelle a beautiful bouquet of her choice. He pledged to himself that, the next time he saw Chelle, that was exactly what he would do. He would buy her the biggest, prettiest bouquet of flowers she'd ever seen.

The old lady sitting inside the booth got up and approached Steven with a handful of flowers, asking, "Flowers for your lady?"

"Sí. I mean no, no. Not today, thank you."

Between the leaves of a tree, Steven looked to the north and could see the huge, hilltop amphitheater the Mexican people called 'Cerro del Fortin' or the 'Hill of Fortin'. The amphitheater was called the 'Auditorio Guelaguetza', and that was his destination, along with eleven thousand other visitors who had been fortunate enough to get tickets.

Steven had much more to see, and he took his time walking along with the other tourists. He found himself enjoying a mariachi band that had set up in the raised gazebo. By the various different languages he was hearing, he could tell that the zocalo was filled with both local and international visitors.

Any one of those visitors could be there with only one objective: kill Steven Westcott.

****

After an hour of walking, Ernie stopped and listened intently.

"I can hear water."

He found an opening into a small clearing off the road with a thin mountain stream running through it.

"The main road isn't too far from here. Let's get you two washed up."

Chelle rested her hand on her gun.

"If you think you're going to 'help' us wash, or even just watch, it's not happening."

"Hey, I thought we were a tight couple! I mean, it's all over the internet."

Chelle's hand didn't move from the gun.

"OK, OK, no big deal, I'll turn my back. You two give me your clothes and I'll wash them while you clean up."

"Ernie, you don't leave my sight. And keep your back turned away at all times if you don't want to get shot."

"Relax, I didn't risk my neck to save you just so I could have a peep show."

"Turn around now, and don't you dare look back."

Adriana and Chelle took off their clothes and threw them in front of Ernie. Ernie did his best to wash the mud off the skimpy garments as Chelle and Adriana washed themselves using the bottles and stream.

After a while, Ernie asked, "How's it going?"

"We're concentrating on our hair and faces. Not much clean water between us."

"I got the worst of the mud off your dresses. They're still dirty, but at least not filthy. I couldn't get the bloodstains out though. Whose blood?"

"A guard; I had to stab him so we could escape."

Ernie held the women's dresses up behind him. The women took them and did their best to wiggle into the wet clothes. Both soon realized that the wet, sheer dresses were almost like having nothing on at all.

"Don't turn around, don't even think about turning around," Chelle said in as menacing a tone as she could.

"I'm guessing there isn't much left to the imagination? Don't worry; it won't take them long to dry in the sun, and I promise I'll do my best to avert my eyes. Let it not be said that Ernie Westcott is anything but a gentleman."

"Now what?" Chelle asked.

"We'll have to get to the main road. We'll hide until we see a farm truck go by. Only a farm truck will be safe to approach for a ride; anything else could be the bad guys."

"Where do we go from here?" Chelle asked.

"Anyplace the truck will take us," Ernie suggested.

"We must go to Oaxaca," Adriana said. "The Guelaguetza is starting. It is the only safe place. I have an aunt and an uncle who sell their crafts there every year. They will help us, and the police of Oaxaca are not owned by El Ángel or any of the cartels, it is too big."

"She's right," Ernie agreed. "There's a lot of traffic going that way right now. It's our best chance, and there's an international airport there to get you back to the US. Acapulco has too many of El Ángel's spies. Trust me, I know; everybody is trying to sell information to somebody, and we'd stick out like a sore thumb. Hell, there might even be a bounty out for us by the time we got there."

"What is the Guelaguetza?" Chelle asked.

"Think of a state fair, sort of, only different," Ernie offered.

Adriana smiled for the first time in the last few days and said, "It is a big fiesta! People from all the neighboring states go there to celebrate Our Lady of Mount Carmel."

Chelle took note that, true to his word, Ernie was keeping his eyes focused on the roadway as they talked.

"A celebration of the Virgin Mary. It sounds wonderful," she said, smiling at Adriana.

"I have been to it before; the festival is much fun."

The thought of seeing her aunt and uncle at the great celebration seemed to lighten Adriana's step.

"How far to the main road?" Chelle asked.

"I'm guessing another mile or two."

"Let's go. Ernie, keep those eyes ahead."

"Yes, ma'am."

They walked along the dirt road, staying to the side, ready to disappear into the jungle the moment a sound was heard. Eventually, they came to the main road.

Ernie looked at a compass he was carrying and said, "This way, and remember: we need to verify who's there before we let them see us."

Several vehicles passed by as the three watched from the side of the road, hidden by the heavy vegetation.

"The last one was a man and woman, probably safe," Chelle said.

"Yeah, probably, but probably isn't good enough. Here comes a truck. Listen, it sounds like it's barely running on all cylinders. Perfect. Adriana, go do your stuff like I told you."

Adriana stepped out and pretended to shoo away some bugs from her long and outstretched leg.

Chelle looked at Ernie and said, "I could have done that, you know. There was no sense in risking her."

Ernie chuckled, "I *never* said you couldn't do it. Merely that Adriana could do it better."

Adriana saw the truck slowing, then she stood up and gave the universal sign for a ride.

"I admit I'm not at my best right now, but I could still stop a farm truck," Chelle said, sounding insulted.

Ernie was watching Adriana intently as the truck's brakes screeched. The young man driving the truck didn't have to think twice about stopping.

"Yeah, but I wanted it done with her legs, not you shooting out their tires." Ernie looked back at Chelle with a smirk then said, "Come on, that's our cue."

Adriana looked up at the open window and the young man peering through it.

"I could use a ride. I had a bicycle to take me to the city, but it is broken."

Chelle and Ernie listened from only feet away.

"We can give you a ride down the road a bit, but we are not going to Acapulco. We are on our way to sell our pineapples at the Guelaguetza."

"That is where I was going too. I was going to get a bus pass in Acapulco. Will you take me?" Adriana smiled with thick, pouty lips. "Please?"

The young man couldn't refuse, nor could he take his eyes from Adriana's cleavage as he looked down at her.

"Why are you so dirty and scratched up?"

"I took a fall when my bike broke. I'm sure I look a mess. I have relations in Oaxaca who will help me."

"Yes, certainly, you will have to sit between my father and me."

The young man opened his door and got out.

"I have two friends – Americanos – they helped me when I fell. I don't know what I would have done if they hadn't helped me. They need a ride too."

Adriana pointed to Ernie and Chelle, who had snuck out of the foliage and were standing by the tailgate of the truck.

The young man was clearly disappointed, but he couldn't change his mind as Adriana smiled at him with all the innocence she could muster.

"They will have to ride in the back. There is only room for you up front."

"I understand. Thank you for being so kind."

Adriana motioned for Chelle and Ernie to jump in. They had both hated to leave the guns behind, but they didn't want to scare their ride into signaling the police.

Adriana climbed into the cab of the truck. On the far side of the seat was an old man who smiled a big, toothless grin and had to forgive his son for making such a rash decision. The young girl was a rare beauty.

Adriana made herself comfortable on the ripped-up bench seat between the two men. Before they started down the road, the young man took the folded-up blanket he was sitting on and handed it to Adriana.

"Please," he said, "what is your name?"

"I am Adriana."

"I am Michael. Please, take this blanket to sit on. The seat is much too rough for you."

Adriana smiled gently at the young man. She was pleasantly surprised by the genuine show of concern.

"Thank you, you are so kind."

Ernie climbed up the tailgate of the canvas-covered truck and then grabbed Chelle's hand firmly and pulled her into the bed of the truck with him. They wrestled some wooden crates full of pineapples around, making room for themselves and seats to sit on.

There was a grinding of gears and a slow chug as the truck struggled to get moving again. Ernie took out his long knife and cut into a pineapple.

"No sense riding hungry."

As the truck began moving along steadily, Ernie pointed to Chelle's legs with his knife, which had a piece of pineapple skewered on its end.

"And you could absolutely stop a truck with those legs, but those curly locks of yours don't exactly scream 'native'."

Ernie offered the skewered piece of pineapple to Chelle, who took it in her hand without acknowledging the compliment. In an awkward silence, Chelle and Ernie shared the pineapple and the rough ride to Oaxaca.

Chapter 30

Steven walked into a small booth that was selling colorfully painted wind chimes and wind catchers. From where he stood, he could see the hotel and the open salon where the meeting would be held. He wondered if he would die tomorrow, not far from where he stood right now.

He reached up to stop one of the wind catchers that was gently twirling. Again, his thoughts went to Chelle, knowing that the colorful chimes would have certainly caught her eye too.

In a couple of hours, the sun would be setting. Tonight was the first night of the official gathering from the seven different regions of the state to dance, sing and play music. It was an affair that was not to be missed for locals and tourists alike.

The Auditorio Guelaguetza wasn't far away as the crow flew, but because of its location high on the hill, a straight path was impossible (unless you were a crow, of course). It was too far a walk, so he had a ride already set up.

Steven checked his watch; Filipe would be along shortly to give him a ride to the base of the hill. He would have to walk the rest of the way along with all the other show-goers. Walking northeast from the zocalo towards the Cathedral of Oaxaca kept him particularly exposed. He passed the corner stone of the old church, noting that it was dated '1535'. At nearly five hundred years old, Steven couldn't help but wonder at what changes both good and bad the old church had seen.

The crowds were much thinner away from the zocalo. At the cathedral, there was a wide expanse of Oaxacan blue stone pavers to welcome the throngs of believers. Steven waited there as visitors and worshipers came in and out of the huge cathedral, which was also built of giant Oaxacan blue stone.

In front of him was the Avenue of Independence. He glanced up and down the wide sidewalk to see if he was being followed. If he was, he didn't detect anyone.

As he watched the patrons of the cathedral mill about, he felt that he looked the perfect tourist, complete with a small camera dangling down from around his neck.

A vintage Dodge four-door, its bright red paint long since faded, stopped in front of him.

"Hello, amigo, do you need a ride to the Guelaguetza?"

Steven opened the door, which squawked from a rusty hinge.

"Nice ride, ten years ago," he quipped.

El Cazador quipped back, "Twelve, and you said you wanted to blend in. Great choice of shirt for that, by the way."

Steven plucked at his shirttail, saying, "This old thing? As an American tourist, I should blend in nicely. And it should make it easier for you and your men to follow me."

"And easier for El Ángel's men too."

"That would be the plan."

The car backfired as El Cazador coaxed it away from a stop sign.

"Are you sure this will get us there?"

El Cazador grinned and shifted the car into gear. Slowly, it picked up a bit of speed.

"If we are being followed, we should know shortly. I have men on the rooftops watching. Our red color, not unlike your shirt, should make us easy to track."

"I was expecting Filipe."

"He was called away suddenly."

"Really? By who? What could be more important?"

"I do not know. Filipe can be secretive at times, even with me. Your successes so far have caused a stir; perhaps he is called away to vouch for you, or perhaps he protects us in another way. We will need it. This is a dangerous game of cat and mouse you are playing. Should I remind you that the cat usually wins?"

"I'll try to keep that in mind. At any rate, I'll bet that El Ángel is here. Somebody told him about the meeting, that's why he had to leave right in the middle of hunting for Chelle. I'm sure he wants to disrupt it somehow to prove he's still relevant. Killing me before the meeting would be the best way of doing that. The only choice to make is do I wait for him to pick the time and place, or do we force his hand a bit by giving him a golden opportunity?"

After two blocks, El Cazador's radio crackled.

"Snipes followed us from the pick-up point to here. He didn't see any sign of a tail."

"If you think that makes me feel better, you're wrong."

"The Guelaguetza will be crowded, and it will be hard to follow you. However, the amphitheater is built into the mountain, and we have many areas of high ground. Because of the crowds, a sniper attack isn't likely. I would be prepared for a close-in assassination attempt with a pistol or knife."

"I agree, and either gives me a chance. El Ángel won't come at me directly, but I'm willing to bet my life that he won't be able to resist watching my demise. Your job is to spot him and arrest him, my job is to not get killed."

"We will be ready, amigo." He pulled the old car to the side of the road. "This is as close as I can take you. The road to the top has been closed off for the parade; foot traffic only."

With a loud creak, Steven opened the door and joined the throng of visitors in the pilgrimage up the mountain to the amphitheater. El Cazador immediately started hearing radio traffic in his earpiece. It announced every step the senator was taking.

Steven watched the red Dodge drive away and checked his watch. The plan was for Filipe to park at the first opportunity and to trek up the mountain to coordinate the arrest (and his rescue, if it was needed). For now, he would have to trust his life to El Cazador and his team. He would feel safer when Filipe was back in charge.

The festival was in full swing. Steven joined a throng of tourists, hoping for the safety of numbers. The participants making their way up the wide boulevard to the amphitheater were a visually stunning display of color and traditional costumes. Many of the costumes were decorated with ribbons and small bells. Alongside the dancers were colorful, ten-foot-tall puppets worked with thin, bamboo sticks to wave at the crowd.

Music seemed to stream from every turn. The street was filled with the mixed scent of fresh-cooked pastries and skewered meat. Just like in the zocalo, vendors were selling handcrafted items of every description.

Every couple that walked by reminded him of Chelle. They should have been one of the many couples walking hand in hand, enjoying all the colorful sights and sounds and smells together. Steven prayed that, next year, Chelle and he would be able to enjoy the festival and everything the city of Oaxaca had to offer.

Steven carried a light jacket in his hand. It was toward the end of July, and the weather was warm, but the dry air up on the mountaintop could cool suddenly. A voice crackled in his earpiece.

"We have detected nobody following you. Perhaps your instincts have failed you tonight. In another hour, the sun will go down; the darkness will not be our friend."

Steven nodded slightly to acknowledge that he had heard El Cazador's comments. The amphitheater wasn't far, and Steven intended on being in his seat before the sun had set.

People were gathering at the entrances for the show. Steven looked at his ticket, which assigned him to a section but not a particular seat. The sun was sinking fast as Steven braced himself against an attack, the crowd all jostling for their turn through the ticket gate, shoulder to shoulder. He noticed an FES soldier not far from him dressed in civilian clothes. Knowing help was close was comforting, but knowing an assassin was possibly even closer was unnerving. At any moment, a handgun could be emptied into him or a knife could stab into his side.

Every time a body brushed against his, Steven prepared for the worst. Eventually, it was his turn at the ticket gate, and a man waved him through. The crowd disbursed towards their own sections and seats, and Steven took a breath as he finally stood alone.

The FES soldier kept his distance and stopped to light a cigarette.

"The mouse is safely inside," he heard El Cazador say through his earpiece tucked nearly invisibly inside his ear.

Steven flashed his ticket as a sign he was going to his seat. He found his section and an empty seat on a bleacher. The rows filled in around him. As soon as the sun set, the show would begin.

That was when a man with a wide-brimmed hat pulled down over his eyes sat next to him.

He smiled gently, leaned over slightly and said in very quiet English, "Perhaps we can share a mezcal together? It is a locally fermented favorite." Steven smiled back at the man. His smile turned to stone when he realized the man was El Ángel. "And if not a shot of mezcal, maybe a cigar, even though I am told you wouldn't share one with the president in his Oval Office."

Steven was dumbfounded by what El Ángel had just revealed. How could he, or anyone but the president himself, know what had occurred within the Oval Office?

"Relax," said El Ángel, "I'm not here to kill you. Not yet. I have some information to share with you before your meeting tomorrow with all the men whose minds and bodies you have hijacked.

"Though I'm sure you wish to harm me, I would advise against it. I have my bodyguards, just as you have yours. If any harm comes to you or to me, the resulting gunfire would injure many. We can avoid that, and that is my wish."

"When did you ever care about the welfare of others?" Steven snapped back, a bit louder than he had intended.

"Ah, the show is starting," El Ángel said pleasantly.

The stage was circular, and the rows of bleachers nearly surrounded it as they climbed into the mountainside. Eight female dancers came on stage, dressed in colorful, ethnic dresses that flowed around their ankles. They were soon joined by eight young men, equally vibrantly dressed in white, silk shirts with wide-pleated sleeves and colorful sashes tied around their waists.

"If you aren't here to kill me, why are you here?" Steven hoped his protectors saw that it was El Ángel sitting right next to him. He was waiting for voice confirmation, but his earpiece was producing nothing but static.

El Ángel produced a small box from his pocket.

"Is there a problem with your earpiece? I'm afraid I might be responsible. Your ears in the sky, though? I have left them untouched. It's just that they may have a difficult time picking us out in the crowd, especially with the music playing.

"Please, El Senador, you have nothing to fear. I just wanted to take this opportunity to talk with you. As civilized men, of course."

"I have nothing to talk to you about," Steven growled, "and there is nothing about you that is civilized."

"I am a businessman who sometimes needs to do uncivilized things. However, you would be wise to listen to me. Have you found your pretty girlfriend yet? She ran into the jungle. I tried to find her and save her from the dangers there, but unfortunately I was unsuccessful."

Steven ignored the comment, saying, "You realize that there are probably no fewer than four guns aimed at your head right now?"

"My men count six, including one sniper with night vision. Very impressive. The FES are extraordinary, aren't they?"

The crowd clapped and roared as the dancers finished in a whirling crescendo of color and music.

"I hope your friends don't get too big of a headache from listening so closely to all this shouting." El Ángel pulled out a cigar from his breast pocket. "Care for one? I doubt anyone will complain."

Steven noticed that the men closest to them had somehow managed to shuffle themselves and the crowds around them far enough away on either side to create a bit of privacy.

"Many people think that Cuban cigars are the best, but that is not true, Señor Westcott. Yes, the Cubans have been making cigars for centuries, and yes, you can find an exceptional Cuban cigar, but they are the exception, not the rule."

Steven was spending his time not listening to the lecture on cigars but rather trying hard to understand how El Ángel had gotten such privileged information about his meeting with the president.

Calmly, El Ángel continued, "These are from Nicaragua. In fact, as you now know, they are only produced in one place and with a proprietary blend of tobacco, all grown in Nicaragua. You see, the difference is that Cuba stopped improving the bloodline of its leaves. It didn't have to; it had the reputation.

"Nicaragua, on the other hand, had to improve on Cuban cigars just to compete. After all, why buy a Nicaraguan cigar if you can smoke a Cuban? And so, they learned how to take the best qualities of Cuban leaves and grow a much better plant. Only, they did this over and over again. Please, take one."

El Ángel held out two in his hand, saying, "By the way, it was brilliant to use my cigars to find me. And now, because of you and my habit, I am less two houses. Two fine and expensive houses." El Ángel laughed. "I guess that would make these very, very expensive cigars, wouldn't it?"

"It would be a fine way to kill me, a poisoned cigar," Steven said, picking one and holding it up in front of his face.

"It would. A fifty-fifty proposition, I guess you could say." El Ángel took the remaining cigar and promptly lit it. "Me first."

He took a long puff and held the smoke, letting it roll around his tongue.

"Ahh," he breathed, "you do not know what you are missing."

"Tell me, Miguel, how do you know so much about me?"

"Please, enjoy a cigar with me. Your brother did."

Steven looked over the cigar and the band around it. It was, as he had suspected, the exact brand that he had found littered around El Ángel's oceanside home in Puerto Vallarta. In fact, the exact same brand as smoked by the president, and which he had indeed been offered and refused multiple times. Steven understood the dare, so he picked up El Ángel's lighter and lit it. He took an equally long puff and had to admit that the cigar was of high quality.

El Ángel smiled and said, "Good, now we can talk as friends."

"You are not my friend," Steven said, steely-eyed.

"Do not be so sure."

"You cut off her toe!"

"See? I did you a favor! As a friend, of course."

"A favor?" Steven fought the urge to strangle El Ángel.

"Sí. I needed information, and I needed it fast. I knew I had little time. Had I not cut off her toe, would you have divulged what I needed to know so hastily? No, of course not. And torturing you would have been senseless, and it would have gotten me in trouble with your country."

"That hardly makes you my friend."

"I agree. My point is, I could have taken much more from your girlfriend. I certainly could have hurt her much more seriously. I could have scarred her pretty face for life. But did I? No.

"Yes, I did you a favor. I only did what I had to, no more. I merely took off her toe, something she will hardly miss. The only one who will notice it will be you, when you bed her. Believe me, I am not normally given to moderation in these matters."

"If you think I'll ever forgive you, you're more unhinged than I thought."

El Ángel blew out another cloud of smoke.

"Well, these things take time, I understand that. However, I am here to talk business. I shared your plan for consolidating the cartels with some business associates, and they think it is a bad idea, a very bad idea indeed. They want me to talk you out of following through on it."

"I'm sure you have *'friends',*" Steven hissed, "who do not want their lucrative and illegal businesses shut down, but that's precisely what I intend to do."

In a low, calm voice, El Ángel continued, "I'm sure it is the patriotic thing to do, but it could be bad for your health. Much worse than smoking, I'm afraid. You do not understand: my friends are *very* powerful, and they are against this. El Ángel nodded his head towards the stage. "Watch, my friend. This region is known for their fine bakery. It is the end of their production, and now they will share with the crowd some of their baked goods."

Steven glanced away from El Ángel in time to see a loaf of bread being tossed to a person several rows in front of them. All of the performers took wrapped baked goods out of huge baskets and tossed them as far as they could into the crowd.

"It is considered a great honor to catch such a gift. Each region will similarly share a product. Be careful of the pineapples," El Ángel laughed.

Steven was trying to make sense of it all and puffed on the cigar as he asked, "Why would you or anyone think I would stop our plan, which, by the way, is to help your country?"

"And yours," El Ángel added.

"And ours, of course, but what's wrong with that?"

"Besides me losing millions of dollars and probably my life? Let me explain it to you. Much of the drugs and human trafficking do not originate in Mexico. The raw materials come from Columbia, Peru, Bolivia, even Afghanistan. These are poor countries; they depend on the illegal American dollars that come in through the cartels.

"As you say, it is illegal business, but it is still business. They hire many people, the money flows, and those people can buy food, medicine and apartments. Thus, this business, though illegal, holds back a more dangerous kind of anarchy. Many, many lives are improved by these businesses."

Steven countered, "And many, many are destroyed. What of the young girls and boys sold into sexual slavery, only to die in some remote country where nobody even knows they exist? What of the millions of drug addicts who have no chance of a life?"

"Those are not our problems; we merely supply what there is a demand for. Not much different than this cigar. A nasty habit, truly addictive, yet the only difference is that somebody somewhere decided it was legal. So, we smoke in public and buy and sell them legally, and governments make money off the taxes."

"You can play with semantics all you like; it doesn't change the suffering and death you bring. We're wasting our time here."

"Maybe we are, but that would be a shame, because by tomorrow night, you will be dead. What I am trying to explain to you is that other governments are involved. Governments that get their money from the sale of all things illegal."

"You mean people who want to amass personal wealth by perverting government."

"I remind you, people *are* governments, and they always have been. Just like your president controls vast amounts of wealth he doesn't own, so do these people. You Americans have a saying, 'there are many ways to skin the cat'. Crude but accurate. Continue on the path you are on, and you will die, you must die. El Senador cannot be allowed to live."

El Ángel watched the current production on stage to let Steven contemplate what he had just said. Steven took a puff of his cigar as he watched a papier-mâché shark chase a fisherman with an exaggerated papier-mâché head. The crowd cheered and laughed as the fisherman avoided the shark's bite. The surreal feeling of socially smoking a cigar and watching a play with a ruthless killer wasn't lost on him.

"Why? Why tell me? Why not just kill me and be done with it?"

El Ángel laughed and sucked another mouthful of smoke, enjoying its flavor for a moment. He exhaled, pointing to the stage.

"The small fish is eaten by the big fish, no?"

He made a gesture of one open hand eating his other.

"I am a small fish, Mexico is a small fish, Columbia, Peru and Bolivia and all the cartels, they are all small fish. The people who want me to talk to you? Now, *they* are big fish. And for some reason I do not understand, they would rather see you alive than dead. It seems they have some use for you, though what that is, I do not know. Like you say, why not just kill you and be done with it? But that is why I am here; to be your friend and ask you not to die."

When a beer vendor walked near their row, El Ángel made a motion with his hand.

"There is one more thing, but first, this cigar has made me thirsty. Care for una cerveza?" Without waiting for an answer, he held up two fingers. The beers were passed down as someone at the end of the row settled the tab with the vendor.

El Ángel handed Steven a plastic cup of beer and said, "Irene told me to tell you that the Woods Trust do not like you meddling in their affairs, and to remind you that Sam failed them, and thus needed to be eliminated. They insist that you do not have the meeting you have planned for tomorrow."

Steven was stunned; he felt the blood drain from his face.

"El Senador, suddenly you do not look so well, my friend."

Steven felt a bit light-headed. He tried to recover.

"Who... who is Irene?"

"I am merely a messenger, I do not know."

El Ángel made the motion of a big fish eating a small fish with his hands again, he said, "I can only guess a very, very big fish."

Steven glanced at a commotion that was happening on the aisles leading to their row. Groups of people on both sides started to converge on them. They moved in as if to squeeze El Ángel between them.

Steven turned towards El Ángel, but he was gone. As quickly as the commotion had started, it ended, and the new patrons sat down on either side of him. Steven was alone with his beer and cigar, surrounded by smiling faces who were happy about their good fortune to have been given the free seats.

Steven knew he was safe, at least for the night. He sipped on his beer. Irene wanted him alive, and apparently Irene got whatever she wanted. Steven stared at the ongoing show, not seeing a bit of it as he thought back to his and Chelle's conversation.

Philip Alan Woods, one of the architects of the United Nations, was the creator of the Woods Trust, but he was a long time passed. Irene and the trust were linked in some manner. Steven's thoughts went back to Chelle. Maybe, in her research of the Woods Trust, she had run across the name 'Irene'.

The president had to be notified. After all, it had been at the same meeting where he had first turned down the cigar that the president had told him not to worry about the Woods Trust. He had, in fact, said that every president since 1944 had known about the Woods Trust. And now somebody named 'Irene', apparently an even bigger fish, seemed prepared to have the president's plan stopped.

Chapter 31

Hours before Steven's meeting, the truck laden with fresh pineapples and three escapees came to a stop. Ernie's back and buttocks were beyond aching. He looked through a hole in the old, ripped canvas covering and knew they were in Oaxaca.

He helped Chelle down from the back of the truck, and they both tried to stretch some of the stiffness out of their backs. The ride had taken over eight hours, and it had been a hot, humid and extremely uncomfortable ride in the bumpy truck, sitting on wooden crates filled with fruit. Yet, somehow, they had both managed to get some sleep.

Adriana came to the back of the truck to greet them. Though still dirty from their trek through the jungle, she looked relatively refreshed. It seemed the young man and father had taken an instant liking to the girl, and she had traveled in relative first-class conditions, her every wish catered to.

Adriana gave the father a hug and an even longer hug to the son. At the last minute, she kissed him on the cheek.

"Will I see you again?" the young man asked, sounding unsure of himself.

"My uncle and aunt sell handmade wind chimes. They set up in the zocalo every year, and the chimes are simple but painted colorfully. Come and find me tomorrow, late afternoon. I will be waiting."

Ernie could see that Adriana was taken with the young man. He hoped that she would find the love and life that had been stolen from her by El Ángel. Working for El Ángel wasn't something he was proud of, and returning a small bit of kindness to the world made him feel just a bit better for the moment.

The trio waved goodbye as they walked towards the zocalo.

They were still a couple of blocks away from the zocalo when Chelle asked, "Now what? Look for Adriana's aunt and uncle?"

Ernie stopped walking and pulled them to the side of a wide sidewalk, out of pedestrian traffic.

"I don't know about you, but I'm tired, sore, hungry and I feel like I haven't showered in a month. You two, no offense, look like crap."

Chelle looked at her dirty hands and reached up to run her fingers through her filthy hair.

"No offense taken," she decided.

"Adriana, you are safe here, and maybe you want to go find your uncle and aunt right away. I would understand that. But, well... I have some money. I think we should all find a hotel, shower up, wash up, and most of all get something besides damn pineapples to eat."

Chelle and Adriana both laughed.

He added, "I'll give you two some money to buy some decent clothes and some shoes or sandals or something. You both look like whores in those clothes, and, Adriana, I don't think you want to meet your uncle and aunt dressed like that."

Adriana and Chelle both eyed each other up, realizing that he was right.

"You're just full of compliments, aren't you?" Chelle chuckled. In a more serious tone, she said, "I need to tell Steven I'm all right."

"Let's find a room, you can call from there. And," Ernie pointed to a sign over his head, "we might as well start right here."

Chelle looked up and saw the advertisement for the Casa del Sueño.

"House of Sleep?" The sign pointed down an alley, towards another dilapidated sign pointing at a single door. "You're kidding?"

"Did I mention my funds are limited?"

"OK, let's give it a try," Chelle agreed, starting down the alley, but Ernie grabbed her arm and stopped her.

"Sorry, you and Adriana need to wait out here. Let me get the room first, then you two will have to sneak in later. Just because it's called 'the House of Sleep' doesn't mean it's not respectable."

"Can't stop with the compliments, can you?"

"Go down the block, I don't want the hotel manager to see you. And try not to look too conspicuous. And try not to get propositioned."

Chelle didn't smile back. She took Adriana's arm and they walked down the street a bit. She turned back to Ernie.

"Please, hurry, this is embarrassing."

"Embarrassing for you, what about me? I've been standing next to you in public for the last ten minutes."

"Not funny, just hurry."

Inside the hotel, Ernie grinned a broad smile at the male manager.

"Hello, good evening. I am looking for a room."

The manager looked up, seemingly uninterested in talking to the dirty and travel-worn gringo.

"I am sorry, but all our rooms are full. In fact, the entire city is booked for the Guelaguetza."

"Look, as you can see, I am desperate. I have been traveling for two days. Certainly, there is someplace I can stay?"

"This is a busy time for Oaxaca. Further away from the zocalo, you might have a better chance."

Ernie turned towards the street, knowing they had few options. He thought of Chelle and Adriana. He had to get them off the street and into some decent clothes. He turned around and went back to the manager's desk, pulling out his wallet.

"I will pay American dollars."

The manager looked with interest at Ernie's palm then looked up at him with disappointment in his eyes.

"Sorry, señor, but I do not have a room."

"Gracias," Ernie said, then he turned towards the door as the manager's phone rang.

Ernie stepped out on the street feeling defeated. If the House of Sleep didn't have a room available, what were his odds elsewhere? And they didn't have a phone, transportation or the time, money or proper clothing to bounce from hotel to hotel looking for a room.

"Señor, señor," the manager cried, rushing out of the hotel door. "I have a room."

Ernie turned, clearly excited.

"What?"

"The telephone call, my guest will be delayed a day. You can have the room for one night. One night only."

"That's great, I'll take it."

The manager opened the door for Ernie and ushered him in. He was excited to have double-booked the room; something his bosses would never need to know. His reward would be American dollars.

Back at the check-in desk, Ernie asked, "How much?"

"Two hundred and fifty dollars."

"For one night?" Ernie asked incredulously.

"Big suite, two beds, television, balcony and private bathroom."

"Two hundred," Ernie tried to negotiate.

"Two hundred and fifty dollars, or I will put up a sign in the window."

The manager took the 'Room Available' sign in his hand.

"OK, OK, I'll take it."

Ernie counted out two hundred and fifty dollars and handed it to the manager in exchange for a key. The good news was that the manager was even less interested in paperwork than he was.

Ernie went up to the room and inspected it. It was everything the manager had said and would do nicely. Unfortunately, it had also eaten up most of his cash. He hastily cleaned himself up a bit and then went down to get the women, knowing they would be anxious to get off the street.

Finding them down the block a bit, cowering in another small alley, he said, "I got us a room. We're on the fourth floor, room four-ten; it overlooks the main street. When you're in the room, signal out the window, and I'll get us some food." Handing them the key, he added, "I'll distract the manager while you sneak in. Go up the stairs to the left."

The women eagerly took the key and followed Ernie back to the hotel.

Just as he had said, Ernie busied the manager with questions about the best places to visit. That gave the women enough time to sneak past the desk and up the stairs.

Ernie thanked the manager once again and went out of the hotel. He crossed the busy street and looked up at the fourth floor. Chelle and Adriana waved at him with huge smiles. Ernie gave just the slightest of salutes to the women and went off toward the zocalo in search of food.

****

Having given the women an hour to themselves, Ernie was sure they would be as hungry as he was, so he purchased some freshly cooked burritos made with the famous mole.

The last rays of the setting sun bounced off the brick of the old hotel building as Ernie entered, a bag of hot food in his hand.

"Ohh, this is unbelievably good," Chelle cooed, tasting it.

Adriana didn't say anything, she was too busy eating the burrito and drinking a cold Coca-Cola.

Ernie had to agree; compared to what they had just been through, they were dining at the Hilton.

With their hair cleaned and brushed, the grime washed off their bodies and their faces clean, both women looked quite attractive. Because both had washed their skimpy clothing, all they wore as they ate were towels.

For the first time, Ernie started to appreciate Chelle's natural beauty. Her dark, curly hair was drying fast, and her smile and easy laugh as she enjoyed her dinner made them all feel more at ease and helped them to forget the dangers they had managed to escape. He could certainly understand Steven's attraction to her.

Chelle had apparently forgiven him, at least for the time being, for any and all transgressions he may have committed in the past. His heroics in saving them must have bought him some grace, he decided. In fact, both women seemed completely at ease with his presence, though they were nearly naked.

Ernie didn't know if he should take that as a compliment or an insult to his masculinity. It was possible, he supposed, that due to the skimpiness of their clothing, they had felt naked beside him for the last twenty-four hours. At any rate, Ernie could sense that whatever attraction Chelle felt for Steven Westcott, it didn't transfer in the least to Ernie Westcott. He had to admit he felt a bit jealous of his brother.

"I'm afraid the bad news is that you two will have to go out one more time in those short dresses. The good news is that there must be hundreds of different booths at the zocalo; they're selling everything you can imagine. You should have no trouble finding something a bit more respectable to wear. I want you to take what money I have left and buy some clothes.

"Unfortunately, this room cost a small fortune, so there isn't much money left. Chelle, I'm afraid that buying some suitable clothing is more important right now than a call to the US. We need the freedom of movement that respectability will give us.

"Tomorrow, after we find Adriana's aunt and uncle, I'll take you to the consulate. I'm sure they'll be able to help you."

Ernie opened his wallet and took out one hundred and ten dollars. "This is all we have, spend wisely."

Chelle took the cash and said, "Thank you, but what will we do tomorrow if this is all the money we have?"

"Let's get through tonight and worry about tomorrow when the sun comes up. Now, you two get out of here so I can shower and wash my clothes too. Be back by ten, please, or I will come looking for you."

Chelle and Adriana gave Ernie a slight peck on his cheek.

"Thanks for everything, and for what it's worth, I'll make sure that Steven and the authorities know what you've done for us," Chelle said as they were closing the door.

"Don't," Ernie yelled back, "think of what it would do to my reputation."

****

Steven didn't wait for the show to finish. He walked out the amphitheater and was promptly met by El Cazador.

"I guess your plan worked. You certainly drew out El Ángel, and you are alive to talk about it. What did he say?"

Steven didn't know what to share and what to keep quiet. He doubted that Colonel Tripp had heard much of the conversation either. The drone had probably been flying overhead during his visit with El Ángel, but between the crowds and music playing, their conversation would have been drowned out.

"He knew far too much about me, and he wanted me to stop the meeting tomorrow."

"That's it, he just asked you to stop the meeting?" El Cazador asked incredulously.

"Yeah, pretty much. He said I should stop the meeting or I would die."

"So, your standard threat."

"Seems that way, just your standard everyday death threat." Steven knew better. Somebody named 'Irene' was privy to his private affairs – the private affairs of a nation – and was sharing that information with El Ángel.

"I would like to share this information with Filipe. Where did you say he is?"

"Filipe is my brother, but even brothers have secrets."

"Strange, I remember Filipe saying he shares everything with you but his wife."

El Cazador laughed and slapped Steven on the shoulder.

"Apparently not everything, eh, amigo?"

Steven added, "I think I've had enough adventure for one night. Mind giving me a ride back?"

"Amigo, I would have it no other way. Sadly, I must first inform you that we have not found Chelle or El Ángel's girlfriend yet. Peculiarly, though, a couple of his men were found in the jungle, dead."

The pedestrian-only roadway was fairly quiet as Steven and El Cazador walked down it to the waiting car.

"You think Chelle killed them to escape?" Steven asked.

"Maybe. It appears that one man was pushed off a cliff and fell to his death. The other was shot twice with high caliber rounds. If it was her, I want her on my team."

"Are you saying somebody else was running around the jungle killing El Ángel's men?"

"It's not impossible that the señora could have done it, but it's doubtful."

"She *is* trained."

"Sí, we know she took a rifle from the guard, but the rounds appear to have come from a different gun. There are still many questions. Please be assured the FES will continue to look for them."

"Tell them thanks from me, will you? I think there should be some guards outside my door tonight. I don't think we should take El Ángel's threat lightly. From now on, place the men on high alert. I'm expecting an attempt to break up the meeting tomorrow. El Ángel doesn't want it to happen, and he may have friends helping him who we don't know about."

"I have seen you walk into the lion's den without fear. Yet, today, you seem afraid."

"Just trust me on this one. High alert, every man you have. Be ready for anything. I'll tell my people the same thing. And no offense, but if you hear from Filipe, tell him to get his ass back here ASAP."

"I understand, I would like my brother in arms here too."

Steven looked at his watch; it was nearing nine. He wanted to catch a quick bite to eat at one of the many food vendors around the zocalo. With his stomach full, he would try to get some sleep.

As they left the area of the amphitheater and approached the road, a heavily armored army SUV pulled up in front of them. El Cazador opened the door for Steven and he felt relieved. It was the first time in the last four hours that he'd felt semi-safe. El Ángel had made it fairly clear. He wouldn't be killed tonight: Irene wanted him alive. For some reason, she was giving him one more chance to stay that way, but if he didn't call off the meeting, he would become expendable. That had also been made plenty clear.

Back at the zocalo, Steven asked El Cazador for a bit of space so he could make some calls. El Cazador slowly held back, pretending to look at some homemade merchandise while four of his men watched over Steven from a discrete distance.

Steven held the phone up to his ear as he walked towards the vendor of the wind chimes. The president had said he couldn't take the risk of talking to Steven once he was aboard Air Force One, so Steven knew that he couldn't and shouldn't try to contact the president while he was in the air.

Nevertheless, the news had said he would be stopping in Hawaii for a few days before going on to Australia. Maybe, Steven hoped, the phone number he'd been given by the president would work once he landed there.

Two women with their backs to him were carefully examining the colorful ethnic dresses at a dressmaker's kiosk. One of them had curly hair, and he reflected that everything seemed to remind him of Chelle. She was even the right height.

Steven did some quick math and calculated that the flight from Washington to Hawaii would take ten to twelve hours, maybe less in Air Force One.

Steven called Colonel Tripp.

"Is the president safely on the ground in Hawaii?"

Immediately, the colonel replied, "Yes, the news had him landing about an hour ago. It's about four in the afternoon there right now; he's in his motorcade heading to some big shindig. Everything OK?"

"Everything is fine, just thought he might want to be updated."

"I see. By the way, Senator, sorry we weren't much help tonight. We got some photos with the help of the lights from the fair, but we couldn't get audio. We were able to identify the man you were sitting with as Miguel Ángel Vega. Are you OK?"

"He kind of snuck up on me, but he was just delivering a message."

"I assumed you wouldn't be smoking a cigar with him if you felt in imminent danger. Still, knowing you..." Colonel Tripp let his words trail off.

"Colonel, based on my new intelligence, I want you to be on heightened alert, especially tomorrow. We need to be firing on all cylinders; I smell an attack. El Ángel warned me not to have the meeting, and I think he meant it."

"Weather is looking good for tomorrow, and the drone is heading back to the ship right now. They'll go over it tonight and we'll be ready here. Good luck."

"Thanks, I think I'm going to need it."

Steven ended his conversation with the colonel and tried the president's number. Almost immediately, he got a text back: 'Sorry can't talk, will call when able.'

Steven found the booth selling the handmade wind chimes. He was more confident than ever that Chelle would be found safe, and he wanted to buy her a 'welcome back' present. Two more guards had been found dead; Chelle was certainly making her mark on Mexico. After all, who else would be wandering around in the jungle killing the soldiers of a notorious cartel leader.

Steven picked out a wind chime that had particularly caught his eye. He was sure that Chelle would love it. He paid the vendor, an older man, with his wife nearby watching the transaction carefully. El Cazador joined him. They strolled as two friends without a care in the world. After getting something to eat, they eventually ended up back at the hotel.

"Get a good night's sleep, amigo. Your friend will be found tomorrow. She has proven herself to be resourceful. You need not worry about her."

Steven held up the small bag in his hand.

"I'm not, I even bought her a present. You get a good night's sleep too. I need everybody on their A-game tomorrow."

"Sí, amigo, good night."

****

For Chelle and Adriana, the first order of business was some decent shoes. Luckily, they found a vendor selling homemade sandals, and then. their next mission was underclothes. Once some proper underwear had been purchased, Adriana giggled like a schoolgirl, thrilled to finally be able to put on some undergarments. Despite being a trained FBI agent and ex-cop, Chelle couldn't deny she felt the same glee, and they ran to the public bathroom with their treasures.

They walked out of the small building, and Adriana said to Chelle, "I know just the dress I want, I saw it down that row."

She took Chelle by the hand and ran with her to the kiosk.

"What do you think?" she asked as she fingered the colorful material.

"It is beautiful."

Adriana explained, "It's the traditional garb of the Zapotec people. They are the largest indigenous group in the state of Oaxaca." She added proudly, "I am part Zapotec."

"Where do I try it on?" Adriana asked the woman in the booth. The woman held up a blanket and asked Chelle to help her.

Adriana looked at the crowds still milling about and back at Chelle. Chelle shrugged and said, "When in Rome."

Chelle and the dressmaker held up the blanket, and Adriana scooted behind it. A few moments later, Adriana came out looking and feeling like a new woman. She twirled around as the bottom of the dress twirled out.

"It's beautiful," Chelle said in genuine awe. The dress reminded her of a European peasant dress, only this was much more colorful. It seemed to have every color of the rainbow and all in the right places.

Adriana came to tears when she saw herself in the mirror.

"It's beautiful! I think it is the most beautiful thing I have ever seen," she gasped. Once she was back in control of her emotions, she looked at Chelle and insisted, "You too!"

Chelle looked at the row of dresses, weaving material through her fingers. Finding a dress she liked, she lifted up the price tag.

"I'm afraid we don't have enough money for two of them."

The smile on Adriana's face faded. She had forgotten they were on a fixed budget.

Adriana turned to the vendor and explained, "We only have fifty dollars of American money, and we need two dresses. I am sorry, but I cannot buy this dress." Adriana started to hand the dress back to its maker.

The old woman looked around, making sure no other potential customers saw or heard her.

"OK, for you only, two dresses for fifty dollars. But tell no one, please. I must sell for more."

Both women ran up to the older lady and hugged her.

"Quick, quick, hold up the blanket. I can't wait to try it on."

The other two women were more than happy to oblige, and soon Chelle was twirling around, showing off her dress as well.

The dressmaker ushered Adriana in front of a mirror and started playing with her long, dark hair. When it was up and twisted just so, she got a few handcrafted hairclips that were painted in tropical colors. She played around a bit more and soon found just the right placement.

Adriana couldn't take her eyes off herself, and for some reason her mind went to the young farmer of earlier that day. How she wished he could see her now.

Adriana gave the old lady a hug and said, "We have no money for the clips."

"Just go!" the old women scolded. "And don't tell anyone, or I will go home with less money than I came with."

The fifty dollars exchanged hands and, with a last hug, Chelle and Adriana bade the woman goodbye.

Above them, on the fourth floor of Hotel Marqués del Valle, Steven took off his patterned shirt and the body armor he wore under it. He left on his undershirt and turned off all the lights, stepping out onto the veranda as a shadow in the darkness looking out over the zocalo.

The body armor would have protected him from a knife attack

and small-arms fire. He would wear it again tomorrow, but he had an ominous feeling that he might be approaching the kind of danger that body armor wouldn't protect him from. In fact, he was surer of it than ever.

He looked down at the carefree visitors to the zocalo and wished he was just a tourist on vacation. Two women wearing traditional, colorful dresses walked below him, leaving the zocalo. He couldn't see their faces, but yet again he was reminded of Chelle.

Chapter 32

The night had been uneventful for Steven; he had even managed to get some sleep. In his heart, he felt that Chelle was all right, but the president had never called, and there was something worrying about his discussion with El Ángel.

Steven couldn't help but wonder if the president who already knew about the Woods Trust also knew who Irene was. He looked at his watch for the tenth time in the last hour; the meeting was set for eleven, with tapas and drinks set out for his guests. There was a lot he wanted to tell them that would be hard to digest. He hoped to disarm them a bit with full stomachs.

Colonel Tripp had confirmed that his man was standing by in Oaxaca with the special imprinting device. Steven hoped that he wouldn't need to make an example of one of the attendees and become an executioner.

****

Chelle, Adriana and Ernie had fallen asleep easily. Chelle and Adriana took one bed, Ernie the other. Even as morning light came, they all were so worn out from the previous days of activities that they slept on late into the morning.

Ernie was the first up at ten after a solid twelve hours of sleep. He pulled open the curtains wearing only his boxer shorts.

"Time to get up, ladies. We had better find Adriana's aunt and uncle, and Chelle, we need to get you to the consulate. I needn't remind you that we have no money for breakfast, so finding someone to help you two as soon as possible is imperative."

Chelle groaned, "If you needn't remind us that we can't eat, why did you?"

Ernie chuckled, "Quit complaining; at least we're not running for our lives through a jungle."

Adriana was slowly opening her eyes and agreed, "Sí, this bed was wonderful. My uncle is a good man, he will give us some food."

****

Steven was inside the first-floor salon area, preparing. He had checked in with El Cazador, who had assured Steven that a mouse wouldn't get near the meeting without them knowing about it.

Still, something wasn't right. El Cazador had confided in Steven that he was worried for Filipe's wellbeing. His family hadn't heard from him either. They agreed that, immediately after the meeting, they would start a search for Filipe.

Snipes was on the top of the hotel, ready to shoot any threat, while El Cazador took a position watching their backs from a lower vantage point. With two snipers in place, the other members of the expanded team patrolled the perimeter of the hotel. Some were dressed as soldiers, automatic weapons in their hands, while others went about their jobs looking like sanitary workers, shopkeepers and casual tourists.

At ten-thirty, Snipes reported over Steven's earpiece.

"The leader of El Dragóns is here; his men are scouring the area."

Breaking in on the communication, Colonel Tripp said, "I can confirm that. We have his radiation signature and he's headed your way."

Steven tapped his earpiece, sending back a signal the he copied the messages. Nobody coming to the meeting would be allowed to be armed. That is, nobody but Steven; his sport jacket was there to hide the Glock 35 he had holstered in the small of his back and to camouflage the body armor he was wearing. He had to admit, it did give him a small sense of security. Ten minutes later, Francisco Delgada Reyes, leader of El Dragóns, entered the salon as the first guest to arrive.

"Welcome Francisco," Steven said sincerely.

"I do not feel welcomed. It is only the threat of death that brings me. I fear I will die regardless."

"I hope not; your men are welcome to watch you from a distance. As you can tell, we will have our meeting here where they can see you at all times. The area around the salon is taped off as an area under construction. That should keep the casual tourist from getting too close and overhearing us."

"Do you think that makes me feel safe?"

"Not safe, just safer."

From the shadows, a man stepped out holding an electronic device.

"Don't be alarmed," Steven said. "He's just going to sweep you for any bugs. Likewise, all weapons will be placed behind this counter and returned after the meeting."

"And why should I give you my gun?"

"Like you said, only because of the threat of death if you don't. It'll also make me feel safer, if that helps."

Colonel Tripp's technical specialist waved his equipment over Francisco and wasn't satisfied until he had collected his knife, gun and two cell phones. One by one, the other guests arrived. The resentment at coming to this meeting under threat of death was universal, as was the reluctance to give up their weapons and phones. Still, one by one, they were persuaded.

****

Chelle, Ernie and Adriana approached the zocalo. Today, their job was simple; find a vendor of wind chimes with the hope that it would lead them to Adriana's aunt and uncle. They had already found two kiosks that sold wind chimes, but neither was the right one. Not disheartened, they continued; they still had rows and rows of vendors to look over.

Ernie had temporarily disappeared, but Chelle and Adriana carried on. After walking another row of kiosks, Ernie found the women and handed them each a tortilla filled with some sort of egg mixture.

The women took the tortillas from him hungrily and started to eat.

Between mouthfuls, Chelle exclaimed, "Oh my god, these are good. How did you get them? We were starving!"

"Don't ask and I won't tell."

"You stole them?" Chelle asked, sounding shocked.

"Did you want to eat or not?"

Chelle took another bite.

"Never mind. But as soon as we get some money, we'll pay them back."

"Sure, but reality says that nobody is handing us a fistful of pesos anytime soon."

The trio finished their breakfast, and Adriana was licking the last bit of food off her hand when she said, "That's them, I'm sure!"

She pulled Chelle towards a tent adorned with numerous colorful wind chimes and wind catchers of all shapes and sizes, swirling in the breeze and chiming their songs. Approaching the kiosk with apprehension, Adriana broke down and cried when she saw her aunt.

"Auntie Lucia!" she cried out as she hugged the women, who immediately recognized the niece she had thought lost forever.

"You are back, thank God, you are back! Papa, Papa, look, it's Adriana!"

"Oh my god, child, we thought you were lost for sure when we heard what had happened to your family," her uncle cried as he hugged her too.

Still sobbing, Adriana managed to say, "I was kidnapped by a terrible man. He did terrible things to me. But these people saved me, they are my friends."

Immediately, Ernie and Chelle became cherished family members and got their own share of hugs. Ernie tried to remove himself from the moment but the aunt and uncle would have none of that.

****

Antonio Cruz Ortega, aka El Pequeño Diablo, stepped into the small salon through the open hotel door.

"El Senador, what a pleasure to see you again."

Antonio smiled broadly at Steven, but Steven knew that it was no pleasure on Antonio's part to be forced to this meeting. Still, there did seem to be a bond between them after escaping El Padrino's exploding yacht.

"Antonio, my friend, I have some good news for you. El Ángel will not be joining us."

"If I am to believe what you promise, that would make him a dead man."

"He is, he just hasn't accepted it yet."

"I heard he treated your girlfriend unkindly."

"What do you know of her?"

"Nothing much, just that he took her toe. I do know that he has spies, but so do I. Do not assume he will not know what is said here today."

"I hope he does. He will hear again how he has made a bad decision by not working with me. Do you know who his spies are?"

Antonio seemed to ignore Steven's question as he looked out over the zocalo and the numerous tourists milling about. He casually turned back to look over the occupants of the salon.

In a low voice, he said, "El Padrino would have the most to gain. I think El Senador may have a problem if El Ángel lives past tomorrow. Many will wonder if El Senador is just an empty myth."

Steven looked over the growing collection of thugs and murderers. He didn't respond, but he understood the warning. Fear for their lives was the only glue holding this coalition of misfits together. If El Ángel wasn't killed for non-cooperation, his threats were empty, and it would all fall apart.

Antonio found a seat and helped himself to some fruit set out on the tables.

Each cartel leader and enforcer looked at the others with suspicion and contempt. In many cases, they had often been mortal enemies with the man sitting next to them.

It was a powder keg for sure, but as more came in, there seemed to be a consensus that they weren't in charge of their destinies and would need to listen to what El Senador had to say. By eleven-fifteen, ten of the most dangerous men in the world were all gathered in the same place.

"Caballeros," Steven started out. Calling these men 'gentlemen' was a bit of a push, but he didn't know how else to start his little speech. He continued in Spanish, "I believe you all know where I stand, and you no doubt dislike the way I forced you all into this meeting. That's why I've brought to you a message directly from your president."

Steven made a point of retrieving a small USB device from a

metal box. He plugged it into a television, and the group immediately hushed. He pressed a button and the large screen was filled by a woman's face.

"This is President Torres, though I'm sure you recognize me. I am here to address you all directly. Please, hear me out. Each one of you has committed serious crimes against Mexico. The Mexican government, your government, has declared war on you. As enemy combatants, each one of you has been sentenced to death. The sentence is to be carried out immediately."

Some of the cartel leaders flexed or even stood, sensing a trap. Others sat confused, expecting a deal for their lives. There was loud objection and swearing at being set up.

Steven used his hands to try to calm them as he paused the message. Antonio didn't move; he calmly smoked a cigarette, watching as things played out.

When he'd had enough, he yelled, "Silence, let her talk."

Immediately, the group quieted, wondering who had the balls to give them an order.

Steven took advantage of the silence Antonio had created and restarted the message.

After a pause to let her message sink in, the president continued, "That sentence shall be commuted if you cooperate with the authorities from now on."

Those who were standing sat down again.

"As you know, the Americans are helping Mexico destroy the likes of your organizations. This is our final solution, and there is no going back. Senator Westcott and President Julius Walker have my complete support in enforcing the terms of your probation. The terms are simple: if you cooperate with us and share your information on every crooked official, who your sources are and how you transport your drugs and human contraband, you will be allowed to live.

"As you know, you are already marked men. The Americans know where you are at all times. Killing you will be exceedingly easy, so I advise cooperation. If you cooperate, not only will you be allowed to live, but you will be helped to prosper.

"Mexico needs entrepreneurs, people willing to create jobs and industry. You have all shown a knack for running organizations. Turn your illegal millions into legal and profitable business within your regions, and you will be allowed to keep your profits. After taxes, of course.

"Senator Westcott will fill you in on the rest of the plan to clean Mexico of the filth you have created, but be warned; I will not falter. For the citizens of Mexico, we must bring law and order to the land. If you want war, so be it, war is what you will get. But make no mistake: five years from now, all the cartels will be gone."

The video stopped. Steven took out the memory stick and dropped it into a small, metal box. He pressed a button and the interior of the box lit up for a second, followed by the smell of burning plastic; a portable electromagnet had just destroyed the contents of the drive beyond all repair. The gangsters might not have understood the precise mechanics, but Steven could tell from their expressions that they understood that the message was gone.

"Each one of you, as you came in, was retagged with another powerful radiation signature. Just to make sure nobody gets lost. It also helps us distinguish you once and for all from your men." He watched the bosses scowl at each other, wondering if they could have slipped away by not attending. It was too late to ever find out, and they knew it. "Each of you will have a handler assigned to you. There is nothing you will not tell them, nothing. Slowly, over the next few years, we will bring law and order back to each region."

"Excuse me, amigo?" It was Antonio speaking up. "How do we build these businesses? We know nothing of running a business."

"Actually, you do. In a manner of speaking, you are all already successful business people. You have employees, pay scales, inventory, account receivables and payables. One small difference is that you can no longer just kill people who don't agree with your methods; that does make it a bit harder."

The group actually laughed at the absurdity of the situation.

"We know you will need help, and each region will have a task force to help you. If violent criminals attack you, you will be defended, and they will be dealt with. It's said that the hardest part of living outside the law is being unable to call on it when you're in trouble. Well, gentlemen, welcome back. We want you to be successful and hire many, many people. Our president, Julius Walker, is on his way to Australia to announce a new North American trade initiative. We expect it to pave the way for many new industries. You help us bring peace and stability to your regions and you will have the willing workers to fill your factories."

"Amigo, that is insane. It will never work," Antonio said as he snuffed out his cigarette.

"It has to work. Don't you see? Mexico is falling further and further behind the industrialized world. The lawlessness that the cartels and gangs create is destroying your country from within. If you continue to be destructive to your country, you will be eliminated. I'm giving you the chance to prosper in a much better world."

Steven sat on the edge of the table that held the large television. He looked over the group of thugs as if they were his best friends and spoke softly and sincerely.

"You all live day-to-day, afraid that you and your families could be killed at any moment. We can stop that. You can stop that. You can do that for your families by making Mexico into a great economic power.

"The people are hungry for jobs – *real* jobs – and security for their families. Isn't that what you want? President Walker's plan is to recreate how business is done around the world. The entire North American continent, Mexico, Canada and the United States will be structured and looked at as one giant trading bloc. Mexico will become a manufacturing giant if companies believe it's safe to build here.

Antonio nodded in agreement, saying, "I did not say I wouldn't try. I just have my doubts."

That was about as close to an endorsement as Steven had ever expected.

"You talk as if we have ruined our country," said another of the bosses, "but Mexico was hard before us. What I have made, I am proud of, and what I did to create it was necessary. You spit on a legacy you do not understand."

"Your legacy is that you reached this point," Steven countered. "Let's not beat around the bush; you're not here despite what you've done, you're here because of it. You fought long and hard, and what you won is a seat at this table. It's a prize that all the men, women and children you've killed will never claim. You get to be rich, powerful and celebrated, but only if you can accept change. Are you wise enough to do that, or are you going to invite death just when the battle is won?"

None of them answered, and a glint in Antonio's eye told Steven he'd found an argument the bosses might accept, especially with a little devil on their shoulders helping to sell it.

"I'm going to introduce you to your individual contacts now," Steven continued. "Remember; you or your men hurt them in any way, you're dead."

****

Ernie and Chelle decided to give Adriana some time alone with her relatives, stepping away from the kiosk.

Ernie said, "Time to get you to the consulate so you can get the proper medical care for your foot and somehow get back to the good old USA."

"Not without saying goodbye to Adriana."

"Agreed."

Chelle felt relieved that Adriana was now safe and back with family. Suddenly, despite all that they had been through, she felt at peace. She looked out over the activity of the zocalo and took in the wonderful sights, sounds and smells as a reaffirmation of the goodness of life itself.

She stepped around the corner to look at the craftsmanship of some homemade leather purses, but the fleeting image of one man addressing an oddly formal group caught her eye. There was something about his stance that just felt... right.

His face was partially covered by a building's overhang, so she moved a bit closer. She couldn't believe it when she saw him. It was Steven. Her heart started to thump. Chelle ran back to get Ernie; she had to let him know.

"That's Steven," she said, dragging him with one hand and pointing with the other. "I know it is."

Ernie looked around the 'MEN WORKING' barriers and said, "Well, I'll be damned."

****

Steven was explaining how the group could use their illegal profits to buy legal business assets. And how it would be overlooked for a limited period of time. Just then he caught a glimpse of someone just outside the range of the 'MEN WORKING' signs. The woman reminded him of Chelle, but she was gone in an instant.

A moment later, he saw her again, and this time she was pointing at him. Suddenly, Steven realized it was Chelle with Ernie by her side. He knew he had to run to her, but if he suddenly vaulted over the half wall separating the salon from the zocalo, his guests would think it another trap and all hell would break loose.

He saw her running towards him. His heart and mind raced; he had to excuse himself somehow. Snipes' voice came over his earpiece.

"I see an RPG aimed at the hotel! I don't have a clear shot: I repeat, I do not have a clear shot. I can't see the shooter."

El Cazador shouted urgently, "Where, *where?*"

"Get out of there!" Snipes bellowed.

"Everyone scatter," Steven shouted. "There's an RPG aimed directly at us. Run, get out of here, *now!*"

Enough of the men had handled a rocket-propelled grenade before that nothing further needed to be explained.

Steven saw Chelle running towards him, then he saw a puff of smoke in the near distance. He hurdled the half wall separating the salon from the zocalo, sensing the cartel bosses all around him. They looked like desperate rats scrambling off a sinking ship.

Ignoring everything else, Steven raced towards Chelle just as a trail of smoke raced over his head. He flung himself at her as a tremendous thunder exploded behind him.

Chapter 33

The explosion pounded in his ears as he tackled Chelle and rolled them to the right. He prayed that one of the big limbs of a towering tree would protect them from the falling debris that had been rocketed skyward.

Steven covered Chelle with his body; losing her again was not an option. Dust poured out of the hotel from where the salon had been only moments before. There was so much dust that Steven could only hear the debris crashing around them. The tree began to creak and groan.

His back was pelted with pieces of cinderblock; the flak jacket under his coat protected him until a larger piece fell on top of his leg. Steven couldn't help groaning loudly as it ripped at his thigh. The breath had been knocked out of him, but after thirty seconds, he knew that, somehow, they had survived.

The dust was still thick around them when Steven took his weight off Chelle and choked out, "Are you OK?"

Chelle coughed from the dust, saying, "Yes, I think so. What *was* that?"

"An RPG hit the hotel; it flew right over your head. I'm sure it was meant for me. We have to get out of here; this is going to be chaos, there are people with automatic weapons everywhere."

Chelle was trying to rub the dust out of her eyes so she could see and said, "Ernie's around here somewhere, and Adriana, we have to make sure she's all right."

Steven was holding his handkerchief over his face to block out the worst of the dust.

"Don't talk. First thing's first; we have to get to safety."

The radio hooked to his belt was gone, and Steven felt around him. He couldn't hear Snipes or El Cazador giving instructions to his men, and his hand flew to his ear. The earpiece was also gone.

People had recovered from the shock of the initial blast and were now panicking. There were people running and screaming through the dust trying to find friends and relatives, while others were trying to find their way out of the zocalo. Still others were injured and pleading for help.

"Steven, you're hurt," Chelle said, seeing the blood seep through the leg of his pants.

"Help me up; we have to get out of here."

Chelle struggled to help Steven up. Steven limped and forced himself to keep up with Chelle as she propped his arm over her shoulder.

"The man that kidnapped you; he organized the attack, and once he sees I'm not dead, his entire army of men will be after me. The dust is our cover, but we have to go now."

Steven and Chelle weaved their way through the rubble the tree had protected them from. There was a man struggling to get to his feet. Recognizing him, Steven rushed to help him up.

He seemed OK, just dazed by the blast. He coughed out some dust, looked at his rescuer, grinned and asked, "Is this part of your well-thought-out plan too?"

"Antonio, thank God you got out in time."

"Most of us did, but not all, I'm afraid." Antonio pointed to the clearly dead Francisco Delgada Reyes. El Dragóns would be in need of a new leader.

"I'm sure it was El Ángel; he threatened me last night."

"I think you should take these threats more seriously," Antonio replied, grinning again.

"Come on, let's get out of here," Steven said, and Antonio saw Chelle struggling to help him rise. Antonio threw Steven's other arm around his shoulder, and the three of them limped away as fast as possible.

One of Antonio's men saw him helping the American.

"Señor Ortega, are you OK?"

"Sí, just a little wobbly on my feet. Do you have a car?"

The man hung his automatic rifle across his back and took Chelle's place, saying, "Sí, it is not far."

Buried in a group of people all trying to escape, the four of them made good time away from the pandemonium of the zocalo.

Steven shouted to the sky, "I'm OK, I have Chelle. If you hear me, follow us; I'm with Antonio Ortega, he has a car."

Chelle looked at Steven, perplexed. Antonio caught her eying the sky.

"You did not know your boyfriend talks to the sky?"

Chelle didn't think it funny and gave a quizzical look at Steven.

Antonio's guard said, "I have a jeep parked around the corner."

Steven looked back at Chelle.

"The navy is tracking me with a drone, but it might be too noisy for it to pick my voice out in the crowd. Once they know I've moved from the zocalo, it'll be easier to search me out."

Chelle had a dozen questions in her head and was just about to ask them when bullets zipped over their heads. They darted around the corner of a stone building.

"Boss, my car is over there."

"Juan, give me your gun. You drive," Antonio ordered.

Chelle and Juan dragged Steven towards the car while Antonio covered their backs. Some feeling was coming back into Steven's injured leg, and he did as much as possible to help them get him to the car.

Juan jumped into the driver's seat, and Antonio hustled into the seat next to him. Steven and Chelle scooted into the back. There were sirens from approaching police, and a military vehicle loaded with armed troops came towards them, but nobody was interested in one more car in the hundreds trying to leave the chaos.

"Where should I go, Señor Ortega?"

"Just drive, just drive."

"Antonio, there's a jeep following us," Steven warned.

"We saw two men get in," added Chelle. "I think they were the shooters."

"I saw them too. Juan, go faster."

The car bolted ahead, and Antonio got the rifle ready, Steven pulled out the Glock 35 he had hidden under his jacket.

"You have to get us somewhere the drone can help us," Steven yelled.

"Juan, head for the quarry park."

"La ciudad de las canteras?" Juan asked, a bit perplexed.

"Sí, sí, and hurry." Antonio turned to Chelle and Steven, explaining, "The people are all visiting elsewhere during the Guelaguetza, so the park and the roads to it should be fairly quiet."

Steven dared to stick his head out of the window and screamed at the sky once again, announcing their plan to the sky.

Chelle was desperately looking for something to tie around Steven's wound. She looked down at the ruffled hem of her dress.

"Damn," she said as she ripped it off.

Steven was looking for an opening to fire back at the riders in the jeep as Chelle wrapped the colorful material around his bleeding leg and tied it tight.

Steven fired off a couple of shots. He looked at Chelle and squeezed her hand for just a moment. "Thanks, and sorry for getting you into this mess."

"You *are* El Senador!" Chelle exclaimed.

Steven looked at her with surprise in his eyes. Antonio fired off another round towards the jeep, half-leaning out of the open car door.

****

Back in the Eisenhower Building, Colonel Tripp was frantic.

"What the hell just happened?"

"I'm replaying it now in slow motion," Lieutenant Kastner said, trying hard to contain the emotion in her voice. It took a few more minutes for her to find the right images. "There, sir, I can see a smoke trail of something being launched towards the hotel."

"Shit. What about the satellites?"

Another technician was typing frantically on his keyboard.

"I have the radiation tags, some moving, some not."

"What about the senator?"

"I have him, sir; he's moving out of the zocalo area."

"Coordinate with the drone, I want a visual on him. Find him."

"Yes, sir."

Lieutenant Kastner said, "I can't isolate him yet. There's a tremendous amount of confusion: people screaming and sirens."

"That's why he's moving away from the zocalo. He's going north."

"I have him moving at a high rate of speed, sir."

"You mean like a car?"

"Yes, sir, and it's moving fast."

"Lieutenant, can you follow the car?"

"I believe I can, sir. Trying to isolate audio now."

Soon, everyone in the control room heard a frantic call.

"Colonel, if you hear me, I need you to take out the jeep following us. They have automatic weapons and are firing on us."

Colonel Tripp studied the video of the cars as they moved through traffic.

"I'm picking up gunfire, sir."

"Damn! There's too much traffic."

****

A burst of gunfire shattered the rear window, and Steven fired back. Luckily, the bullets missed the driver and everyone else had taken cover low to the floor, but the rattle of gunfire was deafening in Chelle's ears.

"Take this," Antonio said as he handed an automatic pistol to Chelle.

Chelle brushed pieces of broken glass from her lap and chambered a round.

"On 'three', everyone fire out the back window. One, two, *three!*"

Three heads popped up and peppered the swerving jeep behind them with handgun fire and one assault rifle.

The passenger side of their pursuer's windshield shattered and was stained with red.

Juan was passing other vehicles on the road at a dizzying rate, swerving one way and then the other.

"We have more company," Antonio announced as a huge, open-backed SUV joined the chase.

Chelle took a peek out the back window and saw three men holding on to the roll bar.

She announced, "It's Miguel driving. I'd know that son of a bitch anywhere."

****

Miguel was directing the attack from the Hummer.

Over the radio, he screamed, "I don't care about the rest, but I want El Senador alive. Shoot out their tires, shoot the driver."

"Oh my god! Miguel, a small plane is heading right for us. It's going to crash into us," one of the men screamed to the driver.

Miguel looked up and saw it.

"That's not a plane, it's an American drone."

Miguel knew its deadly force. Four missiles were clearly visible under the over-sixty-foot wingspan.

The driver of the jeep in front of them started to take evasive action, but there was little they could do on the crowded road.

The drone kept coming closer and closer. It was descending right towards them.

"It's going to hit us!" screamed one of the men, hanging onto the back for dear life.

Miguel saw the jeep in front of them take a hard turn to avoid the plummeting drone. He pressed the accelerator to the floor and the Hummer shot straight ahead.

****

Steven saw the drone descending towards them.

"What the hell are they up to?" he wondered aloud.

The rest of the occupants were equally amazed at what they were seeing.

The drone buzzed over their car and kept descending towards the two vehicles chasing them. The sound of its nine-hundred-horsepower turboprop engine was so close it shook them in their seats.

Chelle dared to peek over the back seat and saw the driver of the jeep swerve as the drone approached. She was glad the drone was on their side. The sight and sound of such a monster coming at you would scare anybody.

Juan sped away as the jeep flipped into the air. However, the Hummer ignored the drone, though the men in back threw themselves to the bed of the truck as it buzzed so close they could have touched it. The Hummer sped past the flipped jeep, whose wheels were still spinning. The men in the back were holding onto the chrome roll bar for dear life.

"Juan, we need an empty road so the drone can use its missiles," Steven said.

Juan turned the wheel sharply to the right.

"I think I know just the place. The Road of the Republic. It is wide and winding, and nobody uses it."

Chelle felt herself swing into Steven's lap as Juan took a high-speed turn. Steven and Chelle's eyes locked.

Steven hugged Chelle and said, "We'll get out of this, I promise."

"Never a dull moment with you, is there?" Chelle looked away to reload.

As their car straightened onto a wide avenue, Chelle asked loudly enough for Juan to hear, "Why doesn't anyone use it?"

There was a huge bump, and the car nearly became airborne. Chelle, Steven and Antonio all bounced off their seats and tumbled down into them again.

"It is too rough, señora."

The Hummer was close in pursuit, but Juan had been right; the traffic was greatly reduced, though he was still swerving continuously to avoid the massive potholes.

They hit another big bump and the car jumped off the ground.

"I have been avoiding the worst bumps."

"You mean that wasn't a bad one?" Steven complained as the car came back down to the earth with a threatening creak. He stuck his head out of the window and screamed to the sky once again.

****

The Hummer turned sharply onto the Road of the Republic, flinging free one of the men in the back.

"There!" El Ángel shouted, pointing at the escaping car as he steered with the other hand. "Shoot the driver, shoot the driver," he screamed to the remaining shooter.

The man in back braced his body against the Hummer walls and aimed as best he could.

El Ángel looked towards the sky and saw that the drone was much higher, though pointed towards them again. The man in back of the Hummer had scored direct hits as the back of the car was peppered with high-caliber ammunition.

El Ángel noticed that the road was nearly abandoned except for them. He looked up at the drone and instantly knew why they had been led here. A vapor trail became visible.

At as high a speed as he dared, he twisted and swerved the Hummer down the open roadway, trying to prevent the missile from finding its mark.

****

Steven saw the vapor trail too.

"Don't stop, Juan. Whatever you do, don't stop."

Antonio's eyes were glued to the incoming missile.

The car sped up; the bumps came harder and faster.

Steven looked back at the Hummer desperately taking evasive action and gaining on them.

A second later, the missile struck where they had just been. Steven saw a great explosion of dust and fire. From out of the dust, the Hummer flew towards them.

"They missed; we have to give the drone time to circle back," Steven said.

Chelle watched in amazement as the giant machine banked and climb away.

"You owe me one huge explanation," she shouted over the engine noise.

"It might take some time," Steven replied.

"Save it for later; I'm a bit busy right now."

Chelle took a shot over the back seat to let the men in the Hummer know she hadn't forgotten about them.

The Hummer's occupants had kicked out the spider-cracked windshield. Now, they had clear forward shots and seemed more determined than ever. A man had climbed from the backseat of the

Hummer and swung into the open back. Once again, two gunmen were aiming their guns over the top of the cab.

"On three, we come out shooting again," Antonio said.

"One, two—"

Before he could say 'three', a barrage of bullets pounded the car. Juan was hit and the car veered left and right as he tried to steer with one hand.

Juan was bleeding badly as he turned the car sharply off the Roadway of the Republic. The car was shaking and steam billowed from the engine. The pursuing Hummer hadn't made the turn in time, and Juan took the moment to pull the car over.

"I won't make it, boss," he said, "but the quarry park isn't far. Run and hide in it." Juan opened his door and fell out to the curb. "Good luck," he said as he crawled off the street and propped himself up against a fence.

"We'll be back for you," Antonio said as he slid into the driver's seat.

Steven yelled to the sky once more, "Man down, get an ambulance here, pronto."

Antonio stepped on the gas and, miraculously, the car shot ahead despite its damage.

****

El Ángel pointed down a side road, shouting, "There they are! Try not to hit El Senador; the damn fools want him alive for some reason. But kill that bastard Antonio and the bitch, she has been way too much trouble."

They could see that the car was compromised. It was throwing steam from its radiator and one side was nearly dragging on the ground.

"Get ready," El Ángel warned. "Steady, not yet, wait." The Hummer was gaining on the car every second. He was so focused on the pursuit that he had forgotten about the drone that was again pointing at them.

"Get ready, steady, OK, *now!*"

A barrage of bullets pounded the car from the rear. The trunk lifted up, blocking the back window, then the rear tires exploded from the heavy caliber gunfire. The car skidded to a stop against a tree.

The Hummer was still moving closer when its occupants noticed the huge drone coming for them once again. The men in back jumped to the ground, sure there was going to be a collision.

****

"On three, we exit," Antonio directed again. "One, two, *three!*"

The three of them jumped out of the car and fired towards the oncoming vehicle just as it was screeching to a halt only yards from them.

Steven's eye caught the incoming dive of the drone. Unfortunately, Steven knew that the truck was much too close to them for another missile strike, but the distraction gave them enough time to run toward the park.

"This way, I know this park well," Antonio said.

Coming up to a carved-out section of the quarry wall, Antonio pointed down to the quarry floor some fifty feet below them.

"Señora, you first."

"You've got to be kidding," Chelle said as she stared down the cliff face with disbelief.

A bullet ricocheted off a rock to her left.

Antonio and Steven crouched down behind some large boulders to cover Chelle.

As they fired back, Antonio hollered to Chelle, "Children do it all the time, and they are not being shot at."

Chelle swung both legs over the edge of the quarry wall and onto a smooth, carved seat.

Without thought, Antonio gave Chelle's backside a not-so-gentle push. Steven heard Chelle scream as he watched her disappear over the cliff.

Chapter 34

You're next," Antonio screamed over ricocheting bullets. "I will be right behind you."

Steven didn't see much of a decision to make, and as Antonio provided cover, he jumped up on the polished ridge and pushed himself off.

Steven saw Chelle sliding down the steep, curved rock face. She was nearly to the bottom. Above him, Antonio had jumped onto the same slide and had pushed himself towards Steven.

Antonio was hurtling towards him fast, clutching his rifle against his chest. The slide twisted and turned around the steep rock face. As terrifying as it was, it had been carved and polished into shape by skilled workers to be used by children and was completely safe.

Steven saw Chelle had safely reached the bottom and was taking cover, aiming her pistol up the rock wall to scare off any pursuers. Steven looked up and saw Antonio, apparently unhurt, still speeding towards him.

The end of the slide arrived, but Steven hadn't prepared himself in time and he flew off the end into a pit of sawdust.

Just as he rolled onto his back, Antonio flew off the end and into Steven's arms, nearly knocking the wind out of him.

Face to face, Antonio and Steven first looked at each other and then turned to see Chelle staring at them from behind a rock.

Chelle fired off two shots towards the upper rim and said, "You two want to stop cuddling? We have company."

Antonio and Steven gave each other a grin as they realized how ridiculous they looked. An instant later, they had rolled behind the boulders with Chelle.

Three of the men on the top of the quarry wall were attempting to descend into the park the same way. Antonio aimed his rifle and took out the man on the slide with one shot. The others scrambled back behind cover.

The shooters had taken up a position on the edge of the old quarry and were taking strategic shots at the trio, but the rocks protected them.

Steven scanned the ridge high above them, then said, "If they move opposite us, we'll have no protection. We can't stay here much longer."

"That other section of rocks would give us more protection," replied Chelle, "but it's too far; we'd never make it."

There was another explosion, and they looked up to see a vanishing vapor trail. The Hummer shot up, flipped in the air and crashed down to the ground, beginning a fiery slide down the rough sides of the quarry. A final explosion disintegrated it when it finally hit the rock floor of the man-made canyon. Anybody near the original missile strike had suffered the same fate.

"Run, now!" Steven yelled.

Chelle threw Steven's arm over her shoulder and helped him limp across the quarry floor to the protection of the rocks.

Once all three were safe once again, Antonio looked at the smoldering wreckage of the Hummer and said, "It looks like El Senador has struck again. El Ángel just lost another vehicle to him, and probably his life as well. If you noticed, nobody shot at us when we crossed the park."

Chelle added, "Yeah, I pick up on small clues like that."

Steven had his back against a rock and was breathing heavily. His pants leg was soaked with blood.

Chelle looked at Steven's leg and said, "We need to get you to a hospital."

Steven looked up, replying, "Too dangerous until we know El Ángel is dead."

Antonio scanned the park.

"This is where most, if not all, of the blue stone used to build Oaxaca came from. When the quarry closed, it was nothing but a huge, filthy hole in the earth."

Antonio stood and swung the strap of his rifle over his shoulder.

"Twenty years ago, they cleaned the place up. Now, it is this beautiful park. I have brought my family here many times to fish and listen to music.

"What you see is just a small part of it, this is the northernmost section, and apparently the least visited." Antonio started walking. "It continues for blocks; the next section is more popular, and there are many places to exit. If we can get to the wall at the opposite side, it will be harder for El Ángel's men to follow, assuming they're still after us."

Steven and Chelle started following Antonio. Steven winked at Chelle then looked up at the sky and said loudly, "Thank you, Colonel. Better tell the Mexican authorities what's going on here."

Chelle gripped Steven's arm and stopped him.

"What *is* going on here?"

Antonio looked back at the couple, then he suggested, "We must keep moving. El Ángel does not run out of men so easily."

Steven was walking a bit better, but Chelle still helped to support his bad leg. They tried to step up their pace to keep up with Antonio as Steven explained, "I guess I can tell you now, after all, you're involved."

"No kidding I'm involved! I lost my toe, remember?"

"I've gained a sort of... reputation."

"Yeah, 'El Senador', Ernie mentioned you're sort of an urban myth."

"You know?"

"We put it together, what with all the explosions."

Antonio was enjoying watching 'El Senador' squirm.

"I'm the point man for the president of Mexico and the president of the United States. They have a plan to put an end to the cartels' rule in Mexico."

"I just saw movement on the ridge, take cover," Antonio shouted.

Just as they started to run, bullets started pounding the rocks around them. All three scanned the rim of the canyon.

"We're on the low ground. We have cover for now, but they can circle," Steven appraised.

"I think those far boulders should be our next protection. We must keep working south." Antonio motioned with his head in the direction of the boulders. "Tell me when you are ready."

Steven looked at Chelle. She nodded in agreement.

"Chelle first. On my count of three, give her cover." Steven aimed his gun with one hand and counted down with the digits of the other.

When his third finger locked straight, Antonio and he fired a barrage of bullets as Chelle broke away and ran towards the next set of boulders. As soon as Chelle was safe, Chelle and Antonio did the same for Steven.

Steven ignored the pain in his leg as much as possible as he dashed for the next set of boulders.

They were just about to provide cover for Antonio when bullets from above pelted them. Only, this time, the shots were coming from the opposite rim.

Antonio twisted his rifle around and fired off a short burst in the direction of the new shooters, which gave him, Chelle and Steven a chance to run to an even more protected area.

Breathing heavily, Antonio said, "The quarry stone forms a natural bridge for the road above. The park goes under the roadway and opens up in the next section. There is a fishing pond and an amphitheater built into the quarry on that side. There is a road the musicians and actors take in and out; it offers the best way out, but we need help from your friends in the air."

"Shouldn't be a problem, if I counted right, they still have some missiles."

"How are we doing on ammunition?" Steven asked.

Not needing to look, Chelle said, "Five shots left."

Antonio pulled out a full rifle clip from inside his shirt, swapping it with the nearly empty clip in his rifle.

"When this is gone, I'm done."

Steven checked his clip, saying, "Three shots. The drone is probably still up there somewhere, following us."

Two shots pinged off the rocks surrounding them.

"They have us on two sides now. Every minute we wait, more reinforcements come in," Antonio reminded them.

Steven peered around the boulder and was rewarded with stone shrapnel exploding around him.

"I think El Ángel is alive and well. Wait, listen," Steven said. "I hear an echo. It's the drone. Get ready. Whatever side the drone is on, fire at the opposite wall and run like hell."

Steven was right; the drone descended and there was another explosion followed by screams of pain. Steven braced himself against Chelle as they took off, and Antonio blasted the opposite side.

A natural rock archway supported a boulevard above them. As soon as Chelle and Steven had the protection of that archway, they provided cover for Antonio. All three ran through the arch and emerged through the tunnel about fifty feet later into the next open expanse of the park.

When they turned the corner, it was as if they had just stepped into another world; a much busier world.

Antonio spoke loudly over the music and pointed to the full amphitheater that was reflected in the pond adjacent to it.

"That explains why the rest of the park was empty. Must be some sort of music festival because of Guelaguetza week. There's the service road; it is our best way out."

Cautiously, they moved from the protection of the arch, searching the rim above them for the attackers they knew would come.

"The men above have to cross the boulevard to reach this side. We have a few minutes at best," Antonio advised them.

"Maybe we can disappear into the crowd?" Steven suggested as he tossed his spent pistol into the pond.

Antonio searched the upper roadway and rim for another attack from above.

"Don't look up," Chelle said. "Steven's right; we need to blend in. You said this park goes on for blocks. They don't know we didn't keep running to the next section. Right now, we have an advantage. I think we need to split up. They'll be looking for two men and a woman."

Antonio looked at the rifle in his hand.

"I guess I should get rid of this."

Antonio swung the rifle around his body by the still-hot barrel and tossed it into the pond as well.

Steven did his best not to limp. The slow walk was much more doable than running. They walked on towards the amphitheater and the crowd.

Chelle said, "There's a hotel, Casa del Sueño, down from the zocalo. Meet back there, five o'clock tonight."

"House of Sleep?" Steven asked, perplexed.

"It's out of the way and has an alleyway to hide in."

"I'm not leaving you again," Steven said.

"Splitting up is our best chance."

"She's right, amigo," Antonio said.

Steven took Chelle's hand in his, replying, "I'm not letting you out of my sight. Not ever again."

Antonio was leading the way in front of them when a bullet ripped through his shoulder. He flew back from the force of the impact, slamming into the ground. Chelle and Steven each grabbed an arm and dragged Antonio with them as they found cover. Breathing hard, they pressed their bodies tight against a sidewall of the amphitheater.

Antonio motioned to them that he was able to stand unassisted. The full pain of the trauma hadn't hit him yet.

Because of the loud music, nobody had heard the shot. Instead, the crowd cheered on the band.

"Antonio is bleeding pretty badly; he needs a hospital," Chelle said as she felt her breath catch up to her beating heart.

Steven nodded as he caught his breath and said, "And you have to get him there. You were right. The three of us together are a dead giveaway. Stay with Antonio, escape into the crowd. We meet at five at Casa del Sueño."

Steven limped towards the back of the stage.

"Wait, Steven. What are you going to do?"

"Chelle, never forget, I love you."

"You're not going to give yourself up? You can't; they'll kill you."

"I'm not going to give myself up, but maybe I can draw them away from you. They want El Senador, not you or Antonio. Besides, I still have my protective vest on." Steven lifted his shirt a few inches to show Chelle and added, "After I let them spot me, I'll blend into the crowd."

Chelle handed Steven her gun.

"A couple of shots left at best, use them wisely."

Steven took the gun and stuffed it into the holster in the small of his back, then he said, "Thanks. Now, hurry; get Antonio to a hospital. See you tonight at five."

Steven disappeared out a backstage door. Chelle found an abandoned jacket and tossed it over Antonio's shoulder. Antonio stood as straight as he could, trying to pretend he wasn't hurt.

Chelle looked up the service road leading out of the quarry. Men with guns were running down it.

She scanned the area for another exit then said, "They'll spot us in a second as soon as we reach the road. There has to be another way."

****

Steven came out of the other side of the stage. He walked towards the edge of the crowd, limping badly. He prayed that El Ángel wouldn't risk a long range shot among so many people. That would undoubtedly create a panic, and Steven's guess was that El Ángel wouldn't want that, because it would make it easier for them to escape.

Steven thought of the gun. What had Chelle said about the shots he had left? *Use them wisely.*

He limped back into the crowd as deep as he could get. He took out the gun and fired two shots into the air. That was enough to panic the crowd, and soon the word spread that a shooter was among them.

****

Chelle and Antonio were still looking for an alternate route when all hell broke loose around them. Chelle had heard several gunshots. Undoubtedly that was what was causing the panic.

She worried about Steven but the panic was providing her and Antonio a way out and they needed to take advantage of it. People rushed in all directions including up the service road.

****

El Ángel saw that the narrow, winding service road to the amphitheater stage they were on was being overrun with panicked concertgoers. The only way off the road was a thirty-foot drop into the pond below.

El Ángel turned around and started running back up the hill, shouting, "Turn around, you fools, or we'll be trampled. Watch the crowd for El Senador, he must be caught."

El Ángel found a protected perch near the rim and he scanned the crowd below, looking for a tall American. After some careful searching, he saw Steven. There was no mistake; he could see him limping through the crowd. He pulled out his phone and made a call.

"If you still want El Senador alive, bring your truck to the service road of the quarry park. I have a plan."

****

Chelle and Antonio were buried deep inside the rampaging crowd. With Chelle's help, Antonio was desperately trying not to fall. One slip and they would be crushed to death under a thousand panicked feet.

The two worked their way up the service road and out of the quarry park. They kept their heads down as the swarm of people in which they were embedded rushed out onto the street.

Chelle was supporting more of Antonio's weight; she could feel him getting weaker. A quick glance told her that El Ángel's men were scanning the crowd for them. Chelle knew that Steven was right; she had to get Antonio to a hospital as soon as possible. She prayed that Steven was somewhere amongst the panicked concertgoers.

Chapter 35

"What do we have?"

Colonel Tripp was scanning the bank of computer screens, looking for signs of the senator.

"One target walking away from the quarry, sir. It's Antonio Ortega," Lieutenant Kastner replied. "Still looking for the senator's radiation signature. The walls of the quarry are blocking the satellite."

"That would mean Steven *is* still in the quarry?"

"It would appear so, sir, but I can't confirm it."

"Sergeant, ignore Ortega for now, try and get a visual of the quarry floor. What's going on down there?"

"Looks like a panic of some sort, sir," Lieutenant Kastner said.

"It sure does. And something tells me the senator is right in the middle of it."

****

Steven was being swept away by the panicked crowd. The concertgoers seemed to be rushing in the same direction, and that was up the winding service road. Though he was still in the middle of the viewing area at the top of the road, he saw men with guns who had turned back up the hill to avoid the rushing throng. As he was pushed along with the crowd, he could only hope that Chelle and Antonio had also taken advantage of the situation to escape the park.

Steven was trying to protect his injured leg from the crowd when a teenage girl screamed and fell in front of him. It took all he had to keep from stepping on her. Steven steeled his body against the push of people, none of whom could know they were about to trample the young woman. He grabbed her arm and, luckily, she was light enough that he could pull her up next to him as he continued to brace against the press of the crowd.

The young woman was just back on her feet when Steven couldn't take it any longer. He used his size to hold the woman up as they both now ran with the flow, away from the amphitheater.

Steven's injured leg was working against him, and he knew he couldn't keep up with the rampaging crowd much longer. The teenage girl was also out of breath. The stress of nearly being trampled to death had taken its toll.

His height gave him an advantage over the young woman, in that he could see an open area. Still in the heart of the quarry, he pointed her to it, and they pressed against the crowd until finally finding a sheltered area against a rock outcropping. They rested under it as the crowd slowly thinned out around them.

"Muchas gracias," the young woman panted over and over again.

"You're welcome," Steven reassured her, over and over again as they both eventually started to breathe easier.

"But your leg, señor, it is bleeding."

"It's OK, I have it bandaged."

It took nearly half an hour for the concertgoers to clear out of the manmade valley of stone. Some had decided that the panic was over nothing and were loitering in small groups.

"It's safe now," Steven said. "I suggest you go home and get a good night's sleep."

The young woman gave the big American a hug and thanked him once again before walking off. Paramedics and police were now filling the quarry park to stabilize the situation and help those who might have been injured.

The young woman turned around one more time and waved goodbye to Steven as she started to climb a stairway out of the park. Steven felt a sting. He reached his hand to his neck to swat at whatever had just stung him. He felt something at the spot and withdrew it from his skin, looking at the small dart for a moment before the earth around him span and disappeared.

****

Ernie rolled slowly from his back to his stomach. As disorientated as he was, he pushed himself into a kneeling position and tried to comprehend the surreal vision around him.

Ghosts were running every which way through a misty fog. He saw them falling and picking themselves back up. They were screaming and crying, but the sounds were all muffled because of the ringing in his ears.

He could smell smoke, and he stared at the blood running down his arm. Nothing was making any sense. There was chaos all around him and, though he thought he might be trampled to death, he couldn't move. He could only watch as if he was in the middle of a movie.

Somebody started tugging at his arm, and he slowly turned to see who it was. He didn't recognize him. The man tugged harder, and Ernie found himself on his feet, being pulled away from where he had fallen.

The young man's mouth was moving, but the sounds didn't make any sense. Soon, Ernie saw a tent, and the tent was full of injured people. There was a tree, a beautiful tree. The young man led him to it, and Ernie dropped down as soon as his arm was released. Some force pulled him up against it, and soon its huge trunk protected him.

Ernie felt himself drift off to sleep, then he heard, "Amigo, amigo. You cannot sleep."

A cold towel pressed against his head and helped to wake him.

"You were hit by some debris from the attack. Here, drink some water."

Ernie stared at the young man, his vision slowly returning along with his hearing.

"What happened?" Ernie was surprised his voice came out in a whisper.

"The cartels are battling in the zocalo."

Ernie looked around and realized that soldiers were mixed in with the crowds, pointing their automatic rifles in all directions. He could smell smoke and see large puffs of it floating through the air.

"Señor, you must help me. Where is Adriana? She said she could be found with her aunt and uncle in the zocalo. I must find her. I must know she is OK."

"You're the farmer," Ernie whispered.

"Sí, I am Michael. My father and I give you and your friends a ride. I need to find Adriana."

Ernie reached out and took the bottle of water, holding it to his mouth and drinking a bit more.

"Help me up."

"You are bleeding badly. I must get help for you."

Ernie reached up and felt the huge bump on his forehead. In a daze, he looked at the gash in his arm, which was bleeding badly.

"Where am I bleeding the worst?"

"Your arm, it needs stitches."

Ernie took the wet towel and pressed it against his arm.

"There are people hurt far worse. Just tie this around my arm as tight as you can." The young man complied, then Ernie said, "Help me up. I know where her aunt and uncle's tent was. Hopefully, that's where she is."

Ernie got to his feet with Michael's help. Slowly, he felt himself returning to the world. He had a doozy of a headache, but his strength was coming back. With his good arm draped across Michael's shoulders, they started to walk towards an area still relatively intact and dotted with tents and kiosks.

"It's all different now, but I'm sure it was over this way."

As they got closer, Michael spotted a series of broken wind chimes scattered across the ground in front of a destroyed tent. He lifted Ernie's hand from his shoulder and ran to it.

Ernie caught his balance and struggled to walk towards the debris. The young man desperately clawed at the remnants of the tent. Ernie caught up and did what he could to help. Eventually, they were able to lift it. Aunt, uncle and Adriana were huddled together under a table that had protected them.

"Adriana, Adriana," the young man shouted excitedly.

Adriana lifted herself and ran to him. They hugged as her aunt and uncle cautiously stood up.

Adriana cried into his shoulder, "I was so scared. There was a dreadful sound and then everything came down on us. I thought we were going to die."

Ernie watched as Michael held her tight and said back, "When I heard the explosion, all I could do was think of you. The soldiers tried to stop me, but I had to find you."

Ernie came up from behind and said, "I think that whatever happened is over. I haven't heard any shots for a while now."

Adriana turned her head; her eyes showed surprise as she recognized Ernie.

"Señor Ernie, you are hurt."

"Thanks to your hero, I'm OK; he found me somehow and brought me to safety."

Adriana took an unbroken chair and sat it upright, insisting that Ernie sit. The aunt and uncle took it upon themselves to further clean and wrap Ernie's wounds.

Soon, a soldier came by and, in an insistent tone, said, "You must leave the zocalo. You cannot stay here."

The uncle protested, "We can't leave, all we have is here."

"Leave now, that is an order."

"We can go to my father's truck and take shelter there," said Michael.

Ernie peered around and could see that the soldiers were clearing out the entire area. Men in army fatigues and flak jackets were everywhere.

"Come, let's go," Michael suggested.

The ragtag group gathered whatever they could carry and started to make their way out of the zocalo. Commands were being shouted to the soldiers and to the populace, who were still trying to find their way out of the chaos.

Ernie saw a face he recognized, "El Cazador, El Cazador! Is that you?"

The soldier turned, surprised to hear his name.

"It's me, Ernie, Senator Westcott's brother."

"Sí, Señor Ernie, I remember."

"Steven was here, and the woman we tried to rescue from El Ángel, she was here too. You have to help me find them."

"Sí, your brother was here having a meeting in that building."

"Steven was in there?" Ernie's eyes gazed at the rubble of the hotel.

"Sí, but he got out in time; I saw him leave with the woman you talk of, but he looked injured."

Ernie thought back to the last thing he'd seen before blacking out.

"I remember; Chelle ran towards the hotel. A man jumped the half wall and ran towards her."

"I do not know where they went."

"Where's Filipe? He might know where they are."

"We are afraid for him; he has been missing for a day now."

"Damn. Look, clearly, I'm out of the loop. What happened here?"

"An RPG hit the hotel, all hell broke loose because every cartel thought the others responsible. It was open war between them. We captured many men, and many were injured. Others were killed. There is no doubt that El Ángel was behind the attack. We captured some of his men; they are not talking, but we do know that the attack on the hotel was meant to kill your brother."

"Of course, El Ángel was out to kill El Senador for messing around in his turf. I sure as hell wish somebody would tell me what my brother is up to."

"I do not know; our mission was to protect Señor Westcott, but his purpose was a secret. Not even Filipe knew what it was. It has bothered him greatly, but he is loyal to Mexico."

"So, whatever it is Steven's up to, the Mexican government is supporting it?"

"Sí, and the American government too." El Cazador looked around nervously and said, "I must get back to my team. Give me your number and I will call you when I know more."

Ernie gave a disappointed grin.

"Sorry, no phone."

"Here, take mine. Go back to your hotel and wait."

Sheepishly, Ernie asked, "Do you have any cash? It seems I'm flat broke too."

El Cazador gave Ernie a disgusted look and then took his wallet out of his fatigues and pulled out a fistful of pesos.

"Here, take this, find a room, you need to rest; you look like crap." El Cazador handed Ernie a mini medical pack that he had in a pocket of his combat trousers. "I will call when I have more information on your brother. Maybe I can get some of El Ángel's men to talk."

"Don't take too long. If he's on the run, I have a feeling he doesn't have much time."

"I'm afraid that I agree."

El Cazador disappeared around a couple of corners and started yelling instructions to straggling citizens.

Ernie looked at the handful of pesos in his hand and counted them out. He didn't have much, and his first thought took him back to Casa del Sueño. The rooms were inexpensive but clean, and with all the tourists leaving town, Ernie thought a room might be available. It was certainly worth a try. Maybe the manager and he could make another deal.

****

Chelle wasn't able to flag down a taxi until her and Antonio had walked blocks away from the pandemonium at the quarry. Antonio was barely able to stand by the time one pulled over. When the driver saw that the man was hurt, he assumed it was from the firefight at the zocalo. News of the carnage was all over the radio.

"We need a hospital, very fast."

"Sí, sí!"

The taxi cab driver could see the emergency, so he stepped on the gas and the old car sped away.

Hours later, Antonio was wheeled out of the trauma room and left on the gurney out in the hall, where Chelle was waiting.

Groggily, Antonio said, "Señora, you didn't have to wait. The doctors said I'd be fine. The bullet passed through me, but it did a lot of damage they had to sew back up. They don't want me going anywhere for a while, but I have to get out of here before somebody recognizes me and the police come."

There was a plastic chair pushed back against the wall. Chelle slumped down into it.

"The truth is, I have no money and nowhere else to go."

With great effort and quite a bit of pain, Antonio pulled out his wallet. He handed it to Chelle.

"Take what you need. My men have been called, and they will come for me as soon as it is safe for me to be moved." Chelle looked at the wallet tentatively. "Go ahead, you will owe me nothing. Think of it as payment for saving my life."

Chelle could see that Antonio didn't travel light. His wallet held thousands of pesos. She took out enough to get her through the night.

"It's still a couple of hours until five," she said, looking at her watch, "but I'll go to the meeting place and wait for Steven. Tomorrow, I'll go to the embassy. I'm sure they're swamped with American tourists looking for answers and protection right now."

"Sí, keep a low profile. I believe El Senador was right. El Ángel was after him and not you or me. But, if El Senador is still alive and El Ángel thinks you could be used as bait to trap him, he could still come after you."

"Thank you for your help. Steven is still alive, I know it, and I'll tell him of your kindness."

"I think I will sleep now. Good luck, señora."

Whatever drug they had given Antonio for the pain was working. Chelle buried his wallet under his back and pulled the covers gently over his bandaged chest. She left to find her way to the Casa del Sueño, hoping Steven would already be waiting for her there.

Chapter 36

Colonel Tripp and his team were going over the drone's video footage frame by frame. Finding out what happened to Senator Westcott had been their mission for the last ten hours. After hours in the air, the drone had needed to go back to the aircraft carrier group that was conveniently in war games off the west coast of Mexico.

The drone's mission profile was listed as fourteen hours max, and Colonel Tripp knew it had been in the air for at least thirteen. It must have landed on fumes.

"Go back to just before the explosion at the hotel. I want to know what caused it."

In front of the team was a large, high-definition screen. Lieutenant Carol Kastner and Colonel Tripp studied the slow-motion video as the lieutenant played it in reverse.

"There, sir, it's a vapor trail."

"I agree. Try to trace its source."

The lieutenant ran the video slowly, keeping the vapor trail in sight. She slowed the video down so much that the RPG itself could be seen.

"Back it up more, I want to see the son of a bitch who fired it."

They could see the RPG leave its housing, but the shooter was concealed by leaves.

"Damn, another dead end. Lieutenant, go back to the video of Steven in the quarry, right before we lost him. Maybe we can figure out where he went."

Colonel Tripp rubbed his eyes. They were sore from studying the oversized video monitor.

"He can't have disappeared into thin air. Not only did we lose video, but the satellite lost his radiation signature at the same time. Play it again, he has to be there. I don't believe in coincidences."

Lieutenant Kastner played the video over and over again. She was studying it for the hundredth time when she said to herself, "It's like a magician made him disappear."

Colonel Tripp overheard her as he studied the same footage.

"What did you say?"

"Nothing, sir. Just tired, I guess. It's so frustrating; one minute he's there and the next he's gone, like a magic trick."

"Freeze the screen, Lieutenant."

The frozen image on the video showed the confusion that was going on around the stage. People ran frantically in all directions.

"What *is* magic, Lieutenant?"

"Sir?"

"A magic act, what is it really?"

Lieutenant Carol Kastner thought for a moment.

"Misdirection, mostly. Sleight of hand, quickness. Confusing the eye and mind of the audience."

"Sleight of hand, misdirection; I agree. So, if Steven isn't where he's supposed to be, we should be looking where he isn't supposed to be," Colonel Tripp mused. "Let's go back to his last known position and the last radiation signature."

The video rolled back rapidly.

"Now, forward, frame by frame, but don't look for the senator."

"Sir?"

"Look for anomalies; the magician's other hand, so to speak."

The lieutenant narrated what they had already discerned.

"He disappears under the stage overhang. That's when we lose him, visually, but the satellite says he's still there."

A few more frames went by and the screen was filled with a rush of bodies.

"Steven could be in the crowd but concealed one way or another," Kastner said. After a few more frames, she added, "Here's where the radiation signature is lost."

"Keep going, but slowly, and look for something that changes," Colonel Tripp said as he stepped back, trying to take in the entire giant screen without focusing on a particular spot.

"Paramedics show up to help the injured, but that's understandable under the circumstances." Kastner continued to narrate what she was seeing. "I see an injured concertgoer on a gurney being wheeled away."

"What, where?"

"Upper right, amidst the crowd. There's two paramedics on either side, but see the line between them?"

"Zoom in."

"A sheet is covering the entire body, sir, even the head and face. Looks like a fatality."

Even as she spoke, she kept zooming in and refining the image until only the gurney and the four paramedics surrounding it were visible.

"That's funny, I don't remember any mention of a casualty. There were many minor injuries caused by the panic, but no deaths mentioned."

Colonel Tripp stepped closer to the large screen.

"Can you zoom in further?"

In answer, the gurney became larger on the screen.

"Could be anyone on that gurney, anyone at all," Colonel Tripp said. "Without letting the gurney out of our sight, run the video very slowly. Let's see where it came from."

Achingly slowly, the video went backward.

"There! It disappears under that rock ledge. Keep going back, but don't move from the ledge. OK, now forward, frame by frame."

There were a few frames where it looked like nothing was happening, then they saw it. A man and a woman darting for cover out of the crowd.

"It's him, Colonel."

"Yes, it is. The woman leaves, and the gurney shows up, but that would have been an extremely fast response."

"Almost like they were ready ahead of time," the colonel thought out loud.

"Sir, the radiation signature is lost when he runs under the outcropping—"

Colonel Tripp finished her thought, "And never comes back, and the senator disappears. But the gurney leaves with a body most definitely under the blanket. Where does it go?"

Faster, now, they followed the gurney out of the depths of the quarry. Four paramedics slid it into a waiting ambulance.

"Stop, zoom there." Colonel Tripp pointed to a particular spot and the image became even bigger. A part of a much larger object came into view.

"Since when do paramedics have rifles hidden under their smocks?" Colonel Tripp asked.

The video continued as the ambulance left the area with lights flashing.

Colonel Tripp patted Lieutenant Kastner on the shoulder and said, "Good job. It looks like somebody who knew about the radiation signature *and* the drone kidnapped the senator."

****

Chelle had managed to find a taxi and was now back at Casa del Sueño. She dragged herself into the lobby. Her body felt as if she had been in a prizefight and lost.

After a quick look around, she sadly came to the conclusion that Steven wasn't in the area yet.

She still had time before five o'clock, so she stepped into the lobby and asked, "Señor, do you have a room?"

"Sí," the manager said. "We were booked, but I'm afraid many of our guests decided to leave Oaxaca. It's a shame to see the festival of the virgin ruined by the cartels."

"I will be here for a night. I am tired and would like a room, please."

"Sí, sí, of course, one thousand pesos or fifty dollars American."

Chelle counted out the money and was rewarded with a key.

"Have a pleasant evening," the manager said as Chelle started the climb up the stairs to her third-floor room.

She washed up a bit, but as tired as she was, she couldn't rest. Steven would be looking for her somewhere near the hotel. Chelle went back down to the lobby and spent the rest of the day and most of the night waiting for Steven. She paced the alleys and streets around the hotel, praying that the next new face she saw would be Steven's.

Finally, she had to give in to her need for sleep. Steven hadn't found his way back to her, and she started to assume the worst. Chelle climbed the stairs to her room and washed her dress in the basin, hanging it on a chair to dry. Hunger, exhaustion and mental fatigue had finally caught up to her. She curled up on the bed and cried herself to sleep, convinced she would never see Steven again.

****

The next morning, Chelle awoke hungry and aching from head to toe. The last few days had been anything but an idyllic vacation in Mexico. She picked up what was left of her beautiful new dress. Though freshly washed, the frilled hem was ripped away, and it was bloodstained all over. The zocalo was closed; the festivities had come to a halt. Finding another dress for such a reasonable amount of money would be impossible.

Chelle sighed; at least she was alive and unhurt. Others in the zocalo couldn't claim as much. Chelle put the dress on, reminding herself that the missing hem had been put to good use.

There was only one thing for her to do. She had to go to the consulate and hope somebody there could help her. She had little money left, no real clothes and no identification.

****

Ernie stood in front of the mirror, examining the bump on his head. It was black and blue, but the swelling had gone down. He peeked under the bandage he had put over the slash in his arm. It looked like the wound had sealed itself overnight. It would leave a nasty scar, but the bleeding had stopped.

After a good night's sleep, he felt halfway human again. His stomach was growling for food, and he was glad he had some pesos left for breakfast. Ernie triple-checked the phone El Cazador had given him. There had been no calls and no messages.

Ernie realized he looked a mess, but after the carnage in the zocalo yesterday, many others probably did too. He didn't know what today would bring, so he took his pack and slung it over his shoulder. He was probably never going to see the inside of the House of Sleep again.

At the front desk, he asked the manager if he knew of a restaurant that was still open after the melee of yesterday.

"I had breakfast there myself this morning. It is two blocks away, and it serves fine food."

After getting directions, Ernie said, "Thanks, amigo, and thank you for the room; it was much appreciated."

"Sí, you are welcome."

Ernie left the front desk and walked to the alley.

****

Chelle came down the stairway feeling tired and worn. She saw the manager glance at her torn dress.

"Ah, señora, good morning." The manager gave a pleasant smile.

"Good morning. I need to get to the American consulate. Do you know where it is?"

The manager gave Chelle the directions, and she turned away just as another man walked up to the desk.

She was about to step out the door when she overheard him say, in English, "I'm looking for an American. A man: tall, dark hair, he is staying here. I think he was injured in the zocalo yesterday."

"Sí, he just left."

"Do you know where he went?"

"Sí, he went to get some breakfast."

Chelle's heart started pounding. She ran back.

"You said there was a tall American staying here last night?" she asked, interrupting the conversation. "What was his name?"

The man quizzing the manager turned to Chelle and said, "Agent Saltarie? Chelle Saltarie?"

"Yes," Chelle said, sounding surprised that anyone would know her.

"Thank God you're OK! We have to talk."

The older man gently nudged Chelle's hand and walked her into the alley.

In the privacy of the alley, he said, "Let me introduce myself: I'm Colonel Tripp, an active officer in the marine corps and an ally of Senator Westcott. I watched you escape from Miguel Ortega."

"Steven was here? Oh my god, is he OK?"

The colonel reached out and took her hand.

"It wasn't Steven; his brother Ernie was here."

"Ernie, here?"

"Yes, he stayed here last night. I thought maybe you knew."

"No." Chelle felt weak in the knees and needed a place to sit down. Steven had suddenly been lost to her again just as she thought a miracle had happened.

Colonel Tripp saw a bench and steered them towards it, saying, "Please, sit, and I will explain what I know."

Colonel Tripp held Chelle by the shoulders, trying to comfort her. She didn't know who the man was, but she didn't fight the comfort of a strong arm around her.

Colonel Tripp explained, "The drone you saw, my pilots were flying it from Washington, DC."

"So, you were the one who buzzed the trucks and shot the missile?"

"Yes. Well, my team was. We saw you and Steven get split up at the concert."

"Where is Steven?"

"He fired a gun into the sky, that was enough to panic the crowd and cover your escape."

"What happened to him?"

"We believe he was kidnapped and taken away in an ambulance. The people taking him were definitely not EMTs."

"We need to find Ernie and tell him. Hurry, we have to find him before he's gone for good!"

"Don't worry; I can find Ernie anytime I want. You see, when Ernie used Steven's ID to travel back into the US, he was marked. The ID is laced with a special, low-dose radiation. Anybody who touches it is tagged so we can follow them."

The colonel's cell phone beeped at him.

"My team has him located," he said, looking at the screen. "He's just where the gentleman behind the counter said he would be. Let's go find him. No sense in me repeating my whole story twice. Besides, we'll need his help to try to rescue Steven."

Colonel Tripp helped Chelle to her feet and they started walking towards the beeping dot on his phone.

"So, you can trace Steven too. Have you been tracking him?"

"Unfortunately not. We only saw him being kidnapped. Somebody was on to us and somehow shielded him from our sensors. We haven't seen his radiation signature since.

"However, if they wanted him dead, they could easily have killed him in the quarry and left him there. The elaborate ruse they used to get him out of the quarry leads us to believe he may still be alive, but that hardly means he's safe. As a US senator, he knows many secrets. Maybe he's being held for information or even a ransom."

"In other words, they may well be torturing him right now."

"We can't and shouldn't speculate on anything right now." The colonel looked at his phone and saw they were at their destination. He looked up at the sign above the door. "This is it."

Chelle rushed in and immediately saw Ernie. She ran up to him and called out his name.

Ernie stood and they hugged for just a moment.

Not particularly caring who overheard her, Chelle said, "They have Steven, you have to help us. We have to find him."

Chapter 37

Wake up, amigo."

Steven thought he was dreaming until he felt a slight slap.

"Wake up, amigo."

He heard the voice again and felt another slap. Steven struggled to open his eyes. They didn't want to open; he was far too tired.

"Give him another half-hour."

Steven tried to focus on the words in his dream.

Another slap.

"Amigo, time to wake up."

Steven strained to open his eyes.

"Welcome, amigo."

Fuzzy images started to appear in front of him.

"Filipe?" Steven whispered through parched lips.

"Give him some water. Make our guest more comfortable."

Steven realized that his hands and feet were tied to a chair. Somebody tipped his head back and pressed a water bottle to his lips. He sipped at the water and worked his eyelids, trying to regain focus.

"Filipe?" Steven said again as his eyes focused on the man giving him water.

"Sí, amigo, it is I."

"Thank God! Quick, untie me," Steven choked out.

"Take some more water, my friend."

"Be careful, don't underestimate him," ordered another voice.

"Sí, he is full of surprises."

"Filipe, untie me."

"I am sorry, Senator, he may not do that."

The few bare light bulbs suspended from the ceiling glared in his eyes. He squinted, trying to block out some of the blinding light.

"Who are you? What do you want?" Steven's voice was raspy.

"I'm sure you have many questions, and I will try to answer them all in time. Who am I? I am not important. The organization I represent, on the other hand..."

Steven had a splitting headache, and the bright light bulbs weren't helping.

"Where am I?"

His throat still felt dry, though the water had helped.

"Ah, now *that* is an excellent question. Perhaps you have heard of the ruins of Monte Albán?"

Steven's eyes were slowly adjusting to the light. The man doing the talking was dressed smartly in a tan suit, white shirt, blue tie and a white panama hat with a wide, black band.

Steven whispered back through raspy lips, "Monte?"

"Monte Albán. Ruins just outside of Oaxaca. We're not far from there. We're actually inside another set of ruins not yet discovered. At least, not by archeologists." The man in the white hat pointed with his cane to several pallets with bundled money on them. "The man you call 'El Ángel' found these particular ruins deep in the jungle. He needed someplace to hide his cash; US dollars mostly. Anyway, this place suited his needs perfectly, and now it suits mine."

The few light bulbs strung together lit the cavernous room enough for Steven's adjusting eyes to make out the man's face. He wasn't young. Steven guessed the man to be in his late sixties or early seventies. However, he carried his five and a half feet pretty well and looked fit, though he used a cane.

Filipe was standing opposite the man in the white hat. He was dressed in his army fatigues; they were dirty, and he had his pistol holstered on his hip.

"Give him more water."

Filipe sloppily dumped more water into Steven's mouth from a plastic bottle. Water spilled from his mouth, making his shirt wet.

"Filipe, what the hell is going on?" Steven asked, ignoring the older man and searching Filipe's eyes for an answer.

Filipe twisted the top back on the water bottle and said, "Sorry, amigo; I warned you not to get involved in Mexico's business."

"You're with him?" Steven's asked, shocked.

"For some time now," the man in the white hat said as he stepped in front of one of the glaring bulbs. There was a glow around his hat and face, but Steven finally had a good look at him. "In fact, it was Filipe who interrupted your little meeting with a rocket-propelled grenade."

"You? You tried to kill me?"

"Sorry, amigo, it couldn't be helped. I was told to stop the meeting at all costs."

The older man's cane clicked on the stone floor as he walked closer to Steven.

"At that point in time, you were expendable, but I'll admit I was pleasantly surprised when we learned you were still alive."

"What do you want from me?"

"Now you're getting to the crux of the matter and a proper dilemma for you. But first, you should know that your friends will not find you here. We know about the radiation signature you're tagged with. After you were tranquilized, you were wrapped in a special blanket that absorbed and contained the radiation trail you emit.

"Taking you alive was the plan all along. I mean, if it was in any way possible. We had anticipated staging an accident, so we had a fake ambulance ready, but we didn't know that you would be providing the necessary diversion yourself. At the concert, with so many emergency personnel around, it was fairly simple to put you on a gurney and wheel you out of the quarry."

The man in the white hat pulled out two cigars from his pocket and waved them in front of him.

"I understand you took an interest in this particular brand of cigar. They *are* excellent but, because of your efforts, El Ángel no longer enjoys them. I would offer you one of my last ones, but perhaps I'll save it for another special friend."

The man placed one of the cigars back in his pocket and used a cutter to snip the end off the other. He pulled out a gold lighter and enjoyed the first few puffs in silence.

"You were brought here, deep underground. This room was

actually carved out of a rather large lava tube. Perhaps you've heard of them? They're formed by flowing lava and often go for miles under a volcanic eruption.

"I'm no archeologist, but my guess is it was the Zapotec that discovered the lava tube which led them deep into the mountain. Here, they found a rather rich layer of obsidian, and then they carved these chambers. As you can see, the sides of the walls are magical; all colorful, volcanic glass. You can imagine the effect it would have when the high priest would bring mere mortals into their lair, deep in the mountain, and the glass walls reflected the light of a hundred torches.

"At any rate, your radiation signature is undetectable here. We also took the liberty of cleaning up and bandaging your leg wound. It took a few stitches. In time, I'm sure your leg will heal up just fine. We used a local anesthetic to ease your discomfort."

"How long have I been out?"

"It is mid-morning. Of course, inside these old ruins, it would be impossible to tell one day from another; I could easily be lying."

Steven scanned the room he was in and deduced that the cave-like conditions were clearly manmade. The explanation of obsidian-lined walls and ceiling made some sense of the strange, blue glow. The light seemed to be coming from within the walls and ceiling. Even with an explanation, the cavern seemed mystical, though there certainly was an old, musty smell to the place.

The man lifted his left hand, and that was when Steven noticed the eagle grip on his cane. He took off his white hat and brushed back his thinning white hair with the other.

"It's warm in here despite the rock surrounding us," he said, replacing the hat. "The jungle heat and humidity penetrate everything."

He took out a white handkerchief from his back pocket, lifting silver-rimmed glasses and cleaning the round lenses. There was an open case of plastic water bottles against a far wall, and he walked over and opened one.

After a long swig, he said, "There would be no point in lying to you, because soon you will know exactly what time it is." He pointed to the small television. "Through the miracle of technology, we can pick up a satellite television feed from anywhere in the world. We can display that feed anywhere we want, including inside thousand-year-old ruins."

Some of the cobwebs were clearing out of Steven's mind, but the headache was another matter.

"What do you want from me? You didn't drag me here so I could watch TV with you. Who are you, and why am I here?"

"I think the question you meant to ask is, why didn't we just kill you? And the answer to that is we want you to work for us. You see, I represent the International Resolution for the Establishment of Nations' Equality."

Steven looked towards Filipe, who remained emotionless. Steven thought about the name and mentally repeated it several times, hoping it would ring a bell. Possibly, it was an organization he had run across as a senator. He thought about the initials when, suddenly, it came to him.

"You're IRENE!"

Chapter 38

The man in the white hat chuckled and swung his cane in a small arc.

"As far as you're concerned, yes. At least, I *represent* IRENE."

"Water," Steven choked out. He had a terrible thirst and needed some time to think. Steven thought about the word 'IRENE' and tried to remember his discussion with El Ángel.

"Water," he asked again. His mind seemed sluggish, but he forced himself to focus.

The man in the white hat nodded, and Filipe tipped the water bottle up to Steven's mouth again. Steven let the water wash and cool his throat, using the time to try and make sense of the situation. He needed more information, and so far, his captor didn't seem to mind providing it.

"Why did you try to kill me if you want me to work for you?"

"As I said, you were expendable and, I might add, still are. But we weren't so much trying to kill you as trying to stop you from dismantling the cartels."

"Let me guess. IRENE makes its money off the cartels?"

"You must think a bit more globally to understand us. You have to appreciate the fact that a lot of countries depend on the illegal drug trade to power their economies."

The man in the white hat talked to Steven as if they were in a parlor having a friendly drink together.

He continued, "To put it in perspective, think about the United States and its nearly twenty-five percent of the world's GDP. Compare that to, say, Columbia's point four. That's right; not even one percent. There are only ten countries above two percent. Ten! The money from the drug trade is critical to millions of people who merely want to survive. This isn't about being able to afford dinner at a better restaurant or the latest designer jacket; they just want to have enough money to eat, to live another day.

"In fact, the cocaine trade accounts for about twenty percent of Columbia's total exports. And you, Senator, want to take that from them. No, I'm afraid they can't let you do that. And, as their agent, we were asked to stop you."

Steven looked up at the man, ignoring the bright bulbs that reflected off the blue glass of the walls.

"You work for Columbia *and* the Woods Trust?" he asked incredulously.

"The Woods Trust? That's how we began, of course, and the source of some of our funding, but no. We represent a higher ideal, and that means our bedfellows aren't who you might expect.

"However, Columbia, Nicaragua, Guatemala, Costa Rica, good lord, thirty percent of Afghanistan's economy is selling drugs! If you stop the smuggling routes through Mexico, it would mean devastation for these economies. People, entire families, would literally starve to death.

"We cannot allow that. For the sake of world peace, and to maintain the small amount of stability there still is, I'm afraid the United States must experience some suffering."

"*Some* suffering? It's an epidemic killing our citizens; our children!"

"You are right, of course, and in due time, it will be stopped. But not right now."

"Because doing so would hurt others or because it would hurt your bottom line? Let me guess, you also believe that human trafficking is important to these same economies?"

"It is, actually – and yes, I can't deny the revenue is useful – but you're still thinking too small. We have many friends in many different circumstances. We help them, they help us, that sort of thing."

"Yeah, I'll bet stopping me will win you all kinds of favors."

"You have no idea. Disrupting the distribution system would topple nations and take a generation to set right. I doubt that you can imagine what Columbia, Nicaragua, Afghanistan and others will give to prevent it."

"So, stopping me will get some dictators in your pocket?"

"Some *more* dictators, Steven, and exactly the ones we need. We've been quietly building influence around the world for the last seventy years, and now we're at a pivotal moment in history. Soon, we'll have enough control to make a crucial difference in world affairs. That's why you're still alive."

Steven watched as the man in the white hat paced back and forth as he talked. He tested his bindings a bit, but they held fast; his arms and legs were immobile. He took note that Filipe, who had been watching him intently, readied his hand over his holstered sidearm and relaxed it only when convinced that his prisoner was still securely bound.

"You want me to be your inside man in the senate?"

"Goodness, no! We already have several. Though, I must admit, in the past, our plan for you was significantly less ambitious. It was to convince you through any means necessary that representing our interests in the senate was also in your interests. But that's in the past."

Steven closed his eyes; his focus was coming back. It took a moment for the implications of the last revelation to sink in. When they did, a rage inside him exploded.

"You're the ones who tried to frame me for murder! You're the ones who killed Destinee!"

Steven's body tensed and his eyes screamed hatred. Filipe sensed danger, and his hand went automatically back to his holster.

The man in the white hat was far less concerned with Steven's outburst and puffed on his cigar. After a moment, he lifted a chair and set it down facing Steven. He slowly lowered his body down onto it, making himself comfortable and straightening the crease in his slacks before continuing.

"We *did* frame you for murder. But you took a... let us say 'unique' route to proving your innocence."

Steven screamed, *"You killed my daughter!"*

"Not me, of course, but the girl's death was necessary to create the confusion we needed at the time."

"'The girl' was my daughter. Her name was 'Destinee'."

"I do apologize. At the time, we didn't know she was your daughter."

"You bastards." Steven strained against his bindings, hoping his anger would give him the strength he needed.

"I know, you are angry at us, and I don't blame you. However, that doesn't change the situation."

"You're crazy if you think I'll work for you. Support the drug trade to help my daughter's murderers? It's perverse."

"I assure you that I am not crazy. You have another daughter; do you want her death on your hands too?"

"Destinee's death wasn't my fault, it was yours, and you lay a hand on my other daughter, the president will know who did it, and he *will* retaliate."

"Against the Woods Trust; against IRENE? Not likely. Perhaps he will blame the cartels, but which? Who would he retaliate against? Why would he do so? In the delicate game of nations, do you truly believe your president will risk anything to avenge a lackey who did his work in secret? Which of us sounds crazy now?"

"You," Steven said between clenched teeth. "But psychopaths usually do."

The man in the white hat stood and calmly paced back and forth again, his cane clicking rhythmically on the stone floor.

Steven knew his situation was almost hopeless, but his rage was real, and it wouldn't let go. He no longer cared for his life if he could somehow also take the life of the man in the white hat.

"As far as I'm concerned," he spat, "you're no better than the rest of the scumbag cartel leaders I was sent to kill."

"Let me remind you that you were more than willing to work with those same people."

"Only if they helped me turn them into legal entities working for the good of Mexico."

"So, it is morally acceptable when, in your words, the 'scumbag cartel leaders' help you accomplish your goals, but we are reprehensible for working with them to accomplish ours? Sounds a bit hypocritical."

"We're not psychopaths."

The man in the white hat laughed.

"All a matter of perspective, I would say. You blow up boats and mountains to improve your economy, we engage in persuasion to prevent the next world war. Can you imagine the amount of carnage and economic damage another world war would create? Yes, we're both trying to save lives, but I'd say our goal supersedes yours."

Angrily, Steven asked, "How are you stopping a world war by poisoning tens of thousands with narcotics and condemning young girls to lives of prostitution?"

"The system is broken; there is hunger and discontent around the world. What you mention is certainly a problem, but it is only a small part of the overall equation. The United States, the richest country on the planet, is paralyzed by its democracy. We want you to help us fix it, to fix things across the world. IRENE believes that action, not words, is what the world needs right now, and we are prepared to deliver it with or without your help."

Steven watched the man pace. He walked with a slight limp; the cane wasn't just for effect. The more the man talked, the more Steven was sure he had a European accent, possibly Spanish.

"As a senator," the man continued, "don't you ever get tired of talk, talk, talk, but never any action? I'm sure you understand what I'm referring to. First, a committee is created, then weeks – sometimes months – spent on who will be in the committee. Then, there are discussions and even more discussions. And then, regardless of what needs to be done, politics come into play. Even good ideas, great ideas, can become politically unacceptable.

"So, even when there is an agreement that something has to be done, agreeing on a single course of action is impossible. The other party is the opposition party even when an idea is good. In fact, especially if it is good. God forbid that anyone help the other side accomplish something for the good of all."

Steven was slowly controlling his rage; some of his training was helping him. Anger could be his enemy as well as an ally. The key was not letting it control you.

He argued back, "Yes, the system isn't perfect and can be frustrating at times. But, eventually, it works. We've been doing it for over two hundred years."

The man in the white hat pointed at Steven with his cane.

"Two hundred years? That's a sliver of time. Look around you! The Zapotec people founded the great city of Monte Albán maybe as long ago as five hundred years before Christ. It lasted for a thousand years as a center of civilization. Imagine that: a thousand years, maybe much more.

"Do you honestly think the United States can survive for even another hundred years under the current way of doing things? Why, in just the last ten years, you have doubled your national debt. Just how long do you think that can continue?"

Steven was tired of the lecture, so he demanded an answer.

"What does IRENE want me to do for them? I'm in no position, even as a senator, to change things in the way you describe."

"Ahh, but you are. You are, in fact, in an extraordinary position to do something about it."

Steven looked up at the man in the white hat. He had no idea what the man could possibly be suggesting, and his face must have shown as much.

"Filipe, please give our friend some more water."

The man in the white hat contemplated how to explain their idea to Steven as Steven accepted the water from Filipe and drank a few good mouthfuls, even though he was more tempted to spit it into his betrayer's face.

"Let me explain. Imagine what you could accomplish if you didn't have to spend half your time trying to get re-elected and the other half trying to convince uncooperative colleagues that difficult choices need to be made.

"What if you could rule the United States with an iron fist for the next eight years, or even longer? The world is in a state of imbalance; our goal is to help it regain that balance, and you are just the man to help us do that."

"You have more ambition than sanity."

"The Woods Trust and IRENE have been around for over seventy years. Our membership has grown exponentially. Many, very many, are now in influential positions around the globe in business and governments.

"With my help, with IRENE's help, you could be their leader. You could become the president of the United States, and we can give you a supermajority control of the house and senate."

"I couldn't win against President Walker, you maniac, and neither could anyone else! He's an easy two-term president."

"That is true; we have cultivated his popularity since before he was elected. We knew, if we got him elected, we would have control of the presidency for a minimum of eight years. You see, we spent nearly half a billion dollars to get him elected."

Steven was left speechless. The man in the white hat took another long puff on his cigar to let the words sink in.

Steven thought it through for a minute.

"No, that's not true. If he's working for you, why did he recruit me to stop the cartels, something you obviously don't want to happen?"

"Let's just say we thought it a good investment at the time. He has turned out to be a disappointment, and that is why he needs to be neutralized."

"Neutralized? You mean assassinated?"

"We paid for loyalty and we expect to get it."

The man in the white hat sat down again. He leaned forward a bit, staring Steven in the eye.

"Senator, we believe you are a pragmatic man. You would have to be to have accomplished so much in Special Forces. You became a successful businessman, and after that, on to the senate. Fortunately for you, you are worth more to us alive than dead. We have a proposition for you. A proposition, in fact, not much different than what you offered the cartel leaders. Join us or die."

Steven looked up at Filipe, hoping that the threat would spur him to action.

Instead, Filipe gave the slightest nod and said, "You would be wise to listen to him, amigo."

The man in white tapped the floor twice with his cane.

"Yes, please do listen. Soon, President Walker will be dead, and we want you to take his place as the next president. That is why we want you to witness President Walker's death on this television. It will be an important lesson, and maybe after you become one of the few people in the world that knows precisely who killed President Walker, you will take us seriously.

"You must ask yourself: if we can kill a sitting president, what chance would you have if you double-cross us? What chance would your daughter have, or your brother, or that pretty girlfriend of yours? What's her name? Oh, yes, 'Chelle'.

"We will show you, now, that there is no escape. After that, you have a lot of work to do. Reason hasn't won you around, so you'll have to persuade me to take any claims of loyalty seriously. For your daughter's sake, you'd better do a good job. Let me warn you, Senator; as President Walker will briefly realize, IRENE punishes betrayal with death."

"Why me?"

"You're already popular. Ironically, that's mostly because of the way you foiled our first attempt to enlist you. So, you see, after the death of President Walker, you will be uniquely situated to become the next president of the United States. We can make that happen; it's what we want."

"I won't do it. Kill me if you will, but I will have no part of your conspiracy."

"Not your decision, I'm afraid. President Walker will die, must die, either way." The man in the white hat gave a nod to Filipe, who turned on the small television. "Within twenty-four hours, you will see the news of the death of President Walker. Like it or not, only you and the members of IRENE will understand it for what it is. That shared understanding can be the beginning of a fruitful relationship, or it can be our parting gift before your death. When I return here, it will be your choice.

"Think about our offer. You want to save a meager fifty thousand people a year from drug overdoses in the United States; IRENE wants to save millions of people a year from war and starvation.

"The world needs stability. Certainly, you understand that? You can be the man to bring peace to the planet. Think of it. As the leader of the free world, with congress willing to do our bidding, and with the wealth of the United States focused on better things, we can make the rest of the world fall in line.

"I truly believe that, or I wouldn't be here. I understand how difficult it must be for you to comprehend the significance of what I am saying. IRENE has leaders in other countries ready to follow, and you can be the man to lead them all. Think of the possibilities. Isn't it exciting?"

"You know, Hitler, Lenin and Stalin all thought they were the saviors of the world too. That didn't work out so well for them *or* for the world."

"I'm not here to debate this; the redirection of the world is already in motion. Nobody can stop it now, but you have a chance to not only save your daughter and friends but, by following our plan, you can save the world and be part of the new revolution."

The man in the white hat nodded at Filipe and headed for the doorway.

"Oh, and Senator?" he said. "I don't want you to worry about your daughter. I have men watching over her this very moment. Apparently, she is a good basketball player, they are enjoying watching her play. Her team was winning the last I heard. It would be a shame if anything happened to her just because her father is a stubborn man. As your friend has said, you would be wise not to underestimate us."

The man in the white hat left the stone vault, the echo of his cane clicking off the floor fading away. For the moment, Steven and Filipe were alone, and Steven didn't waste any time in making his argument to Filipe.

"Filipe, listen. He's mad. He's a certifiable nutcase. Besides, do you think he's going to let you live? You heard their plan to kill the president. That makes you a liability. They don't sound like an organization that leaves loose ends loose."

"Amigo, what makes you think I was given any more of a choice than you? Accept their offer. It is the only way. I do not want to kill you, but make no mistake: to save my family, I will."

"Filipe, untie me. I can get us both out of this."

"I wish that was true, amigo."

"You know I can! You've seen what I can do."

"Yes, but I warned you not to believe your own myth. I know your tricks and that you are as helpless right now as I am,"

Filipe used his radio and ordered two more soldiers into the room.

Once they had taken the positions Filipe instructed, he said, "Do not talk to him, and if he moves off that chair, or tips it, or makes any kind of aggressive move, shoot to kill. I will ask no questions." Filipe pointed to the case of plastic water bottles. "He gets water every hour, nothing else."

As Filipe left the room, he warned, "There are more guards protecting the only passage out." He gave the two guards a stern look. "They have orders to kill *anyone* leaving the ruins."

Steven watched Filipe disappear down a dark hallway. The strain of trying to understand what had been said, combined with his headache and the lasting effects of the tranquilizer, was soon too much for Steven. He was straining to keep his eyes open, but the steady glare of the bare bulbs caused him to lose that battle. His eyes closed.

Chapter 39

Ernie, Chelle and Colonel Tripp huddled at a corner table. They were all famished and ordered breakfast while they tried to come up with a plan.

Ernie asked, "How did you find me?"

Chelle was about to answer, but Colonel Tripp beat her to it.

"The manager at the hotel told us you came here."

Chelle knew that there was more to the story, but apparently Colonel Tripp was playing that information close to his chest.

"You look like hell," Colonel Tripp said.

"I know that; I got banged up pretty good. I had a goose egg on my head, but it's gone down a bit. My arm was hurt pretty bad, I took care of it the best I could last night with a med kit El Cazador gave me. It'll heal up.

"By the way, Chelle, Adriana is fine. That young farmer came looking for her, helped to pull her and her family from the rubble, they're all ok. And that was after he pulled me to safety. Quite a young man, I would say."

"What else do you know about the situation at the zocalo yesterday?" Colonel Tripp asked.

In a low tone, Ernie volunteered, "When I saw El Cazador, he told me they didn't know where their leader Filipe was, so he may have been taken too. He's been MIA for at least twenty-four hours."

"Who's El Cazador?" Chelle asked.

Ernie was a little surprised when Colonel Tripp answered, "He's on the FES team that was protecting Steven. His real name is 'Marco Belmonte'. He's one of the team's snipers, so they nicknamed him 'the Hunter'. He's also second-in-command under Filipe, who was Steven's main contact in Mexico. Now, did he say anything else?"

"He said it was an RPG that hit the hotel. All hell broke loose after, because each cartel leader thought that they were the target of an attack by the others."

"I can confirm it was an RPG, but we didn't have a view of the shooter."

Chelle filled in more of the story.

"Steven told me it was meant for him; he was sure Miguel Vega was behind it. Antonio Ortega helped us escape. Steven was injured, but I don't know how badly. I never had time to look. All I know is his leg was bleeding pretty badly when I wrapped it." Chelle looked at Colonel Tripp and asked, "What do we do now?"

The colonel looked at her apologetically and said, "I'm afraid that, until we know where Steven is being held, there isn't much we can do. Officially, I'm not even here."

Ernie stood and wiped his face with the cloth napkin, saying, "Maybe there's nothing you can do, but I have a few ideas. Give me your number, Colonel; I'll call as soon as I know anything at all."

"But you don't have a phone," Chelle reminded him.

Ernie pulled out his phone and said, "Courtesy of El Cazador. In the meantime, why don't you two hole up at Casa del Sueño? At least I'll know where you are if my idea fizzles."

Chelle suggested, "Let us help."

"Sorry, not an option. If you don't hear from me by tomorrow night, that means the Westcott brothers are probably both dead."

The two men traded numbers.

Chelle, who was still seated, whispered to Ernie, "What are you going to do?"

"Whatever I have to."

"Please, let me come with you."

"You disapproved of me stealing some breakfast. This is going to be a bit worse than that."

Ernie didn't wait for an argument; ten seconds later, he was out the door.

Colonel Tripp watched Ernie disappear through the café window, asking, "What do you know about him?"

Chelle thought about the question for a moment. "Actually, very little. About the only thing I do know is he loves Steven."

"But can he be trusted?"

"He did save me and Adriana. Right now, I'll give him the benefit of the doubt."

"Well, at least we can track him. Something I didn't think he needed to know."

"I think you're a wise man, Colonel."

Colonel Tripp laid some pesos on the table to cover breakfast, saying, "The FES are trying to locate Steven and will call me as soon as they know anything, but I'm afraid that, because of the bombing in the zocalo yesterday, they're stretched pretty thin. And, I might add, their president is no longer so sure that their plan to organize the cartels was such a good idea. Ernie might be our best bet right now."

"Colonel, I need to make some calls to the States, can you help me with that?"

"You bet I can, and let's get you some decent clothes. You look like you've been dragged through hell."

"Trust me, Colonel, I have."

****

A military troop convoy was headed north on highway 1350. It was about thirty miles north of Oaxaca when one of the trucks pulled off onto a side road. It drove about a half-mile on a dirt road until it was fully secluded. El Cazador ordered the men with him to park the truck and start a hike towards the main road.

Ernie Westcott emerged from the side of the road after all of the military personnel were gone. He opened the back tailgate of the canvas-covered vehicle and climbed in.

"I understand that some of you worked for El Ángel," he said in Spanish.

The men in the back of the truck looked up at him. They were all bound hand and foot.

"Let's talk!"

Ernie grabbed the man closest to him and dragged him out of the truck. The man landed on the ground hard, dropping from the back of the truck with a groan.

Loudly, Ernie asked, "Do you know where El Ángel would take a special prisoner?"

"Please, señor, I do not know."

A gunshot rang out.

Ernie climbed back into the truck and said, "I didn't get the answer I was looking for. It seems I need to ask again."

Ernie grabbed another of the prisoners and roughly pulled him out of the truck and out of sight of the other prisoners.

Again, he asked loudly, "Where would El Ángel hold a special prisoner?"

"Please, señor, do not shoot me. I work for El Ángel, but I do not know of such a place. I would tell you if I did. Please, please, I beg of you!"

Inside the truck, another gunshot was heard.

"I sure hope one of you talks soon; I'm getting a bit warm jumping in and out of this truck."

Another man was dragged out of the truck.

Ernie asked in a loud voice. "Do you work for El Ángel?"

"Sí, sí, but I work for him only so my family can eat. He pays me more than I can earn in a year farming. Please do not shoot me, amigo."

"You seem like a reasonable fellow. You see, I have a family too. My brother and a friend are missing, so you understand that I am very determined. What I'm wondering is, if El Ángel wanted to take somebody someplace nobody else would find them, where would he choose?"

"Amigo, I am new. I have just worked for him for a month. I don't know such things."

Another gunshot was heard. A minute later, Ernie climbed into the truck and grabbed the next prisoner in line. The man grunted loudly as he hit the ground.

"Look, amigo, I hope I'm not wasting my time. It's so fucking hot out here, and I just want to go home. But, you see, I can't do that until I'm sure that none of you know where my brother is. So, let me ask again: if El Ángel wanted to take somebody someplace nobody else would find them, where exactly would he take them?"

"I might know! Please don't shoot me."

Ernie chambered a bullet, saying, "I'm listening."

"I helped El Ángel hide some money in a cave. It was in the jungle near Oaxaca. There was a jungle path that was hard to follow. It was secluded, but I think I could find it again."

"You know, I might just believe you. You get to live for another five minutes."

Ernie climbed back into the truck, he looked at the remaining five prisoners, lit a cigarette and asked, "OK, I only need one other volunteer; somebody who knows where El Ángel's secret hiding place is. The rest of you, well, I guess you got shot escaping. So, who will it be?"

"Three of the men shouted, 'I know!'"

"OK, I'm going to ask all of you for the directions. If any of you don't tell me the same thing, well, I'm going to have to assume you're lying to me."

Ernie dragged them out of the truck one at a time. After three men had been pulled out, a single shot was heard.

Ernie came back into the truck for the remaining two prisoners, dragging them into a shaded area alongside the road. He pulled the men right up against the rest of the prisoners he had interrogated. Each was lying in the dirt with their hands and feet still bound and duct tape over their mouths.

"Don't move; the military will be back to get you, but there's a sniper who has his gun aimed right at you. You move, you'll be shot for real. He doesn't miss." Ernie took a bottle of water, set it on top of a rock and said, "Just to prove my point."

He stepped off to the side and pointed his finger at the bottle. In an instant, it disintegrated. A moment later, the sound of the shot echoed in the distance.

Before getting into his jeep, he called El Cazador on the radio.

"Great shot. I think I got what I need. Three of them independently gave me the same directions to a spot they claim El Ángel uses to hide his money." Ernie repeated the location to El Cazador, adding, "I'm hoping your man Filipe is being held there with Steven. I should know for sure within two hours. I'd appreciate it if you could keep the prisoners here until I can confirm it. I might need to have another talk with them if I come up empty handed."

"Sí, but hurry. I can only keep my men away for so long."

"I understand. Do the best you can. If you don't hear from me in two and a half hours, take them to Mexico City for trial."

Ernie sped down the dirt road back to the main highway towards Oaxaca. The instant he had cell coverage, he called Colonel Tripp.

"Colonel, I might have a lead on where Steven is. Meet me outside of town. There's a dirt road north of the city off of highway thirteen-fifty. Go exactly five miles from the last gas station out of town. I'll meet you there. And Colonel, bring Chelle. We'll need all the firepower we can get. Steven's FES partners are being recalled to Mexico City and can't help us. Colonel, I have supplies."

****

Chelle and Colonel Tripp were having a late lunch at a small, outdoor café. The colonel had spent the morning with Chelle, making sure she got the clothing and shoes she needed.

Chelle had opted for a more practical outfit of summer-weight, light-brown slacks and a darker-brown button-down top. Her shoes were white, heavy-canvas type sneakers. All were courtesy of the colonel's charge card.

They were walking out the store when Colonel Tripp's phone chirped. The colonel spoke softly into the phone as he walked from the crowded street to an unoccupied and shaded street bench.

After his conversation, he clicked on an app on his phone and studied it for a while.

As Chelle approached, he said, "That was Ernie; he thinks he has a lead."

"Did he say how he got it?"

"No, and I wasn't about to ask."

"According to the tracking device, Ernie is coming down from the north. He gave me directions to where he wants us to meet him. It appears that we're Steven's best chance of rescue. The FES detail have been called back to Mexico City."

"What about weapons?"

"Ernie insinuated that he had what we needed."

Chelle asked, "Any reason for us to doubt him?"

"Not that I know of."

"Then let's go. I have a debt to repay El Ángel"

****

Chelle and Colonel Tripp had pulled their car off the road and followed Ernie's jeep into the concealed area. Ernie got out of his jeep and quietly closed the door, carefully listening to the sounds of the jungle before eventually motioning for them to quietly leave their car.

Once they were closer, he whispered, "Colonel, I'm sorry, but your rank means nothing out here. This is the way it has to go: this is my territory and I call the shots.

"Same with you, Chelle. If this is where they're holding Steven, we'll only have one chance to save him. I know how these guys think; they're quasi-military but not as disciplined. We can use that to our advantage."

Colonel Tripp nodded his consent and, with an eye on his response, Chelle also agreed.

Ernie handed out rifles and equipment satchels from the back of his jeep, explaining, "So far, what I see checks out with the directions I was given. Doesn't mean much, but it's a start. The vehicles should be off the road far enough. Colonel, you and Chelle cut some brush and try to cover the tracks better.

"I'm going to scout ahead, so wait here. The radios are for absolute emergencies only. Turn them off; one crackle of static at the wrong time and we fail. If you hear shots, get back to the cars and get the hell out of here, because shots mean I was discovered. If that happens, my best chance will be to disappear into the jungle, and that will be way easier if I don't have to worry about you. Either way, if I'm not back in thirty minutes, leave."

Colonel Tripp stepped closer to Ernie and said, "I'm afraid that I haven't been completely honest with you. I can help. I didn't know if I could trust you or not. Now, I believe I can." He pulled out a tablet computer. "I can get you all the surveillance you want, with no risk."

He turned on the tablet and a bird's eye view of the three of them appeared on the screen.

"You have a satellite tracking us?"

"Better: a drone. Specifically, a Reaper."

Ernie looked up at Chelle in amazement and said with a smile, "Our chances just improved, a lot, but I doubt they'll be able to spot the path from the air; the jungle growth is just too thick."

"Colonel," Chelle said, "can that thing pick up heat signatures?"

"You mean of people moving through the jungle? Yes, but I'm not sure if that will be enough. The canopy is so thick, it may mask body heat."

"Tell them to try," Ernie suggested, "because if the information I got is accurate, El Ángel hides his cash in an old cave near here. He takes great pains to keep it hidden and to protect it. If he's hiding a person of importance, they might be there. We can expect the way there to be booby-trapped and guarded. Here, put these leather gloves on.

"Our first clue that we're on to something would be other heat signatures. Tell the people flying that thing to warn us the moment they see anybody besides us."

Colonel Tripp whispered instructions into his satellite phone, then looked up and said, "They're using as wide a field of view as possible; so far they only see us, but they'll chirp my sat phone at the first sign of other heat signatures."

Chelle said, "In other words, they may or may not be able to warn us."

The colonel clipped his phone onto his belt, replying, "Pretty much." He gave Chelle a wink and said, "But that doesn't mean they can't track us at all."

He looked at Ernie, saying, "Do you have Steven's ID? The one El Ángel gave you?"

"As a matter of fact, I do," Ernie replied. "How do you know about it?"

"It's actually a tracking device. May I see it, please?"

"Son of a bitch," Ernie said as he pulled out the ID. "You've been tracking me?"

"Not actively, you weren't a priority, but yes, in theory."

The colonel took the ID from Ernie and handed it to Chelle, saying, "It's perfectly safe but, if we do get split up, my team will be able to track us. I want you to hold it for a minute, and then I'll do the same. It will tag us both with a radiation signature, and my team will register us on the tracking system."

"Didn't think that little tidbit of information was important for me to know until now?" Ernie asked once the colonel passed back the ID.

"Sorry," the colonel replied, smirking, "need-to-know basis."

Chelle asked Ernie, "Do you think you can find the path? I don't see anything but jungle."

"I found you and Adriana, didn't I? It's about fifty feet in that direction." Ernie pointed. "Step where I step, single file only."

Ernie led the way, followed by Chelle and Colonel Tripp. Ernie took measured and cautious steps. They all had guns slung over their backs, and each was wearing a backpack full of supplies. The leather gloves helped them keep the lion's share of the thorny bushes out of their faces.

Ernie whispered, "Sorry about the thicket, but we can't use the machete. I don't want to make life easy for anyone following us."

The giant leaves surrounding them trapped the midday humidity. The heat of the jungle was stifling, even though the thick foliage protected them from the beating sun. Birds squawked overhead, and Ernie took that as a sign that they were doing a fair job of being quiet. No one talked as they cautiously marched on, each acutely aware of the pending danger and waiting for the slightest chirp from Colonel Tripp's phone.

Branches hung low in their faces. The smell of rotting leaves hung so think in the humid air that it permeated their clothing. The trio stopped for a brief rest near a rock ledge.

Ernie whispered, "This path has been used recently. See the deeper tracks in the ground? Looks like some of them were carrying a heavy load."

Colonel Tripp took a deep swig of water and asked suspiciously, "You mean like a man on a stretcher?"

"Or bundles of money. I'm telling you, these guys can make so much money they literally don't know what to do with it. Especially when spending it is a quick way to prison."

Chelle leaned back against the rock wall and brushed back her hair. It was so saturated with sweat and humidity that her normal curls were plastered to the sides of the face.

She asked, "Any idea at all how much further?"

Ernie took a swig of his own water and said, "Not a clue. We could be right on top of it. When the trail ends, we'll be there, but not before."

Ernie stood and carefully proceeded in front of them, but Chelle touched Colonel Tripp's hand and held fast against the rock.

When Ernie disappeared around a large tree, Chelle whispered, "I haven't seen any trail. We could be going in circles for all I know."

Colonel Tripp nodded, saying, "Let's give him another half an hour. After that, I'll check in with my people and find out exactly where we are, whether he wants me to or not."

Chelle nodded in agreement and they caught back up with Ernie.

It was only fifteen minutes later that Ernie motioned for them to stop immediately. Ernie crouched down and crawled back the few feet between him and Colonel Tripp in the rear.

"Shit!" he whispered. "We can't go any further."

Chelle crouched down next to Ernie and whispered, "What? We came this far and have to turn around?"

"Not turn around, but we can't go any further."

Ernie looked the colonel in the eye and pointed at his last position.

"Just three more feet and we're in an open field. Manmade or natural I don't know, but the path continues through it."

"Why can't we keep going?" the colonel asked.

"It's a killing field. My guess is that this path is guarded. Their plan is that anybody following them goes halfway through the open field and then all hell breaks loose. With nowhere to run, anybody in the field dies."

Chapter 40

Colonel Tripp took out his sat phone and said, "Sounds like a good time for some bird's-eye reconnaissance."

"I couldn't agree more."

It didn't take long for the colonel to make a satellite connection, then he said, "Looks like you were right, Ernie. There's a mountain that starts rising suddenly left of us. Four heat signatures, my people are trying to get some visuals." The colonel listened some more, and Chelle and Ernie heard him say. "Send them to me."

All three crouched down, looking at a photo image of the heat signatures.

Ernie studied it for a minute then said, "I'm going to crawl downfield a bit; I need to identify their exact position. If I'm spotted and shooting starts, backtrack out of here pronto. They have the high ground, and we don't have a chance."

Ernie crawled off, leaving Chelle and Colonel Tripp alone.

"Son of a bitch!" Colonel Tripp said, adrenaline in his voice. "The son of a gun was right! I guess he *can* be trusted. That Reaper has some special equipment on it. My guys are going to analyze the entire area with a fine-tooth comb."

It was some long, quiet minutes later when Ernie appeared through the brush.

"They're dug in pretty good, but I saw two of them. There's a rise not far from here, and they're about halfway up. Wherever we were headed, we're there."

Chelle asked, "Now what?"

Ernie looked back at her with a question in his eyes.

"We can't attack them. If there are four outside guarding the field, you can bet there are more. My guess is there are two relief guards to rotate guard shifts and at least a couple of others for camp duties."

The colonel suggested, "I'm a pretty good shot, couldn't we take them out?"

"If all three of us got three of the luckiest shots in the world off, we would still be mowed down by the survivors. I'm guessing that, besides being out-manned, we're also seriously out-gunned."

The colonel's phone gave a nearly imperceptible chirp, and the colonel whispered into it, "Great work, Lieutenant. What does the infra-red show? Can you digitally erase the foliage around the mountain? Great!"

Colonel Tripp looked at Chelle with a smile.

"We found Steven."

Chelle was about to ask how they knew when Colonel Tripp held up a finger to silence her.

"Stand by," the colonel ordered into his phone. He explained, "After they found the four heat signatures, they concentrated on picking up their audio."

Ernie looked to the sky and saw and heard nothing.

He asked, "Are you telling us you picked up their conversation?"

"Exactly, and they were talking about the prisoner inside the old ruin; they're nervous because they think he's the famous El Senador. When they digitally scrubbed away the vegetation from the mountain, it clearly shows some sort of manmade structure underneath."

"That would make sense with what I was told. My sources said they put the money in a room carved out of a cave."

Looking relieved, Chelle said, "That means he's alive. We can't turn back now. We're his only hope!"

The colonel smiled, replying, "We're not turning back. I have a plan."

****

Alejandro stood up and rubbed his backside. He stretched his legs and back; he was stiff from sitting on the same rock for the last hour. The other three men standing guard over the grassy field below them followed his actions with their eyes, glad of the distraction. Alejandro gave his compadres a small wave. The last two days of guarding the prisoner and El Ángel's money had been filled with only boredom.

Only once had he seen some activity below him, and that was when two deer had leisurely crossed the grassy field. He carefully strained his eyes around the edge of an outcropping of rocks to see if Filipe was watching the watchers. The hillside provided a nice arc around the open field; forty meters to his right was another watcher, with two others roughly opposite Alejandro's position. From their perches, they had an open view of the field.

Alejandro checked his watch. It would be another boring two hours before he was relieved. Slowly, he walked back to his post, not anxious to resume sitting on the rock. That was when his boredom came to an end. A single unarmed man was walking out of the jungle, disturbing the high grass of the field.

He picked up his radio and shouted excitedly into it, "Filipe, Filipe, there is a man walking across the field. Do you want us to shoot him?"

Filipe came running out of the cave entrance with a pair of binoculars and scanned the man daring to approach them.

"Mother of Jesus," he said out loud. He knew the man: it was Ernie Westcott. Filipe shouted more orders into the opening, and all of the available men resting in the comparable coolness of the ruins ran out with their guns.

Ernie wasn't even halfway across the open field yet. Filipe thought for a moment. *Would another Westcott be a welcome hostage?*

There was a clatter of steel as all the men around him readied their weapons and scattered in an arc to give each of them a clear shot at the man below. With eight rifles pointed right at him, Ernie Westcott would be dead the instant Filipe gave the order to shoot.

Filipe remembered the man in white's orders: 'kill anyone approaching the camp.' The man in the white hat had left little discretion.

Filipe looked one more time at Ernie. It would be the last time he saw him alive. Filipe watched Ernie approach the halfway point of the field. Filipe was just about to shout the order to shoot when Ernie did something strange. He turned around and started running back towards the jungle.

Out of the corner of his eye, Filipe saw a flash of something heading toward them. He was by far the closest to the opening into the old ruins and the only one to immediately understand the destruction that was coming. He ran as fast as he could into the cave as explosions and fire raged outside.

The obsidian that made up part of the mountain shattered like broken crystal. Dust filled the opening and rocks dislodged and fell all around him as he ran deeper and deeper into the cave. Filipe could only imagine the total annihilation befalling his men on the outside. It appeared that another Westcott was in charge of the missiles now.

****

Ernie hadn't made it back to the protection of the jungle before he heard all hell break loose behind him. He dared to turn and look as the mountainside crumbled. The barrage of missiles had turned it into a fiery inferno. Rocks had been turned into projectiles, flying in all directions; many of them were going to be falling in his direction any moment. Ernie ran like his life depended on it.

Just inside the jungle, he found the rocky overhang where Chelle and Colonel Tripp were already huddled. He flung himself towards them, and they grabbed his body and pulled him as far under the overhang as possible.

The crescendos of the explosions were growing like a thunderstorm. Rocks pounded the jungle around them and bounced off the ledge above them. As fast as it had started, the crescendo of rocks stopped raining down on them, and the sound of thunder echoed away as fast as it had approached.

Speaking into his satellite phone, Colonel Tripp said, "They saw nine heat signatures before the missiles struck. It's too early to know casualties or damage."

Ernie rolled off his saviors and stood, saying, "Congratulations, Colonel; it seems your plan worked."

"You were the one who took the risk by exposing yourself."

"True, but the point is that I'm not dead and we managed to draw out more of the men before the strike."

"Let's hope it was enough. There's still plenty of risk to go around."

"Doesn't matter, Colonel, it's now or never. We have to get across that field and climb up that mountain as fast as possible, before they can recover from the blast. Let's just hope that Steven was far enough inside the ruins to be protected."

As Ernie helped Chelle to her feet, she said, "It would be a miracle if anyone survived that. I pray that we didn't cause a cave in."

"Let's just hope the Zapotecs deserved their reputation as builders."

Colonel Tripp offered some hope, saying, "The missile strike was designed not to penetrate, but—"

"But there are no guarantees," Chelle finished.

With their rifles at the ready, the three of them ran towards the devastation, fairly confident that, if anyone had survived, three intruders would be the least of their worries.

****

Steven coughed and tried to spit out more of the dust.

"Untie me," he shouted to the two clearly scared guards.

The lights had flickered off, plunging them into pitch blackness until the guards found a couple of flashlights.

"You know that wasn't an accident; they're coming for me. If you want to be just as dead as your friends outside, do nothing. I guarantee you that my people are coming in guns blazing unless I stop them. I am your only hope."

One of the guards shouted to the other to check the passage. As one of the guards left, the other kept his gun trained on Steven.

"I can help you. You have certainly heard what El Senador can do, and I am El Senador. Now, untie me so we can both get out of here before this place collapses."

The guard looked more uncertain than ever. He took his flashlight and started to examine the crumbling ceiling.

"If you let me die in here, El Ángel isn't going to be happy about that."

"If we let you go, the man in the white hat will not be happy," Filipe said as he was helped into the inner room by the guard. Filipe looked hurt and was covered in dust.

"You heard him," argued Steven. "He wants me alive!"

"He also said I should kill you if you try to escape."

"Filipe, I thought we were friends. I can help you. Whatever they promised you, I can do better."

The guard carefully walked Filipe to the chair, two flashlights shining through the dust lit the room.

"You're injured," Steven insisted. "You know they're coming for me. The FES will kill you. Do you want to force your own men to shoot their captain?"

"The FES is not coming for you; they were recalled to Mexico City after the terrible carnage at the zocalo, but I did see your brother approaching the hillside. As far as I could see, he was alone, and I suspect that he is now dead or gravely injured. He was much too close to the blast to have survived."

"It was Ernie?"

"Most certainly. It seems he now has, or at least had, control of the drone that shoots the missiles. I only just barely escaped by running deep into the passageway; a passageway that is now blocked with sharp rocks." Filipe pointed to the guards. "Go, see how badly we are blocked in. And take your weapons. We need to get out of here. The drone operators will try to get a rescue party organized. The missiles were only a first strike."

The two guards left, leaving only one flashlight. Filipe drank some water and tended to his injured leg.

"Why, Filipe? Why did you turn traitor?"

Filipe found an old cloth, ripped it and tied it around his leg.

"Maybe I will ask you that same question in the near future. What will you do now that your daughter's life is on the line?"

"I can stop them. *We* can stop them."

"Ha, look at you, tied to a chair. Can you truly tell me that, given the choice between becoming president and your daughter's death, you will choose to lose everyone you love? I think not. I'm afraid, amigo, that when I thought about it, I didn't have a choice. And, I'm afraid, neither do you."

Filipe finished bandaging his leg and drank some more water. He lifted himself from the chair and limped over to Steven. He helped Steven with a few big gulps of water out of a plastic water bottle to clear the dust from his throat.

Filipe continued, "We will get out of here, hide in the jungle and then I will make contact and let El Ángel know that I still have you alive. They can decide what to do with you, and they will know I am a man of my word. We are not that different, amigo. We have good intentions, but other, more powerful people control us. In the end, we are just pawns."

Grateful for the water, Steven said, "I don't believe that. We've been in tough situations, Filipe, and we've always found a way out. We can do it again."

One of the guards came back excited and nearly out of breath.

"We think we can dig ourselves out; we can feel fresh air."

"Take some water and work hard, my friend. We need to be out of here before nightfall. A rescue party for our prisoner will be arranged, and we need to be gone before they get here."

"Sí, Filipe, we will work hard."

****

Ernie, Chelle and Colonel Tripp inched their way up the mountainside. The newly loosened rubble made the going treacherous. The glassy rocks were razor sharp and easily disturbed, causing a small landslide if and when they weren't careful enough. If there had been a path, it was now obliterated.

Suddenly, Chelle let out a scream. Colonel Tripp was immediately at her side and saw what was left of a gruesome face staring up at them. Tripp used his body to block Chelle's view of the severed head and guided her past the carnage and up the mountain.

Ernie led the way, with each of the trio helping the other past particular difficult terrain.

From time to time, the colonel would slow down to consult with his team back in Washington. Each time, the answer was the same: no further heat signals detected.

He advised the group on the latest report, "The drone has to go back to the ship. I do not have authority to bring in helicopters or US troops, and the FES don't know we're here. That means we're on our own until morning. The good news is, I can get the drone back to help us then."

Ernie scanned the sky and said, "Night comes double fast in the jungle. We can't be stranded on this rubble overnight, and we can't attack any remaining guards in the darkness."

Chelle looked down the deep slope and said, "Going back isn't an option either."

Without further conversation, the trio continued their careful trek up the sharp rocks.

****

Steven was searching for the right words to convince Filipe to let him free when a guard rushed in.

"We can see daylight; we can get out of this accursed mountain."

"Keep your gun pointed at him," Filipe ordered. "If he makes one quick move, shoot him. Don't think, just shoot. Got it?"

"Sí."

Filipe cut Steven's hands loose, leaving his legs bound.

"Put them behind you, *now!*"

Steven couldn't help but rub his sore wrist for a moment. That was all it took for Filipe to swing the butt of his pistol hard against Steven's shoulder.

"I won't tell you again."

Steven cooperated, and soon his hands were securely fastened behind him with a thick plastic tie. Filipe cautiously cut the ties securing Steven's legs. What he didn't see was Steven removing something from his back pocket.

"Let's move. And I warn you, amigo; I am taking a risk keeping you alive. Don't make me regret that decision."

In the darkness, Steven dropped the white handkerchief before they moved down the tunnel.

Three flashlights lit the tunnel out of the mountain, which was more surreal than the glass-lined room. It had a flat floor, but the top and sides looked like he was walking through a tunnel created by an immense worm. When a beam of light struck the sides, it was refracted back at them with an eerie, blue iridescence.

Once outside, Steven could see that it would soon be dark. He guessed they had an hour at most. The devastation around the opening was complete. He could only imagine what the outside of the cave had looked like only hours earlier. The three men guarding him also stopped to scan the destruction. Their mouths were agape, and it was easy for Steven to imagine their mixture of sorrow for their friends and disbelief at their own good fortune.

Filipe surveyed the area and said, "We can't go down. Find a way up the mountain."

The four men picked their way up the mountain. Steven was pulled and pushed along. Several times, he found himself falling on the sharp volcanic rocks. With his hands tied behind him, he was helpless as he slid down the rubble. Each time, he would be roughly lifted up to resume the climb. After half an hour, they were out of the debris field, though the journey to the top of the ridge was still arduous.

When darkness came, they proceeded along the ridgeline as best they could using the flashlights. Eventually, they had to succumb to the night and made camp. Steven's legs were aching, and he gladly dropped to a sitting position when told to do so. He propped his back against a tree and didn't even hope for his hands to be untied.

****

Once at the top of the rubble field, Colonel Tripp led the group to the one area that appeared comparatively undisturbed.

"There's the opening," he said, "it has to be! If Steven is here, he's inside, and the odds are that he isn't alone."

Chelle checked her gun, took off the safety and said, "Maybe whoever was in there got trapped?"

"The lack of daylight won't hurt us inside the cave," said Ernie, looking at the sky one last time. "Let's proceed with extreme caution."

With guns ready and flashlights leading the way, they cautiously entered the cave. The smooth, round sides were mysterious, and they were greeted by a mystical, blue shimmer. After fifty feet, they saw the cave in, but rocks had obviously been moved. Somebody had been trapped, but now they were free.

Silently, step by cautious step, they worked past the pile of rubble and deeper into the mountain. Eventually, they found their way to the large, ceremonial room. The light from their flashlights created a strange blue glow and seemed to reflect back at them from every angle.

"Look," Chelle said excitedly. She shone her light on the chair and the discarded restraints around it. "He was here."

Chelle rushed over to the chair and picked up a white handkerchief.

"It's Steven's! It has his initials on it; I gave it to him for his birthday."

They scanned the rest of the room with the flashlights.

"I see one chair for one hostage," Ernie observed. "I'm sure it was Steven. That leaves the question of what happened to Filipe."

Colonel Tripp sat in the chair and shone his flashlight straight ahead.

"Strange place for a television; they were making him watch something."

Ernie sat down on one of the pallets of cash. He took some of the bundled hundreds in his hand and added, "The good news is that he was protected inside here. And we have plenty of paper for a fire."

Colonel Tripp and Chelle turned their flashlights towards Ernie and the cash.

Chelle said, "There must be millions here."

Ernie shined his light back at the chair and said, "They left this here because they had something more valuable to take, and that was Steven. My guess is it took them an hour or so to clear the cave in and get out. We probably missed them by an hour or two, max."

"What now?" Chelle asked.

Colonel Tripp said, "Wait for morning and the drone. We didn't cross paths on the way here, so we pretty much know what direction they took. We let the drone find them and we pursue."

"I agree," Ernie said as he re-arranged a pile of cash to make a pillow.

Chapter 41

The trio woke up the next morning somewhat refreshed. Each had used the bundled cash for a makeshift bed. It hadn't been comfortable, but it had served to insulate them from the cold, rock floor of the cave.

Colonel Tripp stood and said, "I'm going out to call my team."

As he left, Ernie asked Chelle, "Did you get a million-dollar sleep last night?"

Chelle looked at the bundles of money on the floor and laughed.

"Well, the next time someone says they slept like a million bucks, I'll tell them I'm sorry to hear it."

Ernie pulled two energy bars from his pack, offering Chelle one and saying, "We should get moving. I'm assuming they had to rest overnight, just like us – traveling through the jungle would have been too dangerous – but they're obviously going somewhere, and they're probably in a hurry to get there.

"Steven's injured leg is probably slowing them down some, so I think we have a chance of catching them if we move quick enough."

Chelle caught Ernie's eye, asking, "So you believe Steven is still alive?"

"They want something from him. So, yes, I believe he's still alive."

"Ernie?"

"Yeah?"

"Thank you. Whatever I thought... Well, I mean. I was wrong. You're one hell of a brother to have. No wonder Steven is so proud of you."

"And do you think Steven would do any less for me?"

"Not for a second, but when you walked out in that field yesterday to bait them into a trap, you went above and beyond. I just wanted to let you know that I respect what you did."

"You're no chump yourself. You handle yourself pretty damn well. But, Chelle..." Ernie paused as he looked her in the eye.

"Yes?" Chelle realized this wasn't mere conversation.

"Make no mistake, I want to save Steven from the cartels. But I'm telling you, something strange is going on, and I'm going to get to the bottom of it."

"Bottom of what? You believe Steven is doing something illegal? How could that be? We know he has the support of the president and the military."

"That doesn't mean it's legal. It seems to me that the president has stepped way past his authority. Maybe Steven got caught up in something by accident. I mean, you can see the amount of money involved. Whatever they're up to just doesn't pass the smell test for me."

"As someone who's so concerned with legality, you mean?" Chelle snorted.

"I have my reasons." Ernie zipped up his pack and said, "Let's see what the colonel knows."

The sun was above the mountainous horizon, and the air was fresh and clear and cool.

Ernie asked, "What's the word, Colonel?"

"We're still alone. They moved the drone out and are scouting north-west. I have a satellite searching for Steven's radiation tag. It may take some time, but we'll find him."

He pointed at the rubble below them, saying, "I doubt they went down. We would have heard them and possibly seen them. They went up, I'm sure of it, and here's where I think they went." His gaze shifted. "It's the only logical place. I say we don't wait for the reconnaissance to get back to us first. I say we start climbing."

Chelle began walking immediately, turning her head as she went.

"Well, what are you waiting for? Let's go find them."

****

Filipe roused his two surviving men and roughly rolled Steven onto his stomach, checking his bindings to make sure he hadn't somehow worked them loose during the night.

Satisfied, he said, "Amigo, time to get up."

Steven rolled onto his backside and then sat up and asked, "How about some food? I know you took some supplies from the cave; feel like sharing?"

"Sí, you will need your strength today. We have a great distance to cover."

Filipe fed Steven some food and water and, as they sat, Steven talked.

"Filipe, the drone is probably looking for me right now. It's not too late. Untie me and we can walk back as friends."

"The drone can do nothing but watch. Its missiles are useless; it won't attack with you next to us. As soon as we reach the rendezvous point, they will know how to make you disappear once again.

"And I *do* consider myself your friend, even now, but that doesn't mean I am willing to trade my family's life for yours. There are only two solutions to my dilemma. Delivering you to El Ángel and his associates is the best one for me."

"What is the other?"

"Maybe someday I will tell you." Filipe stood and lifted Steven by the arm. "And what of your daughter, Tracy? Escaping me does not save her life. They are watching her right now. Amigo, they are dangerous men."

They started walking over the ridgeline. Filipe and Steven were alone while the other guards scouted the way ahead.

"What of their offer? Just think, my amigo, the presidency! Why wouldn't you take that? As if you daughter's life was not persuasion enough."

"Filipe, I have lost two daughters already; one murdered by your boss and another lost to the cartels and their drugs."

"Sí, I remember."

"I made a promise to myself that I wouldn't fail Tracy like I failed them."

"Does that mean you will accept their offer?"

"So far, I feel forced to do what I must versus what is right, but you said there's another path. Will you share it with me?"

"The only thing I can tell you is that the other path is not welcomed by me, and I am afraid that I do not see that same path for you.

I'm afraid, amigo, that if you wish to save your daughter's life, you have no choice."

****

Colonel Tripp studied the map on his satellite phone.

"It looks like they have a two-mile head start. The problem is, they're moving as fast as we are. It's definitely him, but there's no way to close the gap."

Chelle studied the colonel's high-resolution picture as he zoomed in on Steven.

"He's OK!"

"He's definitely being held prisoner, though. Let's see by whom." A moment later, Colonel Tripp's face turned ashen. "Oh my god!"

"What, what?" Chelle asked.

Ernie rushed to look.

"I can't believe it."

Ernie and Colonel Tripp looked at each other as they both exclaimed, "Filipe!"

"Who's Filipe?" asked Chelle.

Ernie answered, "He's the FES commander in charge of protecting Steven."

Colonel Tripp studied the photo some more, saying, "Obviously, he's been turned. No doubt Steven is his prisoner; you can tell his hands are tied."

Chelle picked up her pack, saying, "We have to hurry."

The three moved on, guided by Colonel Tripp's men in Washington.

"There must be something we can do?" the colonel suggested as they walked. "What about a missile strike in front of them to slow them down?"

Ernie responded, "Filipe knows that we won't risk hurting Steven, but we could have an advantage if we knew where they were going. If your people in Washington could take an educated guess at where they're heading, they could study the topography and give us the best way to get ahead of them."

"Head them off at the pass, so to speak."

"Exactly; if we keep chasing them, we'll never catch them. But we might have a chance with a shortcut, if your people can find one."

****

Mile after mile, mostly following the ridgelines for defensive reasons Steven and his three guards trudged on.

"Filipe, I need a rest," Steven huffed.

"Bullshit! I've seen you keep up with the fittest of my men. We will keep moving."

"We all need a water break, come on. Your own men are going to collapse from dehydration."

A look from Filipe's men confirmed that Steven was right.

"All right, a short rest; five minutes. Daniel, give El Senador some water, but no food."

Daniel set down his weapon and twisted off the top of a water bottle, holding it up for Steven.

Steven lunged like an attacking snake, jabbing his open hand into the man's throat. The man dropped his rifle as he instinctively reached for his throat, gasping for air.

Steven grabbed the dropped rifle with hands that were slippery with blood. During one of his falls, he had managed to slip a razor-sharp piece of obsidian into his back pocket. The sharp stone had been effective, but it had cut his hands badly.

Out of the corner of his eye, he saw Filipe and the other guard lifting their rifles, preparing to shoot at him. Seeing no other choice, Steven body-slammed the remaining guard.

They tumbled off the ridge. Steven was more prepared and tucked and rolled past a few trees, but he lost his grip on the rifle. The guard landed flat on his back, the wind knocked out of him as he continued to slide down the steep mountainside on his back, upside down.

Filipe pointed his rifle downslope, trying to catch a glimpse of Steven through the trees.

Steven tried over and over again to gain a footing on the sharp slope. He looked uphill and saw the guard slide hard, headfirst, into a tree. It looked like his neck had snapped, but Steven couldn't be sure. He could see Filipe taking aim at him, followed by a flash and an immediate splintering of the tree just inches from his head.

Steven decided to keep his profile low and continued to roll down the hill, keeping as many trees between him and Filipe as possible.

****

A steady chirping sound came from Colonel Tripp's satellite phone.

"What do you have for me?"

The voice on the other end of the conversation excitedly said, "It's the senator, sir, we have him on visual, or at least we did. He's making a run for it. He took one guard down and grabbed his weapon. He pushed another off a cliff and followed him down. We lost him in the trees, but we can see that Filipe is shooting at him." Colonel Tripp looked at the dots on his phone's map display. "He's moving in our direction.

"Lieutenant, superimpose all known combatants on my map. I need to know where everybody is at every moment. Mark our location too. Good guys green, bad guys red."

By the time Colonel Tripp looked back up, Chelle was already running in the direction of Steven's dot. Ernie was right behind her.

"Lieutenant, what about a missile strike against Filipe?"

"Too close, sir, Filipe is moving in the same direction. One of the other combatants seems to be on the move too, sir."

Colonel Tripp uttered, "Damn!" as he holstered his phone and started running as fast as he could.

****

Steven ducked behind a tree near the bottom of a ravine.

As he took a precious moment to get his bearings and decide on a route, he heard Filipe shout, "Amigo, you are hungry, tired and thirsty; you can't outrun me. There is a reason I didn't give you any food these last few days."

Steven knew that Filipe was baiting him to better guess his position, but that worked both ways.

There was a relatively flat area along the bottom of the ravine. Slowly, he stepped away from the tree and put another between him and Filipe. Carefully, he worked from tree to tree, increasing the distance. It was a dangerous game of cat and mouse; Steven moved silently, but Filipe made no sound either.

A rock turned to his right. The sound came from further up the hill. He heard a grunt as someone slipped on the loose terrain. It wasn't Filipe, so now he knew there were two attackers after him. He was pretty sure that he'd crushed the one guard's trachea, so it had to be the other who was after him.

Steven inched his way towards the next tree. If he didn't make a sound, he reasoned, they wouldn't know which direction he took out of the ravine. That meant they would have to split up to search both directions, and they would have to move equally cautiously, knowing their prey could be waiting to ambush them behind any tree.

The next cover was at least ten feet away from him, on the edge of a dry creek. There was some thicker vegetation uphill that he hoped would be enough to conceal him, because he would be a convenient target as he moved slowly, picking each step carefully.

He found the next tree safely and listened intently for any sound. He heard nothing; even the sounds of the jungle had stopped, which meant that the jungle itself sensed imminent danger. Looking for his next source of cover, he realized that the dry creek bed would be his quickest path. Unfortunately, it offered no protection. He heard a branch snap. It was small but close.

The tip of a rifle barrel edged just past his eye. Steven grabbed it and flung the holder three hundred and sixty degrees around, slamming them against the trunk of his covering tree.

The man groaned and his grip on his weapon relaxed. Steven pulled it out of his hands and then slammed the butt against his assailant's head. The man went limp against the tree, and Steven hit him again. Now, two were down for the count, with only Filipe left hunting him.

A bullet whizzed past him. His only chance at cover was back up the hill. Maybe it was time to take the high ground, he reasoned. With the rifle in his hands, he had evened the odds at last.

The scuffle had given away his position; it was time to disappear once again. No more bullets followed him as he moved tree to tree, always climbing higher.

Steven rested, keeping his breathing as shallow as possible and trying to still his heart. The adrenaline coursing through his veins kept every one of his senses on the highest alert.

A bullet splintered a nearby tree, but he held fast, keeping his breathing shallow and trying to hear the shooter's footsteps. He turned the slightest amount, trying to spot the shooter, and heard a rustle behind him.

He had nearly raised his rifle when something struck the back of his neck. His knees went limp and things turned dark.

****

Chelle heard the shots. She didn't need to look at Colonel Tripp's GPS to know what direction to run in. She had one more ridge to climb; she was sure the shooting was on the other side of it.

Ernie caught up to her, grabbing her shoulder to slow her down.

He warned, "Rushing to our deaths won't help anybody. Let's wait and take a look at the colonel's phone before cresting the hill. The bad guys could be just on the other side."

"That might be time Steven doesn't have!"

The colonel came into view, climbing the ridge towards them.

Ernie asked, "What's the latest?"

"Looks like he got another of them; I only see one enemy combatant still moving, but he's uncomfortably close to Steven. They don't know who it is yet; they can't get a visual." The colonel studied the map a bit and pointed at the screen, "We're *here*, Steven is *here*, so I think we have time to flank them. Be careful with any shot; they're in close proximity, so you could easily hit Steven. And remember, Steven doesn't know we're here. He might shoot first and ask questions later, so use whatever cover you can.

"OK, let's go. Chelle left, Ernie right. I'll go head on and draw the combatant's attention. You'll need to climb up the next hill about half-way to flank him."

Chelle peeked her head over the hill and watched as Ernie and the colonel did the same. She picked her path and ran down into the ravine, from tree to tree, as fast as she could.

To her right, Colonel Tripp was edging his way down the hillside, giving her and Ernie time to get out in front. She saw him fire into the air to draw attention.

Chelle raced down the hill on her side and was soon crossing a dry creek bed. She looked back and saw the colonel taking a huge risk by exposing himself and firing into the treetops. When the tree beside him cracked, followed by the boom of a gunshot, he knew he had the combatant's attention and ducked behind it.

But the ploy had worked: Chelle saw where the shot had come from, and she worked her way back up the next ridge, hoping Ernie was doing the same.

Chelle could still see Colonel Tripp from time to time. He was inching his way down the hillside, shooting sporadically into the treetops. From the shots their target returned, Chelle could tell she was positioned as intended, and she prepared her rifle, stepping more and more carefully as she got closer.

That was when her heart sank, as a voice called out, "You can all come out now. I know there are three of you. I have a gun to Steven's head and a knife to his throat. We are stepping out into the open."

Chelle froze in place. It didn't take long for Filipe and Steven to step into view. Steven's hands were tied behind his back, and Filipe held him tightly with the knife. Any movement on Steven's part would immediately cut his throat.

Filipe shouted, "I'm serious! I have a feather trigger on this thing. You shoot me, he is dead with either the knife or the gun, maybe both."

Unseen, Ernie shouted back, "You have nothing to gain! If you kill Steven, we kill you."

"If I let the senator escape them, I am dead anyway. I am not bluffing: show yourselves! Put your guns down and step out unarmed."

"Filipe, if you try to kill us, I guarantee that you will die," Ernie negotiated. "Give up Steven, and then we can help you. Whoever you are afraid of, they are not here. You have a chance with us."

"First things first, step out," Filipe shouted.

"No, Ernie, don't," Steven protested.

"We are not coming out into the open," Ernie said as he tried to get just a bit closer.

"That may be your decision, but understand that you are forcing me to kill Steven. If I am captured and he lives, my family dies. If I die fulfilling the wishes of IRENE, my family will be taken care of."

"We can get to them first. Look, Filipe, I don't know who Irene is, but we can stop her. She won't even know Steven is alive until after your family is safe."

"Tell them, El Senador, tell them. Nobody can escape IRENE." Filipe shot the gun just over Steven's head and shouted, "Now, or I will kill you and myself. I will not give them the chance to kill me."

"Ernie, listen," Steven tried to explain. "IRENE is an organization with many eyes. They're powerful, and they have Filipe's family. He has no choice; it's either delivering me or killing me. If he doesn't do one or the other, they die. Filipe is right, they *will* know. I don't want any more deaths because of me. Please, go, I'll be all right."

Chelle shouted, "If I come into the open, how do I know you won't kill me?"

"I want you alive. I want you to tell your superiors what I have done."

"Why? Why would you want that?"

"When you make a report of what happened here, IRENE will know I served them well. Please, do as I say; it is the only way El Senador lives. If you are bound and we can make an escape, I can keep Steven alive. But if I am faced with no other choice, understand that I must kill him, even though it will mean my own death."

"Don't shoot, I'm coming out." Chelle stepped into the open with her hands in the air.

"No, Chelle, no!" Steven pleaded.

"I won't force this man to kill you, and I believe he will if we continue this standoff for much longer."

Filipe kept his knife tight across Steven's throat as he tossed a ring of plastic hand ties towards Chelle.

"I do not wish to hurt you or Steven. Tie your hands around that tree."

Chelle bent down to pick up the ties, never taking her eyes off Filipe.

Steven begged, "Let them go. You want me, you said that yourself. I'll go with you, no tricks."

"I won't kill them if they cooperate. They will eventually free themselves, but we will be long gone."

Chelle backed up to a tree and slipped both of her hands into the loop of the plastic tie, facing out.

Filipe nervously moved him and Steven towards the tree. His knife was cutting into Steven's throat. With a quick tug of the plastic tie with his gun hand, Chelle's wrists were tightly bound together.

"I need another volunteer, *now!*" Filipe shouted. "One at a time."

Colonel Tripp stepped out with his hands in the air.

"Put your back to the tree," ordered Filipe. "Now, stretch your hands behind you."

It didn't take long before the colonel was tied in the same way as Chelle.

"Señor Ernie, if you want your brother to live, you must give yourself up."

Ernie slowly did as he was told, using every second to try and come up with a plan.

Filipe pointed to another tree opposite Chelle.

"As you can see, my knife is sharp. Any quick movement will cut his throat. Do not make me do that."

Ernie backed up to the tree and slipped his hands through the plastic ring supplied by Filipe. Filipe pulled the ring tight and double-checked it.

"OK," Steven said. "You said you would let them live if I went with you, so let's go."

Filipe pushed Steven out in front of him. As they walked away, Filipe held his gun pointed squarely at Steven's back.

Steven wasn't expecting the gunshot. Strangely, as it rang out, he wasn't worried for himself, but that Filipe had turned on Chelle. Instead, he turned just in time to see Filipe drop to the ground.

Steven rushed back towards him, but he could see that Filipe was mortally wounded. Filipe looked at Steven, and his eyes had the look of impending death.

"Amigo, you asked me what my other option was for escaping IRENE. I have found it. You will file your report, and IRENE will have no reason to harm my family. I have found the final solution to protecting my family, but amigo, what is yours? I do not have a final solution for you. They will kill your family first, and then you shall die. I am sorry, amigo, I do not see another path."

Filipe took a last, deep breath. Steven stared into the lifeless eyes and shed a tear for his friend. Behind him, his rescuer worked on freeing Chelle, Ernie and the colonel. Chelle's hand landed on Steven shoulder, and he stood to have his ties cut.

Once he was able, he gave Chelle a well-earned hug. Nearby, Ernie patted El Cazador on the back in reassurance.

"How did you find us?" he asked.

El Cazador's eyes had sadness in them.

"I thought I was on a mission to save my compadre, not kill him. I told my team to continue on to Mexico City without me and followed your directions to the cave. When I saw the damage and no survivors, I followed your trail here. When I heard what Filipe was saying, I did what had to be done, but I have many questions."

"Filipe was trapped," Steven explained. "If he didn't do what he was told by a powerful group called 'IRENE', his family would die. Filipe felt he had no choice."

"He was my brother, why didn't he tell me?"

Steven looked at Ernie, who had picked up Filipe's weapon.

"Telling you wouldn't have helped him, and it would have put you in jeopardy. He felt he couldn't risk telling anyone. Even with his dying breath, he hoped that IRENE would look at his death favorably and his family would be spared."

"I also have many questions," Ernie said, suddenly pointing the rifle at Steven. "You are under arrest, Senator. Don't move, or I *will* shoot. I don't want to kill you, but I'm taking you in."

Chapter 42

Steven froze in place when his brother turned the gun on him. He looked around, trying to understand, but everyone else was equally stunned.

"Ernie, what in the hell are you doing?" he asked.

Ernie glanced at Chelle, calmly saying, "Chelle, I'm with the Drug Enforcement Administration; I've been working deep cover for the last three years. My job was to infiltrate the cartels. My handlers at the DEA have already contacted the FBI. You can use the colonel's phone to verify it."

Steven looked at Ernie, perplexed.

"You're DEA?"

Ernie stood firm, replying, "Yes. It took years of risking my neck to infiltrate these guys, and you blew my cover in a matter of weeks. Many people are *not* happy, including me. They want you brought in and whatever you're up to stopped."

Chelle, Colonel Tripp and El Cazador exchanged glances. The colonel walked towards Chelle to hand her his phone.

As he moved, he said to El Cazador, "You and I were both ordered to protect Steven by the highest authorities our countries have. Train your gun on his brother until we have this sorted out."

El Cazador promptly pointed his weapon at Ernie, and Chelle stepped away from the group and made her call.

Steven argued, "This is crazy, Ernie; I'm on a top-secret mission for the president of the United States to stop the cartels."

"By organizing them even further? And what is IRENE? You know, the people who want you back so bad, dead or alive?"

"They want to stop my work with the cartels too. Trust me, I can explain, but we don't have time. The president's life is in grave danger."

"I'm afraid you'll have to make the time. Because, right now, trust is in short supply. I don't believe a word you're saying, and neither should anybody else."

After five minutes, Chelle came back and said, "Ernie is telling the truth. I was transferred pretty high up the food chain, and I was assured that it all checks out. Ernie *is* DEA."

"The DEA doesn't know what Steven is up to down here, but it's nothing we sanctioned," Ernie explained. "After I alerted my superiors to Steven's odd behavior, they concluded that he somehow got and used our intel to organize the cartels for his own profit. Intel that I risked my life to gather!"

Sadly, Chelle added, "The FBI doesn't know what Steven is up to either."

Colonel Tripp motioned to El Cazador that he could lower his gun.

Chelle looked at Steven with pleading eyes, asking, "Steven, what are you doing here?" She felt the detective in her come out. "What is 'IRENE', and why do they want you dead or alive?"

One by one, Steven looked everyone in the eye. The sounds of the jungle were nonexistent to them as they all waited for his response.

"I was sworn to secrecy by the president, but I guess the cat's out of the bag. Please, let me explain." He pointed to a rock not too far from him. "Do you mind if I sit? This might take a while."

"Sure," Ernie agreed, but he didn't take the gun off him, and nobody seemed to care.

"You all might want to sit too. It starts with the president asking me to the Oval Office."

Steven's audience sat spellbound by his tale. When necessary, El Cazador and Colonel Tripp confirmed what they had and hadn't known. As the story progressed, the military men seemed glad to hear that they hadn't backed the wrong horse.

"I heard Steven give the exact same explanation to El Ángel under threat of Chelle's torture," Colonel Tripp said eagerly.

Ernie, a little more relaxed, asked, "OK, so what is IRENE, and what does it have to do with this?"

"That's a new development. Or, at least, one I only just realized was in play. Chelle, you remember the discussion we had about the Woods Trust?"

"Yes, it was started by Philip Alan Woods after World War Two. We, or more like *I*, believed they had something to do with the murder of Sam Kreiser."

"I just found out a day ago that, in fact, they did. Sam was killed to prevent him from implicating them. It seems the Woods Trust and IRENE are pretty much the same thing; one grew from the other. They're also the ones who killed Destinee over a year ago. They were trying to force me to work for them via a scheme to blackmail me for her murder. Apparently, they had a fall guy, probably Sam, to take the blame if I agreed to work with them."

Steven took a breath, looking at Chelle.

"The reason we couldn't find anything about the Woods Trust is that all of its money goes to support IRENE. You see, IRENE is an organization, and apparently a big one."

"That was then, what about now?" Chelle demanded. "What do they want from you?"

"They want me to become the next president of the United States after they kill President Walker. Apparently, they have the resources to make it happen."

Ernie kept the gun pointed at Steven and said, "That's one hell of a story. Why do you believe it? Why should *we* believe it?"

"You said you were in the room I was held in, is that right?"

"Yes," Chelle agreed, "we all saw it."

"Did you see the television?"

"Yes, of course. A little strange, we thought."

"They wanted me to witness Walker's death. If I still didn't agree to their demands..." Steven looked up at Chelle. "Besides me, those closest to me would be eliminated, including Tracy." He glanced at Filipe's body. "It was the same threat Filipe was dealing with."

Colonel Tripp asked, "Why do they want Walker dead?"

"I guess he didn't play ball with them. I don't know to what extent they might have helped him get elected, or if he even knew about it, but this whole cartel eradication scheme of his wasn't part of their plan. Apparently, IRENE makes a ton of money from the illegal activities of the cartels."

Chelle added, "Yeah, literally a ton of money, we saw it."

"I believe the president's life is in immediate danger; it may already be too late. It was yesterday when I was told he would be dead within twenty-four hours."

Ernie leaned the rifle against the tree, saying, "If you're lying, you deserve an award for creativity, that's for sure. What I do know is that, inside the cartels, there was always the mention of someone or something bigger than them, pulling the strings. Still, have you considered the possibility that the president is lying to you? What if President Walker and President Torres are scheming together for a piece of the cartels' profits?"

"I took President Walker at his word. They want the leaders to go legitimate over the next five years. I do believe it's an honest effort to destroy their hold on the country."

"Sorry, bro, I'm not buying it. After what I've seen the last three years, I don't trust anybody."

Colonel Tripp pulled out his satellite phone and said, "Either way, we need to inform the Secret Service, but how? Who would believe us?" Colonel Tripp turned to Chelle. "You have contacts at the FBI. Let's start there?"

Steven stood up from the rock and said, "We do have to try and warn the president. However, I'm afraid we can't trust anybody but ourselves. The man in the white hat knew too much. He knew what had happened between the president and I privately in the Oval Office. Somebody close to him is an agent of IRENE."

"Or it was the president himself," Ernie suggested.

Colonel Tripp volunteered, "Or his chief of staff, Mitchel Waters. I can tell you this: for having appointed him personally, President Walker doesn't trust him much."

"Obviously, the president isn't in on his own assassination," Steven reminded him.

"I trust my people at the FBI," Chelle objected

"I'm not questioning the integrity of the FBI," Steven replied. "I agree that we need them to notify the Secret Service that the president is in danger. I'm just saying we can't trust that they'll take us seriously or that somebody in the inner circle won't quash the warning. I'm sure the president would believe me if I could only talk to him. Also, we can't let IRENE know that I escaped; Tracy's life is on the line. That could speed up their timetable."

Chelle offered, "We have to tell the FBI of a credible threat against a senator's daughter's life and at the same time warn them of a credible threat against the president."

"What if they don't get to Tracy in time?" Steven asked.

"I'll make sure they understand the urgency, but we can't withhold the threat to the president until after she's safe, we can't take that chance," Chelle insisted.

"Damn it!" Steven said angrily. "And we can't tip our hat by sequestering Tracy. They would immediately know I somehow escaped."

"Maybe that would be a good thing," Colonel Tripp suggested. "They'd know we've already disrupted their plot?"

Steven shook his head, saying, "Any group that can control the cartels the way they do won't quit easily. We'd just lose the element of surprise."

Chelle said, "I'll call the bureau. They can contact somebody they trust within the Secret Service."

Colonel Tripp paced while Chelle made her call, saying, "The president is eight thousand miles away in Australia promoting the US and Mexico's new trade agreement with Australia. He's a little far away for Steven to just tap him on the shoulder and tell him he needs to be careful."

Ernie did some quick calculations, replying, "From here, I'm guessing it would take at least twenty-four hours to get there. First, we would have to get Stevee back to the road, then we'd need to find a flight to the US out of Oaxaca, because I know there are no direct flights from Mexico to Sydney. LA is probably our best shot."

"There's something else," Steven insisted, "something he said. He told me that only he and I would know what had really happened. If he had to tell me about it in advance, that makes me think it's going to look like an accident, like what they did to Sam."

"Harder for anyone to guard against than an outright attack," Colonel Tripp added.

"The man in the white hat also said he had to leave, but that he'd be back for my answer."

"You think he went to Australia personally?" Ernie asked.

Steven paced nervously and agreed, "That would be my guess. We might already be too late."

"*That* I can find out," said Colonel Tripp.

As soon as Chelle was finished, Colonel Tripp made a short call. Everyone held their breath as he asked a few short questions.

"My people say that, so far, the president's visit is going like clockwork. They have real-time information and haven't heard anything to the contrary."

"Thanks to Ernie's boss," Chelle informed them. "I'm back in good standing with the bureau. They're taking me seriously and will notify the Secret Service that there's a credible threat against the president. I also told them there was a credible threat against your daughter. I warned them to protect Tracy but to stay in the shadows."

"Thank you, Chelle. Hopefully, we can stop the threat before they realize I'm free." Steven looked at his watch and did some short calculations. "Australia is seventeen hours ahead of us, which means it's tomorrow morning; the president's last day in Sydney. It has to happen sometime in the next eight hours, before he leaves. He'll be attending meetings for most of that time, so I'm guessing they'll strike as late as possible, when he's in a bigger space and harder to protect.

"That still doesn't help, though. I can't see any other way around it: *I* need to warn him personally; he'll believe me and it's the only way we can be sure the message gets directly to him. There's so much in play that no-one else knows, and anyone could be working with IRENE, or answer to someone who does. If someone's able to get close enough to properly protect the president, they're exactly the type of person IRENE would have compromised. It's not even a matter of loyalty; Filipe was my friend until his last breath, but he was willing to kill me to further their agenda. *Damn it!* There's no-one to trust and no time for me to get there."

"What if I could get you there within the next four hours?" asked Colonel Tripp, stroking his stubbled chin.

"Are you going to use the *Star Trek* transporter to do it?" Steven asked.

"Well, something like that. Do you remember meeting Lieutenant Colonel Richard Pratt?"

"No, I... Wait, yes, the astronaut I met outside your office?"

"He has a sweet little ride you might like to try."

Chapter 43

You're serious?" Steven asked incredulously.

"I have a letter of authority to use governmental assets to help you in any way I deem necessary. Let's just see how good my special presidential authority is. None of you have heard any of this, of course."

The colonel stepped away from the group and, in hushed tones, made several calls. He came back to the group with a smile.

"I hope that was the most time-consuming part of this whole endeavor. The Mexican government has authorized a rescue mission, and there's a chopper on the way. My team back in Washington has already found a clear landing zone nearby."

"You'd better come with us," Steven said to El Cazador.

"Sí, but what will I tell my commander?"

"That's the problem; you *can't* tell any of this to your commander. If we save the president's life, he'll square it with President Torres."

El Cazador asked, "And if he dies?"

"Let's not think about it."

Steven looked at the colonel, asking, "Are you sure about this?"

"Absolutely not, but if you want to get to Sydney in the next few hours, this is your only chance."

Half an hour later, the group of five arrived at the clearing just as the helicopter touched down.

"Are you kidding me?" Ernie asked, amazed. "We're going to ride in a Seahawk? What a rush."

The colonel smiled, replying, "Nothing but the best for the DEA. In a half-hour, we'll be out on the USS Carl Vinson."

Wind from the still-rotating rotors made the prairie grass around them dance wildly. Military men ran up to the group and took Filipe's body off the hastily built stretcher. He was placed in a body bag and lifted into the chopper. Next, the soldiers rushed everyone into the cargo strap seats. The now full Seahawk lifted off the field.

The single rotor, which was powered by two seventeen-hundred-horsepower turbines, whisked them over the treetops and towards the waiting aircraft carrier off the coast of Mexico.

The mountains of the west coast came and went. The helicopter dropped towards the sea and skimmed along the ocean. Steven peered out the window and saw the numerous ships of the aircraft group come into view.

Steven asked, "How can you possibly get me to Australia in four hours? As you know, I'm on the Armed Services Committee. Nobody on the planet, including us, has a plane that can go eight thousand miles across the ocean in four hours."

The colonel realized that nobody but Steven could hear him in the noisy cabin, so he answered, "You're right; we don't have one that will take you to Australia in four hours; we hope to do it in less than two. Hopefully at Mach seven and a half, or better."

Steven's eyes widened.

"Why weren't we told about this?"

"Strictly experimental. This is top secret, and generally we don't tell you guys about something in development until we know it works."

"You don't know it works yet?"

"Not exactly. So, how do you feel about being a test pilot?"

The Seahawk settled down on the steel surface of the USS Carl Vinson. The crew of the aircraft carrier hurried the five passengers against twenty-knot winds.

Once below deck, the colonel pulled Steven to the side and said, "They told me you have ten minutes, then they'll find you and get you into your flight suit. You'll be riding in the flight engineer's seat of a highly experimental, incredibly dangerous aircraft. One chance to back out, and that's right now. What do you say?"

"What would you do if you were me?"

"Are you kidding? I wouldn't miss this ride for anything in the world!"

"I thought you said it was dangerous?"

"It is, in the extreme, but if it works, you'll be making history."

"Not exactly the encouragement I was looking for. But it's the only way to get me to Sydney, so I only have one question. I haven't eaten in two days, I'm starving; can I have a sandwich first?"

"That would be inadvisable, Senator."

Steven caught up to Chelle, who was on Colonel Tripp's phone.

As soon as she saw him, she said, "They have Tracy and her mother under protective watch. They won't let them out of their sights."

"That's great, but Lucille isn't going to be happy about this when she finds out."

Steven glanced at his watch; he knew he didn't have much time. He took Chelle's hand and gently held her back as the others were ushered through the narrow, steel corridor to the personal quarters.

"Chelle, I don't know how I can ever make this up to you."

"You don't have to. I make my own calls; it's called being an adult. You aren't responsible for me."

"That's nonsense. You lost your toe and suffered a great deal because of me. You risked your life to save me. How can I not feel responsible for what you've been through?"

"You've been through a lot too. Who are you blaming? President Walker? President Torres? The cartels? Or did you know what you were getting into when you made the decision to take on this mission?"

"Point taken. Damn, you *are* good." Steven gave Chelle a hug. "I don't have much time, but I need you to know that I love you."

Steven tentatively brought his lips to hers, not knowing if they were welcome.

Chelle reached up and ran her hands over Steven's back. She pressed him towards her and they kissed long and hard.

"Good luck, and please be careful."

"I will. And Chelle, one more thing, if you could do it for me?"

"Yes, certainly, what?"

"Time, sir," said a sailor, tapping Steven on the shoulder. "We need to get you prepped."

Steven nodded and said to Chelle, "If something does happen to me, please tell Tracy how much I love her."

Chelle kissed Steven one more time.

"Of course. And I'll tell her how brave her father was, but I'd much prefer you come back to both of us."

Steven started walking for the far door but looked back down the cramped hallway, needing to see Chelle one last time. He could see the worry in her eyes. They both knew that however he was getting to Australia, it would be dangerous.

****

On the flight deck, Colonel Tripp met Steven and instantly started giving him directions. Steven was used to the organized commotion on the flight decks of aircraft carriers, as he had been invited on many as a senator. However, today the top deck was oddly quiet.

The wind was blowing hard against them as Colonel Tripp explained, "We must be traveling at least twenty knots, and the captain has put our back to the wind, so for your departure you should have over forty knots over the wings before even starting up, and you'll need it."

At the far end of the ship was a single plane. The wind was noisily whipping at their clothes and blowing them towards it as they fought for footing.

"The plane is an experimental hypersonic. Lieutenant Colonel Pratt can give you more info once in flight, but the basics are that it takes off with the under-mounted jet engines. They'll push you to Mach one, then they drop off and the rockets kick in. *They* push you to Mach five and then drop off, which is when the scramjet kicks in."

"If this is experimental, how come I don't have a parachute?"

"There's no ejection system. You would disintegrate immediately at those speeds. Sorry; you're in it for the duration, however long or short that is."

Steven looked at the plane, thinking that it looked like the tip of an arrow. He saw the two mounted jet engines and the two rockets. Underneath the fuselage was a box-like structure but no other engine components.

"Where's the scramjet engine?"

"That box *is* the engine. It diverts the super-compressed air at Mach five and above so that fuel can be injected into it. It has no need for any moving parts; it's all about controlling the already compressed air. It doesn't need to carry oxygen like a rocket motor because the compressed air has enough for combustion."

"Hello, Senator, I'm Lieutenant Colonel Richard Pratt. You might remember that we met briefly."

"Yes, outside of the colonel's office, back when he couldn't tell me what your assignment was because my security clearance wasn't high enough. I guess I just got a higher clearance. At least now I understand the astronaut wings."

"Yes, sir, and you just got assigned to me as a flight engineer on a highly experimental aircraft. I'll need your help to capture some of the data we'll generate on our test flight. Just punch the buttons I tell you to *when* I tell you to and leave the flying to me. Otherwise, please don't touch anything.

"And I hope this little jaunt to Australia is as important as Colonel Tripp says, because both of our lives are on the line."

"It is, Lieutenant Colonel, it is."

"Good, and I hope you haven't eaten for a few hours."

Senator Westcott looked at Colonel Tripp and then assured the pilot, "Not a problem; I haven't eaten in days."

Colonel Tripp and a deckhand helped them get strapped in. Senator Westcott saluted as Colonel Tripp and the deckhand took cover.

Through the headset, Colonel Pratt asked, "Have you ever been to space?"

"No, sir."

"Well, we're going to get damn close, and we're going to get there damn quick. Take a deep breath and try to force it out through your feet. The catapult doesn't screw around. It's going to take us from zero to 170 miles per hour in two seconds. Here we go."

Steven's body was plastered against the back of the seat. An instant later, it seemed like they were shooting straight up into the sky.

"In two minutes, I will jettison the jet engines and kick in the rockets. Just want to warn you. If they don't both ignite at precisely the same time, we'll rip off a wing. At four hundred knots, that won't be a good thing."

Two minutes later, he saw the signal that they had successfully jettisoned the jet engines. An instant later, he felt another jolt of power pressing him to the back of his seat. Only, this time, the feeling persisted for much longer.

"We're going up to forty miles high; welcome to the astronaut's club. At Mach five, we drop the rockets and kick on the scramjet."

Steven was overjoyed that he hadn't eaten for the last two days, as he knew there was no way it wouldn't have come back up.

He answered, "Roger."

"I'm impressed, Senator. The money was against you still being conscious at this point."

"I hope you bet on me."

"Sorry, sir, I put my money on a heart attack as we kick up to hypersonic flight."

"So, how long do I have to live?"

"About three more minutes. We drop the rockets and, hopefully, the scramjet starts. If it doesn't, we become a billion-dollar glider with no place to go."

"Are you telling me this just to improve your odds? Is there anything *else* I should worry about?"

"Oh, yeah, tons. But the biggest is after we get to Mach seven point five. The air friction at those speeds has been a problem."

"What do you mean 'a problem'?"

"Melts the aircraft, sir. We think we found a workaround; we're pumping water through the leading edges of the plane. That should keep things cool enough not to melt."

"And if it doesn't?"

"That's why we're paid the big bucks, sir."

"Right!"

"Hang on. Mach seven point five, here we come!"

Two lights flashed, marking two rockets dropping away. Steven felt a much smoother acceleration taking over. A digital display over his head indicated the Mach number, and he saw it climbing.

"That wasn't so bad," he remarked.

"No, not bad at all. Just don't pay any attention to the glowing airframe outside the window."

"You're trying to give me that heart attack, aren't you?"

"Wouldn't dream of it. You're doing great, Senator. Enjoy the ride. In an hour and a half, we should be landing in Sydney at RAAF Base Williamtown."

Steven looked out of the side window and could see the curvature of the earth. The red-hot leading edges seemed to be glowing steadily, and Pratt didn't seem to be concerned, so Steven reasoned he shouldn't be either.

"It's starting to get dark out."

"Yes, sir, we're approaching night. Soon, you'll see the most fantastic starry sky you've ever seen. In an hour, it will be morning light."

"How close to space are we?"

"Twenty miles higher and we'd officially be in space and officially be in a lot of trouble. We are in the sweet spot right now, low enough for oxygen to compress and burn but high enough that the thin air is our ally."

True to his word, the clearest, brightest starry night appeared. Steven couldn't believe he wasn't in space.

The next hour went by as a blur. Steven did his best to keep up with the fast-paced instructions the pilot gave him. He pressed buttons and used recording devices that were monitoring the airplane's every move.

He was surprised when he heard the pilot say, "Prepare for landing."

"Landing? Where? We're out over the ocean, and I don't even see land ahead."

"That little spot ahead, sir, is Australia. We're traveling at five thousand, seven hundred miles per hour. We'll start slowing down when I turn off the engine, but we need several thousand miles to descend to land."

"Turn off the engine?"

"Yes, sir. From here on, we're a glider. Just like the space shuttle."

Before Steven could ask another question, the hypersonic plane started gyrating. A moment later, he saw the ocean under his head; the plane was inverted and dropping towards the sea. There was another roll and a violent pitch up. Steven's body was pressed hard against the back of his seat. He couldn't breathe, and the g-force made his eyes feel like they were pressing against his brain. The earth fell away and the sky became suddenly black; they were in space, and he was looking at billions of bright stars for an instant before he blacked out.

****

Alfonso Lucas stepped off his private plane and walked the short distance to a waiting white limousine. His eagle-topped cane clicked against the concrete tarmac. Unfortunately, he'd had to leave his white panama hat on the plane. He had become accustomed to its feel and missed it.

Today's event dictated he wear a white shirt, black tuxedo and black bowtie. He didn't expect to be at the state affair inside the Sydney Opera House for long; he only needed to deliver a small gift, and then he would be off again. Hopefully, he would have time for a few days of relaxation in Hawaii before heading back to Oaxaca, unlike the quick fuel stop they had made on the way to Sydney.

Alfonso felt rested and relaxed. He'd been able to get a fair amount of sleep on the long flight from Oaxaca to Sydney on his jet. The weather in Sydney was transitional; the Australian continent was going from their winter to summer, so instead of the high heat and humidity of the Oaxaca summer, it was pleasant both in temperature and humidity.

Alfonso slid through the wide door of the limousine, which was held open by its driver. He would be the only passenger today and had more than ample room and privacy behind the tinted windows.

He took out the engraved invitation from his tuxedo pocket and opened it by gently sliding his fingers under the already broken seal. Alfonso ignored the traffic around them as the limousine sped away from the private airport. He scanned the invitation for the second time; the first had been when he'd boarded the plane and found it waiting for him. He had checked that everything was properly done, and now he double-checked that his access to the black-tie event would go smoothly. It was a simple document; just words with his name on it, he mused. A simple piece of paper would give him access to the president of the United States and, with it, the power to assassinate such a powerful man.

Alfonso slipped it back into his pocket. He guessed that his ride to the Sydney Opera House would take an hour. He noticed a bottle of Champagne had already been uncorked and took it out of the ice bucket, pouring some into a tall glass. It was much too early to toast his own success, but just the same, he had no reason not to enjoy the ride.

****

Steven woke up to the sound of his name and an unpleasant smell attacked his nostrils.

"Senator! Senator Westcott!" he heard again.

Slowly, his eyes opened, and the awful smell was taken away.

"What happened?" he asked, noticing he was still in the back cockpit of the experimental plane.

Lieutenant Colonel Pratt was on a ladder next to the plane; the canopy was raised and he was holding smelling salts in his hand.

"You passed out when the rudder malfunctioned. We did some serious g's while I figured out what had gone wrong. We nearly shot into space!"

"I remember seeing the darkest sky and the brightest stars I ever saw."

"Part of the rudder burned off. Using full deflection, I was eventually able to control the aircraft and land it in Australia. You have your astronaut wings now, sir."

"Senator Westcott?" shouted a solider, running over.

"Yes, that's me."

"I have a helicopter waiting to take you to HMAS *Canberra*."

"I'm sorry, I can't go out to sea. I have to get to Sydney immediately"

"Yes, sir, we understand. We were told time is of the essence. The fastest way there is by helicopter, but because of the president's visit, there's a temporary flight restriction in place around the Sydney Opera House. Luckily, we got a military clearance to fly to the Canberra, which happens to be in port fifteen minutes from the president's venue. We have a military escort waiting for you there. We can get you to the Opera House, but getting in to see the president will be all on you, sir."

Lieutenant Colonel Pratt tapped Steven on the shoulder and asked, "When you were coming around, I heard you say you needed to warn the president. Is his life in danger?"

"I'm certain it is, and I believe somebody close to him may be the assassin. I need to warn him in person."

"That would explain the multimillion-dollar ride here. Let me come with you, sir; I'll help any way I can. After all, he is my boss."

Steven cursed the grogginess that had robbed him of his

discretion, but Pratt had no direct connection to the president; if he could trust anyone, it was probably the man before him.

"I might need some help," he admitted, "but make no mistake, the people we're trying to stop play for keeps."

"Understood, sir."

"And Pratt, do you have a phone?"

"Yes, sir, never leave home without it."

The three of them raced across the tarmac to a helicopter that already had its rotor blade spinning up.

Chapter 44

On the helicopter, a soldier wearing the uniform of the Royal Australian Air Force handed Steven a package.

"Clothes, sir. Somebody called in your size and said we were to get you clothes suitable for a black-tie event at the Sydney Opera House."

Steven tore open the paper wrapping and saw a complete set of clothes; Chelle's work, no doubt. He didn't waste any time putting them on, right down to the black, patent leather shoes.

Steven searched the suit for an invitation, but to no avail.

"What's wrong, sir?" Lieutenant Colonel Pratt asked, noticing Steven's panicked look.

"No invitation. Getting in to see the president just got a lot more difficult."

The helicopter touched down on the flat-top deck of the HMAS *Canberra*.

As they were rushed to the waiting cars, Lieutenant Colonel Pratt said, "I feel completely underdressed, sir." He pointed to his orange flight suit and flight boots.

"Nonsense," Steven said, straightening his tuxedo. "I'm sure all the other hypersonic pilots will be wearing exactly the same thing."

Three black cars clearly marked with the Royal Australian Navy insignia – an oval with an anchor and chain centered in it and the royal crown above – raced away from the pier.

The sailor sitting alongside Steven and Richard said, "We have no official standing, hence no sirens. We can make a good show of it, but that's all we can do."

"Please turn on the radio to a news station, any news station. I need to know if the president is still OK."

The three cars followed the speed limit down the four-lane boulevard that ran parallel to the harbor. The air along the shore smelled of salt water. Turning a corner, the taller buildings of downtown Sydney came into view. They went through a series of tunnels before exiting out onto a narrow boulevard.

Looking official, the fleet of cars weaved their way past a host of other vehicles being checked and turned around. Fifteen minutes later, the giant, white, concrete-clamshell design of the opera house came into view. The three cars pulled up to a small roundabout, which was the final automobile checkpoint. Three officers approached the lead vehicle.

The navy driver announced, "We have a United States dignitary traveling with us. He's here for a meeting with the president."

"Let me see the invitation."

Senator Westcott and the lieutenant colonel were in the middle car, but they heard what was being said to the lead vehicle through their open window.

"That invitation would be real handy right about now," Lieutenant Colonel Pratt observed.

"It sure would, but even without it, I have to get through those gates."

Pratt said, "I'll create a distraction. Good luck, sir."

"Pratt?"

"Yes, sir?"

"I need you to call Colonel Tripp and tell him to immediately have the FBI take my daughter and her mother into protective custody. One way or another, the shit is about to hit the fan, and they'll need protection."

"Yes, sir."

Before another word was said, Pratt boldly stepped out of the car.

"I am Lieutenant Colonel Richard Pratt of the United States Navy." Richard pulled out his identification and loudly announced himself again, pointing to the name stitched on his flight suit. "I was sent here specifically to officiate at a luncheon recognizing the cooperation between the Royal Australian Navy and the United States Navy."

"Sorry, sir, but our orders are that nobody gets past this point without an invitation."

Richard pointed to his flight suit once again and said loudly, "You want an invitation, how about this flight suit? How about twenty years in the US Navy? How's that for an invitation?"

The lieutenant colonel's confrontational tone was attracting more policemen and a crowd of onlookers.

Steven opened the opposite side door and slid out of the car as the policeman said forcefully, "Sir, you need to leave immediately."

"Oh yeah? And who's gonna make me, you? I'm here representing the United States Navy and I'll be damned if I'm going to let some Aussie tell me what to do."

"Look, mate, this is your last chance. One more word and all us Aussies will wrestle you down and haul your clever arse down to the remand center."

Senator Westcott had nestled himself in with the crowd that had formed watching the commotion. His black tuxedo, white, ruffled shirt and black bow tie made him blend in like just another penguin at a beach full of them as he inched his way past the gate.

Lieutenant Colonel Pratt noticed the senator staring at him from three rows behind the entrance gate and said, "The president is going to be pretty upset that you treated one of his officers so poorly."

Job done, he slid back into the car and slammed his door closed. Thirty seconds later, all three of the vehicles twisted around the roundabout and returned to the base.

The group of onlookers and the assembly of police disbursed, and Steven walked with a group of invited guests towards the broad expanse of steps that led up to the opera house. While the actual guests chatted about Pratt's scene, Steven was on the lookout for the man who had taken him prisoner in Oaxaca.

Steven approached the stairs. From a past visit, he knew they also served as bleachers for outside performances. Up the grand staircase were five unique show houses, each designed to host various types of venue. Today, security gates prevented anyone without a proper invitation from entering.

Steven walked past the wide staircase towards a view of the harbor; there was no point in climbing those stairs without an invitation in hand. He had literally flown halfway around the world, and he was too close to give up now, but he still needed to get past the security gates. He searched the crowd for anybody who might be able to provide him with a way past security and into the opera house.

That was when he noticed two men off to the side, ready to climb the grand staircase. One of the men held a cane. Though today he wore a tuxedo, Steven recognized him immediately as the man in the white hat.

Steven looked out over the harbor. He was sure his face hadn't been seen, but he needed to verify the identity of the other man, so he covered his face, pretending to cough, and risked another look.

His first assumption was proved correct, the other man was Mitchel Waters, the president's chief of staff. The men broke company as the man with the cane walked towards the exit. Steven thought about Colonel's Tripp's suspicions about Waters.

Chief of Staff Waters climbed up the staircase regally and was waved through the security gate. Steven was surer than ever that the president's life was in danger, and he now suspected that Mitchel Waters might be the assassin.

After he saw Waters disappear inside the huge building and watched the man with the cane go off in the opposite direction, Steven decided to take his chances further up the staircase. He prayed that somebody he knew would walk by.

On the other side of the security fence, he saw an opportunity; probably the only one he was going to get. He had spotted Bruce Benet, the president's press secretary, alongside Allen Coleman, the current United States ambassador to Australia. Both men knew him, and both could possibly get him inside the event.

Steven went as close as the protective fence would allow and yelled their names. They were too far away to hear his calls, but a security guard did and went up to Steven to quiet the commotion-causing tourist.

"Sorry, sir, but I must ask you to not shout so loud, you are disturbing other guests."

"Look, Officer, I am US Senator Steven Westcott, and I need to speak with those two gentlemen."

"Please, sir, just present your invitation and you will be able to talk with them in a more gentlemanly manner."

Steven pulled out his ID, saying, "Look, this is me, OK? My

invitation blew out of my hands and into the harbor. Those guys can help me. The president is expecting me to be with him today."

The officer examined first the ID and then the face of the senator.

"Perhaps I can help you," he said eventually.

He took the ID and walked up to the two men just as they were about to retreat back inside. Steven watched the short discussion and, thankfully, they both descended to the security fence to talk with Steven.

The officer handed back Steven's ID as Bruce said, "I didn't know you were going to be here today. What a pleasant surprise!"

"Hi Bruce, I mean 'Ambassador'. I'm afraid my invitation blew out of my hands. I'm hoping you could get me past this security checkpoint."

"Of course, Senator. You've been a great proponent of this trade deal. Let me see what I can do."

It took a bit of explaining to various security personnel, but eventually Steven was admitted through the security gate. Once inside, he asked for one more favor.

"Bruce, could you tell the president I'm here and that I need to talk with him immediately. I believe his life is in danger."

"Senator, he has the best protection on the planet looking out for him. We've been advised by the Secret Service that a credible threat has recently come to their attention. As you can see, they've increased security a few notches. I assure you, the president is being properly protected and is aware of the recent threat.

"He's also extremely busy. Besides, I doubt I could get past Mitchel Waters right now. If it makes you feel better, I can assure you that Air Force One is being prepared for an immediate departure as soon as the noon reception is over."

"Bruce, you don't understand. I have to see him."

"I'm sorry, Senator, I just can't do that."

"Listen, he's been waiting to hear from me, so just give him a message. Tell him 'Irene is here'. You have to trust me, it's life and death important, but you must give him the message in person. Tell only the president; not Waters or anybody else."

"This is all very strange, Senator. However, I do know that the president thinks highly of you. OK, I'll try."

Steven watched helplessly as Bruce proceeded without him. A good distance away, Bruce stopped to talk with the president's chief of staff. Mitchel Waters seemed to be shaking his head and denying Bruce further access.

It certainly looked like a heated discussion; Bruce even stepped around Waters, but the chief of staff pressed him back. Steven remained out of Water's sight, hoping that his name hadn't come up in the discussion.

People were starting to gather, several recognizing him as they walked by. Steven picked up a stray program from a tabletop. It was for the noon luncheon, and the president was the featured speaker. Steven felt desperate; he stared at the program, hoping it would somehow present a solution.

He considered that maybe he could gain the president's attention inside the dining room but then discarded that idea immediately. Private discussion would be all but impossible, even before the risk of triggering an early assassination.

Nervously, Steven looked at the giant wall clock that showed it was nearly noon. That meant time was running out. The dinner would start soon, and the president would have to be in attendance. Steven was afraid that, whatever the plan was to kill the president, it would have to happen soon, before he boarded Air Force One for the trip back to the states. The luncheon would be the least protected and thus most likely space.

Just as he was beginning to panic, the ambassador appeared around the corner, clearly flustered.

"You were right, the president wants to see you immediately. Please, follow me, hurry, we don't have much time!"

Steven realized that it wasn't just Bruce; two burly Secret Service agents were walking alongside him. Then, Steven caught Mitchel Waters staring at him. He was clearly upset, though it was unclear whether that was because he was the assassin or whether he just resented them for going over his head.

A steel door was opened, and Steven was lead down a narrow staircase. A maze of hallways and doors followed. They were clearly inside the arteries of the massive opera house; arteries not meant for the general public.

Eventually, he was hustled into a large reception area. Multiple sets of swinging glass doors led out of the room, and one set was held open for him. He stepped outside into the sunshine and humidity of the peninsula the opera house consumed.

"Senator Westcott, welcome!" said President Walker. "What a pleasant surprise. I thought you were away in Mexico."

The president held a lit cigar in his left hand while extending his right to Steven. The two shook hands and the president said, "That will be all, Bruce. And thank you for seeing the senator to me."

"Yes, sir," Bruce said, then he added, "I would like to respectfully remind you that the luncheon is about to start."

"Please tell Mitchel that I will be unavoidably detained for fifteen minutes."

"Yes, sir." Bruce nodded respectfully and disappeared.

Bruce and the Secret Service men left the area. Steven was sure they were lurking nearby, but they knew how to disappear from immediate view. Finally, he was alone with the president.

They were standing outside on a wide patio alongside the massive opera house. Opposite that was the harbor and the magnificent Sydney Harbor Bridge.

"We have the whole place to ourselves for a precious fifteen minutes. I asked for a bit of privacy to smoke a last cigar before the luncheon and heading back to the states. I have to say, I'm surprised to see you. You had some pressing business in Mexico I hoped you were attending to."

The president sucked a deep puff of smoke into his mouth, enjoyed its flavor for a moment, then blew it out over the harbor waters.

"I would offer you one, but unfortunately I only have the one, and I have to thank Mitchel for that. Too bad, because I believe this time you would have joined me. It's the same brand as the ones you found at Miguel Vega's home. Indeed, they're the same ones that allowed you to trace his footsteps. Very clever, by the way."

"Sir, no disrespect; I came here from Mexico to warn you that I believe you're in grave danger. After we last talked, I was kidnapped and held by a group that calls itself 'IRENE'. I escaped but not before they threatened me with death if I didn't comply with their demands. Those demands included me running for and becoming president after your death. They promised me you would be dead before twenty-four hours were up, and that time is nearly over."

"An organization called 'IRENE', you say?"

"Yes, sir, and I take them seriously. I believe they have the resources to do it."

The president examined the harbor waters and the wide bridge connecting the sides of the bay. He took another deep puff.

"You understand that there are death threats against me every day? I'm not saying I or the Secret Service don't take them seriously, but they do become a bit passé after a while."

"Sir, they had detailed knowledge of you, your whereabouts and even private conversations between you and me."

"Are you implying a mole?"

"Yes, sir, and I believe they intend a clandestine attack. It's going to be made to look like an accidental death. If that's their intent, it's something they'll have needed to set up in advance, not some lone gunman the Secret Service can outdraw. The pieces must already be in motion."

An inch of ash clung to the cigar's tip. The president flicked it into the sea with the snap of a finger as he leaned against the railing.

"I appreciate your efforts to save me, but what do you propose I do about it?"

"I don't know, sir," Steven reluctantly admitted, "but you need to take extra precautions."

"Perhaps I shouldn't be standing out here alone with you. After all, you could be an agent of IRENE. What would stop you from taking that knife off the cheese platter over there and stabbing me with it? Perhaps a drone is flying overhead and will soon rain down missiles on both of us. I'm not being flippant, Steven; life is full of risks, especially for the president of the United States."

"Yes, sir, it's just that I sense real danger here. This is not just another idle threat. I'm positive I saw Mitchel Waters talking to the man who kidnapped me."

The president suddenly turned to Steven.

"You saw Waters talking to who?"

"I don't know his name, but he had a cane just like the man who kidnapped me, and when he walked away, he had the same limp. He walked one way and Waters the other."

The president became more interested, asking, "Did the cane have a silver eagle handle?"

"Why, yes. You know him?"

"In a manner of speaking, yes. And you're right; he's dangerous."

The president took another puff of his cigar as he thought.

Steven asked, "Mr. President, did you say that Mitchel gave you that cigar?"

"Yes, he said he found me some time and a place to enjoy a guilty pleasure."

Urgently, Steven asked, "Please, sir, may I have that cigar?"

Chapter 45

The president handed the cigar to Steven with suspicion.

Steven went over to the table that held the hors d'oeuvre and the cheese plate. He extinguished the end of the cigar by touching it into a glass of water. Placing the extinguished cigar on the table, he used the cheese knife to gently slice it open.

"Oh my god!" said the president.

"Thank goodness you didn't get the cigar down to that point yet."

Steven used the knife to edge out a green, toothpick-sized sliver of material a half inch or less from the charred cigar end.

"Thank God you found it. Another couple of puffs and I would have started to inhale whatever that is."

"We need to get this analyzed immediately; you may have been poisoned."

The president pushed a button in his pocket. Three Secret Service agents were almost immediately at his side.

"Senator Westcott probably just saved my life. He found this remnant in the cigar I was smoking. I need it analyzed immediately. Also, have my physician join us inside, and detain Mitchel Waters in secure quarters on Air Force One. He talks to nobody, do you understand?"

"Yes, sir!"

"And do it all discretely."

The agents made calls over their radios while others arrived to escort the president and Senator Westcott inside the reception area, which was now secured from probing eyes.

Soon, the doctor arrived, wasting no time in checking the president's vitals.

"Mr. President, I can't find anything wrong. The device seems to be intact. However, it's critical that we find out what it's made of. I've been assured that the poison control center on Air Force One is state of the art. Fortunately, this is one of the contingencies it's prepared for, but they still need to know what they're dealing with."

"Doctor, would it be OK if the senator and I have a few private moments? I promise, no more cigars today."

"I see no reason I need to be at your side. However, I'll be just around the corner if your condition changes. I do need to warn you that I don't want to leave Sydney until we know what we're dealing with. I'm putting the poison center in Sydney on call; it's one of the best in the world."

"Thank you, Doctor." The president shook the doctor's hand firmly, letting him know that he had his strength. The doctor was escorted out of the inside reception area, and Steven and the president were once again alone. The president sat down, looking relieved if a bit ruffled.

"Thank you, Steven, I believe I owe you yet again. I'm convinced you caught the poison in time."

"Sir, I'm afraid this isn't over. I believe IRENE have great resources. You and I have discussed the Woods Trust, and I believe they're funding IRENE. They've promised retaliation against my friends, my family and myself for not cooperating in their scheme. I'm afraid that they can and will carry out those threats.

"I don't think it wise to underestimate their capabilities. Sir, I believe you're still in danger. I have no reason to think they'll stop their attempts, and foiling them each and every time may not be possible. After all, they only have to be successful once."

The president stood up and realized his shirt was still unbuttoned from his examination. He turned from Steven and nonchalantly buttoned it, tucked it back into his pants and started retying his tie. All the while, he was quiet.

As he slipped his tie around his neck, he said, "Steven, now that I understand what is happening within IRENE and who is responsible, I can stop it."

Steven's eyes flashed a look of astonishment.

"Stop it? How?"

"You had better sit down. Please, Steven, just sit and listen to me for a minute."

Steven took the president's advice and sat on a cushioned dining chair next to one of the reception tables. The president poured him a glass of water and Steven took the opportunity to sip some.

"Steven, I *am* IRENE."

Steven nearly spit out the water.

"What?" he choked. "What are you saying?"

"Not in its entirety, but I am its president. No matter what you think now, I can and will assure you that it is not a sinister organization. Every US president becomes its president for at least part of their term. At other times, prime ministers, kings and presidents of other countries take on that role. And yes; it is funded by the Woods Trust."

Steven couldn't help himself; he stood and paced the length of the glass dining table.

It took a while for him to gather his thoughts, then he asked, "You are the president of a secret organization that promotes its interests at the expense of the United States?"

The president laughed, saying, "Sorry, nothing so melodramatic. Have you heard of the Bilderberg Group?"

Steven chuckled knowingly.

"Yes, the super-secret club for all the movers and shakers of the world to plan the one-world society."

The president didn't laugh.

"Exactly, founded in 1954 by Joseph Retinger, among others. It is, to this day, one of the most un-secret secret societies around. Denis Healey was a Bilderberg Group founder and a steering committee member for 30 years. In 2001, he said, 'To say we were striving for a one-world government is exaggerated, but not wholly unfair. Those of us in Bilderberg felt we couldn't go on forever fighting one another for nothing and killing people and rendering millions homeless. So, we felt that a single community throughout the world would be a good thing.'

"Henry Kissinger, Bill Clinton, Tony Blair, David Rockefeller and David Cameron are or have been members. The list, of course, goes on and on. At any rate, it is real, and they do not keep notes on what is talked about. But that's the point."

"Sir, what does this have to do with IRENE?"

"Think of it as the Bilderberg Group on steroids."

Steven's eyes bulged.

"And you're its president?"

"This year, yes. My role is to set up the annual meeting: where, when, who, that sort of thing. Next year, it will be the Grand Duke of Luxemburg. There's nothing sinister about it. Much like the Bilderberg Group, IRENE was created in the aftermath of World War Two, and its mission was to be an incubator for some of the world's greatest leaders and greatest minds to share ideas on how to achieve world peace.

"Philip Alan Woods, a seasoned diplomat, and a leader of humanitarian efforts during World War Two, is the original trustee and creator of the Woods Trust. He had seen the travesties of two world wars, and he couldn't stand the idea of another just because of a lack of open communication. He also saw the pitfalls of the newly created United Nations and felt that the incredible scrutiny it was under meant it was doomed to failure if it wasn't supported by a sister organization. Unfortunately, I agree that as an organization created to prevent war, it has been abysmal."

"What you're saying isn't that far off from what the man with the cane said," Steven replied. "He wanted world peace, and my efforts on your behalf in Mexico were interfering with that."

"So, now I'm a wrench in IRENE's works? Well, I hope that vindicates me a little, at least. You see, when we get together to discuss world affairs, no minutes are kept and nothing is released to the press. Because nobody even knows about our organization, we can speak openly and candidly. That means we can debate, persuade each other, even back down from a position without worrying about the strictures of political correctness and the glare of immediate public scrutiny. It's refreshing, but more importantly, it's necessary.

"Example: Haiti, one of the poorest countries in the world. Let's say somebody suggests we help Haiti initiate a minimum wage to increase income. A noble objective, and it would be political suicide for somebody to argue against that.

"However, inside our organization, somebody could. Somebody could freely argue that, by raising their minimum wage, you would not only not help the population but condemn them to starvation, because what little industry they do have would leave for an area of the world where total cost would be cheaper.

"Through IRENE, we can talk about what might be the best way to help without making things worse, such as better education or increasing the population's value to investors. Or, we might talk about encouraging a more stable government, to make investment less risky. More than that, we're free to have bad ideas and talk them through without political factions instantly seizing on an undeveloped position. Do you know how difficult it is to make sensible decisions without private counsel?

"Another example is the total debt of the United States and how even a small default could affect the world's economy. Again, some of the greatest political and economic minds of the world can explore the subject objectively. All because they are free of political distractions and without the worry that the discussion itself could affect the world markets.

"You see, there are many reasons IRENE is necessary. But, as a group, we control nothing; we don't want to."

"You're wrong, sir. The attempt on your life is real, and it came from IRENE."

"No, it didn't; it came from Alfonso Lucas. He's the man with the cane, and I do believe I know what is going on now. Unfortunately, I should have seen it coming. I didn't realize the internal dissent had gone this far, but it makes sense to me now.

"You see, the actual running of the organization has always been left to the directors. It was, I'm embarrassed to say, a way to ensure no one figure had too much power, as well as a matter of practicality. Shifting presidents, such as myself, are too fluid for continuity and too busy to have time to run a clandestine organization.

"Alfonso is the executive director. He runs the day-to-day maintenance of the organization, including our funding and investments. More and more, he has expressed the idea that we are all talk and no action. I'll admit, he's even suggested we use our resources to force the changes we often talked about, but it was always taken in the spirit of firm debate that makes IRENE so useful. Unfortunately, it seems the tail wants to wag the dog."

"So, kill you and replace you with me," Steven said, beginning to understand, "but not just within the presidency; within IRENE?"

"If he had you compromised enough to pull your strings in both positions, he and IRENE would indeed have great influence over world affairs. In fact, in the political climate following a modern-day presidential assassination, I dread to think how he could have leveraged his position.

"But what he didn't count on was the resilience and diligence of the man he had targeted. With the intelligence you've brought me, I believe we have the advantage and that we can squelch their insurrection."

There was a knock on the door.

"Yes?" the president answered.

A Secret Service guard opened the door. Once the president's doctor was a few steps inside, he closed it again.

"The lab on Air Force One called. They believe that what you nearly inhaled was a fairly common compound. It's used to induce sudden cardiac arrest in test animals. They also sent the spectrum analysis of the compound to the FBI lab in Quantico, Virginia, who came to the same conclusion."

"So, somebody wanted me to have a heart attack?"

"Yes, and they went about it the right way. Via inhalation, the effects would likely have been fatal and probably undetectable. The effects wouldn't have become severe until you were in the air, flying back to the States. We wouldn't have known what was happening, and you would have probably tossed the evidence into the ocean when the cigar was spent.

"Thankfully, they checked the tobacco around the compound, and we're as sure as we can be that nothing left the ampule. In short, you didn't inhale anything but tobacco, not that I recommend that either."

"I guess you're right, Doc; smoking can be bad for your health. So, we're cleared to go back to Washington?"

"We'll need to keep checking your vitals over the next few days, but yes, sir. On your order."

The president slipped on his black tuxedo jacket and said, "We have a luncheon to attend first. I hope you're hungry, Senator; I insist on you joining us."

"As a matter of fact, Mr. President, I am."

"I also assume you could use a lift back to Washington?"

"That would be greatly appreciated, Mr. President."

Epilog

Colonel Tripp, Steven, Ernie and El Cazador were riding in the communication center of a US Navy EP-3E Aries signals reconnaissance aircraft. Escorting them was an EA-18G Growler electronic warfare aircraft and the Reaper drone. They were flying at twenty thousand feet over the Gulf of Mexico.

Steven hoped that this would be the last of his secret missions. He was here to deal with a loose end that El Senador had left undone.

"It looks like we found the homing device you planted," Colonel Tripp said to Ernie. "The plane it's on is headed for Cuba. It seems your plan worked."

"After you told me how you could track Steven's ID, I thought I might as well put it to good use."

El Cazador nodded, saying, "It was clever to place it inside the bundles of money; money that El Ángel was sure to reclaim."

"Cuba makes sense," Steven said. "Share some of the loot with the government, get some plastic surgery and then get lost in Africa. But how can we be sure El Ángel is on the plane?"

"His private plane never goes anywhere without him. Certainly not with his money on it, and certainly not now," Ernie replied.

"We have to be absolutely certain," Steven insisted.

Colonel Tripp said, "I have an idea. Lieutenant, use plane-to-plane frequency to hail the pilot."

"Yes, sir. Let's see if they have their ears on."

A moment later, a connection was established and then immediately confirmed by the cursing of a startled pilot.

"Tell the pilot that, if he doesn't put his boss on the radio, we'll blast him out of the sky," Colonel Tripp ordered.

Shortly, Steven heard El Ángel's voice come over the loudspeaker.

"What is it you want? We are on a humanitarian mission, en route to special, life-saving medical procedures in Cuba. We are under the protection of the Cuban government."

Colonel Tripp used another radio to talk to Lieutenant Kastner back in Washington.

"Lieutenant, does the voice print match?"

"Yes, sir, identical. It's him, no doubt."

"Steven, is there anything you would like to say to him?"

Steven grinned and spoke into the headset.

"This is your amigo, El Senador."

Steven couldn't see the dread on El Ángel's face, but he could hear it in his voice when he answered.

"So, you have found me and now need to make an example of me."

"The footage of your plane dropping into the ocean should be convincing to anyone who doubts the word of El Senador."

"Amigo, please, I am sorry about your friend; I only did what I had to. IRENE gave me little choice."

Steven gave a nod to Colonel Tripp, who issued an order over his headset.

"Let's test out that new air-to-air SACM."

The Reaper that was shadowing them dropped underneath and sped out in front, unleashing two missiles.

"Adios, amigo," Steven said into the headset.

El Ángel's plane began immediate evasive maneuvers, but there was no outrunning the SACM. There was a magnificent, mid-air explosion and Steven's team watched as what was left of El Ángel's aircraft hurtled into the ocean.

Steven had never liked taking lives, but he had no remorse for El Ángel or his lackeys.

"Let's head home," he said.

****

Steven and Chelle were escorted into the Oval Office and told the president would join them shortly. Steven looked out at the Rose Garden through the east door. He had been inside the Oval Office before, but today he had time to enjoy its true magnificence.

He smiled as he looked at Chelle, who seemed paralyzed; afraid to touch anything, including her red heels to the giant oval carpet with the insignia of the United States embroidered into it.

Steven took time from his admiration of the Oval Office to admire Chelle. She was dressed smartly in a pantsuit bought for this meeting. He remembered her asking, over and over, if its baby blue color looked good on her. Obviously, he had agreed over and over that it suited her just fine.

Her hair seemed more curled than usual and bounced on her shoulders when she moved her head. Chelle often didn't wear make-up, but she hadn't held back for today's meeting. He had to agree, it suited her. She was a rare beauty.

"Tradition has it that each president designs their own unique version of the great oval carpet," he said. "The first time I entered this room, I was afraid to step on it."

Chelle looked down at her high heels, parked just inches from the carpet.

She said, "So, I'm not the only one?"

Steven pulled her onto the carpet and gently brought her to his lips.

"You deserve to dance on it," he said as their lips parted.

They had a few more minutes of privacy before the president walked in, saying, "Chelle Saltarie, how wonderful that you could meet with me today."

The president shook her hand. He reached out and firmly shook Steven's hand as well, putting his other hand against Steven's shoulder.

"Senator Westcott, congratulations, you did the impossible. I think our little scheme is going to work. Maybe even better than we hoped."

"Thank you, sir, I believe you have the right man taking over from here."

"So, you talked with Ernie?"

"Yes, sir, we decided it was time for a brotherly talk. We agreed to no longer keep secrets from each other."

"Ernie is becoming El Senador?" Chelle asked, looking surprised.

The president laughed.

"Ah yes, the legend of El Senador! Yes, in a way, you're right. Ernie is representing the United States and our firepower. He was suspicious of the plan, but in the end, I convinced him he would be in charge and could work in concert with the DEA."

Steven smiled at the president and said, "You can be very persuasive, Mr. President. With his knowledge of how the cartels operate, I'm confident you couldn't have a better steward."

"Agreed, though it's not all on your brother's shoulders. The man you call 'El Cazador' is spearheading Mexico's takeover of the cartel strongholds."

"Then I'll rest easy, sir."

The president turned to Chelle and said, "Both America and Mexico owe you a great deal more than we can give. I have, of course, been informed of the ordeal you had to endure. For that, I am truly sorry. In the end, I doubt our success had you not been there when you were."

Chelle's face flushed as she accepted the compliment, "Thank you, Mr. President. I know I stuck my nose into a place it didn't belong."

"Maybe where it didn't belong, but where it was needed. Isn't that what good cops do? At any rate, thanks to you, Ernie, the FES and Steven, Mexico has a real chance of reclaiming law and order.

"President Torres is using the new trade agreement as her springboard for a manufacturing initiative to replace the cartels' money with legal, well-paying jobs, and, I might add, new cash crops. My own efforts have facilitated a new trade arrangement with Australia, setting up Mexico as a major exporter of crops and giving them access to minerals they'll need to support industry. In short, the whole world benefits."

The president opened his palm and motioned to the couches immediately in front of the Resolute Desk.

"I'm letting enthusiasm overtake me. Please, have a seat. Does anybody need a coffee or water or something?"

The sat down but declined the refreshments. When his guests were settled, the president sat in an open seat on the couch opposite.

He relaxed his frame into the back of the couch and said, "Aside from our victories, there's something I need to talk to you about. You have been exposed to extremely confidential information. Now, I must remind you that, because you are both government employees, I am your ultimate superior. It is with this in mind that I say, as your commander-in-chief, you may not divulge anything that I'm about to tell you. This is for national security reasons, and confidentiality is enforced, by law, through the contracts and agreements you have already made to serve this country. Do you both understand?"

They nodded and the president handed each of them a letter.

"Inside these envelopes are what amounts to a presidential pardon for each of you, if you should ever need one. This administration considers you patriots, if not heroes, but you will be required to keep your efforts on the country's behalf secret, even if doing so puts you in legal jeopardy in the future. Give the enclosed documents to your attorneys. I couldn't bear to think that, after serving your country so bravely, any of you could come under attack from a future administration."

Steven and Chelle accepted the envelopes, but they glanced at each other, clearly uncomfortable.

"The assassination attempt has to remain a secret, and I expect both of you to help me keep it that way. An inquiry into an assassination attempt would lead to discovery of our escapades in Mexico. We, *you*, didn't risk so much to have it fall apart now. We just can't risk it."

Steven hadn't thought of the ramifications of a full-scale investigation.

After a moment, he asked, "What about Mitchel Waters? He attempted to kill you!"

"After what you told me about our friend with the cane, I instigated an investigation within IRENE. While his reach wasn't as extensive as he claimed, there *were* some major officials on his payroll. All have been removed from office, and most have agreed to plea deals that will prevent them from ever again holding public office. Their sentences will only scratch the surface of their crimes, but tomorrow's news will reveal multiple officials caught selling influence and investing illegally.

"Mitchel has agreed to plead guilty to severe breaches that will land him jail time, and to playing an active part in corrupting others. All true, in fact; just not the whole truth. He won't be locked up for anywhere near as long as he should be, but that was all the justice I could get under the circumstances."

"What about Alfonso and IRENE?"

"You must both understand that I can't prosecute anybody. In any trial, our activities over the last several months would be exposed. Successful or not, there are aspects of our involvement in Mexican affairs that could be considered criminal, or at least beyond my authority. On top of that, if even half of the steps we took were revealed, America's diplomatic standing would crumble, possibly for generations."

Chelle and Steven both looked at their letters, realizing how important they were.

"As for IRENE, active members have been made acutely aware of what happened. The parties involved have been detected and dealt with, and as IRENE's current president, I have initiated a complete review of our investment policies and funds. The review isn't complete yet, but it appears we have much more wealth than we were led to believe. Again, the perpetrators won't answer for everything they've done, but they will be dealt with."

"'Dealt with' how?" Steven asked awkwardly. "Alfonso Lucas admitted to killing my daughter and Sam Kreiser. They threatened all of us, my daughter, even you. I can't imagine how many crimes they committed, including the attempted murder of a sitting president! Being 'dealt with' doesn't seem sufficient."

"I hope you can appreciate the delicate situation IRENE is in. Exposing Alfonso and his underlings, bringing them to trial, would also expose IRENE. It has been a secret society for nearly eighty years, doing important work. Work we can't do, conversations we can't have, gatherings of individuals who normally can't even be seen together.

"IRENE does good work, noble work. In the past, our members brought dangers to light ahead of time. Because of the foresight of our members, millions of people's lives have been saved. We can't destroy that."

"I'm sorry, Mr. President," Steven argued. "I appreciate your dilemma, but this is *not* how our laws work. We bring in the accused and let the courts decide what's justice."

"IRENE is an international group, and this is an international problem. I'm telling you that the guilty parties, including Alfonso, have been brought to justice. It was just done internally, to protect the organization."

"With all due respect, sir," Steven replied, his voice shaking, "that sounds like you're making your own laws and enforcing vigilante justice. IRENE already killed my daughter to blackmail a United States senator, they—"

"No, they didn't," the president growled. "Alfonso and a small group of his supporters did that. I can assure you that we did *not* authorize it. Steven, I like you. My god, you literally saved my life! But this is not your call."

The president briefly turned to view the Rose Garden. That was when Chelle slipped her hand onto Steven's knee. It was a gentle warning to contain himself.

The president turned back towards his guests and continued in a much calmer voice.

"Let me be clear, Senator: this is not up for discussion. I am telling you, I am ordering you, that for national security reasons, you, neither of you, can reveal what you know or think you know about IRENE. That would make the envelopes in your hands worthless.

"I can tell you that you and your families are safe from retribution. Those responsible *have* been dealt with. Within IRENE, you are regarded as heroes. And I hope at some point, Senator, you will be invited to attend a conference yourself, so that you can see IRENE for what it really is."

The president walked up to Steven and Chelle and they stood, understanding the meeting was over.

"Steven, Chelle, I can't thank you enough for the service you have done for your country. Rest assured that you both have a friend in me."

Steven and Chelle each graciously accepted the president's hand, though they were all clear that Steven hadn't been satisfied with their discussion.

The president pressed a button by the door, and it immediately opened. Chelle and Steven were ushered down the long hallway as the president took his seat behind the Resolute Desk.

****

The roller coaster clicked and clanked to the pinnacle of the mountain. The menacing eyes of a huge Yeti looked down on Steven and his daughter Tracy, the track in front of them clearly destroyed by the monster. The car they were in suddenly dropped backward away from the Yeti. Tracy and Steven screamed as the coaster fell. The coaster descended into a dark tunnel and a strobe light flashed in their eyes.

They emerged from the roller coaster laughing about who had been more scared. Tracy saw it first; their photo displayed on a huge, electronic board. She started giggling.

"Look, Dad; you look terrified. You're such a wimp!"

Steven laughed and had to admit that the camera had caught him off guard. He ordered two prints, one for him and one for Tracy. The impromptu visit to Disney World was the medicine he'd needed after the stress of his mission in Mexico.

Tracy shouted, "Dad, the line is so short, let's do it again!"

Steven didn't have any choice as Tracy dragged him along.

The trip to Disney World was more for his benefit than hers, allowing him to reconnect with his daughter and, in a way, life itself. Steven thought of his friend Filipe and his ultimate solution to saving his family.

Steven glanced at Tracy's smiling face and thought about his own solution. He remembered his promise not to fail her like he had failed Destinee and Rebecca. Had Chelle and Ernie and, most importantly, El Cazador not come along to save him, Steven knew that he couldn't have failed Tracy any more than Filipe could have sentenced his family to their deaths. Away from the immediate danger of his mission, and with the president covering up crimes of staggering significance, he was no longer so sure about the morality of his actions. He hated Alfonso and IRENE for killing Destinee and threatening Tracy, but hadn't he done the exact same thing to the cartel leaders?

The line was short, and they boarded the coaster cab. The ear-to-ear grin on Tracy's face was priceless. Steven thought about the gut-wrenching ride in the hypersonic aircraft and knew he could endure another bout on the roller coaster.

He had a feeling that IRENE wasn't out of his life just yet. The president's solution had left a lot of powerful people untouched in the name of a lesser justice, and Steven now felt his trust might have been misplaced.

The coaster started the long ride to the pinnacle of the mountain with a *click-clack* and a look of excited anticipation from the riders, especially Tracy. For now, Steven promised himself that he would put his cares and concerns behind him. He lifted his hands high into the air and dared his daughter to do the same as the coaster fell backwards once again.

The End